THE FOUR SEASONS

THE FOUR SEASONS

HEIDI HARRISON

SAPPHIRE BOOKS

SALINAS, CALIFORNIA

Editor - Heather Flournoy
Book Design - LJ Reynolds
Cover Design - Treehouse Studio

Sapphire Books Publishing, LLC
P.O. Box 8142
Salinas, CA 93912
www.sapphirebooks.com

Printed in the United States of America
First Edition – July 2018

This and other Sapphire Books titles can be found at
www.sapphirebooks.com

Dedication

To my dad, who was like snow in a parched desert. And to my mom, with whom I share a love that has seen no limits.

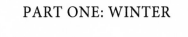

PART ONE: WINTER

Chapter One

I rene Alborz stared out the window, watching the rain fall. In the Northwest, they called it slanted rain, when the lashing wind combined with the water falling from the sky, making the rain look like half of a V as it tumbled to the ground. Regular umbrellas were useless, as the flipping-up syndrome would generally occur, making for an embarrassing moment. Getting soaked was simply what happened.

On those kinds of rainy days, it was best to stay inside.

Irene looked at her syllabus, thoughtfully written out during those balmy days of summer, when slanted rain was the furthest from her mind. She remembered the moment well, sipping lemonade in her voluminous Capitol Hill garden as she watched her plants grow, flowers blooming everywhere, all colors and shapes and sizes. They were planted from seeds she'd sowed years ago, mulched and fertilized with her own hands. Indeed, she was quite proud of this garden she had created from the mound of dirt and weeds ten years earlier when she had bought the place.

Her mind drifted, back and forth, like a swing. She stared again at the words on her computer screen and recalled today's lecture at the University of Washington's Music Building, the impressive 200-year-old structure with the rounded arches, leaded windows, and Gothic spires. This was her home away from home; she was as much grounded in these illustrious walls of music as she was in her garden with the soaring vines, which, left unkempt, could reach all the way over the fence, cascading down the block. Her neighbors, the kind souls they were, smiled when she occasionally brought out her clippers and trimmed her trumpet vines before they took over the forget-me-nots two houses down.

That day, as the wind and rain pelted outside, hitting the leaded windows like tiny tympani, a glockenspiel, perhaps, she spoke of Vivaldi's *The Four Seasons*, illuminating the fourth movement, "Winter." She looked up at her class, their eyes awaiting her words, their fingers poised over the keyboards of their tablets, laptops, and iPads. She smiled to herself, remembering her earlier days of teaching when notepads and pens created a silent acknowledgment of words. Now, as she spoke, the tip-tapping of her students' hands replaced that seemingly long-ago silence.

She loved teaching this class, Classical Music 101. The students, all freshmen, were so open and receptive to a subject 90 percent of them knew nothing about. For many years, the University of Washington, affectionately known as "U Dub," had discussed the need for students to know more about classical music, and finally this past year, Music 101 became a required course for all incoming freshmen. Irene leapt at the chance and volunteered to teach this one course, lecturing up to 300 students per class.

"We are in winter. I purposely wanted to begin here, in the last concerto of this series of four that he wrote in 1721, since that is the season that envelops us as we speak. Most people know the 'Spring' concerto, the one that is light and frivolous, the one that invokes birth and of course, sex, and all things that are life-giving." Irene listened to the quiet giggles of her students. Teachers saying the word "sex" has been taboo for generations, she thought to herself.

"In 'Winter,' this brilliant concerto of Vivaldi's, there is a raw sensuality present with each turn of the bow. He is describing the edginess present in nature, the stark reality of the cold, the icy rain, hibernation, and the accompanying violins and violas, especially in the first movement, 'Allegro non molto in F minor,' possess a visceral intensity where there is a vulnerability of the barren fields covered in snow. The music is influenced by Italian sonnets, maybe even written by Vivaldi himself, but it has been shown that he was inspired by paintings done of the four seasons by a man named Marco Ricci. The solo violin resounds in a sweetness that violins naturally create, and in this interpretation, the composer seems to delight in the harshness of the cold, like the snow queen perhaps, coming out to dance, adorned with her robes of fur. Let me read to you a bit of the sonnets that inspired the music for the winter concerto.

"'Shivering, frozen mid the frosty snow in biting stinging winds...We tread the icy path slowly and cautiously, for fear of tripping and falling...We feel the chill north winds course through the home despite the locked and bolted doors...This is winter, which nonetheless brings its own delights.'

"Let's listen again to each of these three movements, and see if you can envision what Vivaldi intended, or maybe create your own version of his music. See if you can truly feel the winter, feel the cold as you listen carefully."

ல.ல.ல.ல.

Irene turned on the kettle, putting a lemon-ginger tea bag in her mug of a maroon and lavender glaze, a gift she gave to herself when she visited her favorite pottery studio on Orcas Island several years back. She sighed, listening to the rain thrashing outside, knowing her day was done. She put on the "Winter" concerto, letting the surround sound encircle her living room as she put her hot cup of tea on the table and plopped herself on the couch. The rain was cold today, whipping through every crevice of her skin. Even with her thick scarf, hat, boots, and her warm jacket, she sensed winter's omnipresence. Now, she slipped onto the softness of the couch, relishing the warmth of her living room, the fire she had made, home. She loved the texture of her silken long underwear, sensual and light, yet also warm and holding the curves of her body. She undid her ponytail, letting the waves of her dark hair unleash as the violins etched out a need for mercy in a tarnished, cold world, an intensity of carnal expression throbbing with desire for release, for sun, for warmth.

Irene's nipples hardened.

She let her hand graze the softness of her breasts. As the violins continued their pulsing intensity, her fingertips circled around her nipples, first on her right and then on her left, and as she did so, her body screamed for more, for lips on her breast sucking hard, a swirling tongue. She took her finger to her mouth and licked it, letting her nipples harden further, imagining her own lips on her breasts, sinking into them, to the flesh that beckoned. One by one, her mouth moved up and down her fingers as the other hand circled around her labia, the wetness pouring out of her like a warm rain, inviting her inside, to her own tantalizing cave. As the violins and the violas and the cellos continued their lament, their celebration of all that is winter, the rawness of the flesh, Irene found herself moaning voluminous chords of satisfaction as still the rain continued outside.

Sitting up, feeling deliciously satiated, Irene sipped her tea, letting the lemon swirl around her mouth like a dessert after a fine meal. She looked out at the gingko tree in her garden, swaying with the wind like a dance, as the rain cascaded all around its bare branches. Its autumn leaves were the talk of the neighborhood; in October, Seattleites would converge in front of her house, cameras in hand, and photograph her tree from every angle.

In her dreamy mind, visions drifted through of soft beaches and warm waters, crystal blue, so blue that they dazzled the eyes, the water so perfect in temperature, the air so deliciously hot, that one could lie on one's back, floating, naked from head to toe. The mere thought of this made her want to stroke herself again.

She glanced at her phone and saw a message from her best friend and colleague, Bob. Their common denominators were being gay, single, and timid about dating, and as a result, they easily fell into becoming each other's "safe dates," mostly in the form of concert buddies, where they lapsed into regularly going off to events all over town, and sometimes in Vancouver, BC. Their musical tastes were the same, so it never was difficult to decide which concert to go to.

Hannah Zinga tonight plays Beethoven violin concerto. Remember? Meet you at Benaroya Hall 7:30 p.m.? Dinner before?

Oh my God, I completely forgot, Irene said to herself. *And on this night where I feel so content staying home.* She looked at the time, 5:30 p.m., and thought about her empty fridge. In her haste to get home and be warm and comfortable, she had neglected to go to the store to get something for dinner.

Right. Looking forward to it. Can't wait to see what she is wearing! Lol. Have no food in the house. Meet you at 6:15 at The Gastronomical Garden for a quick sandwich or...?

Perfect. See you then. I could use a good sandwich, check out the sandwich-making guy. Not sure if he works tonight:)

Irene whisked herself into the shower, willing her body into an energized state after her luscious late afternoon. Her clothes off, her body now freezing again, she let the hot water pour down onto her awaiting skin. She knew if she stayed in the shower too long, though, she would not be able to get herself out the door. Two minutes later, she was out, toweled off, and headed to her room to find something decent to wear.

Opening her closet, Irene looked at the choices before her. She did what she always did, such a creature of habit she was, and chose the outfit she wore to the last concert two weeks ago. Her tight corduroy jeans, hemp-linen ivory-colored blouse rolled slightly at the neck with a little cleavage showing, but not too much. She had to remind herself she wasn't twenty anymore, and modesty was acceptable at her age. As she slipped on her cashmere-lined pants, she enjoyed the softness of the delicate wool grazing her legs, the tightness in her thighs and around her buttocks, a bit of a pull to make her feel alive, defined, and sensual, yet not so tight that it felt like a chastity belt. She put on her earrings—the same ones as two weeks ago, the gold and malachite—and loosely wrapped the gold lace scarf around her neck. She looked at the clock. Five fifty. She messaged the Lyft driver. They would be at her door in five minutes. On went the silver pillowy down coat and her up-to-the-knee boots. She looked out the window—the driver had arrived. She turned off the house lights, turned on the porch lights, and into the pouring rain, the car sped off. *Ahh.* She sighed, sinking into the heated leather seat as the streets of her beloved Seattle breezed by.

Irene stepped into the café right as Bob arrived.

"Hello, gorgeous!"

"Hello, handsome!"

That was their typical greeting. That and the warm hug. Bob gave great hugs, big ones, right out of his rounded self, like a bear, Irene always thought. If they were straight, they would have been married years ago. They would have had 2.5 kids, a house with a white picket fence, and a dog. The kids, by now, would be entering college. Combined, their tenured faculty salaried positions would have produced an amazing sum in the bank, enough for them to retire early and travel around the world, listening to concerts in cities all over the globe. They often laughed about this, Irene and Bob, sitting in a tree, except that they tried once to kiss, way back when they first met, and all that came out of their mouths was *yuck*! In their early twenties, they already knew they were gay, but they knew about the research done on the gay-straight continuum, where each person falls somewhere: definitely gay, definitely straight, or somewhere in the middle. Upon reflection and examination of this theory, they decided they had yet another thing in common: each was definitely gay, and therefore, them getting married was definitely out of the question since sex was kind of important. Sometimes, when they were out together, they pretended to be married, and laughed at the ludicrous conversations they came up with. Their banter was always interrupted when a hot single woman would walk by, or an adorable man on his own would saunter past, and then after the subsequent subtle flirting, Irene and Bob would resume their incessant jabs at each other, adoring each other's company and the stability it provided, letting it let them hide behind their own intense shyness at finding the right person to actually meet and possibly marry.

"Turkey sandwich on rye with a bit of cranberry sauce and avocado?" Bob smiled and giggled to himself, no doubt because Irene always ordered the same thing. As he went to the front counter to order for the two of them, he looked around, presumably to check for the cute sandwich guy, and frowned when there was no sign of him. Irene found a table and got comfortable. She enjoyed listening to the happy conversations around her, and one of her favorite things to do was listen in on beginnings and middles and ends of conversations from people around her.

"…and you'll never guess what he put inside of her last night…" A big man arrived—maybe the man who did the deed, Irene thought—and the conversation abruptly ended at the table next to her. If it were polite to guffaw loudly in public, she most certainly would have done so. Bob then joined her, and she texted him the conversation. That's when the guffaws came out, together.

Still laughing, Bob returned to the counter once his name was called. Bringing back the plates, he placed the infamous turkey sandwich in front of Irene. She smiled to herself as she watched him almost wink at the man at the table next to theirs. He did have a thing for big men, she noticed, and the one that he almost rubbed shoulders with was decidedly in that category. She remembered how he once went on a camping trip in northern California, in the mountains, with the society of gay bears. He had told her, upon his return, that he had felt like he had died and gone to heaven, and that all the men around him were quite round and hairy and deliciously voluptuous. That was so long ago, she reminisced. Maybe he was twenty then.

"Thank you, darling, for this most delicious sandwich. How did you know this was exactly what I wanted?" She winked.

"*Pour toi, madame, je te donne le monde...*" He seemed to get a kick out of teasing her in French, sounding like a waiter in a restaurant in Paris. It made her giggle, and often began a round of banter. Irene would always win with her perfect French.

"And what did you get today, Monsieur?"

"Reuben. Lots of sauerkraut."

"Oh God. I shall definitely not be kissing you tonight."

"Of course not. You are saving those ruby lips of yours for Hannah. Her soft, round shoulders...in the middle of her cadenza..."

"Now there's a thought. Audience member descends onto the stage as artist is playing her solo piece, and said audience member rips off her dress, bit by bit of course..."

Their guffaws continued.

Irene looked at her phone. "It's a little after seven. Lyft? Or walk?"

"Walk in this rain? Not me." Bob sent a message from his phone. "Driver will be here in eight minutes."

"Quick pee, then." Irene scurried away as Bob finished her sandwich. Another one of their little "matrimonial" rituals.

When she got back, the car had arrived, and off they went to the concert hall.

As soon as they walked in, Irene sensed the buzz of the audience filling their seats. This was one of the things she loved about Seattle. It was a big city, but it had a small-world feel to it, and when a major artist was in town, it was such a thrill for the spectators. The city was not blasé, not full of a certain snobbishness that other big cities sported. The people appreciated good things, quality art and performance, and when such quality walked into their town, this beauty was not taken for granted. It was kind of like the sun, interestingly, Irene thought as she looked up at the people and the smiles on their faces. After days and days of endless rain in this town, when there was a sunny day, the people noticed, smiled, and made comments to anyone who would listen about how lovely the day was, even if it was freezing cold.

While Irene carefully read the program, Bob scrutinized the crowd. This was also part of their ritual when they went to concerts. Bob was an expert on Medieval and Renaissance Music—on all genres and periods, really—but she had grown accustomed to him putting his brain aside for most of the time he attended concerts while his eyes and all his other sense organs seemed fixated on the men around him. Of course, Irene was guilty of this, too, and she couldn't help her own lustful gaze when a woman she was drawn to stepped into her field of vision. Yet she was also able to let her brain step in and comment on the concert or the interpretation of the music. She loved to engage in interesting discussions with Bob, but sometimes it was like pulling teeth to get him to talk about anything except what his crotch was telling him. She knew, from watching him teach, that he was completely professional when he was lecturing or with any of his students, but, good old Bob, as soon as he wasn't in a work environment, he let all scruples go to the frenzied wind outside. Mostly, to avoid conflict, she let herself be amused by him and his ways. Actually, it was good for her, too, as he let her often intensely thinking mind be free, relaxing into the ways of simply having a good time.

Sinking into the velvety chair in the Orchestra section, she looked up at the magnificence of the concert hall, feeling transported to another time and another place where music and the arts of geniuses surrounded the listener. In her mind, she recalled concerts in Paris, where the echoes of this genius filtered still in her ears. Here in Seattle, just a young city, still she often wept inside before a concert, just knowing that brilliance was about to enter on stage.

The audience hushed. Bob looked at her, and they exchanged smiles. Irene disappeared into the folds of the concert, into her private world between herself and the artists and the music itself. The orchestra entered, an organized mass of women and men all in black, announcing the formality and seriousness of what they were about to do. She loved this part, this entrance of the musicians, each one holding their beloved instrument, ready to play more than notes, but their expression of feelings, passion, sadness, joy, and above all, the beauty of life itself.

Once every musician was seated, and the bassists stood like sentries behind their instruments, the conductor made his entrance, accepting the applause, bowing. Then Hannah emerged from the wings at the left of the stage, dressed in an emerald-green dress of splendor, a plunging neckline, diamonds glittering around her dress, underneath her breasts, illuminating them, the soft curves blending perfectly with the silken folds wrapped around her.

Irene gasped, her heart beating wildly as she stared, and wanted immediately to take that woman off stage and place her hands on that silken dress, unzipping it carefully in the back and watching the diamonds glisten as the dress slid ever-so-sweetly off her tantalizing body.

Not a sound came from anywhere as the conductor raised his baton and the orchestra began. From the initial entrance of the winds, the oboes, clarinets, and bassoons, to the tiniest hint of the string section, there was a silvery magic feeling. Irene sensed it as the hush continued around her, people holding their breaths for almost four minutes as sections of the orchestra sang back and forth to each other, the strings, the winds, and the faintest sounds of the tympani giving the lengthy introduction until finally, the first angelic notes of the solo violin began. When Hannah entered, it was, for Irene, as if the angels had arrived. Her fingers on the strings transcended regular life as she knew it to a place of the sublime. Her highest notes, in the beginning, left not a scratch, but slid under her fingers, sweetness embodied in an expression of passion, innocence, yet not. Listening to her play was like witnessing the most beautiful love scene that could ever exist, beyond sex, coming together of beauty and passion that met no limits. She couldn't stop crying, tears flowing down her face, lacing her neck, as the first movement flowed into the second, the larghetto, where everything slowed down, the notes pulled out of the air, like fine thread, light and delicate, sweet, yet keeping a sensual intensity, like fingers on the nipples, stroking them like velvet, and bringing out the sumptuousness of the breast itself. Her eyes closed. Irene felt like Hannah had put everyone into a trance as only the music came from her bow, her soul pouring out from her violin into every one of the listeners. The orchestra, quietly accompanying her, allowed her to create whatever she wanted to. Beethoven knew this magic, he knew the violin, every aspect of it, and how to transform the world into that place of ethereal beauty. Irene imagined herself again on the beach, the sun and the warm water bathing her. When the third and final movement began, a dancing frolic after the rain, after the lovemaking, Irene opened her eyes again and felt like she, too, was dancing, following every stroke of the bow, not wanting to miss a single passage. She imagined flowers everywhere, fields and fields, as the violin followed her into the dance. Herself free, naked, she imagined Hannah, the game she was playing, flirting with Irene as Irene begged for more and more, laughing, loving the seduction, Hannah all to herself. In the cadenza, the solo where only the violin spoke, the game almost over, the notes were ones of play, yet a certain wistfulness was present, for always there was an ending to things, and always there were the last notes to savor as the orchestra made their concluding sounds, enveloped by the solo violin. The audience clapped and stood, wanting more. Irene bolted up from her chair, the buoyancy of this bolting mirrored in the audience around her. Bob bolted up too; she had forgotten about him. In her total immersion in the concert, her own bubble had expanded to only herself and the musicians. As her hands moved together to make sound, she turned to him, beamed, and let out a very loud contented sigh. He smiled back, his face looking like that of a little boy who had been given all the cookies he ever wanted.

"Now that was one of the finest renditions of the Beethoven that I have ever heard. Her interpretation was flawless."

"Like gold shimmering on the water," she added. "Yes, I don't think I have ever seen such magic on the violin with that concerto. It gave me a renewed appreciation for that piece of music. Such brilliance, that Beethoven."

"Okay, her dress? I thought of you when she came out. Were you drooling like I thought you were?"

"I was working hard not to run down to that stage and grab her and whisk her away, all for myself, if that's what you mean." She laughed. "Our next concert here is Luc Francois playing the Brahms. Your turn to drool. I know you lust after those French men. That's in March, I think."

"Right you are. I can't wait. Hey, want to get a piece of cake, glass of wine? I have a sweet tooth right at this minute."

"You know, so do I. Let's see if it's still raining. If not, I would love to walk and get some fresh air. Head over to Le Vin Fou?"

"Great."

Irene and Bob made their way to the front door and were immediately greeted by a clear sky, the moon's luminescence almost blinding. A brisk wind whipped around the steps as they descended onto the street.

"Brrrr," Irene said with a laugh. "Winter in Seattle. You gotta love it."

"All my parts are frozen. Not good. Let's walk fast before I lose something valuable from *mon corps*."

Irene broke out in the loudest laughter, and people walking by simply stared, perhaps thinking to themselves, oh God, one more downtown crazy as high as a kite.

Le Vin Fou, translated as the crazy wine café, greeted them with an inviting hot brick oven, where they made their own cakes from recipes passed down to the owners from their French grandparents and beyond, living in small towns in the provincial regions away from Paris where things were simpler and down to earth. Their wines also were all French, from caves that also belonged to family members, some still alive, some long gone. Irene and Bob loved this place, and it, like many things and places in Seattle, had become a stable ritual in their friendship. Bob always joked that going there saved you a ton of money and the annoyance of jet lag. If you had any inclination to go to France, it was all right there. Cakes and wines, and French music in the background—who needed anything more?

"Let's sit for a bit by the oven, if you don't mind. I need to thaw out my boy."

Irene was tempted to guffaw even louder, but she

didn't want to risk getting kicked out of one of their favorite places in all of Seattle, so she worked hard to stifle her outrageous laughter as she stared at the menu.

"Hey, look at this. Something new, apricot mousse cake with almond and raspberry coulis. I have got to try that one! What about you?"

"Mmm...think I will go with the tarte aux pommes. Going simple tonight. A Vouvray moelleux?"

"Sounds lovely." Irene sat back in her chair, feeling warm and delicious all over, the sounds of Edith Piaf filtering in her ears. Her thoughts remained on Hannah and her silken dress. Slowly, with the music and the smells of sweet things wafting around her, she imagined taking that zipper in her hand and deliberately, carefully, pulling it down, listening to the soft moans of the violin as she did so.

The waiter, the son of the owner, arrived with the desserts and the wine as he greeted his regular customers and told them the story of this new mousse cake his father had discovered on his most recent trip to the Limoges region of France, where his family was from. He was excited about it and insisted they each take a bite. Irene placed her fork in the soft, luscious texture, taking a piece and putting it into her mouth, where she was instantly transported into a different time, a different place. The mélange of the apricots and the almonds and the raspberries blended so perfectly on her tongue that it was as though her mouth were having an orgasm and only wanted more. Instead of devouring that cake as she wanted to, she held herself back and told the waiter that indeed this was truly the best cake she had ever tasted. The waiter, Georges, beamed as he glanced at Bob, who looked entirely engrossed in his piece of torte, and if Irene was not mistaken, had likely become quite hard under the table. When he came to, he gazed up at Georges with eyes that spoke of nothing but extreme satisfaction, and told him he agreed with Irene—that this was the most delicious dessert he had ever encountered, and to *please* keep making it. A delighted Georges skipped away, almost tripping on his own feet.

After the apricot mousse torte, they shared the apple pie, a simple cousin, they decided, but good on the palate and a nice ending to a lovely day. As they sipped their Vouvray, they were each quiet for a moment, tasting the mellow aromas and letting them slide down gracefully, a perfect complement to the still lingering taste of the desserts.

"I have had now, twice today, two fantasies of being on a warm beach, soft sand, air so perfect that it must be summer," Irene blurted out, breaking the silence.

"Hmmm..." Bob muttered in his distinct Bob-muttering-hmmm tone. "Well then, I think, if you want my opinion, you need to listen to these fantasies of yours. I mean, come on, you never go anywhere, except when you have to give a lecture, and you only stay one night. Oh yeah, on occasion you go to your dreadful aunt's house and come back thoroughly depressed."

Irene thought for a moment. Yes, her aunt. Living in suburbia in southern California. She had most assuredly voted for Trump in the recent election, which made Irene sick to her stomach.

Bob continued, his speech not quite done. "So, yes, a trip is in order, all by yourself, and make those arrangements pronto as winter break is less than two weeks away. Go to that beach, sink into that warm sand, let the perfect waters surround you, and maybe you'll even find some gorgeous woman to add to that most lovely vision I have now painted for you, inspired of course, by your vivid fantasy world." Bob sat back in his chair, looking quite smug, and glanced up at his best friend, who was staring into her empty glass. "I saw that smile," he added. "You can't hide it."

Irene looked up. "I was thinking hard about your words. You are right. I completely forgot about winter break coming up. Your idea is a good one. I can't even remember when I last went away. I mean away, away. As in not coming back the next day. I am pathetic, aren't I?"

"Takes one to know one, dear. We both have dusty suitcases, don't we?"

Irene smiled. "So, what are your plans for break?"

"You know, I'm not sure. I was planning your life, not my own. Do you want to plan mine?"

"No, but I'll sit here and listen to your ideas. It would only be equal if you do something quite fun and out of the ordinary. I would hate to fly away to someplace exotic knowing you are staring at the walls as the rain pellets like stones against your front porch."

"Well, I was thinking about the gay bears the other day. They're having a winter retreat at some lodge in the Sierras. The deadline to apply is tomorrow, I think. It's been more than twenty years since I did something with that group. The hairy chests might all be gray by now, for all I know."

"Oh, there will be some young cute things, I'm sure. Now, I think that is a marvelous idea. Being in the snow, in a warm lodge with all that fur and flesh and all the boys getting hard merely looking at you. It will be like in the eighties, but now, with protection—which of course you will be using—no one will be getting sick and dying." This last statement brought tears to Bob's eyes. Irene put her hand on his, remembering how many friends he had lost to AIDS.

"You made me go back for a bit, Irene. Things have changed a lot, haven't they? I think I didn't do all those crazy things for so many years because I was, like everyone, so scared. I like to think I cannot be so hidden from what I want, you know? Yes, we do have protection now, and we are smarter and wiser, I think, but still we want to get off. That doesn't change, even if so much else has."

"And I think ultimately you want a partner, don't you?" Irene said quietly, appealing to the vulnerability that her friend was showing her.

"Yeah. Like you."

Irene smiled and blushed, looking down. Bob knew everything about her. She didn't have to say a word. She loved that about him. They both knew it was so hard to meet people, a partner, yet they both yearned to be met. She looked up into Bob's eyes, the person she could trust the most on this planet. He met her eyes, and it was one of those beautiful moments in a friendship that identifies it as a connection made of gold.

"It's late," she said, noting the sleepiness in her own body, seeing Bob's eyes begin to droop. "I have a nine o'clock class to teach tomorrow morning."

"Yep. Time to go." He reached for his phone and messaged a driver. She did the same.

Five minutes later, each had their coats on and into the cold night they emerged, giving each other a warm, long hug and a kiss on the cheek as they each stepped into their awaiting cars.

❧ ❧ ❧ ❧

Irene intended to throw herself into bed and fall immediately to sleep after her long day. But once she stepped inside her house, she was energized and had a second wind, most likely after talking to Bob and listening to his rather assertive comments about getting away, finding a sandy warm beach somewhere. She ran a bath, a hot one that would last a good long while as she relaxed and sat with this vision of a winter's holiday where she would be transported to a balmy summertime.

Her skin burned and tingled as she slipped into the hot water, rather fishlike, wanting nothing to do with land and earth, only water to bathe her parched cold skin, to quiet her busy mind. All was quiet except for the Chopin on the radio, piano sonatas that serenaded the quiet spaces of her brain. She loved live-streaming her Australian radio station; the classical music programming was superior to any classical station she listened to in the US. While it was Thursday night in her bath, it was late Friday afternoon in Melbourne. She closed her eyes, finding calm in simply being, with nothing to do or to think about, the piano drifting in and out of her consciousness, moving in and out of places of being that were nothing and everything. The notes wove themselves around something that felt like joy and bliss, or maybe a marriage between the two.

"Om shanti. Shanti Om," she mumbled, taking a deep breath in and a long breath out.

A calm sweet voice answered back, with an accent that lulled her again into another inhale, another exhale.

"And we would like to offer," her sultry voice continued, "a free round-trip ticket on Qantas Airlines from anywhere in the world to Melbourne, and then on to Tasmania, to the first person who can answer the following question: What was the name of the painter who inspired Vivaldi to write his very famous *The Four Seasons*? If you know the answer to this question, please phone us at 7010 1099."

"What?" Irene screamed out, jolted from her state of quiet ecstasy. "I know the answer. Where is my phone?" She jumped out of the bath, letting water drip everywhere, as she almost slipped in her drenching puddles. There it was, in the pocket of her pants, thrown on the floor, now a soggy mess. With her genius memory skills, she recalled the country and city codes, as just this morning she phoned the University of Melbourne's music department to arrange for their visiting faculty member's lecture in May.

011.61.3 she began, dialing out of the US, and then to Australia. And then to Melbourne. She recalled the actual phone number: 7010 1099. The numbers flew out of her fingers as she held her breath.

It rang. The out-of-country ring. The one that signals one is calling very, very far away. Irene's heartbeat was so fast she thought said heart would bulge out of her skin and plop into the bath.

"Hello. You have reached ABC Classical. You are the first caller. Do you have the name of the artist?"

"Yes. Hello. It was Marco Ricci."

"Correct! Congratulations! You have just won one round-trip ticket to Melbourne. Included in that is a live studio tour of our radio station during our Vivaldi festival with artists from around the world, plus first-class lodgings in Melbourne, and then on to the resort at Wineglass Bay, in Tasmania, which was voted one of the top ten beaches in all of Australia. The journey begins in one week and the return is ten days later. Congratulations. Who, may I ask is the wonderful winner of this prize, and where is the origin of your travels?"

Irene's mouth dropped. She forgot her name for a second, and then somewhere, her speaking voice reemerged. "My gosh, *thank you*! Irene. Irene Alborz. Seattle, Washington is my closest airport. But I would be more than happy to leave out of San Francisco. Thank you, thank you! This is indeed the most amazing news."

"Please hold and we'll gather all your information. Don't go away."

Irene could barely breathe as she waited for the voice on the other end to return. *Australia?* "Thanks for holding, Irene. Will you be ready to leave in one week?"

Irene looked at her mental calendar. The last day of school before winter break. There would be finals to give. She would be done at 5:00 p.m. "Absolutely. When would the flight leave?"

"We could definitely arrange for a flight out of Seattle. Usually our flights leave after eight at night. I am doing a quick Qantas search here, and I see that on the tenth of February there is a flight out at 20:50. Perhaps we could get you out on that one. I'll have our flight representative confirm with you in the next twenty-four hours, and they will send you all the details. Will this work for you?"

"Yes, absolutely. Again, thank you!"

"Well, congratulations. I look forward to meeting you in Melbourne. My name is Nathalie."

"Yes, I listen to your show all the time. I just love it. It is always so inspiring, and I look forward to it every week."

"Why, thank you. I am glad you enjoy it. It must be Thursday evening for you?"

"Yes, it is. Do enjoy the rest of your Friday and your weekend! And thank you again. I am speechless."

Irene stood, naked, holding her phone, whose battery had just died. Goose bumps covered her body; she did not even realize that some time ago, she had begun to shiver. The bath water was now cold, the room temperature a mere sixty degrees at most. As she wrapped her towel around her, she ran through the house, howling with delight.

In bed with a hot water bottle clutched to her chest and three down comforters, her flannel sheets, and her thickest flannel pajamas shrouding her, she still shivered. Yet despite the cold, the thickness of joy wrapped itself around her, tickling her, taunting her, keeping her mind in a place of boundless energy. Meanwhile, her body was exhausted. She tried everything she could to relax, but the day, this most amazing day, was too amazingly wonderful to let go of. *I am going to Australia*, she said to herself. *I am going to Australia. I am going to Austral...I am going to Aus...I am going. I am. I.*

Chapter Two

Six hours later, the alarm clock chimed. Irene pressed snooze. Five minutes later, she was still mostly comatose, but the chimes were relentless, and she had it set so that it would not turn off unless she manually pressed the Off button, which she absolutely could not do that morning. The chimes continued, like church bells on a Christmas morning in France. She was in France. She was drinking wine and eating cakes. No. She was not in France. She was home. It was what? Friday. Friday! Oh no! She glanced at her phone. 8:00 a.m. She had a class in an hour. She had never, in all her years of teaching, been this rushed to make it to class. *I can do this. Shower, I have to take a shower. My hair is a mess. No, I don't. I will just get it wet and brush it out. Dry it a bit. Breakfast. Coffee. Oh God, I am so tired.*

At 8:25, Irene was out the door, and happy that Lyft existed to get her to work on time. There were many moments, and now was one, where she was very happy to be part of the One Less Car Movement in Seattle, having sold her car many years earlier. She sighed, and closed her eyes. *I never again have to maneuver rush hour traffic.* By 8:55 she pranced into her classroom, looking relaxed and content. She had the amazing ability to kick whatever was going against her away from her, so all the lack of sleep and morning stress somehow vanished when she walked in the door to her awaiting students. Today's lecture, with a different class, of course, would be the same as yesterday's. Winter. In twenty-four hours, however, Irene's concept of winter had dramatically changed. As she opened her laptop to begin her lecture, she said to herself, *In just one week, I will be flying away from winter, into the balmy arms of summer.* Her face glowed at the thought.

As she came to the end of her lecture, she reminded her students that as usual, she would be holding office hours that day from 2:00 to 5:00 p.m. in preparation for next week's midterm exams.

"And please don't let me see blank expressions on your faces the day of the exam." She laughed, and her students did the same. She loved the rapport she had with these not even twenty-year-old human beings, whose age was as close to infancy as she could imagine, but whose lives showed an incomparable wisdom and sophistication. The millennials, she reminded herself, who had the knowledge and the wherewithal to do whatever they imagined on this planet.

All afternoon, Irene welcomed a host of students into her office. She looked forward to this part of her job, to listen and to help students, one by one, who came in with all kinds of questions related to music. They wanted to learn, they wanted to know, and they wanted to incorporate classical music into their programmed life of anything but classical. They saw the parallels between the old and the new, and they could envision a better world with the marriage between the two.

At 4:45, a student she barely recognized shuffled in. She always sat in the back of the lecture hall, hidden away with her long hair that she deliberately used to cover her face. Irene beamed when she saw her. She had always wanted to talk one-on-one with this girl. With a heavy sigh, the girl sat down. Irene waited for her to begin.

"Ms. Alborz," she began. "I just loved 'Winter.' I played it for my mother on Sunday. She smiled, and it looked like she was having the sweetest dream. She died the next day. She had cancer. I have been taking care of her for six months. She left so quickly, but on that last day, when I played the Vivaldi for her and she had the earbuds in her ears, she seemed so happy, like she was going to a place where the violins were."

She sat quietly, looking into Irene's eyes, which were full of tears. Irene realized that this girl's mother was probably her age and died the same age as her own mother did.

"Oh, I am so sorry. I am just so sorry."

"Only six months ago, we were all in Pakistan together, the whole family, and she was fine, happy to be with her mother and all her sisters. I did see her face looked sad and more tired than usual when we had to leave. My dad works here at the university. He teaches in the Department of Middle Eastern Studies, and the term was about to begin, as you know, in September. One week after we got back, the doctors confirmed she had pancreatic cancer and would survive maybe a year. She didn't get through even half of that. Her body simply gave up."

She sighed. Irene sighed with her. Sometimes a sigh is all you can do. Irene knew that without her mother at such a young age, life would be so much harder than the college kid whose mother was always there at the other end of the phone.

"Music, you know, heals. I lost my mother, too, at the same age as you are now. That's when I followed the path of music and it has led me to some wonderful places of healing and happiness. I can't imagine a world without music in it."

"Yes, I feel that, too, Ms. Alborz. Vivaldi will always be kind of a hero for me."

"I can see why. He took your mother to a very special place. You can always keep that memory safely inside you."

She looked again into Irene's eyes and scanned her face. Irene thought perhaps she felt comfort in the color of her skin, wondering if it was the same shade as her mother's. "Thank you," she said as she rose to leave.

"I am always here, you know. Remember this. And if sadness gets too much, remember that music is always there for you."

"Okay. Thank you, Ms. Alborz. Have a nice weekend."

"Thank you. You, too." Irene noticed the girl's footsteps down the hallway seemed a tiny bit lighter than a few minutes before. She listened to those footsteps, the echoes of them on the hard floor, as she imagined that moment that the girl's mother passed listening to Vivaldi. She sighed.

Irene looked at the clock in her office. It said 5:00 p.m.. Normally, on a Friday at this time, she would race out the door, wanting to leave the space of learning. She stared out the window, caught in the swirls of rain, cascading around the barren trees, hanging on to life from their deep roots, gravity pulling them down and even farther. She couldn't get up from her chair, as she thought of this girl's story and thought of her own mother, gone before Irene graduated from college. Loss enveloped her as tears emerged, drop by drop, her gaze still focused on the rain, tumbling down with an effortlessness that reminded her of the day she got the call.

She was in her dorm room at Cornell and she had been studying hard that day for her midterm exams. A winter's day in New York, snow was everywhere, silent wisps of winter falling from a light gray sky. Her mother had been depressed for years, ever since the love of her life, Irene's father, died suddenly of a heart attack when Irene was quite young, only eight years of age. They had met in college, in their course on Romance Languages. He was as handsome as a painting, her mother always said, Iranian born, with a smile that melted her to her feet. One kiss, and she knew this was the man of her American white suburban dreams. She always wanted out, and here she was given the opportunity. After college, they settled in New York for good, and they both taught at NYU, both in the language department. Her mother said that she, her only child, was conceived while her dad was reciting Rumi poems of love and devotion, and thus her middle name evolved. Her mother told her indeed she was a child of love and tremendous passion, and when she told this to her daughter, her face would always turn a bright red.

The day Irene's father collapsed in the hallways of NYU after a regular teaching day, a massive heart attack that killed him instantly, was the day that Irene's mother barely held on to a thread of life. Everything vital in her being dissolved that day, and never returned. Her heart suffered, and she had all kinds of medical interventions, but nothing can fix a wounded heart when it is connected to grief, and little by little her heart shriveled to a useless organ that eventually gave out.

When Irene got the call from her aunt, Irene heaved a sigh of relief. Finally, her parents would be reunited. It had been twelve long, grueling years for her mother, and now she could be at peace, back with the love of her life. Irene had begun grieving when she was eight, for even if she had a mother, she felt like an orphan. At her mother's funeral, she was light, somehow free, and found a release from her grief. It was then that she firmly decided that music would be her lifelong calling. Her father had inspired that in her. Poetry and music were his muses in life, and Irene, watching the casket get buried under the soft earth, saw in herself a fervent desire to surround herself with the comfort and the beauty that the written word and music could eternally provide the soul.

After her mother's death, her studies became everything to her. She would go on to get her bachelor's degree, her master's degree, and her PhD all with accolades and distinctions. When the University of Washington grabbed her in a second, offering her a tenured faculty position in the Department of Music, she flew. Her greatest wish was to be away from New York, the snow, and the painful memories. Her home became the West Coast, and she knew this was where she belonged.

Hearing her student's story and reminded of her own painful past, Irene completely forgot about her own present life and what awaited her in one mere week. As she slowly put on her thick scarf, jacket, and hat to venture into the darkened wintry world, in her head she stirred up her own version of "Amazing Grace." In her mind, she sang it silently to herself, hanging on to every word.

Amazing Grace, how sweet the sound...I once was lost, but now am found...

As she walked in the now empty hallways, her own life fluttered before her. She pondered the loss of her own parents, when she was so young, and how she found her own way to rise to the challenges of simply being alive. As her mental singing turned into a low hum, and turned still louder once she went outside, she sensed her own strength at having mastered the huge act of creating a life, creating a self, and creating something beyond even her own flesh. And that strength was reflected in each purposeful step she took across the many puddles in her path on that rainy Friday night.

＊＊＊＊＊

When she got home, she threw off her work clothes and put on her running gear. Though tired from the week, her body still needed to move, work itself through the mental challenges that she'd face in a week. She often did this on Friday nights, stopping for a burrito on the way back. As she began her run in her own neighborhood, her limbs began to loosen up, slowly, as she let her body move into her own rhythm, a meditation on her feet, moving to the music of Beethoven's Ninth Symphony, his last movement, "Ode to Joy," composed when he was completely deaf. Irene felt like she was flying at one point, as her whole body felt its own levity, as she experienced her own joy in this day, in surviving, in being alive.

When she reached the burrito shop at the corner of East Broadway and Olive, she realized she was starving. Devouring a chicken burrito, she ordered another one to take home.

Once inside her front door, she finally discovered her exhaustion. She got in the shower, and from there her bed called out in voluminous tones. Collapsing under the sheets, she fell into the depths of slumber and did not stir one inch until the sun poured in through her windows sometime around noon the next day.

She picked up her phone. Bob had called, then had left a text.

Thought you might want to have a wee bit of breakfast. Guess you have flown the coop. Later.

Just woke up. I have news. Call me when you can. I will be grading papers all day, but I'll pick up when you call.

Grading papers, Irene thought to herself. Yes, sleep over, papers were calling. Irene did love to grade papers, but she always loaded down her own responsibilities the week of exams. While her students studied, she read and graded their papers. Three hundred students, three hundred papers. Well, in truth, she only read one hundred of them. She divided up the other two hundred between her two dependable teaching assistants. As she moved through the kitchen, toasting a bagel and making coffee, she did the math in her head: Saturday to Thursday, six days, one hundred papers, roughly sixteen papers to grade a day. Approximately thirty minutes a paper meant around eight hours each day. Now it was close to 1:00 p.m. *I'll be done today around nine.*

She sighed. Gone from her head was the vision of her trip. She knew herself all too well. If she spent time daydreaming, she wouldn't be done with today's work until midnight. As she poured her cream into her coffee, she put on the news.

"Seattle, prepare yourself for the biggest blizzard in a century."

Irene turned up the volume.

"Today will be the last day of our so-called balmy weather."

"What balmy weather?" Irene asked, talking to the radio.

"Beginning Sunday evening, the temperatures will be dropping gradually, each day getting colder and colder, with light snow flurries by Wednesday. Then, on Friday morning, get out your boots, get your flashlights and generators in order, because by early Friday evening the biggest blizzard since 1914 will be hitting the Pacific Northwest. It will send several feet of snow out our way, with winds gusting up to forty miles an hour, and according to the Port's official website, it will most likely close down Sea-Tac airport, disrupt all air travel, train travel, and major highways and roads, causing severe power outages in the region. And now, for sports. The Seahawks..."

Irene turned off the radio. She slumped on the couch, tears welling up inside her. As she let the warm, smooth coffee slip down her throat, she tried to coax her own wisdom into her muddled head. *It's only Saturday*, she said to herself. *Six days from now, everything can change. If you are meant to be on that plane, you will be. Now, get to work. Your students are depending on you.*

Irene stared into her mug, the one with the blue-and-green swirls that made her feel like she was drifting onto another planet. She could make herself another cup of coffee and sit and brood, or she could open her laptop and begin. She thought of the assignment she gave: *Pick two composers of different genres and historical time periods. Compare and contrast the two. Find three similarities in their music and three differences. Illustrate with examples pulled from their music. Optional add-on: Imagine the two sitting down over dinner, talking about music and how the times they are living in reflect what they have composed. Show their conversation and illustrate it with examples of each composer's music.*

All of a sudden, curiosity filled Irene's mind. She truly wanted to see what her students came up with. She flipped open her laptop and got into her first student's paper.

Hildegard von Bingen Meets Johann Sebastian Bach in the Most Beautiful Love Story One Has Ever Encountered. Irene laughed and laughed at the title. Hildegard von Bingen, living in the twelfth century, was one of Irene's greatest musical heroes of all time—a musicologist, spiritual healer, and mystic who wrote polychromatic, one-melodic-line Gregorian chants. It was assumed that she was a lesbian. And J. S. Bach? Irene couldn't refrain from laughing again. From the historical records, he was as straight as they come. She found it amusing that this first essay moved to a love story, an improbable one at that. She was intrigued if the student had gone into their music at all or had immediately turned it into a screenplay made for Hollywood.

The essay did speak briefly of the music, but the student crafted his words quite expertly and convincingly. He even created his own music video that combined the music of Hildegard von Bingen and

J. S. Bach, one of her chants flowing effortlessly around one of Bach's solo partitas for the violin. The student did this recording in such a way that when Irene listened to it, she really did see a marriage between the two artists. He had created a true love story in music without them even meeting and having a sex scene. Genius, Irene thought. Not the assignment at all, but true creativity in the making. *Ah, these millennials. What will they think of next?*

She made comments on the love story student's essay, and even if he didn't follow the assignment, she couldn't help but give him an "A." She then pulled up the next title, eager to see what brilliance would show up on her screen.

Vaughan Williams and Vivaldi: Taking the Violin to a Place where the Lark Really Does Ascend and Where the Snow Queen Reigns over the Mountain.

Wow. What a title, Irene thought. Obviously from the brilliant and gorgeous "Lark Ascending" and "Winter," from *The Four Seasons.*

She glanced at the name of the author. It was the student she'd talked to yesterday. The one whose mother had recently died.

As she read the astounding words, the poetry of this eulogy she had written for her mother, seeing the violin as the means for transcendence from this world to the next, tears welled up inside of her. Her writing was stunning. But not only that, she completely got the context of the music, the power of how music connects with the human experience and moves the soul to ascendant places. She'd followed the assignment exactly, described the historical significance of each piece, and compared and contrasted each work. Music was the girl's calling, this was clear. Irene was a puddle of tears by the time she finished reading her essay that was so rich in metaphor and seized what music was all about.

Irene stopped for a moment before reading the next essay and recalled a moment in high school, so many years ago, where the first love of her life, a girl with flaming red hair, had played *The Lark Ascending*. She remembered wanting to stare at this girl for life, her violin, the way she played this ethereally dazzling piece of music with such finesse. Later, the girl had sent her a love letter, with a peacock feather laced on the envelope. And then she moved away, never to be heard of again. *I wonder where she is now.*

The afternoon turned into evening as Irene read one essay after another. Although the essays did not move her as much as the first two, each one was unique, entertaining, well-written, and well thought through. Each one grabbed her attention and made her think and marvel at the students' intelligence and creativity.

Before she realized it, it was already 8:30 p.m. She checked her phone, and Bob had indeed called. It must have been when she was listening to some of the music that corresponded with the essays. As she warmed up the burrito that thankfully she had gotten the day before, she dialed his number. He did not pick up. "So sorry I didn't hear your call. I have been swimming in essays and music and must not have heard the ring. Call me this evening before I collapse into sleep. I am done grading for the day."

Munching on her burrito that was indeed better yesterday but was still food today, she looked out the window at the dark skies, the wind swirling like a Van Gogh painting. She tried to visualize the upcoming blizzard floating away like the wind moving out to sea. She wanted to get on that plane. She did not want anything to stop her.

The phone rang.

"Hiya hoya."

"So…what's your news?"

"So, after we had dinner the other night, I thought about what you said, and while I was in the bath, they announced a contest on my Aussie radio station, and I won. I had to answer a simple question, something I'd talked about in lecture that morning."

"What did you win?"

"A round-trip ticket to Melbourne first, where I will be part of their big International Vivaldi thingy, and then to Tasmania, where they are sending me to some resort that was voted one of the best beaches in Oz. And I leave on Friday when the blizzard is supposed to close everything down. So, you must help me visualize that I get on that plane and take off, no matter what."

"Irene, well done sweetie." Bob was laughing so hard, she could almost feel the spit coming from his mouth through the phone.

"It's all because of you. You were the one who put that harebrained idea into my head that I should do something about my little fantasies."

"No, don't give me credit unless a masterpiece evolves from it."

"So, any news about the bears went over the mountain?" she asked.

"Depends on this blasted weather. If they shut down Sea-Tac, then I don't get out to meet those old grizzlies. And I definitely will not be driving. I might write a novel in a week. I have had some great ideas. And this morning my old publisher friend—remember,

Harry?—called me and asked when I was going to write my next book. He said he has a craving for my sex scenes."

"Well that's a good thing to do when all is shut down and the world of winter is inescapable…after, of course, I have made my escape."

The two laughed, echoing each other.

"How's grading going?"

"Good. Those students are truly inspiring. How's your grading going?"

"Yeah, good. There was one today where a student wrote an entire screenplay to his adaption of *The Canterbury Tales*, and the music he thought up was breathtaking. He got every nuance he possibly could muster."

"Thrilling. These students are brilliant."

"They are. Are you at it all week, the grading?"

"Yeah, pretty much. Like always. I don't know why I do this to myself, do all the papers at once. I should stagger the assignments."

"Well, maybe. But we all know that you do well under pressure. Everyone loves you for that."

"That might be good for everyone. But since you seem to know me so well, I will have to trust you on that one." She laughed and yawned—a full resounding yawn. "God, I feel like I am eighty-nine. I have got to get to bed."

"Okay, old lady. Off to beddy-bye you go. I'll check on you tomorrow. And hey, congrats for your amazing win. I will dream of storms abating."

Irene chuckled. "Thanks. Have a good night yourself."

⁂

Sunday followed, and then, as was par for the course, so did Monday, Tuesday, then Wednesday, and soon it was Thursday. While her students took their exams, Irene sat in a quiet corner of the classroom and graded papers. By late Thursday evening, all the papers and most of the midterm exams were graded. The next day she would finish grading the remaining midterms.

Completely spent and an exhausted wreck, Irene looked out the window at the freezing sky. The forecast had not changed one tiny bit. Light snow in the morning, turning to medium to heavy snow by 2:00, and turning to blizzard-like conditions by 5:00.

Still she hoped; still she dreamed as she went to her closet and pulled out her suitcase. She gasped.

Bob was right. But there was more than dust on that suitcase. When she pulled it down from the shelf, it fell apart. It literally broke into two pieces of fabric, sitting clumsily on the floor. It was almost midnight, and her flight was to leave the next day. Tomorrow she had to teach and grade papers all day until 5:00 when she would call the Lyft driver, whereupon she would definitely get herself to the airport.

This is completely ridiculous.

As she thought this, she went to her kitchen drawer and took out the duct tape. She only had a bit left. Coming back to the pitiful suitcase, she put the two pieces together and with her hip pushing and connecting them, she carefully rolled out the precious remains of the tape and got the two pieces into a solid one piece, right as the end of the roll ended up in her hands.

Okay, this is a sign. My life is a mess. A huge blizzard is on its way, but I have a suitcase that is in one piece.

She went through her drawers and smiled as she pulled out her summer clothes. She thought it was incredibly wonderful to not have to pack a single pair of long underwear, no scarves or hats or gloves. And everything was so light. All her dresses and shorts and tank tops barely weighed a pound. When she was done and zipped up her bag, she was tempted to toss the suitcase in the air and bounce it around the room. But she didn't dare. She had no more duct tape.

At midnight, she pulled the covers over her head and thought about sleep, but it was a mere thought. She was way too excited to even close her eyes, let alone drift off into the dream state. Somehow, she did, though, and when the alarm went off at 6:30, she jumped out of bed, danced into the shower, and did not bother to look out the window at the dark, very dark sky.

As she prepared to dress, she fumbled through her underwear drawer. The only bra that was remotely clean and did not smell like sweat and who knows what other bacterial organism was her oldest, gangliest, and thinnest poor excuse for a bra. When she put it on, she laughed in front of the mirror. *I guess it's nipplitis for me. Oh God.* She could wear her thick sweaters at work, but when she got to Australia, she would be one big embarrassment.

Grabbing her coffee and downing it in a few minutes, she was out the door, placing her incredibly light suitcase in the trunk of the Lyft car.

The day passed in a haze. She did administer the exam for her Friday students. She did grade the remaining midterms. She did hold office hours. But her consciousness in all these activities was somewhere in another place, far away from where her feet touched the ground. Not once did she look out the window at the sky or listen on the phone to the forecast.

It was 5:00 p.m.

She spun out of the Music Building like a marionette without its strings, heading outside to a world that was surprisingly quiet. The snow was light and delicate, a tinkling of jewels that softened the world of the city. It was gentle, not heavy at all, and was more of a decoration, a nuance, than a troubled mass of ice that the forecasters had all predicted. People were smiling, loving it, and the usual Friday evening frenzy seemed absent as she loaded her taped-together suitcase into the trunk of the Lyft car and felt its tires quietly pull away from the curb.

"Supposed to be bad tonight," the driver reminded her.

"Yeah, that's what they say. We'll see. It's beautiful now."

"It sure is."

"Sea-Tac?"

"Yep."

"Well, let's cross our fingers."

"Great idea."

The radio was fixed on the weather report. The driver switched to another station, and there, too, was a weather warning. After the third station and yet another weather report, he turned off the radio entirely.

"That's a good idea." She laughed.

He started to hum.

"Farsi?"

"Yeah, an old song my grandmother used to sing."

"My grandmother, too. She's dead now. But when I was a little girl, she sang that song to put me to sleep."

"Mine did, too. Iranian?

"My dad was."

"Hmmm. Nice. All my family except me is still in Iran."

"You miss them?"

"All the time. But the work is better here."

"Yeah, I imagine it is. Do you ever go back?"

"It's been five years. Do you ever go there?"

"No, never. I was going to go, but then my dad died suddenly a few months before we were all going to go as a family."

"I'm sorry."

"One day, I'll get there."

"It's a beautiful country."

"Yes, I imagine it is."

"Well, here we are. The snow is just as pretty and light as when we started, and let's hope it stays that way. Safe journey to you. Salaam."

"Thank you so very much to you. Salaam."

Irene got her bag out, gave the man a generous tip, and headed into the check-in line to get rid of the old bag that absolutely had to make it to the other side of the world.

It was 6:45 by the time her bag was checked, 7:30 when she finished going through security. She couldn't see the world outside and had no idea what the snow was doing. She let herself move through the waiting area to her gate with a gracefulness and an ease. She did not pick up her phone to look at the weather report. She did not ask anyone if her flight would be cancelled. She did look up at the monitor and saw that Flight 88 to Melbourne was scheduled to board at eight o'clock, with an on-time departure of 8:50 p.m.

At 7:55, she heard her name called at the boarding

gate.

She went up to the counter, and the Qantas flight representative in the bright red dress told her that since she was a Qantas prize winner, if there were any available business class seats, she would get one. In fact, she said as she scrutinized her computer screen, there was one left.

At 8:00, Irene boarded the plane and was ushered to her first ever business class seat on a plane that was headed to Australia.

As soon as she was ushered to her seat, a roomy space next to the window, she thought perhaps this was a novel, and she was the main character of the most luxurious fantasy she had ever experienced. The seat was plush and soft and there were dozens of buttons that slid the chair forward and backward, to the right and to the left, and if she wished, she could make the seat fully recline. There were blankets and pillows, and whatever else she wanted, a very gorgeous woman would give her. First there were the pajamas, a hopping kangaroo on the top, and roomy bottoms. Then there were the fuzzy slippers with the matching gray kangaroos. Then the champagne and strawberries. Then the menu for dinner that consisted of the finest and creative concoctions. A newspaper, the *Australian Times*, one of her favorite international newspapers, promised her hours of lovely reading.

Irene sat back in her seat, resplendent with comfort, and sighed. How did I get here, she wondered to herself as she looked out the window and saw the snow building with intensity. Surely within the next few hours, maybe less, the storm would take over, and the projections of closing the airport would be true. As she sat, buckled in her seat, she assumed that everything would happen the way it was meant to happen, that her plane would take off in a mere twenty minutes, and then it would soar up and away and off into the night, crossing over the equator, into the southern hemisphere.

Yet as those thoughts slipped through her mind, there was an announcement on the loudspeaker.

"Welcome to Qantas Airlines. We are experiencing some technical difficulties related to the weather and the Pacific Northwest storm system that is affecting flight visibility all over the West Coast of the US. We appreciate your patience as we are checking in with our air traffic controllers who are, at this time, carefully monitoring the safety of takeoff. If it is deemed unsafe to leave this airport, we will inform you and assure you safe travel when the storm is over. Thank you again for your patience."

Irene picked up the newspaper, trying to find distraction from the tears building in her eyes. She recalled the time when she was barely five, and she had a beautiful blue balloon that she treasured more than anything. One day that beautiful blue balloon flew out of her hand and up into the sky, floating and floating away from her so high until it vanished. She remembered the devastation of that day, so fresh on her mind, as the Qantas representative announced the possible end to a dream—a silly one at that—to leave winter, to find a beach and sit surrounded by summer. Yet, still that stubbornness of the dream, the blue balloon, the quiet warmth of a beach, represented more for her than the object itself. It was a sense of magic, of finding something purely in the fantasy world and making it real.

Then her mind maneuvered itself to the

conversation with the driver. Just saying the word "Salaam" to him as she exited the car conjured up a myriad of feelings, memories of her father's mother whom she had adored. Whenever Irene wondered where she got the passion for music, she would turn to her grandmother's image, for there was a woman who sang with the voice of an angel, whose smile would light up a little girl's heart for decades. She hardly knew her grandparents. They had come to this country with their tiny son, her father, hoping to give him a good life, a better opportunity. Their hard lives were only about this, providing for their one and only child. When, at the age of forty, Irene's father suddenly died, his parents in their complete devastation knew there was nothing holding them there in the US, and they quickly returned to Iran to "grow old and die in our own country," as they told her. For years, Irene begged her mother to take her to Iran, to be with her beloved grandparents, to see the place where her father was born, to go to the mountains that belonged to her last name. Her mother always refused, too sad and depressed to even leave her own apartment. Then, one day, the phone calls came, first one announcing the death of her grandfather, and then, six months later, the death of her grandmother.

Irene, in her early teenage years, wept and wept for months after that. A huge part of who she was had been ripped away, the side of her that spoke a different language, had a different color of skin, went back centuries and centuries ago to a land that was always, to her, mystical and full of poetry and wisdom, a land whose language itself was like a song, the most beautiful love ballad that ever floated into her ears.

In her ears, she still had the song the Lyft driver

sang, her grandmother had sung to her, caressing her mind, when the intercom interrupted.

"Ladies and gentlemen, please fasten your seatbelts and prepare for takeoff. At this time, please fold up any seat tables in front of you and turn off your cellular devices. Thank you for your patience. Air traffic controllers have now cleared this flight for takeoff."

A collective sigh filled the plane. From all regions, from first, to business, to coach, the sigh seemed like a leaf, fluttering, finally free from the wind-whipped tree. Everyone on that plane was off to the world of summer.

Irene stared out the window, watching the snow build and build, now coming down with winter's ferocity. She wondered if this might be the last plane to leave the airport.

Although she wouldn't find this out until hours later, she was indeed right. After her plane's takeoff, Sea-Tac shut down completely until the following Monday morning, when the storm was finally over and the runways were cleared.

She closed her eyes and let the plane do what it needed to do and the pilot do what he needed to do to let this huge vessel slowly gain speed, gaining speed, still gaining speed, to finally the moment when it lifted off the ground, heading south, toward warmer air currents, and even farther south, where the storm would be over, and higher and still even higher past the thick clouds, and farther up to where there was not a single cloud and all was clear. From there would be the ocean, the long expanse of ocean that would lie quietly beneath the plane for hours and hours and hours. Irene's eyes grew heavier and heavier as sleep came, a light one, just enough to let go of anything that had held on to her mind for the past week.

When her eyes opened an hour or so later, her dinner was ready, with a white linen tablecloth spread in front of her, a glass of wine, a steaming plate of baked salmon with all kinds of colorful accoutrements, and even a crème brûlée for dessert. The gorgeous flight attendant had done everything for her, and all she needed to do now was eat.

The food slid down her throat with delicacy and grace. The tastes blended perfectly as she sipped her wine and looked out at the limitless sky. No music came from her brain, no thoughts, only a fine silken quiet that made her smile as she finished her wine and the beautiful woman cleared her table and helped her with the button that let the seat turn into the softest bed. Then came the down comforter that the beauty queen wrapped around her, tucking her in. Her eyes closed again, this time, heavier and heavier. As her body sank into the softness woven around her, sleep came deeply and without stirring, Irene drifted away.

Chapter Three

When her eyes opened, they were flying over Australia.

As she munched on her gourmet breakfast and drank her coffee, waiting for her on her bedside table, she looked out the window, seeing land very much like land in California in the summertime—dry and arid, large expanses of barren earth that seemed starved for water. She chuckled at the irony of it all, the earth, the seasons, the starkness of winter, of summer, and how, wherever we are, we learn to endure.

And then, with a calm exit from the world of the air to the world of the earth, the plane landed. It was over. Just like that. A few meals, a long sleep. And here she was, on the other side of the earth. She turned on her phone, realizing she had not even looked at it since Friday morning, before she left for work. There was a message from Bob.

Welcome to the land of Oz! Your plane was the last to leave. Sea-Tac has been closed until who knows when. The storm is crazy here. I have my generator ready if I need it, all the food I need, and my novel is pouring out of me. Sending you lots of love, sweetie. Enjoy! Enjoy! Enjoy! I will hear everything when you get back. Hugs!

She wrote quickly back:

I am here. Flew in business class, treated like a pregnant queen. It's summer...oops. Sorry...Let all the erotic muses fill you up and write that best seller, dear! Xx.

Exiting the plane, Irene was instantly hit with a blast of hot air and wondered why they sent so much heat into the building. It hit her, in a rather surrealistic fashion, that it was summer, and that wasn't the heater, that was the air outside. She felt so stupidly innocent, like a child who had never experienced anything different from her own backyard. She took off her jacket, obviously useless, and her sweater, too, another futile article of clothing.

Standing in the customs line, she listened to all the accents, the multitude of languages, saw the colors of skin, and was soothed by the varieties of people who had flown from all over the world to land here, in Melbourne, Victoria. She eyed one of the customs officers, obviously a lesbian, as cute as they come, dimples hidden in her officious expression. She had the urge to pull her aside from her governmental rules and regulations and kiss her right there in the airport. As her eyes drifted toward the woman's eyes, the sexy lines of her hair, Irene felt her nipples harden, pushing through her threadbare bra. No sweater or jacket to cover her up, she felt like she was completely naked as she walked up to the counter. The customs officer took her passport, looking first at her face and then down, straight down to her breasts, staying for a brief second on Irene's nipples that were getting harder in that fleeting moment.

"What is the purpose of your visit?" she asked, simply trying to do her job.

"Vacation. I won a trip here. First Melbourne, then Tasmania."

"How long do you plan on being in Australia?" she asked, perhaps silently wanting to kiss those breasts.

She wrote something down on a piece of paper and slipped it inside of Irene's passport.

"Have a good stay. Enjoy Australia," she said. No doubt, she was watched by her superiors from above.

Flushed, Irene stepped quickly toward the baggage line, the next step before the baggage inspection. Her suitcase, moving around and around the carousel like an abandoned log, had fallen apart entirely, its contents spewing out like a volcano. The duct tape had worked only so long, and she had no idea which, if any, of her belongings had made it to the southern hemisphere. She picked up her ridiculously misshapen bag, holding it to her chest as she walked up to the border patrol agent. He looked at her with a mixture of disdain and amusement.

"Well, I guess we don't have to ask you to open your bag, do we?" He laughed, his charming accent making Irene laugh with him.

"Time to get a new suitcase, I guess."

"Any food, water, anything to declare?"

"Nope. Just clothes. Toiletries. If even they made it without falling out."

"Enjoy your stay."

"Thank you."

First stop, bathroom, Irene thought. She was ready to burst.

Locking herself in her stall, she pulled out her passport and held the paper in her hand.

"Harriet. 0491 570156."

Oh my God. She could get herself entirely out of a job if they discovered she did this, she thought as she held the paper and wanted desperately to phone her that evening from her hotel room. Her body was screaming out for touch. Her hands shook, waves of desire flowing through her, her nipples wanting only Harriet's lips on them. As she got up, finishing her business, the piece of paper fell in, becoming quickly submerged in a toilet that she dared not reach into.

She tried to recall the numbers. Usually she was so good at this. The best she could get was 0481 and 570136. She knew this was not right. She grudgingly flushed the toilet, grabbed her cumbersome suitcase, washed her hands, and exited the bathroom, convinced that another adventure was surely waiting for her and her body that had only now begun to experience a deliciously freeing sense of longing.

She stepped outside, and one foot out the door of the airport was all she needed to have an immediate rush of happiness. At eighty-five degrees, Melbourne was, for Irene, paradise. With her dilapidated suitcase hanging over the edge of her wheelie cart, she hailed a taxi, her bare arms shuddering with delight as the warm sun embraced her skin. As she watched car after car stop, and stop and go and stop and go, people coming in and people coming out of cars, impervious to the sun that was so indescribably lovely, she realized it had been six months since those arms of hers had seen and felt the sun on them.

When she climbed into the taxi, it occurred to her to see what time it was. She had no notion of time or day or season. Coming from winter to summer all in a few hours already felt like being in a dream. She figured her time away would be rather ethereal, and jet lag would emphasize this fact. But for now, it seemed like she was swimming somewhere between two hemispheres, and she loved the feeling of this amorphous type of existence.

Still, she looked. Two o'clock in the afternoon. It was Sunday. Saturday the eleventh of February 2017 got eaten up, gone, never to be experienced in her lifetime. She chuckled at the fact.

"The Royal Hotel?" the taxi driver asked.

"Yes, thank you. Beautiful day, isn't it?"

"Yes, sun's out. Can't complain. We had so much rain here last winter and that dreadful cyclone. The world is changing."

"Yes, it is. I hope you were okay last winter."

"Yeah. Melbourne got hit with so much rain and wind, but no casualties."

"The earth is screaming out, isn't it?"

"That's for sure. What part of the US are you from?

"Seattle."

"I have an aunt who lives in DC."

"Oh, yeah?"

"Have you been there?"

"No. Not yet. One day."

"First time in Oz?"

"Yes, it's lovely here. It is such a beautiful thing to leave winter and to arrive in summer." Irene sighed. She thought she would never tire of saying this, feeling this most amazing phenomenon. By the end of her stay, she might have to take her own broken record home with her in her suitcase. Which reminded her— she needed to find an old thrift shop sometime soon and get a bag that would stay together.

"Well, here we are. Enjoy your stay."

"Why, thank you. I will. You enjoy this beautiful day."

A palace greeted her. Never in her life had she been a guest at such a spectacularly gorgeous hotel. She checked her phone to make sure indeed it was the right place. Yep. Two nights' stay at The Royal Hotel. Tomorrow would be the day at the radio station. Today, for the rest of the day, would be hers. *Okay. Check in. Go find a shop that is open on a Sunday. Buy a suitcase. Rest of the day, whatever. You are in the land of Oz, girl.* Irene kept pinching herself in her mind as she stepped into the luxurious foyer of this most beautiful castle hotel. It was summertime. The lobby itself felt like a grand exhibition hall, with chandeliers and sumptuous bouquets of flowers and bands playing and magnificence in every corner. She smiled as she felt her record getting very well-used. After checking in, she made her way toward her room, accompanying the porter, who thankfully took her heap and put it on the elegant cart that probably had never had such a monstrosity in its wheeled life.

If this hotel was a palace, her room was indeed palatial. A king-sized bed greeted her, with a dozen windows surrounding it, each one displaying a sparkling view of the beautiful city of Melbourne and beyond. She plopped onto the bed, laughing as all her travel clothes came tumbling off, and, in her summer underwear, without a stitch of thermals, she giggled, sensing her own giddiness in this otherworldly existence that lay right in front of her.

She looked up thrift shops on her phone, called op shops or opportunity shops in Australia. Quite fortuitously, there was one right down the street from her hotel, and it was open on Sundays until 4:00. She had forty-five minutes. Quickly, she pulled out one of her dresses that had now become rather a wrinkled mess. She pulled out another that was no better. The third and final dress looked remotely presentable, so she put it on along with her sandals, and felt like dancing to the sky and back as she did so. With nothing to carry but her tiny handbag, she pranced out of the hotel and onto the bustling street below.

Thank God for Google directions and smartphones, for in fifteen minutes, she arrived at the magical op shop that would indeed have her beloved suitcase waiting for her. She looked around at the rather smallish shop, finding nothing remotely suitcase-ish. There were a few laptop computer carriers, small backpacks, baby carriers, and toilet article bags.

"Pardon me," she asked a saleswoman, who didn't seem to have too much to do right before closing on a Sunday afternoon. "I am looking for a suitcase. Might you have any, please?"

"No, I am sorry. We're all out. Check back in a week or so."

"Are there perhaps any other op shops in the area?"

"Nope. Not open today at least. Try tomorrow. Across town there might be a few."

Irene's heart sank, thinking about her mess of a bag at the hotel and how more than anything she longed to get rid of it. Tomorrow would be a full-on day at the studio, from 10:00 a.m. to 8:00 p.m. As she slowly headed toward the exit door, a tiny woman, reaching perhaps up to Irene's shoulders, ran up to her.

"Excuse me, but are you the one looking for a suitcase?"

"Well, yes I am, indeed!" Irene's face lightened.

"Well, this morning this one came in. It apparently had been sitting in the main warehouse for years and they were about ready to dump it, and then one of the helpers brought it in here, trying to give this poor old bag one last chance. It's a bit dusty, been on the shelves for I don't know how long, but it's roomy inside, and the wheels work fine. Kind of looks like the wheels were added on. It's a rather old-looking bag. Zipper works great. Take a look."

Irene almost skipped to the front counter, where an emerald-green suitcase glowed, waiting for her. Upon first look, she knew it would be the one. For practical purposes, she opened the zipper, and gave a quick look inside. Perfect. It would hold her things. No more duct tape. No more heaving a large falling-apart piece of junk through airports. She paid the woman and must have thanked her at least twenty times, then wheeled the bag back to the hotel.

Once back at her imperial palace, she decided to properly pack her new bag. First, she dusted it off carefully, getting some stray cobwebs out. Then she ironed all her clothes and put them back into her new magic emerald bag. She sensed something unusual about this suitcase, but besides its lovely color and obvious age, she couldn't put her finger on it. She attributed it to her rather surrealistic frame of mind, and with that, she took her mass of a mess and tossed it in the trash bin at the end of the hallway. She felt light and airy and descended again to the street to see the sights. Famished, she hoped her travels would lead her to a small, intimate place to have a bite to eat.

Meandering through the exquisite Fitzroy Gardens and its adjoining Conservatory with its stunning array of plants and flowers, she once again was transported, her mind wandering, her body alive and vibrant, summer's queenly gaze upon her. She entered the café, in the midst of the blooms around her, and ordered a sandwich as her eyes focused on exotic flowers she had never seen before. Her ears perked up to birdsong that was, at first hearing, loud and boisterous—calls that seemed insistent and in voluminous tones, fortissimo chords in a raucous sort of symphony. *Carmina Burana* came to mind, Carl Orff's elemental resonance to peace in the midst of human conflict, his notes striking and distinctive, shattering the quiet, deceiving moments in a troubled world.

As Irene sauntered out of the café and around the gardens before they closed, she was peaceful, relaxed, open. She found herself changing, much more than merely being on a vacation, away from it all. Like the suitcase, she couldn't quite describe it, but something shifted deeply within her core, filling her senses, her mind, her psyche. Waves of a highly charged sensual energy wove themselves around her being, calling forth an awakened self, an opening that creates elemental change in a human being. She liked this sensation, the warmth on her skin even as the day was waning. The sun still beckoned her to an invitation to newness, to this exploration of gardens, those around her, and the mysterious ones inside of her.

When she returned to her hotel, she showered and slid into her luxurious bed, the soft bamboo sheets gently wrapping around her naked skin. As she slept, her breasts gently rose and fell with each breath, her summered body feeling caressed in her deep—very deep—sleep.

᪣᪣᪣᪣

At 8:00 a.m. on Monday, Irene wasn't quite sure what time of day it was, for in her body, there was a transitional feeling: it could be day, it could be night. When she pulled open the drapes, a brilliant day greeted her, sun majestically beaming as the city was already bustling its way into the beginnings of a workweek. She stretched out her body like a cat, and currents of energy ran through her. Sleep had rejuvenated every part of her, and as she let her back and her legs and her whole body move into yoga pose after pose, she found in her a flexibility she had not had since she was twenty. She went to the bathroom, did her toilette, looked in the mirror at a face she hadn't recognized in a long time. She liked what reflected at her as she brushed her teeth, her hair, dark and long, silky to her fingers. Even her hair felt softer. She put on her dress and sandals and headed downstairs for breakfast with a bounce in her step as she took the stairs, ten flights down.

She ordered Tasmanian yogurt with fruit and muesli. Coffee, of course. As she was waiting to be served, she remembered, as a young child, the yogurt her father would bring home from the Iranian grocers in New York. It was like having a piece of heaven in her mouth, the smooth, creamy texture that slid down her throat as the sweetness of the milk enveloped her tongue. She always wanted more and more, and her father would laugh at her insatiable appetite for this yogurt. Since then, Irene did not eat a lot of yogurt as she did not particularly care for the American brands that were either too sweet or not creamy enough, or both.

When her breakfast arrived, she dipped her spoon in the bowl, put a bit of yogurt on her tongue, and felt a shiver go down her body. It reminded her of her childhood. The taste was perfect, the creaminess exactly what she remembered, what she thought yogurt was supposed to taste like. She ordered another bowl and devoured it, relishing the sensuality of the creaminess. It felt like a woman, like the smoothness of a woman's body: soft, elegant, luscious.

❧❧❧❧

When Irene arrived at the radio station and alerted the woman at the front desk that she was there, she looked around her, amazed. She had been listening to this station for years, relishing their classical programming, which always had a degree of sophistication and real knowledge about classical music from all the eras. She had gotten to know all the broadcasters by their kind voices, and when one of them had to leave the station for retirement or to have a change of pace, Irene would experience a sense of loss. These people had become like family to her, regular presences in her life, providing her, from across the world, with music and commentary about music during all times of the day and night.

A tall, stately woman approached, gray hair tied back in a bun-like thing that allowed her stray hairs to emerge loosely, as if they were wanting to escape and fly onward, south maybe for the winter. She held out her hands and took Irene's in hers.

"You must be Irene. Hello. Warmest greetings to you, truly. I'm Nathalie Brown, the one you spoke with on the phone."

Nathalie was one of those people whose voice was like gold. Her interviews with people from all over the world moved Irene. They were captivating, and there was always a wonderful warmth of spirit. And here Irene was, holding her hands in Nathalie's.

"You cannot imagine what an honor it is to be standing in your presence, Nathalie. I have been listening to your program since I was up to your waist."

"Oh, my goodness. I haven't been alive all that time, have I? When you do the same job in the same place year after year, you somehow forget about how time really does pass. One day you look in the mirror and you wonder who is staring at you." She chuckled as Irene laughed, too.

"Without even knowing it, Nathalie, you have been with me in all kinds of ups and downs in my life. You are like the invisible mother on the radio. But I am sure that for every one of me, there are thousands out there whose lives you have touched. Somewhere, I assume you must realize this."

"I actually have never thought about it like that. That moves me. Thank you. Sometimes you do a job because you absolutely love it, and it is your life, and you can't think of anything else you'd rather do. Altruism doesn't even come into the brain. It's more of a narcissistic perspective." She laughed again, obviously the type to always make others feel good inside. There was an art to doing this, Irene thought, a genuine art that was part of her makeup. Lovely. *If more people like that could be on this planet, imagine the kind of world we would have?*

"So, shall we get started? Have you eaten? If not, there is plenty of food always at this studio. No one leaves here emaciated."

"Thank you, but I have been indulging in so much Australian yogurt here that I am ready to burst at the seams."

Nathalie laughed. "Yes, the Aussies do know their yogurt. Well, if you have an inkling for more later today, check out our fridge and you will laugh. Many of us like it here, too."

The laughter flowed; it was so light and happy here. It felt like a home. A happy little home where music was their domain. Wonderful, Irene mused.

"Have you seen the program for the day? We are quite excited about our Vivaldi festival and all the artists who have made their way across the world to perform on-air today."

That morning in the hotel, Irene had carefully looked over the program for the day. It was quite impressive. From the UK, Academy of St. Martin in the Fields chamber orchestra and the London Concertante Chamber Ensemble. From Melbourne, The Australian Chamber Orchestra and the L'Astrée ensemble, from Italy. From the US, The Sage Chamber Players. From Switzerland, the Camerata Bern. And the list went on.

"You are free to make yourself at home here, Irene," Nathalie said, warmth in her face. "You are part of the family, so today feel free to come and go in each of our recording studios. You can follow the program or meander within these lovely walls. Nathan is coming down in a few minutes to give you a tour of the facility and all that we do here, and after that, the day's concerts will begin. We are scheduled to begin at eleven and go straight through until eight this evening. Meals and all food are provided here, so you can stay here and get to know us, and most of all, enjoy the music today!"

"Can I give you a hug, Nathalie? This is so amazing, and I am so honored and happy to be here."

Nathalie reached out her arms and Irene slipped into them, feeling her kindness, her motherly warmth. Tears sprang in her eyes as they separated.

"It would be lovely to chat with you later, Irene. I would love to get to know you and what brings you so closely to the world of music."

"I'd love that. Do enjoy your day, too. I am sure it will be busy for you."

"Yes, but these kinds of days fill me immeasurably. See you around, and bon appetit!"

Nathalie disappeared into the elevator as another kind-looking soul approached Irene.

"Hi there. Welcome to Melbourne! I'm Nathan, one of the interns here. I would love to give you a tour of the studio. Oh, and congratulations for being our honored guest here today. You are all the way from Seattle, in the US, I hear."

"Yes, across the pond a bit. And how lovely to be taken on a tour here. I have been listening to this station since I was a young girl."

"Wow. That's impressive."

Nathan indeed knew every corner of this major Australian radio station. He gave Irene a quick tour, showing her all the rooms where the news was broadcast, and music was recorded and performed. He showed her where live audiences observed the shows and where everything happened so that listeners anywhere in the world could hear the station. After showing her where the food was served all day long for employees and specially invited guests, he ushered her to the auditorium, where the first concert of the day was to be performed.

Irene stayed in that auditorium most of the day. Mesmerized by the music that flowed into her ears—all Vivaldi—she was transported back to the seventeenth century, and she experienced an agelessness in the music itself, all performed on period instruments to preserve the authenticity of each note.

Sitting in the back of the auditorium, at first her eyes were fixed on the instruments, their age and the beauty that came from the wood. She could tell that some of these string instruments came from centuries ago. Their sounds were different from contemporary violins; the older violins had such a sweetness and an airiness in tone. She sat back and let the music fill her, her eyes closing as the notes and phrases turned this way and that, melodic harmonies that resonated with her sense of calm. Her eyes opened once, but jet lag and the comfortable chair eased her into a space of slumber, the music opening into spaces of a luxuriating lusciousness, her body merely a vessel.

Harriet arrived in her dream. She floated in, unannounced, surprising Irene, as she kissed her, first on the neck, sweetly, as violin music serenaded each kiss. Harriet seemed to know Irene's body as she sucked on her hardened nipples gently at first, then harder, quite hard as Irene writhed under her, wanting her everywhere in all the folds, Harriet knowing by her moans exactly where her mouth and her tongue and her hands would go. The Australian woman pinned her down, with a gentle hand that said, you will be loved, let me love you. Irene felt herself succumbing to this hand, her lips, as she squirmed for more, ached from the insides, a relentless ache that excited Harriet, her nipples as hard as engulfed balls, round and throbbing, starving for Irene's ache as their wetness merged, and

*this grasping for more and endless more finally subsided,
as the moon rose in the sky, their wails, together, as one,
their nectar oozing in the space of the skin, the softness
that came from it, from the music that adorned all.*

Irene woke up to the roaring applause from the
audience all in front of her, she a mere speck in the
back of the room, smiling, the wetness between her
legs reminding her of the visitor she had in her sweet
slumber. She stood up with the rest of the listeners,
begging for more, more, music they loved. Irene, too,
begged for more of all that was sweet here in this
country where it seemed everything beautiful poured
into her and did not want to stop.

The audience quieted as the musicians again
picked up their instruments and played. Then the next
group came in, and they, too, eagerly serenaded Irene's
ears, and again, slumber moved its gentle folds around
her and around her and back again.

The next time she opened her eyes it was six
o'clock. Still the music continued, still the standing
ovations, the encores.

Her stomach interrupted the applause with a
vast grumble. She giggled to herself. Never had she
done this, slept the day away in an auditorium filled
with baroque music that beguiled her as easily as it
beautified all the spaces inside of her. Quietly, she got
up and made her way to the cafeteria, where, quite
fortuitously, Nathalie was sitting with a cup of tea.

She saw her and waved, a movement in the air
back and forth that resounded in warmth, a beckoning
toward friendship. Irene bounded toward her, her
smile huge as she wrapped her arms around her new
friend.

"How lovely to see you, Irene. I was hoping you

might pop in for a bit of tea and something delectable to eat. How are you enjoying your day?"

"Ahhh...it's amazing, this music, the ambience. It is truly one of the best days I have had for years...all thanks to you, Nathalie, for making this all happen." Irene felt young, like a child, around Nathalie, and even the words she used gave her a sense of being someone young and innocent. Nathalie seemed so maternal to her and brought forth a sweetness she'd had with her mother way back, years ago, when she was still small, when her father was still alive.

"Yes, this is definitely a superb day. You know, when you organize something like this, you don't often know how it will turn out, and when the audience is swept off their feet, and group after group keeps astounding them with musical brilliance, you know there is a light out there, and music lets it happen. All day, we keep getting emails and tweets and calls from all over the world, loving these musicians and what they are doing to people's souls. Brilliant. Truly."

"Antonio has been here all day. Do you feel his presence?"

"Absolutely."

"The instruments. All of ancient wood, most probably of his time or close to it."

"Yes. That is what is amazing, too. It is the musicians. And the instruments. Do you play an instrument?"

"You know, people often ask me this. I teach music at the University of Washington. I teach from a place of passion for music, and while I have indeed put my hands on and made notes from mmmm...maybe twenty different instruments, I have never been all that interested in seriously playing one. Sometimes I find that quite odd, like something is wrong with me, a frustrated wannabe musician who teaches instead, but then I have to let it go and do what I love to do and not what I think I should be doing."

"I completely understand. I interview musicians from all over the world and love to get caught up in the passion of music and what it can do to a life, but I have never wanted to play an instrument. My mother had me take piano lessons when I was young, and I lasted all but a year. I refused to practice, and instead spent my free hours listening to piano music and music from all kinds of instruments. That is what made me happy."

"Yes, kindred spirits then." They smiled.

"Ah, Irene, it is so lovely to have you here. I wish I could talk to you more. I do sense a kindred spirit in you. Alas, though, I need to attend to the next group, an Aboriginal group from Alice Springs known for its diversity in styles. They will be combining digeridoo and Vivaldi. Should be captivating. They will be starting in twenty minutes. You must eat and come back to the auditorium."

"Oh, gosh! Absolutely."

Irene found all kinds of sweet and savory pies, yogurts, and fresh summer fruits, and with a smile on her face, she sat down and ravenously ate everything, finding again the happy place in her belly. She pranced back into the auditorium just as the digeridoo began playing an introduction that then blended with Vivaldi's "Summer" concerto, making an indescribably rich and delicious duet between the two styles, giving Vivaldi an earthy resonance that made Irene want to dance in the aisles.

When they were finished, they brought out on stage all the musicians of the day, all fifty or so of them who had played during the festival. In a Baroque music style that blended with folk and world music rhythms, they all jammed together, prompting the audience to get up from their seats and dance. Irene joined the ecstatic crowd, her feet bouncing to the energy of the music. Everyone was smiling, loving it, the blend of styles bringing together people, the collective energy of a love for music, for what it does. The encores spilled into the evening, way into the dipping of the sun on a summer's night. As finally the last note was played, and applause echoed in that auditorium and into the streets of Melbourne, there was in each person, as they walked and drove away, a joy in the soul, a feeling of peace.

Irene floated back to her hotel, showered, and folded herself again in the soft sheets, still hearing music in her head as she gently stroked herself, quieting her mind, the rhythms of her own body gently quieting until sleep came sweetly, lending itself to a deepening of her slumber, deep into the night.

♫ ♫ ♫ ♫

Her eyes opened early, the sun beckoning her wakefulness. She opened the curtains to another brilliant day, the horizon calling her, the blue sky and its endlessness awaiting her travels to Tasmania.

In ten minutes, she was dressed and ready, suitcase packed, as she made her way downstairs for breakfast. Again, yogurt and coffee welcomed her and filled the necessary spaces of her belly. She called an Uber driver, and within minutes she was in the car and headed to the airport, swiftly moving through traffic, the bustling of a summer's day early in the morning.

She felt giddy inside, a bounciness in her heart, in her step, as she checked her emerald-green bag, went through the security line, and made her way to the gate.

The familiar red outfits of the Qantas staff greeted her on the plane, as they took off into the air, one hour later arriving in Hobart. When the plane landed, a grand ebullience filtered itself around her, an excitement that felt uncontainable. As instructed, she looked for her name on a sign, and once recognized, she was graciously whisked away to the resort shuttle, which arrived once a day at the airport to take passengers the two-and-a-half-hour drive to the resort at the majestic Freycinet National Park.

Mesmerized, Irene was transported to a different reality on that bus. Driving through a landscape she had never encountered, her eyes feasted on perhaps the most beautiful journey she had ever taken in her life. Leaving the city of Hobart, most of the drive along the Tasman Highway's terraced arid wilderness was bordered by sages and spinifex that blew in the warm breezes. The hills and low-lying mountains on this east coast of Tasmania held boulders of colors that mimicked the earth—reds, oranges, pinks, and browns that together created a kaleidoscope of shading. They allowed her mind to wander to an existence way beyond the current one, a time when Aboriginal culture was the only culture, and the land and the humans blended as one. When the water appeared, the glorious plunging coastline of the Freycinet Peninsula, Irene leaned into the windows, wanting to be a bird, to fly over the crystalline waters, the white pure sand that beckoned all her senses. She pinched herself, wanting to prove that this was indeed real, that she was here, witnessing this magnificence. Tears moistened her eyes as she took in the beauty that surrounded her, beauty she had never witnessed before, one of the great wonders of the world. As they entered the park, she again felt that same giddiness, the majesty of the mountains and the blue-green water and the rocks all blending to form a landscape that quite literally took her breath away.

She checked in, and the attendants showed her to her private cabin. Immediately her focus was drawn to the view of the water that met her back door. Once the attendants left, she opened the doors and all the windows, letting the gentle breezes lap against her skin. She plopped herself on the pillowy bed and stared for what seemed like hours at the view: perfect water meeting gentle land. Her mind quieted as her senses felt alive, she was a part of the magnificence of the natural world that surrounded her.

Rested, she left the bed and took the path from her private deck down to the beach, letting her feet sink into the sand, warmed from the day's sun. The silky white texture greeted her toes with their sensual calling as she walked and walked, loving the feeling of her bare feet exposed, experiencing the threads of softness billowing around her feet.

Far down the beach, away from all people, she sat, her warm thighs enveloped by the softness of sand, such a different texture from the coarseness of the sand at the beaches near Seattle. Here, she felt like she was melting, and had a craving to sit and never leave. As she put her legs out, letting the silky whiteness cover up her skin, she sighed. She never thought that life could be this good. She completely forgot where she came from only a few days earlier and found herself contentedly immersed in this resplendent dreamy experience.

As the sun lowered itself over the horizon, she headed back, feeling a bit peckish after her long day of travel. The last time she'd eaten was early that morning, a small bowl of yogurt. *Yogurt...I am in the blessed land of yogurt.*

She returned to the resort and headed immediately to the restaurant, where she ordered grilled salmon cooked with watermelon, pomegranate, feta, and asparagus. The combination of tastes put her mouth into a state of orgasmic euphoria; each bite was like kisses on every corner of her body, wanting more. She finished with a bowl of simple vanilla bean ice cream that had the same wondrous sensual texture of the yogurt.

Floating back to her cabin, a flow of delight ran through her. *Can there be anything more wonderful than this? I dare not think so.* She giggled to herself.

She decided to settle in and put her things away in drawers and closets, making this cabin her home for the next five delicious days. She carefully folded each item, and at the end, she noticed that something seemed to be missing. At dinner, she made the decision to go on a long hike the next day to a waterfall that was said to be one of the most pristine in Australia. She didn't know the rules on nudity here, so she thought she'd bring along her bikini top and bottom, just in case. She found the bottom in her emerald bag, but the top seemed to be gone. *Probably fell out when my old suitcase exploded*, she thought, but for the sake of it, she took the bag and shook it over the bed. Nothing of course fell out, but she heard a faint sound of something crinkly. She shook it a second time, thinking this was all quite ridiculous, and again, she heard the same crinkly sound. Irene stared into the suitcase, listening to silence as she inspected every corner and opened the small zipper pocket inside that she hadn't used. It was a bit dusty, but empty. *All this euphoria has made me go most definitely insane. I am now hearing sounds. Oh goodness, this most definitely is not good.*

She went to the bathroom and brushed her teeth, returning to the mystery on the bed, convinced she did not make up the sounds. She inspected the bag once again, and this time she noticed a strange kind of fold that the fabric made at the side and along the entire perimeter of the suitcase. She lifted the dusty folded fabric and found a zipper, a smooth, hardly even used hidden zipper.

"Oh my God!" she screamed out loud as she found the end to the zipper and carefully followed it from start to finish. When she had reached the end, there, awaiting her was a double bottom, a secret space to put things. As she completely revealed this surface, there, in plain view was a tattered and weathered envelope taped to the back of the first bottom of the emerald-green bag.

She carefully took off the tape, and in her hands, which were now shaking, she held the envelope that obviously contained something.

Sitting down on the bed, she lifted open the flap that was sealed shut. Inside the envelope there were two envelopes. The first one she opened contained money. Lots of it. They were pounds, in denominations of 1,000. She counted out the bills; there were twenty of them. She knew that pounds were replaced by the Australian dollar in the early 1960s. Her hands shook even more as she realized she was holding someone's savings from before she was born. Next, she opened the second envelope, and there were pages and pages of writing, poetry it seemed. She looked for a name, some identification, and as she scanned each wrinkled page, noting the beautiful handwriting, she saw, at the bottom of one of the pages, the name "Hilary." Irene screamed inside to find the last name. She had to know who wrote these voluminous poems that she would later read, word by word. She found nothing. She looked inside the bag again, and in the first envelope, she saw what she needed: on a slim, folded piece of paper, folded were the words *To L. L., from Hillary Hanover. Forever...*

L.L., Irene mused. Who was that? A woman or a man? And why on earth was there so much money and all these poems attached to this suitcase?

She began to uncover, word for word, the mystery that would permanently change her life.

Chapter Four

Empty houses I have seen, I have walked in,
I have smelled the remains of memories
Trapped in empty rooms, the vacant stare of walls,
The quiet whisper saying hush,
Saying so many things in the night where
everything is so dark,
So very very dark.
I've tasted those empty houses,
The bitterness that lingers on the tongue
Where the furniture has all been carted away.
I gave you lemons once.
So many you couldn't hold them all against your
white blouse.
Your nipples hard, grazing the yellow that
blended so perfectly.
You smiled then, so full of life you were,
Your house a pulsing emblem of all the poems
you wrote,
All the conversations clipping along like
Trains going from Paris to Marseille.
Gone, you're gone, long gone.
Only blank stares laugh at me for loving.
For yearning for the impossible,
For striving for that perfect art form
Eclipsed around false dreams.
Empty houses surround my soul
As I remember the souls I have ever loved

Who have moved away,
Without saying goodbye;
Ghosts in the night
Whispering hush
As floorboards creak.
And hearts sit quietly on lonely windowsills.

࿄ ࿄ ࿄ ࿄

Footprints in the snow
I headed to her, always to her.
Her fragrance captivated me
drawing me closer and closer
her voice I hang on to
even when she is not there.

I knock on the door of her small cabin
deeply hidden in the bush, ghost gum trees with
the fragrance of pine,
her lingering smell mingles with resin and the
earth.

Where did she go?
I am panting
an animal, waiting.
It is her birthday today.
My lips long for hers
wanting to run away with her
under the soft down comforters
letting the dreams of our bodies meet our souls.

Tears come down
flowing like the juices between my legs
as I search for her everywhere

here in the snow
footprints and handprints and voices in my head
that are only echoes of a time where she was
everywhere
all over me
surrounding my smallness, letting it grow.

I will wait for her
the rest of my life
and I will continue to walk in the snow
following her tracks
until the warmth of her breath meets mine again
and the sun dazzles on the pristine earth
making white even whiter.

☙ ❧ ☙ ❧

The veil is thin
I am so close to the truth
to the world of spirit
to endless possibilities.

I reach out
my fingers gently graze skin
it frightens me
yet I must remember it is only fear.

My hand strokes the boulder that I stand on
the one that crashed to the sea
or so I thought.
But here it is
under my feet
as I stare at the sky
and the stars

and I remember your voice and the sound of it
as I feel protected somehow by this voice
and the memory of it that resides in my heart.

All I have to do is take that breath
believe in the circle
and let go of the line
finding that depth again inside myself
knowing that the mountain is always there
even if it is covered by mist.
And knowing
that the tide always goes in
and it always goes out
as I step from that boulder
feeling the wind that is you reminding me
that the universe is there to catch me all over
vagain.

❧ ❧ ❧ ❧

Irene felt her tears well up, cascading down her cheeks to her chest.

"They were lovers," she said, out loud, holding the aged paper, crinkling in her hands. Two women. For some reason, L.L. vanished, and then she died. Hillary was so in love with her. Oh my God, what a tragic story, she thought.

She clutched the stationery, feeling like she had been let in on a secret love story whose mysteriousness gripped her as much as the beauty of their love in a time where it was most probably quite unheard of for two women to love each other. Who was L.L., she wondered, and why did she leave? How did she die? And who was Hillary? A Tasmanian love story that ended so tragically. L.L. was a poet, there were references to being in France, and the eroticism made Irene want more, more poems, more words of these forbidden desires, the hardened nipples against the white blouse, holding all those lemons. She could picture that scene, the longing in Hillary's eyes, the animal-like passion she had for this woman, wanting to devour her. Yet, the pathos of her grief was immense. She held on to this woman all her life, or so it seemed, and when L.L. vanished and later died, all she wanted was to be reunited with her beloved.

Irene was exhausted, saddened by this story. She took a shower and lay in bed, the poems strewn around her, lives partially revealed after maybe decades of obscurity.

Sleep met her instantly, fatigue from the day mixed with all these recent emotions sweeping her offshore, to the distant world of her dreams.

Lined up in a row, outside in a garden filled with flowers, there are suitcases, hundreds of them, each one a different color, each one containing different items, lives unveiled, as Irene goes down the line, in her green and purple uniform, inspecting the contents, deciding which ones to keep, which ones to put aside. Gum trees line the path as hundreds of pink and gray galahs squawk to their heart's content, flying and landing in the trees. Kangaroos jump freely, fearlessly up and around her, showing off their muscled haunches. Irene has a job to do and ignores the life around her as she attempts to sort through the pages and volumes of material flying out of the suitcases, the wind picking up speed, sending people's lives away from their bags, their homes to unknown destinations. She catches a piece of paper in her hands. It is old, frayed at the edges, and coffee stains mar many of the words. There are lists of names on it, like a family tree. The names all begin with "H." At the top is Hillary's name, and beside it, a line marking a marriage to a man named Henry. Another line comes down from that which connects these two. The name inscribed is Hal. A line connects Hal with Hortense, and the line down from that line spells out Helena. Irene holds this paper in her hand, clutching it, as all the contents of all the suitcases spill out and away, down the hillsides and through the garden. All that is left is the emerald-green bag, sitting alone.

⚜⚜⚜⚜

The sun shone on Irene's face, waking her up. It was late in the morning, perhaps almost noon. The galahs were flying back and forth from her deck, singing and shouting to each other as the air was still. As she looked out on the horizon that stretched to infinity, she felt herself pulled from the present moment, drawn to the dream world that wove itself around her awake brain.

Throwing on her hiking boots, she began walking as the gentle breeze from the ocean met the sun, warming her neck. All around her was water, the limitless ocean with the greens and blues that drew her mind away from her feet, the earth, to the watery substance of her imagination, her dream. Her heart was healthily pumping blood as she climbed up the hill, arriving at a waterfall, a towering mass of rocks spilling water down toward the beckoning ocean. She was hot, sweat pouring from her navel as she stripped off her clothes and stood in the cascading pools of water, movement and stillness combined, cool and warm merging together as she felt the aliveness in her body. In her nakedness, every part of her became stimulated, caressed, blending hard and soft, desire and hunger as she came with the swirling movement of water around her.

Afterward, she lounged on a sun-warmed boulder, the gentle rays of summer drying her cooled skin, warming her again to the perfect temperature. She pulled out her lunch from her backpack, three yogurts and a sandwich. The dining room had carefully put the yogurts in a bucket of ice when she told them she would be going on a hike, and as she put the spoonful into her mouth, she sighed, smiling, as the cool, slippery, perfect texture slid down her throat.

I had a job to do, she mused, reflecting on her dream. *Deciding which ones to keep, which ones to let go of. Then there is the wind, blowing everything away except one piece of paper. I am supposed to figure it out, why this piece of paper that lands in my hands, why the family tree? Why?* The name Helena rang in her brain as Irene bolted up from the rock.

She pulled out her phone to see if perhaps she might have internet access. An idea had popped into her mind. Her phone gave her a vacant stare when she looked at it. *Ah, no need to be in such a hurry. Put that silly phone away*, she silently admonished herself. With a deep sigh, she lay on her back and listened to frogs croaking in the distance. Lizards came up to her feet, doing their sensory push-ups, tickling her toes. She giggled. From a gum tree nearby, she heard the distinct call of the kookaburra. She had always wanted to hear this call in the wild. It was a rather eerie sound, and indeed it did sound like a laugh, the way the song suggested—the one she had learned as a child:

Laugh, kookaburra, laugh, kookaburra, gay your life must be.

It sounded like a nervous laugh, as in someone was out to get it. She wondered if it was indeed a predator of some animals. She sat up and looked around her and perked up her ears. From way in the distance, she heard a dreadful screeching sound, like that of an animal in the middle of killing another. She listened carefully, trying to discern where it was coming from. It appeared to be heading closer to her. A Tasmanian devil, she wondered. Not only were they an endangered species in Tasmania, she had heard that they screech at full volume when they approach their next meal, and they were known to have voracious appetites. She pulled out her binoculars and scanned the horizon. She didn't know if she was imagining it or not, but her keen eyes, together with the magnification, spotted a very stalky, black rodent-dog-looking thing that matched perfectly all her mental photos of the Tasmanian Devil. Then, as quickly as the sound appeared, all was silent, the staging of the natural world around her coming to an intermission. She dressed and packed up to leave. Her footsteps quietly sank into the earth as she walked, the afternoon waning, as the sound of cockatoos squawking, their shrill, vibrant voices filling the air. A family of gray kangaroos hopped noisily in the bush beside her, scavenging for bugs and other crawly bits. Irene had been watching kangaroos since she arrived—they were a regular presence in the park. She had grown quite fond of these animals, the strength in their haunches as they leapt so high, fearlessly soaring into the air. Their facial expressions were a mixture of jovial and serious, with a comic air, as if they, too, were all part of this theatre that was their life. Irene watched the family, two adolescents and the mother, leap away, off to find more tasty morsels as she smiled to herself, feeling like she, too, could leap into the air in this world of what seemed to her an endless imagination.

She got back to her cabin, tired from the long hike but extremely content. As she sat on her deck drinking glass after glass of water, she pulled out her phone, scanning the pictures of the day, smiling as she reran the cinema in front of her. Then, with internet access in her hand, she did a simple search: Helena Hanover.

On the screen in front of her was this name, the owner of a dairy farm in Colorado.

Irene laughed loudly, a mixture of a screech and a laugh, one that begged her to continue her search, finding again a clue, an amusing one at that. She scrolled down, looking for another Helena Hanover.

The dairy farmer was the only one.

She got into the site, and written in one line was the name, "Tassieyogo."

She felt her heart racing fast, and she thought she would burst off her lounge chair and soar into the water below.

The yogurt got its cultures from Tasmania, it said. It was noted that it was the best yogurt that had ever hit the US. There were product descriptions and Colorado retail locations, and there was a "Contact Us" link. Irene, sweating, pressed this button and wrote.

Dear Ms. Hanover. This might be a very strange message, but are you the granddaughter of Hillary Hanover? If so, please contact me as soon as you can.

I have some news to tell you. I am in Tasmania at the moment. Irene is my name.

She pressed Send, staring at the site and the pictures of happy cows in the mountains.

Irene stared off at the beach, thinking she saw perhaps some penguins. With her binoculars she scanned the beach, and sure enough, there on the sand was a group of the tiny fairy penguins, little birdlike creatures, the smallest in the penguin family. They, too, were looking for food as it was low tide. Their waddling movements were altogether adorable, and Irene giggled quietly, feeling akin to the magic of penguins right outside her door. Her phone zinged.

She looked down, forgetting for a moment about these things called phones. There was a message labeled urgent. It was from Helena.

This is amazing. I am at the airport in Denver, and my flight to Melbourne is boarding in five minutes. I am flying in to Tasmania, to Swansea. Where are you? I would love to meet you!

Irene gulped. *I am in Freycinet National Park. At the resort.* She pressed Send and gulped again.

Oh my God. I will be right around the corner, more or less, the next town over! My Skype name is TASSIEYOGO and I'll message you my phone number. I can meet you for dinner on Thursday. Have to go now. This is completely amazing, Irene. Oh, I so hope to see you! Helena.

Irene held the phone in her hand, which was

now shaking like a leaf in the wind ready to launch out of its autumnal tree. She made a giggle kind of laugh that was more connected to a sense of disbelief rather than to humor, but there was laced in that laugh a bit of mockery in the ridiculousness of it all. The whole thing seemed like something out of a novel, completely made up, to imagine that in that suitcase were words, and connected to those words was a woman who made yogurt from Tasmanian cultures, and here she was standing right in the middle of Tasmania, as kangaroos hopped blithely by, holding a phone that would, in twenty-four hours or so, bear a message from a woman from Colorado who would be at her front door asking her to dinner.

This was too surreal for words. Her life never operated on surrealism or surprise. From her idyllic life with her parents to the stark emptiness of life with only her mom, to her escape to the Northwest and her didactic teaching job, where structure and regularity were the main course of her existence, she never had entertained anything different. Bob was her one friend, and her own company provided the rest. She was content, or so she thought, and life was simple, without much adventure to speak of. So, why on earth now, did she have that fantasy of a beach in winter? She never had such inklings to expand her horizons all that much.

As penguins and kangaroos lived their banal existence around her, as the Tasmanian devil's cry returned to her memories, as she stared out into the vastness and spaciousness of water, the ocean, the deep blues and greens a painting to her eyes, now vulnerable and exposed, she, the traveler journeying to a place that had existed for thousands of years, she felt her own suppleness, a bending of the spine that allowed her to stretch her own life beyond what any novel could ever accomplish.

She walked down the stairs from her deck to the beach, letting her feet sink into the softness of the sand. She could do this every day. *I should like to live here in Tasmania one day*, she said to herself, reaching back into that sense of place that resounds in the psyche. A slight breeze grazed her face, her hair falling into her eyes. As she stood, brushing hair off her face, her eyes filled with tears, this knowing, this sensing that every bit of her was at home here on this land whose symphony was loud and vivacious, yet whose effect on her was quiet and calming. The early evening birds arrived, some en masse and some all by themselves, announcing to all their entrance into the scheme of things, their own predictability juxtaposed with their spontaneous cries of delight at finding the right food for their bellies.

Irene sat on the sand, her legs wanting softness. She sighed, then smiled at what was right in front of her and what was waiting for her tomorrow. She had no expectations about Helena, yet she also knew in herself that a giddiness had spread throughout her being as she thought of the yogurt stranger from Colorado who truly wanted to meet her. Irene had to admit, she wanted to meet this woman, too.

Hunger met her, all forms of hunger, even though in part she felt completely full. Her stomach, however, reminded her that it was time for dinner, so she ventured away from the sand to the restaurant to see what specials of the day they might be offering.

❧❧❧❧

The evening was quiet, and a luxurious fatigue spread through Irene after dinner and her long bath that followed. She sat on the deck, watching the late summer sun dip down behind the horizon, the colors off the mountain reflecting oranges and pinks that allowed her eyes to rest, as though she were immersed in a warm painting, yet cool enough to create a calm inside of her, a gentle hum, a sense of gratitude for the abundance in the world around her. Her silk robe slid off her shoulders as she picked up her glass of wine and sipped it slowly, as she let everything slow down, her hair loose, gently grazing the softness of her skin. She sighed.

Day birds vanished, as the beings of the night emerged. Bats swooped up and around, out of nowhere, attentive always to the signal that this was their time for foraging, when the darkness began its rule. From a distance, Irene heard owl calls, a courting pair, one song to another hooting from tree to tree. Down on the ground she spotted some possums, with their long tails, beginning their hunt for dinner. The sounds of the night created a different kind of symphony, one that was more modernistic, she thought, more of a squealing, eerie kind of cacophony. The waves of the ocean, the regular calming rhythm of water accompanied all.

Soon it was dark, and Irene looked up at the stars, each one carrying its own story, brilliant beacons in the sky. With a yawn, and then another, she headed off to bed, letting the soft covers lightly graze her sultry skin. As the animals of the night continued their lives in their world, sleep met her gracefully in hers.

Chapter Five

When Irene opened her eyes, the afternoon had arrived. She bounced out of bed, greeting the day with exuberance, the sun, already halfway across the sky, coming down in a gentle heat, warming the earth. Rosellas and cockatoos sang cheeky and belligerent songs to each other, voluminous conversations from the trees. A teenage kangaroo grazed outside her cabin, oblivious to everything except for the food that was slipping down its throat.

Starving, Irene brushed her hair, threw on some clothes, and headed to the café for breakfast. Two bowlfuls of creamy yogurt with muesli and a café au lait later, she walked, but more so skipped, to her cabin. In just a few hours she would be meeting Helena. The mere thought of this made her heart race, her feet poised to leap into the sky like one of her companion kangaroos.

She pulled out her phone and sent a text message. *Hope your long flight was a good one. Safe travels to Swansea. Can't wait to meet you. Irene.*

Then, she sent TASSIEYOGO a Skype invitation.

She put on her swim bottoms under her clothes, placed her book and water and a towel into her bag, and with her boots on her feet, she headed to a trail that would take her to the long stretch of a beach that she had wanted to venture on. This would be a perfect day to be a beach bum, she thought—a hike and a swim and a lollygagging afternoon in Tasmania.

Energized by the thought of her rendezvous that evening, Irene hiked for quite a distance along the beach bluff trail, surrounded by mountain peaks and the pristine water on all sides. The trail gave in to a steep slope, descending to a private cove, a breathtaking secluded beach. She accepted nature's invitation to spend the rest of her afternoon right there on the sand. The tide was far out, and according to her tide chart, it would not be coming back in for several hours. Perfect, she thought.

Warmed by the walk, she headed into the water, an undoubtedly ideal temperature, so unlike the frigidly cold ocean waters of the Pacific Northwest. She sat in the water, half of her body submerged, her shoulders heated by the sun. A smile spread across her face as she looked out, the water lapping on the shore behind her, and in front of her an endless mass of energy that headed all around the world. As she looked beyond, way beyond, she noticed movement in the water, a fin arising from the bulbous waves that extended miles away from the shore. She wondered if it was a shark, and she looked closely. No, it was decidedly a dolphin—actually, there were two that were rising and falling from the water, swimming in tandem, the curves of their backs perfect arcs in the air. Irene left her spot and swam closer, wanting a better view, yet not wanting to frighten them. She was a good swimmer, her strokes even and strong, muscled movements through the waves. Treading water, she got closer to the dolphins and quietly observed. They did not venture away, but stayed in proximity to her, as if playing a game. They were not afraid, and neither was she. In the presence of fear, they would have most assuredly swum away, but they must have sensed a safe human, and they began to swim around her, circles and spirals. She beamed, loving this game, her legs moving in the water like a dance as they themselves danced with her, a *pas de trois* in the ocean. The two made sounds, dolphin music, uniting human and animal with their water duets. And then, as quickly as they arrived, they disappeared, their massive fins curving and sinking as their bodies became transported through the gravity they created. Elated and tired, Irene swam to shore, took off her suit, and lay naked on her towel, letting the sun surround every part of her bare skin, warming all her curves and folds and seeping inside of her contented being. When she got too hot, she ventured back into the water, finding a place that was half-shaded and half-sunned to spend the rest of her afternoon.

The day waned, and the tide returned to its evening pose. Irene put on her clothes and packed up her backpack, heading back up the trail. She glanced at her phone and saw it was almost five o'clock. Picking up the pace, she ran up the hill and across the bluff. Her years and years of running made her moves effortless, as she arrived at her cabin at 5:45 and threw her sweaty body in the shower.

At six, she picked up her phone. Her hair was wet, glistening in the early evening light. Her black summer sleeveless dress curved around her body, flowing to her muscled thighs. Her skin, darkened by the Australian sun, glowed and gave off a healthy sheen, smooth and soft, beckoning to be touched.

A message zinged in.

Hi. I am in the lobby.

Well, here's someone who believes in being on time. Irene chuckled. This was one of her worst vices, forgetting about the time on social occasions. She never was late for work, but everything else seemed to be eclipsed around a vague notion of the clock.

Her footsteps were a blend of walking and skipping. When she opened the door to the lobby, her heart skipped a beat. She felt unmistakably nervous. The woman who was clearly staring at her was stunningly attractive, her red hair a mess of curls that begged to be played with. Irene was instantly pulled toward this woman, the chemistry in that first sighting of each other proving to be an insanely voracious magnet. Helena's eyes moved up and down the graceful lines of Irene's body ending with her gaze into Irene's eyes as they walked toward each other.

Shifting quickly into formalities, they put out their hands to shake, introducing themselves, as if they really needed such a trivial welcome. They each laughed, already finding a secret between them that was indeed laughable.

"It is amazing meeting you, Irene. This seems very unreal that here we are, in Tasmania, shaking hands at one of my most favorite places on this planet."

"Really?"

"I have always loved this park. I've always thought it is rather magical."

"It is." Irene blushed, feeling tongue-tied, caught up in this moment of incredulity.

"What do you say we go for a drive? I have a restaurant I want to take you to, another one of my absolutely favorite places to have a nice meal." Helena's cheeks were bright red and glistening, radiant and puffed out like a partially inflated balloon. Irene didn't miss a beat, was even more drawn in to her adorableness when she was excited about something. "And," she continued, "I am dying to find out how you encountered the spirit of my grandmother and what in the world brought you here."

Irene smiled as they walked out to the car, not ready to talk and chatter away. She was in the moment of an astonishing delight that had no words yet. Helena seemed to sense this and relaxed into the comfort of silence. Soon, they stepped into the emerald-green car she had rented.

They drove in silence along the steep coastal road, curved and vivacious, lending itself to majestic overlooks. The energy between the two women was intense in its silence, and the newness of this allure created a fizzing sensation inside Irene. While she couldn't tell yet what Helene was feeling, she thought she would throw all caution to the wind. She wanted out of that car, wanting Helena's hands on her and not on the steering wheel.

"Would you mind if we stop here? It is just so beautiful. I want to breathe it in."

"Absolutely. I was thinking the same thing."

They stood on the barren cliff, the ocean stretching on for an infinity. On all sides there were mountainous peaks, boulders, and rocks jutting out to the ocean and higher, so high it seemed there was an endlessness in their ascension. The ocean breezes were gentle, blending with the soft ending to a warm day. Irene stood, her hair flowing against her back and shoulders, her neck exposed to the last rays of sun for the day. She loved the feeling of Helena standing next to her, sensing the movement of her hair, like a dance around the curves of her back. Side by side, the energy between them seemed to contain a life all its own as the seals below barked like dogs, inviting giggles from the women. Irene breathed it all in, this delicious sensation inside her and the majestic landscape all around her. Instinctively, she reached out her hand, and Helena clasped it and brought it to her mouth and kissed it gently. Irene purred as the two stood, her hand joined with Helena's, intuitively knowing life had shifted its course and would never be the same again.

As they got back into the car, all nervousness dispelled, there was a calm, this knowing, this trust that everything that was supposed to happen, indeed was happening, and would happen. There was no rush, no need to speak, to act, to do anything except what the inner voice and the body communicated. Irene had not experienced this before and somehow, she sensed it was the same for Helena. The newness of this knowingness was as beautiful as the discovery itself. As they got to the restaurant, their hands came again together. They walked from the parking lot to the door and then to their table, outside on the deck; it jutted out over the cliff that illuminated the setting sun's resplendent colors. They looked in each other's eyes, gazing, familiarizing themselves with the nuances and the depth that each mirrored to the other. Their smiles were like a talisman of what lay ahead, the joy in their faces reflecting an awakening into the current of lives transformed, two energies calling to each other with all the fierceness and sublimity that their journey would deserve.

Still gazing, Helena broke the silence.

"Okay, so tell me, what? How? Tasmania?"

Irene laughed. "So, you are one of many words and complete sentences."

They both laughed, and Irene cherished this sound, their laughter that linked them to surges of desire; Their eyes locked, and she felt herself inescapably connected to something beyond words.

Irene began her story, the details of her life flowing out of her like water, gentle, rhythmical, melodious bits and pieces that created who she was.

ตั้ต้ตั้ต้ต้

Helena watched and listened to Irene, all her senses alive and open as she felt drawn into a life that was so different from her own, yet somehow not. She stared at the beauty of Irene—not just her story, but the essence of her. She fixed her gaze on her face, the softness in her eyes, the way her mouth moved. It was like a song, with harmonies laced into the weave of her life. It would be too cliché to say she dreamed for years and years of meeting this woman, but in that moment when Irene got to the dream of the beach, when she had brought her to nearly the present, when perhaps an hour or maybe just five minutes had passed, Helena felt like she was swimming with this nebulous feeling that in that space of time, everything was as it was planned. The excitement that ran through her, in massive waves that flowed up and down her body, surging in every corner of her being, was only a mere sign that pointed the direction to her awaiting heart. As Irene finished her story and the period was placed ceremoniously at that place where Helena's gaze was firmly locked with Irene's, she felt like she was reaching in, fitting like a perfect pose. She sensed that it was like a *pas de deux* that could perhaps last forever if one were to allow it.

Helena took Irene's hand, finding the curves in it, and brought it to her lips, letting the grazing of a mouth sink into the skin of another's. Irene moaned gently and smiled. Helena sensed that she wanted more, but also detected that she wanted to stay in this moment of stories, unveiled.

Helena knew it would have been easy, completely natural, to have left the restaurant at that moment to explore the other, to graze the lips in other places. In one quick look, she sensed their mutual feelings. That moment would surely come, but better to feed a body that is starving, and not one that is growing in its hunger.

"Your turn," Irene said. Helena noticed mocking in her eyes.

"I'm not sure if I can tell as riveting a story as yours was."

"Enough disclaimers. Go."

They each giggled.

Helena took a deep breath.

"It began before I was born."

"These things usually do."

"I love your quick wit."

Irene nodded for the story to begin, her eyes riveted on Helena's face, waiting for the first sentence.

"Hillary, my grandmother, the one whose letters you found, met my grandfather in England. They were both students at King's College Cambridge. They sang in the choir together. Henry had the voice of God, my grandmother once said, when she heard him solo one day in practice. He was studying Marine Biology, and my grandmother was studying Literature, with an emphasis on Virginia Woolf and the modernist classicists. She got to hear Virginia speak several times, apparently, in guest lectures she gave at Cambridge. They graduated and got married. My grandmother really wanted to stay in England and be in the thick of the Bloomsbury entourage, but my grandfather got offered a prestigious position to teach and to eventually launch the Institute of Marine and Antarctic Studies in Tasmania. They almost separated because of this, as my grandmother really did not want to be in Australia. The University of Tasmania knew this, and because they wanted my grandfather so much, they wooed her by offering her a tenured faculty position in the English Literature department. Everything was new then, and the founders were mostly recruiting graduates from universities in the UK."

She paused, staring out the window at the passing birds.

"So, the story goes," she continued, "that one of my grandmother's students seduced my grandmother one day off campus in the bush somewhere outside of Hobart where my grandmother liked to study and read. Her name was Laure, and she was French. Laure Lyons. This began a two-year-long affair that my grandfather never knew about. My grandmother was crazy about Laure, as you figured out, and their relationship was as passionate as it was fraught with tragedy. One day, I heard, she simply vanished, and my grandmother had no idea what had happened. Years later, she found out, through a letter she had sent her, that her parents caught wind of their daughter's lesbian seductions, and they shipped her immediately back to France and married her off to a suitor they had chosen, a withered older man from their hometown. Apparently, Laure fell into a deep depression after that, and shortly after she wrote that last letter to my grandmother, she drowned herself in the river that went through her village in the center of France."

Helena paused, thinking to herself about how awful it must have been for her grandmother when she heard this news. Her eyes drifted away again, to the water below as Irene also looked out. After a few moments, she continued.

"My grandmother, a few years after the departure of her beloved, was pulled into motherhood with the birth of her fraternal twins—my mother, the youngest by twenty minutes, and my uncle. As a full-time mother, she almost entirely lost her connections to the university and was given the status of 'Professor's wife'—a title which she, in her feminist ways, abhorred. My mother seems to think that she never did get over the loss of Laure, which of course neither she nor her brother knew about for all those years until her last days, when, as the story goes, in a state of predeath delirium, she revealed to my mother the name Laure, and as she was sleeping, she pronounced, 'I am coming, my dearest Laure, wait for me...' She died that night."

Helena sighed, imagining again her grandmother in that state of distress. She took a sip of wine and continued.

"While my mother and my uncle were growing up, my grandmother, they said, was always very distant, and my grandfather became absorbed in his work, often leaving for weeks at a time to go on excursions to Antarctica to further his research. My mom and uncle made a pact that as soon as they completed high school, they would leave Tasmania for good.

"Indeed, at age eighteen, my uncle went to the University of Melbourne, married an Aussie, and had three kids with her. They still live in Melbourne. My mom went to the University of Sydney, where she focused on urban architecture and design, and was one of the main architects for the Sydney Opera House. While she was completing her studies, she met and married my dad, an American, who was smitten with her. They lived in Sydney for a few years until he got a call from his mother telling him his dad had suddenly died from a heart attack, and she needed him to be there to take over the dairy farm in Colorado. She couldn't do it alone, and he was their only child. In a way, their lives repeated my grandparents' story. My mom resisted going to the US. She was at the beginning of her career, and the Opera House was in its groundbreaking stages. She didn't at all want to be on a dairy farm, but dutifully followed her husband."

Helena finished the last bit of wine in her glass, looking for one last drop, and seeing that there was none, she resumed.

"Meanwhile, my grandmother withered away and died young. My mom, right before she moved to the US, stayed for a month with her, and when she died, my grandfather became steeped in his work. He lived for about ten years and then died of cancer. I remember meeting him when I was a little girl. He seemed like a wise person who held sadness deep in his pocket. After he died, my uncle had no idea what to do with all their things, so they shipped them over to Melbourne and stored them in their emptied-out garage and sold the house in Tasmania. The emerald suitcase was my grandmother's, from England, and the money in it was all her personal life savings. Their joint money—hers and my grandfather's—got distributed between my mom and my uncle. I think in her almost dead and demented state, she thought she would take a trip to see Laure, who she imagined was still alive, and give her everything of value that she had."

Helena glanced over at Irene, taking in her gorgeous, focused eyes.

"One day," she continued, "my uncle phoned me, telling me that his wife was fed up with all that stuff in the garage, and she insisted my uncle get rid of it. He donated almost all of it to charity, which is how you got it when you went to the op shop in Melbourne."

Helena shook her head.

"Anyway, my parents settled in Colorado together, on the family farm outside of Boulder. While my dad took care of the entire farm, my mother sat and brooded and painted cows. For years, that's all she wanted to do—stare off into the mountains with her easel and her watercolors, and cow after cow emerged on canvas after canvas. My grandmother, my dad's mom, couldn't stand my mother, as she did nothing to help with the farm, but still, my dad was so in love with her that he never made a comment about her lack of participation.

"When I was born, my mother took a bit of interest in me, but mostly left the caring of my needs with my grandmother, who was happy to have me in this world. When I was five, she pretty much left my dad and me, venturing to Boulder, and was offered a position to help design a state-of-the-art concert hall. She would only come home on a few weekends a month, and when she was home, she seemed bored with the life of the farm as she now had her passion in front of her with her work."

Helena paused for a second, took a sip of water, gulping it down. In the back of her mind, she had a flashback of her mother, driving away, her eyes on the road, as she sat on the porch stoop and cried. She didn't want to stay in that memory. She glanced up at Irene, scanning her face, the soft lines, her dark hair that looked like the color of the rich earth. She sighed and continued.

"I loved the farm, unlike my mom, and from my grandmother and my dad, everything I learned excited me. Our focus in life was yogurt. As I got older, I loved to research new methods for making yogurt, and several years ago, after a visit to Australia to see my uncle and tasting the brilliant Aussie yogurts, I had the brilliant idea to see if I could use the Australian cultures, export them, and create an American version of the best yogurt in the US. My dad loved this idea, and he and I began a new venture.

"Zip ahead the story by several years. He died, only a few years ago."

Helena stopped, and Irene took her hand, her face expressing compassion. Helena held back her emotions as she tried to finish her story, the hand in her hand only reminding her of how many tears she still had left.

"I wanted to go back to my roots even more after he was gone, so I lived in Tasmania for a year, rented an old house, and made connections with farmers. I discovered the region we are in now and I fell in love with this landscape, the richness of this soil. I come back here every chance I get."

She was silent then, her story done. Helena stared out the window at the sea, feeling called to reach it somehow, her dad, his voice, the legacy they created that she now held in her heart. Irene stared, too, at the water.

"I feel a voice sing, a requiem, cadences and harmonies that align with the dead, our fathers, their spirits, and what remains they leave for the living, the daughters, us," Irene said, her own voice drifting toward the water as they both stared at it.

"That's beautiful, the way you say that." Helena squeezed her hand.

Irene reached in her bag and pulled out the tattered envelope, the paper so thin it seemed like a wisp of a wind would blow it away.

"This is the reason we have met," she said gently, handing it over to Helena.

Helena grasped the folded paper, her hands shaking. She pulled up the flap and pictures of the Queen came tumbling out, one after another, in all colors. The former monarchy of Australia laced the table, each bill reminding her of the past—the Australia that belonged to former generations, stories that were locked up in old suitcases with doubled bottoms.

"I think I discovered that in total you have the equivalent of several thousand US dollars," Irene announced.

Helena reached in and pulled out the pages of poems, tattered paper stained with age. She held her grandmother's poems in her shaking hand, her mind going back to the day before she died, and Helena was in the room all alone with her, and the truth of her life came spilling out, secrets revealed, as Helena sat quietly, stunned.

"You know," Helena began, thumbing through the cadenced words in her hands. "These poems aren't really all that great in terms of the writing style. I don't think my grandmother was that much of a poet." She laughed. "Now, Laure was the writer, so I have been told. I would love to get my hands on her writing. I wonder if there are any of her poems sitting in hidden suitcases."

"Does your uncle have any more of your grandmother's stuff?" Irene asked.

"I don't think so. What you have brought me is the gold mine in the family—the family's jewels, so to speak."

They both giggled, following the play on words.

Helena put everything back in the envelope, a quiet ritual, letting history fold back up into an aged and creased piece of paper.

She took Irene's hands into hers, and held them for a moment, looking into Irene's eyes.

"These are the jewels of my past. Finding you is, for me, the only thing that matters now."

Dinner arrived, steaming plates that held delicacies from a continent that was foreign yet also very familiar.

"Well, it's a good thing that service is so slow here." Irene giggled after the waitress had left. "You got to tell your whole story without choking on your food."

She raised her wineglass, meeting Helena's as they gazed into each other's eyes.

"Here's to old Australian money and bad poetry that brought us together."

They laughed, their eyes twinkling, their faces lit up, like a sunrise over a cliff, a canyon bejeweled by resplendent colors.

❧ ❧ ❧ ❧

By the time dinner was in her mouth, Irene was so hungry that no sooner had she taken her first mouthful, the second one was already down her throat. Neither spoke as they ate gluttonously, as if they hadn't had a bite to eat in a year. When they were done, they laughed together at not only their silence, but also the speed in which they devoured the finely cooked food.

"So much for mindful-based eating," Irene chuckled.

"No, I don't know about you, but I tasted every morsel with gusto."

"Okay, so tell me, what exactly did you eat? Describe the spices, seasoning, textures, and the overall feel of your dinner." Irene winked at Helena.

"Well, there was salmon, and it was delicious."

"Beep. Beep. Beep. No description. Try again."

"Okay, let me take a spoonful of the remaining sauce with the leftover crumbs, now that you are grilling me in your culinary university." Helena giggled as she closed her eyes. "Okay. Wow. There's a hint of horseradish, combined with a bit of what is this? Cinnamon…Oh my…Never would I have thought to combine those two spices…Ah, the cinnamon must be from the mango on the side. Yeah, that's it. And the horseradish must be what was mixed with the marsala for the rice dish. The salmon itself is light, subtle, melts in the mouth, with the aroma of the Pacific Ocean filtering through. An altogether most amazing dish."

She opened her eyes, and Irene let out a laugh.

"You are indeed mocking me."

"Uh-huh."

"God, you are gorgeous when you laugh. I mean, you are stunning to look at any moment, but when you laugh, there is a flame that alights all through you. Me. Hmmm…delicious." Helena took Irene's hand and borrowed a finger, gently kissing it, swirling the tip on her tongue, and then, boldly, put it inside her mouth. Irene closed her eyes, purring quietly, her body on fire. They stayed like that until seconds before the waitress returned to take their plates.

"Would you like a dessert?" she asked, catching their intimate moment from the other side of the room.

"You know, I did notice crème brûlée with peach and mango sorbet. Sounds delicious." She looked up at Helena. "Care to share one with me?"

"Absolutely."

"Perfect. Any coffee or tea or something else to drink with your dessert?"

They each shook their heads. "Thank you, no," they uttered simultaneously.

The waitress smiled and walked away, as again Irene and Helena giggled.

"So, what is it, now, we even speak at the same time? Is that the equivalent of lesbians bringing out the U-Haul on the second date?" Helena was beside herself with her own joke as she got up, laughing all the way to the restroom.

When she returned, the warm brûlée was sitting in the middle of the table, and two spoons lay waiting.

"Now," Irene said, "the fun is making the crack. Let's see if we can do it at the same time. On your mark, get set, go!"

The two women slammed their spoons on the hard, warm surface, letting the gentle ooze of the egg mixture run amuck on their plates. Eyes twinkling with delight, they mixed the brûlée with the sorbet, the cold summer fruit melting on their tongues with the warmth of the caramelized egg mixture, the textures of hard and soft blending delicately on their tongues.

"Oh my God, I am in heaven. This is orgasmic. Truly. Here." Irene took a bit on her spoon and brought it to Helena's mouth, delightedly watching her taste it slowly, her tongue dancing around, her eyes lighting up with the mixture of sugar and passion, summer and ecstatic gastronomical moments.

Helena did the same. Irene took the spoonful and grinned, the flavors decidedly even more intense when the passion of another across from her was jumbled seductively together with the taste of good food. She moaned, feeling for a moment the urge to take their dessert to bed with her, Helena at her side, this dessert on her body...Her fantasies exploded in her head as she felt her nipples harden—severely harden—underneath her thin cotton dress.

The waitress arrived with the tab.

"Is she a lesbian?" Helena asked, hissing and laughing at the same time once the waitress had left. "She keeps coming over to our table when there is a particularly ummm...strong, ummm, loaded moment."

"*Ménage à trois*?" Irene laughed, feeling the heat run down her body as she stared at the empty plate, the dessert over.

"Fancy a walk on the beach?"

"Absolutely. It has been inviting us this entire time." Irene's voice was soft, yet whimsical.

Helena insisted on paying for the meal, and Irene, usually stubborn about this, let her, as she took hold of her hand, letting the suppleness of hers meet the fine lines of Helena's. As they walked out of the restaurant and onto the awaiting beach, joining the water with the flaming reds and oranges of the sky ending its day, Irene felt herself slide gracefully into a place of a sweet vulnerability. As she took off her shoes, holding them in one hand, with her other in Helena's, she relished the softness of the sand between her toes and sensed with a perfect intuition that she could trust this woman with her heart, with the intricate psychology of her, as well as her body, with all the folds and caverns, the latter of which were craving entrance by this woman who had now, effortlessly, entered into her life, craving a kiss as much as she was herself.

As if there was an innate cue into the innermost workings of Irene's mind, Helena turned toward her and brushed back a wisp of her hair that had been blown around by the light summer breeze. Her lips met Irene's and she slowly tasted the remnants of the fine meal that had formed on the subtle corners, finding a home on those lips that begged her to fold into them. Over and over, their tongues met, dancing for the first time, as their lips parted, mouths inviting more, tongues swirling even more as their bodies edged closer, so close that their nipples touched, Irene's hard and vibrant, Helena's becoming so. Helena's hand reached around and stroked the side of Irene's soft buttocks, pulling her in even closer as her hand reached down and under her dress, the lightness of the fabric flowing gently, giving her hand freedom to move exactly where it wanted to go. Their kissing continued as Irene's moans grew sweeter. Desire ran like a train throughout her body, her wetness flooding her thighs.

They pulled away, their lips parting as each took a breath. They stood, side by side, watching the sun descend, the flowing patterns in the sky mingling with the oncoming darkness.

"And this is the beginning," Helena said with a sigh.

"Today, our worlds changed, didn't they?" The pulsing in Irene's body calmed as waves of contentment filled her. She knew in that moment that she would crave this woman next to her for the rest of her life.

Helena yawned.

"Jet lag has hit you, hasn't it?"

"I guess so. I could keep kissing you for hours."

"Me, too."

"Are there any words to describe these feelings?"

"Oh, probably. But sometimes silence meets silence and speaks volumes. We have begun a story, you and I, and I know it is a story that begs for more and deliciously gets what it wants, but each story needs a pause to capture the breath that gets taken away with every installment we put into this story."

Irene's words, the truth behind them, the poetry that laced itself around this truth, brought Helena's lips again to Irene's, who tore at them, a lioness opening its mouth to passion, as their tongues turned to fire, the burning inside of them for more, an endless more. Helena reached for Irene's nipples and squeezed them between her fingertips, the hardness becoming even harder as their bodies swayed into each other, their mouths moaning into the space that blended with the waves that crashed at their bare feet.

Again, they pulled away, catching their breaths. Breathing, slowly, deeply, it was now night, and bats swirled their winged bodies in the distance.

"You should go. Get some sleep."

"Yes, you're right. I should. How about if we meet early then and take a long leisurely drive to the Wineglass Peninsula and around. I can show you everything I know and love so dearly about this area."

"There is nothing more that I want to do. I will ring you in the morning. What time?"

"Wake me up if I am still asleep," Helena answered. "I want the whole day with you."

They got back into Helena's rental car, and with one hand in Irene's and one hand on the steering wheel, Helena drove back to Irene's cabin. They were silent, each of them, and Irene sensed the hugeness of what had happened. She let the tape replay in her mind, each moment since they met at the lobby only a few hours earlier.

When they arrived, a family of possums was grunting outside her door. They laughed, scaring them away as they stood under the waxing moon, Irene reaching for Helena's neck, letting the softness of it meet her lips. Her kisses continued as Helena reached and pulled Irene toward her. Their lips met again, this time with a softness, hiding their innermost urgency, letting it wait as they kissed, flowing in and around each other, until their own symphony came to a gentle finish for the night.

❧ ❧ ❧ ❧

After leaving Irene safely in her cabin, Helena drove an hour in the dark night to her hotel. Her eyes yearned to close as much as the rest of her body yearned to curve itself around Irene. She opened the window, listening to the calls of animals living in the trees, familiar southern hemispheric sounds that always made her smile, welcoming her back, her home away from home. That night, the calls of tree frogs and nocturnal marsupials sounded louder, more vibrant than ever. Perhaps it was her, Helena's interpretation from her experience that day of falling, indescribably falling into the fabric of Irene. Never in her life had she felt like this. She'd had lovers and girlfriends and partners of all kinds—women, of course—but never had she known from the instant she approached one of these women that she would feel such a connection. As she wrapped her mind around kissing Irene, listening to her moans, she felt a starvation curve its way through her as if she had never been fed before, never in this way. She was tempted to turn the car around and end up at her cabin, letting her body, inflamed with an insatiable desire, swim all over Irene's. Her lips wanted only this woman she had met merely hours earlier.

This only happens in the movies, she thought to herself, or in novels, as she squelched her longings, knowing she—and Irene—needed sleep.

Sleep. Helena yawned, craving it, realizing she had started the day somewhere across the equator, had lost a day, changed a season. She had done this often, this across-the-world journey, and always there was a bit—actually, a lot—of bizarreness in the act of being somewhere between the hemispheres, and then completely in a different one, flanked by a cacophony of sounds and textures and accents that made it seem like she was doing science fiction time travel.

Irene. Her mind drifted back to Irene. Her long, dark hair that cascaded around her shoulders and down her back and flitted in the wind; the way she laughed; her gentle sarcasm; the quick wit that put her, Helena, in her place. In a few short hours, Irene had figured out how Helena worked, how to seduce her exactly how she wanted to be seduced. She gripped the steering wheel, trying to rationalize the intensity of her desire, wanting desperately to turn the car around.

Her eyes became heavier as she saw the sign that indicated she was ten minutes from the town where her hotel was. Her lids closed for a second and then bolted open.

She rolled down all the windows in the car, feeling the summer night's chill on her neck.

Irene's kiss on her neck, Helena felt it still, gently, but with an insistence that demanded more later. Later.

Later, Helena felt insatiable as she caught a whiff of Irene's fragrance from her body, embracing her, not a feigned one, not of a chemical smell or a perfume, but the essence of an earthiness, a musk scent that Helena was drawn to instinctively like an animal. She recalled stroking her buttocks, the roundedness and tightness of skin, Irene's skin, the softness enveloping her as her hand moved itself up her thighs, under her dress, feeling her wetness. Helena put those adventurous, questing fingertips into her mouth, tasting what lingering, delicious essence remained. Licking her fingers, she felt an orgasm approaching. As her fingers had tasted Irene everywhere, as Irene's scent was all around her, she moved her hand to her pants and stroked and stroked the fire inside. Irene was there, everywhere.

Helena screamed.

Her car swerved off the road, missing a ditch by two inches. Bats flew up and around her, screeching, frightened, as her quick reaction time hit her, forcing her to grab the steering wheel hard, and even harder, as she got the car back on the road, finishing the drive to the town and to the lights of her hotel.

Turning off her ignition and sitting in her car in the parking lot, Helena took a deep breath, thinking to herself how stupid she had just been *Even if I am completely crazy about Irene, I will never do that again,* she said to herself, quite rattled by her potential near-death experience.

Once inside her room, she threw herself onto the bed. Sleep grabbed her instantly, letting her body calm, her mind become still, allowing her entire being into the space of a healing and restorative slumber.

Chapter Six

Irene woke to a sun-dazzled morning, an ebullient profusion of light greeting her. She went outside to her deck and stared at the pristine smoothness of the blue and green ocean surrounding her. She began sun salutations, her body flexible and supple, letting each yoga pose fill her as her mind cleared itself, her breath perfectly in tune with each salutation, welcoming the day ahead. In the back of her mind, she knew it was almost time to return to the US, but she kept this firmly in the farthest recesses of her brain as she focused on the moment and the beautiful day that awaited her.

In the shower, she let the warm water flow over her body. She had instantly loved this shower, the fine mist that sprayed from the walls that joined with the harder spray that surrounded her. The water cascaded down her nakedness, following the curves of her body, down her neck, her erect nipples, her back, and into the innermost crevices of her sensual caves, down her muscled thighs and calves, all the way down to her feet, ending up in the multicolored, tiled drain. It was easy to waste water in this shower, to lose complete track of this precious natural resource and let one's mind drift off into a beautiful, sublime space. She had to remind herself to turn off the water, to be responsible here on earth.

With her towel wrapped around her body, she

sauntered over to her deck and, staring out at the
sea, phoned Helena. The heat in her body expanded,
moisture developing between her legs as she pushed
the send button and listened to the ring, waiting for
the voice on the other end.

"Mmm...Hi, gorgeous..."

"Hi, you. Good morning."

"Sleep well?"

"*Comme un rocher en hiver*. Like a rock in the
winter."

Helena giggled.

"You?"

"Yes, I fell into something that was definitely
called sleep."

"Beautiful. Are you just waking up?"

"Umm, looks like it. I can be there in a bit. An
hour or so?"

"Perfect. I won't keep you. See you soon then.
Can't wait."

"Ditto."

Irene pressed the red button, listening to the
ding of a call ended. Holding the phone in her hand,
she stared at it, mesmerized by the sound of the voice
that elicited such a thrill, the newness swimming
everywhere, like a fish released into a gigantic pond.

She headed to the restaurant, where she devoured
two bowlfuls of yogurt, muesli and fruit, and a cup of
coffee, made the way she liked it. The hostess had come
to know her likes and greeted her each morning with
a warm smile and her cup made to perfection. Irene
imagined herself coming back here every year.

An hour later, back at her cabin, Irene stood
on her deck, staring out, something she had grown
accustomed to doing, this staring at blues and greens,

the water a mesmerizing meditation into the vastness of her soul. On each side of her, the rolling hills, surrounded by jutting peaks, spread itself out for what seemed like infinity. She just loved this land, and she imagined living here with Helena one day. She smiled at her audacious self. As the morning breezes filtered around her, lifting her cotton summer dress slightly, she became oblivious to the corporeal vacillations around her, not noticing the goose bumps that had developed on her arms. She sensed another presence and was not surprised when Helena tiptoed up the stairs and stood behind her.

Irene purred, and gently Helena folded her arms around her, softly pressing into her, placing tender kisses on her neck.

"Mmmm. Don't stop."

"Never. The breeze is floating through your hair like feathers. How could I ever stop breathing in the magnificence of what is in front of me?"

Helena folded even tighter around Irene as her lips pressed into the softness of her neck. Her hands were light, insistent, as she wrapped them around Irene's breasts, letting the nipples rest against her second and third fingers of each hand. Irene writhed, her body pulsing like a stream released, as she moaned louder, her nipples filled with blood that demanded Helena's hands, her fingers dancing wildly on their hardened peaks.

She turned around and pressed her lips against Helena's, her tongue thrashing inside of Helena's mouth, finding the deepest caverns it could reach. Their mouths and their tongues together contained an unstoppable fire as their bodies pressed into the other, nipples like glistening rocks grazing each other's, feeling their own heat as the sun bathed them, rising higher in the morning sky.

They pulled away, breathing hard.

"Good morning!" They each laughed.

"Now that's a way to start off a day...Can't say I have ever in all my years started off a morning like that." Irene giggled.

"Nor have I. I could get used to this."

Irene kissed her on the cheek. "Could you, now?"

"Rhetorical question?"

They found each other's hands again, gently fitting one with the other. Standing side by side, they breathed in the freshness of the air in front of them.

"I smelled the first scent of autumn this morning."

"Now that you mention it, I did, too. The sun is a tad softer."

"Ready for a drive? I have so many places I want to show you."

Laughing, Irene loved the layers of nuance filtered in that comment.

"Yes, let me grab my sweater. Take me anywhere."

"All right. That I will do."

They kissed briefly, lips placed on lips, knowing there would be more.

"Hop in, madame, the limo is ready."

Irene, feeling like she was drunk on champagne, slid into the car that Helena had magically turned into a convertible.

"Oh, you...I don't need such extravagance. Simple is fine."

"Okay, I don't need to impress you?"

"Not in the slightest. In fact, if you do I will think it's fake, anyway."

"Yeah, you got a point." Helena guffawed.

"So, you know what I'd love to do? Find a little bakery or something with fresh bread and get some cheese, and summer fruit, and find somewhere along the way for a picnic."

"Perfect idea. There's a little shop about an hour from here. Everything you want is there. We will be taking Coles Bay Road down to Fleurieu Point, over to Wineglass Bay and then looping around the Peninsula, Cooks Beach, and then back up. Here's a map if you want to have visual bearings."

"Wonderful. Ah, to be a passenger, I must say, is just delightful. I am so looking forward to this road trip."

"It's one of my favorite places to drive and just look out. The world is just stunning here in Tasmania."

For the next hour, neither spoke, as eyes were open, wide open to the majesty that surrounded them. Granite peaks of faded pinks and oranges greeted them on all sides of the road, reminding them of the mountainous region that Tasmania was known for. The Swan River met the road, a sleepy curved body of water, transporting a state of calmness and an array of wildlife unsurpassed. They stopped for a good while with their binoculars, Helena pointing out that this part of the region was known for spectacular bird life, some of them on the endangered species list, and endemic to just Tasmania. "The wattlebird and the honeyeater are two of these. I have always wanted to see them."

They sat, side by side, peering out into the trees. In a bit, a beauty flew by and into one of the many eucalyptus trees nearby. It had a blazing yellow chest.

"Shh...Oh my God," Helena whispered. "I think that is one of them. It is! It's a yellow-throated honeyeater. Here, look."

She handed the binoculars to Irene, who gasped at the brilliance of the yellow chest.

"It's like a sun has blazoned her chest. God, that's gorgeous!" she whispered.

She stared into the lenses for a time. She noticed some movement. "I think she's making a nest. What do you think?"

Helena took the binoculars. Peering for a moment, she uttered, barely audible, "Yes, I see tiny scraps of grasses in her mouth that she is placing around and around. She is indeed weaving her home for her babies."

Helena teared up, whispering, "I have always wanted to see this. You are bringing me this joy." She reached over and kissed Irene. Irene's lips met hers, briefly, as they heard the honeyeater call out, a sweet sound that sounded like a mating call. Indeed, they looked over and the male had just arrived with fresh grass in his mouth. The two sang to each other, she obviously delighted with his shopping trip. As the two birds proceeded to create a nest together, Irene and Helena couldn't keep their lips away from each other, nature eliciting courtship that seemed of a contagious nature. As the female honeyeater made faint squealing sounds, seemingly overjoyed with their creation, a home for the babies that were about to come out of her, Irene moaned quietly, a sweetness enveloping her mixed with desire as Helena kissed her earlobes, a gentle pull on them, sending waves throughout her body. *I want this woman to kiss me like this for the rest of my life.*

Then, with a tiny swoop of the wings, both birds flew up and away, as the two women looked up into the sky around them, witnessing one of nature's miraculous paintings, the yellow burning in the sky like fire.

"Wow!" they said together, their voices raised.

"Now that is something to remember," Helena shouted to the breeze.

"Completely!"

They walked back to the car, driving again in silence, taking in what they just saw.

In a bit, the bakery that Irene had requested emerged out of the clearing. They had arrived at Coles Bay, a small village of shops, mostly, and in the center of town was a place called the Dancing Dog Bakery, Delicatessen, and Organic Food Shoppe.

"Well, will you look at that," she exclaimed. "A shop out of my own heart. Everything one needs under one roof."

Smiling, they left the store with a huge bag full of freshly baked breads, just pulled from the oven, cheeses made from goats and sheep that grazed the hills of Wineglass Bay, and fresh organic fruit, ripened from the Tasmanian heat. Back in the car, with the breezes flowing around them and the midday sun warming their shoulders, they traveled on a dirt road toward Fleurieu Point and Hazards Beach. At the point, they got out, and Irene had the feeling that the world had invited them to an endless oasis. The ocean, which they hadn't seen that morning since their departure, greeted them with an expansiveness that made her sigh, as if she was a witness to a painting that only grew in its elaborate, sweeping brushstrokes.

"So much wildlife underneath those waters that we can never see," Helena mused.

At that moment, something flitted out from the blue-green calmness, making waves that headed toward the shore. As they looked out, they saw a pod of dolphins swimming past, a family of many sizes. Irene related her dolphin encounter just the other day.

"You do attract wildlife, don't you?"

She grinned, not exactly sure why this occurred. She rested her head on Helena's shoulder and took a contented breath, looking out at the now empty blue where just moments ago dolphins had been.

"This must be a good place to see whale migration, I'm thinking."

"Yeah, I would think so. We need to come back here during migration time." She put her arm around Irene, squeezing her close. Irene imagined coming back here with Helena, revisiting this memory. Just the thought of it made her weep a bit inside.

They walked back to the car, and once in, their lips came together with a ferocity that urged their bodies close, their hands searching, reaching, caressing as their lips tore at each other, their tongues merging in a dance that seemed unwilling to reach its end.

They laughed as they were forced to distance their bodies.

"The car and its limitations."

"Our bodies definitely have a voluminous language, don't they?" Irene laughed. "We are bottomless pits, aren't we?"

Driving over the Isthmus Track into Wineglass Bay would exhilarate even the most depressed person on the planet. With the mountains on the left and the lagoon on the right, the road descended from a heightened place of wonder down into the mystical and stunning depths of the bay, the luminescence of the aquamarine greeting them in the shape of a wineglass, the curves and flow of the land and water like a woman's body.

Irene held her breath, feeling all through her waves of euphoria, absorbed in the nature around her that made her want to leap in the air, becoming a part of it.

"Lunch? On a secluded beach that hardly anyone knows about, where the water is as stunning as this vista?" Helena asked, as if she had read Irene's mind.

"Mmmmmmmmmmm...yes. Yes."

They headed down the road, past the tourist spots and onto a rough dirt road, turning left in the bush. Careful not to end up in a pothole, Helena used her expert driving skills to forge her way to the end of a road, a small desolate parking area. They leapt out of the car with their towels and the bag of food, scampering down a dusty wooded trail to an opening where the earth and the trees opened to water, the sublime of the browns and greens meeting the limitless blue.

They found a spot near a tree for some shade, and placing their towels in the sand, Irene immediately tore off her clothes and ran into the water. Helena stared at her, her eyes focused on the stunning curves of her body, a goddess naked, running like a gazelle into the soft folds of the water, jeweled from the sun. Irene splashed water all over herself, cooling the heat from her body, and then ran back to Helena, throwing her wet, sandy body all over her.

Helena laughed, getting sand in her mouth, as the two tumbled down to the towels, Irene laying her wet, dripping body on top of Helena, loving every minute of the laughs that came from below. Throwing her dress back on, her wet nipples standing like beacons, she chuckled. "Let's eat! I'm starved!"

They opened the bag and produced two loaves of bread, five small packets of different kinds of cheeses, peaches, apricots, cherries and mangoes.

"Do you have a knife?"

"No. Oh, I do somewhere, but not here," Helena laughed.

"Teeth and fingers were made before knives."

They began a picnic where Irene fed Helena, and Helena fed Irene, their lips devouring the other, tasting and feasting. Peaches and apricots, cherries and mangoes, deliciously ripe and oozing with sugar, slid down their chins as their tongues licked their faces like puppies, their lips continuously coming back for more, more kisses, more summer's nectar. There was an endlessness to their feasting.

At some point when the sun was at its highest, the yawns began, deep and full, their bellies satiated, and as crumbs laced their bodies and their towels, Irene lay down and placed her head on Helena's chest, her hair cascading around her shoulders. Helena stroked the stray strands of hair, her fingertips gently caressing the softness of Irene's forehead. Together they fell asleep, as the shade from the tree cooled their faces, and the sun warmed their toes, partially hidden in the sand.

❦ ❦ ❦ ❦

Sometime later, maybe an hour, Irene opened her eyes and looked around. All was still; even Helena was still fast asleep. It was as if all her surroundings were engaged in the most serene of siestas, the essential quieting of the busy existences that all animals—humans included—seemed to live by. She lay still, feeling the transition between sleep and wakefulness, that place where the smile from the unconscious lingers with the smile from the conscious self. She felt Helena's arms around her, perfectly still, embracing her, holding her close. In twenty-four hours she already felt the normalness of all of this, waking up to her, falling asleep with her, and during sleep, finding the path that was just hers, and hers alone. Her waking brain began to function as she thought about this dance, this being with another and then being alone, and that the two places could exist simultaneously. She wondered why it took her this long to find someone, and when she could put her mind around it, she realized she had been frightened of the idea of losing her independence. She saw her mother wither away right before her eyes when her father died, and at some level, mostly unconscious, she vowed to never allow herself the experience of depending on another, because if they go, she thought, then all life dissolves, and there is an empty, completely empty shell that remains. As she realized this, as she put the pieces of her past together, she also felt something quite significant waking up in her, finding this woman who was holding her like it was the most natural thing in the world. Irene felt tears gather in her eyes, grief and joy mixed together like two spices in a cake. She listened to Helena breathe, in and out, the vitality of it all, this life that had met hers, so easily they fit together, so much they had in common, so much fire between them that just happened without the faintest bit of trying.

Irene wondered what day it was…The days had slipped so easily from one to another that no day really had a name to it. The timelessness of it all worked its magic in unfolding tension that had existed inside of her. Her brain was about to work into its own mental calendar when Helena stirred, her fingertips moving effortlessly up and down Irene's arm, letting her mind cease its rumblings as her body became engaged, purring. In a half-sleep, half-wake state, Helena's fingers gently stroked Irene's back, up and down; then her hand, the softness and warmth from sleep and the sun, moved itself up and down the sides of her thighs. Irene's purring turned to moans as she pulled off her dress, wanting skin on skin. She rolled herself on top of Helena and, pressing into her gently, took her fingers and softly stroked her face, examining her eyes, her nose, the way her cheeks were molded, the curves in them. She ran her fingers through her red locks of hair, loving the way the curls bounced and danced with their own rhythm, as if each strand was on its own frivolous planet. She felt Helena's nipples harden through her shirt as Irene moved her fingers under the fabric and stroked her breasts from the base to the point, each particle of skin a beautiful moment between. Helena opened her eyes and smiled, taking off her shirt and bringing Irene close to her, moaning, as their lips joined.

The nakedness, the freedom of their breasts meeting for the first time, sent exhilarating waves of joy through them, and as their nipples played innocent games of touching each other, their kissing intensified, letting out the lions again to roar with delight. Irene pressed herself harder into Helena as their tongues thrashed inside of each other's mouths, deeper and even more deeper into the cavernous hidden places.

"Let's go into the water," Irene suggested, feeling their playfulness surround them with a wonderful fizziness.

"Yes, absolutely," Helena responded as she threw

off her shorts and underpants. Irene grabbed her hand. They ran into the water like children, laughing and laughing as the heat from their bodies met the perfectly warm, yet also cool water. They leapt in, embracing and holding, their naked bodies mixed with the water sending a euphoric wave through them. Not like children, but two grown women crazy about each other, they kissed. Their lips craved the other's, and their breasts did the same, and the motion of the water between them made this craving even more powerful as their hands reached and pulled and stroked and felt and moved inside of each other as the gentle waves enveloped them, and they ran farther in the water, splashing, letting the mere fact of getting wet devour them. They roared and laughed and pulled themselves close as their hands again went inside and stroked and created fire with water as they came together, wailing and screaming as the birds overhead did the same, only perhaps even louder.

Then, all was quiet. They took each other's hands and walked to the edge of the water and lay on the sand, letting the hot sun and the cool water bathe them as they held each other, celebrating what had just happened between them, the vulnerable spaces of passion. Irene was crying and so was Helena, tears released from this letting go, letting in, the first time, newness and sweetness mixed with their own ferocity.

Their arms embraced, they rocked each other back and forth, the movement mixed with the waves that lapped around them, the soothing feeling of being held.

"This is love."

"Yes," Irene murmured, bringing Helena even closer to her, the softness of her skin, her beating heart.

They lay quietly, letting the stillness surround them, as the sun moved ever so carefully through the sky. An early evening breeze flitted around them, and they moved their towels into the sun to lie like satiated tigers, together, folded around each other, letting the waning heat of the day warm them.

Helena dozed off again for a moment as Irene stroked her back, feeling the muscular ridges and curves. A deep purring remained inside of her, a completely contented sensation that she had never experienced before.

She looked up at the sky, seeing the sun begin its ceremonious dip into obscurity, as Helena opened her eyes.

"Shall we go?" Helena asked, seeing darkness approach.

"In a bit."

Irene placed her purring lips on Helena's, slowly, sweetly, caressing the fullness of them. Her lips moved up her face to Helena's earlobe which she kissed and licked, and her tongue found the inside of her ear, gently seducing Helena all over again. Helena moaned and grabbed her, pulling her close, as they kissed deeply, their lips on fire as their bodies writhed underneath.

"I want you tonight. All night," Helena murmured.

"Yes. Yes."

"Let's leave now before it is completely dark. Find a place for dinner, and then your cabin?"

"Only that," Irene answered. "We obviously have a bit more exploring to do, don't we?"

They both laughed as they threw on their clothes, grabbed their things, and made their way to the car.

⚜⚜⚜⚜

As Helena carefully drove through the bush toward town, Irene noticed some movement on the side of the road.

"There's something there," she said.

Helena slowed the car, looking around.

A family of kangaroos hopped, frightened, in front of the car, moving from one side of the road to the other, two females with two joeys stuck firmly in their pouches.

When they had passed, the two women exhaled, realizing they had held their breaths the entire time.

"Wow! You did it again. You bring on the wildlife."

Irene giggled quietly to herself. Images of kookaburras, Tasmanian devils, wombats, endangered birds, and dolphins floated in her head. As they drove in the dark, she shared her stories of these encounters. She was quite the storyteller, and her elongated passages extended all the way to Coles Bay.

They got out in front of the Trumpet Café. Wood-fired pizzas, fresh organic ingredients.

"I read about this place," Helena exclaimed excitedly. "They just opened recently to rave reviews." The two women bounced into the café, a half-skip lacing their steps.

They sat down, opened the menus, and the "Tree Hugger Pizza" enticed them. That plus two rocket salads and plenty of water, as they realized they were extremely dehydrated.

As they waited for the pizza, Irene's brain had an inkling of activity.

"I am supposed to leave Freycinet and go to

Hobart tomorrow for an early Sunday morning flight back to Melbourne. My itinerary has me taking the bus tomorrow late afternoon and staying the night in a hotel. My flight back to Seattle from Melbourne leaves at noon on Sunday."

There was silence after this comment, the tremendous weight of these words hitting hard.

"No," Helena flatly said.

Irene smiled, loving Helena's balking at rules and limits.

"I don't want you to leave tomorrow. Absolutely not." She looked up at Irene, who smiled, waiting for her alternative idea.

"Early Sunday morning I can drive you to the airport here in Swansea. Let me see when I can get you on a flight to Hobart." She pulled out her phone. "Okay, good, there is a flight out at six thirty, arriving at the airport in Hobart at seven thirty. What do you think? We could leave here at four thirty Sunday morning. Four forty-five at the latest."

"That's got to be crazy expensive."

"It's on me. It's my crazy idea because the thought of you leaving tomorrow afternoon is the last thought I want to entertain."

"But I have to leave anyway." Irene's voice was laced with resignation. She was not used to being given such a generous gift. She wanted to accept, but it was hard to. At the bottom of it all was an infinite sadness; she didn't want to leave.

"Can you ponder it for a bit?"

"Yes, I will."

The pizza came out, and they both realized how starving they were.

The fresh, slightly spiced lettuce, and then the

roasted peppers and grilled zucchini, three different kinds of Tasmanian mushrooms, feta, and mozzarella melted in their mouths, along with the wood-fired, crunchy crust that made for a perfect gastronomical end to a blissful day.

Arm in arm, they exited the café, feeling happily full, yet silently pondering the conversation before dinner.

An hour later, they stood on her deck, taking in the sound of the water that lapped gently from all directions. Irene took Helena's hand, kissing it. She took a deep breath and exhaled, and put Helena's hand to her lips, letting the palm of it graze her cheeks, her lips meeting each finger as she gently placed a kiss on each one. She felt the stirrings in Helena.

"It's been a beautiful day, Helena." She opened her mouth, putting one of Helena's fingers in, gently kissing and sucking. Helena breathed hard.

"I won't be able to leave you tomorrow. I know this. I will accept your generous offer for the flight out on Sunday."

Helena took Irene's hand, kissing it. "Thank you." She sighed. She pulled out her phone and quickly made a reservation for the flight. She called up the front desk of the lodge and paid for a Saturday night stay for Irene and called the hotel in Hobart and cancelled Irene's reservation. Irene stood watching her, amazed at her speed at organizing her life, amused by it.

Helena stood quietly again, behind Irene, folding her arms around her, pressing into her, as the almost full moon shone down on them. Her hands reached for Irene's breasts, hardening with her touch as her hips swayed into her. Irene moaned from deeply within. Her knees weakened, and she could barely stand. Helena took her hand and led her inside to the bed. She pulled off her dress, gently stroking her breasts, kissing her neck, carefully holding her as she let her collapse onto the bed. She lifted her shirt, throwing if off. She slid Irene's underwear off, caressing the firmness of her buttocks as she gently placed her entire body on Irene, kissing her neck, up and down, exploring every crevice. Irene would have succumbed to anything at this point, and moaned and moaned, feeling herself trust anything that Helena wanted to do to her body. Helena moved her lips to Irene's for just a moment, and then quickly left them, exploring the other side of Irene's neck, slowly, deliberately waiting between each move she made. Irene felt Helena's wet thighs press harder into her as her nipples became hard and fiery. Helena's lips moved down to Irene's throat, kissing it. Irene writhed under her, breathing hard, wanting her. Helena moved her lips back up, and again, for a moment, thrust her tongue, like a snake, inside Irene's mouth. Irene could tell that Helena knew what she wanted, and as Irene panted for more, Helena moved down to her swollen breasts as her tongue swirled around and around her engorged nipples. Irene screamed for more as Helena descended, feeling her kiss her belly button, her tongue inside as her fingertips swirled her nipples. Irene writhed with desire, her breath on fire, as Helena descended lower, to her thighs, her tongue licking up the river that was pouring out of her, juices everywhere. Irene's moans were voluminous as Helena thrust her tongue inside, devouring her. Irene's moaning turned to still louder screams as Helena swirled her tongue in the labyrinth of Irene's core, circling and circling deeply, then returning to the surface and then back inside, still deeper, as far as her tongue could go.

Her fingers moved back to Irene's nipples, and again her mouth returned to Irene as she screamed a final crescendo.

Helena held her then, her arms around her, as Irene cried deep tears from places hidden inside. Aftershocks hit her once and again as Helena held her, rocked her, their bodies slipping together, sliding, as Helena wouldn't let go, Irene needing her there. There was quiet for a moment, and then, from a fire that wouldn't subside, Irene took Helena's hand and kissed it, each finger sliding gracefully into her mouth. Helena moaned as Irene kissed harder, sucking each digit as Helena panted, her thighs soaked. Irene took her mouth to Helena's breasts and sucked hard, harder, and the harder she sucked, the more Helena panted, her breath filling every space. Irene couldn't stop, her mouth glued to Helena's nipples growing harder as her tongue on them gave relentless thrusts and swirls. Irene reached her hand down and farther down, not waiting for a moment to go inside where she then found a home, desperate for her, as she put first one finger, then the entire hand, deeply in, reaching for juices and nectars that Helena kept making over and over. Irene knew she wanted more, this insatiable appetite meeting her hand, as orgasm after orgasm erupted from Helena's body, bursting, as slowly the fire subsided and the screams shushed, and together, their slippery, love-filled bodies held each other in silence.

With a final, mmmmm from each of them, they fell asleep, their breathing slow and deep, their bodies fulfilled, beckoning them even deeper as their arms wrapped around each other, holding the space of sacred slumber. Even the stars were quiet that night, halos around the moon, migrations of planets, lulled.

Chapter Seven

The sun began its ascent as Helena opened her eyes gently, viewing Irene's face in a sublime pose, smiling as she slept, her arms around Helena's, draped in such a way as to show all her vulnerability. Helena lay quietly in bed taking it all in, every moment they had shared since they had met not even forty-eight hours earlier. Her half-awake brain rested on last night, their lovemaking sumptuous, tantalizing. She had read about this in books, seen films where actors had pretended, but never had she experienced passion like this—not even remotely. She listened to Irene sleep, the deep breaths that emerged, slow and even, like a melody in pianissimo, sweet and quiet. Just listening to her, feeling her arms on hers, made Helena desire more. She stared at Irene's chest, the curves of her breasts, the soft, rounded nipples when she was not aroused, sleeping peacefully. Just watching her, the rising and falling of her breath, the contours of her body, gave her a throbbing sensation all through her as she lay motionless, not wanting to wake Irene until she was ready to wake up on her own.

She turned her head and stared at the sun rising behind the mountain, faint oranges and pinks swirling in the sky. The forecast predicted rain all day. After a brief morning glow, a faded sun, the clouds would emerge little by little, she had read. This would be the first rain since the beginning of summer. Helena thought of something, putting this thought in the back of her mind to ask Irene later, perhaps on Sunday morning.

Staring at the clouds, still feeling a continuous pulse throbbing deliciously throughout her body, she felt Irene stir, sensing the minute beginnings of wakefulness entering her being. Helena felt a thrill run up and down her, a playful twist and jolt, as she turned her head back to watch this awakening of the goddess she was holding.

A faint moan came from her lips, her smile ever so slightly widening. Helena ran her fingers down Irene's back, her palms decidedly wanting skin. Her hands moved up and around, effortlessly, gently massaging and opening places in Irene. The sublime softness of her skin worked its way into Helena's hands, and like a master masseuse, she stroked every particle of Irene's back to its full suppleness. Each rounded fold of her body she stroked, small and large sweeps of her hand, feeling each place like a sand dune, gentle and fine, rolling and smooth. Irene moaned louder, entering a space of greater wakefulness. She reached her head up and met Helena's lips with hers. Slowly, waking, her lips caressed the smooth contours of Helena's lips. Her kisses continued all around her face, her nose, her cheeks, and over to her ears, where she lingered, waking up even further as her tongue emerged, licking the earlobes, inside the ear, she breathed, blowing air like a balloon, and then kissing harder, breathing in, and upon the exhale, gently blowing out a gentle breeze. Helena gripped her buttocks, breathing and moaning, her hands now moving up Irene's thighs with fervent strokes. She was entirely on fire, and her wetness met Irene's hand that pushed her over onto her back as Irene moved onto her. Completely awake now, Irene pushed her mouth onto Helena's. She moaned, allowing Irene this time to be completely in charge. Irene moved her lithe body up and moved her breasts into Helena's mouth, letting her suck to her heart's content as her nipples hardened even more as Helena licked and devoured what Irene had placed into her mouth. She then removed her throbbing breasts from Helena's grasp, letting Helena pant for a bit, starving for more, as her flexible body effortlessly moved upward so that her vulva was now on Helena's mouth. Irene arched her back, as Helena sucked and licked, her tongue like a serpent, as Irene moaned, the fire between them uncontainable. Then, when Irene was about to come, she stopped, moved her body again, and placed her mouth on Helena's river, her thighs, licking and tasting as Helena writhed under her, the strength in Irene's body holding her down. She moved her head around Helena's labia and burrowed inside, her tongue a seething mass of muscle as Helena feasted, licking and sucking on Irene's labia. Together, in this position of eating and sucking and licking and devouring each other, their moans became overwrought, starving, and they craved each other incessantly, their bodies squirming with ecstasy as they came together over and over, their mouths famished, their bodies energized. They couldn't stop coming, until finally, one last time, their screams made a melody and a harmony, a unifying note. And then there was silence.

After a few minutes of quiet, bodies resting, Irene murmured, kissing Helena on her wet thigh, "Well, good morning to you." She giggled.

Helena squeezed Irene's buttocks. "Wow! Good morning, dearest sweet Irene."

Irene un-contorted herself and lay on her stomach, propping herself up on her elbow.

Helena got up to pee, and when she returned, Irene did the same.

When Irene returned, she found Helena propped up in bed, spreading out all the pillows. Helena took one look at her and lunged, her body a mass of unbridled passion, wanting more. As if something in them had turned on a switch that just couldn't stop, the throbbing sensations in their bodies took hold of them. The bed was their paradise, but the bed was only the beginning. Their urgings took them to the table and to the chairs in the room and to the floor, and then, finally, to the shower where water met their passion all over again as their lips and their hands and their mouths sought to devour the other, embracing every part of their demanding bodies.

❧ ❧ ❧ ❧

Sometime in the afternoon, they realized they were famished, this time for food.

They got dressed and headed to the café down the road for some food, watching the rain come down gently, and when they were done with their lunch they quickly headed back to Irene's cabin.

They ran a bath to get warm again, not able to ever get enough of each other. When the water cooled, they headed back to bed, their bodies deliciously warm, and began all over again to devour the other. Irene felt her own primitiveness, hardly speaking a word that day. It was so unlike her, this silence, this appetite for another, for sex, for this insatiable pull toward another. She had no idea where this had come from, had never experienced this before, and she was amazed at her stamina. She felt pulled into what seemed like an insane direction, this lust, this desire for the other that had no limits. Yet, in the back of her mind she knew that there was a limit.

When she emerged from the bathroom some time later, drying off her hands on a towel, she saw Helena's phone in her hand. Her face fell at the thought of an alarm being set for their early morning departure.

It was sometime in the evening. Night had fallen. The rain continued outside. She cuddled up close to Helena, feeling cold all of a sudden. They wrapped blankets around themselves and sat up in bed, folded around each other, listening to the rain outside, a steady musical rhythm that made the idea of departure even harder.

"There have been so few words between us," Irene began, Helena's arms softly embracing the curves of her. They both sighed.

"My body is so relaxed, held by you. I have never experienced this sensation, this ability to feel so calm with another, this willingness to let someone into my most vulnerable spaces. There is such balance between us, isn't there?"

"Our bodies have done all the talking. We have allowed ourselves to trust each other, haven't we?" Helena smiled, pulling Irene closer. "There is indeed so much trust involved with passion. It's strange in a way how simple it has been to want nothing in this world except you," Irene said, her voice soft, melodic, almost like a lullaby.

"I can't imagine anything else—you, me. It does seem like an effortless change in my life."

"Someone once told me that if one works too

hard at something, it's not meant to be. And if it comes without effort, then that is where one should be." Irene snuggled her head even closer into Helena's neck.

Silence surrounded them as they both pondered this statement.

After a bit, Helena asked, "So, what do you have to do when you get back?"

Irene laughed. "Live without you. How crazy is that? I have to teach already on Monday. Talk about insanity. It's going to be full-on, too. It always is from February until May. What about you?"

"Yeah, likewise. I have several meetings here in Tasmania with my distributors, then when I get back to Colorado in early March, I have to begin production on a new line we are starting, a special formula for babies."

"Really? How young?"

"As young as day one, for infants who are not breastfeeding. It's one of the dreams I have had for a while. A good friend of mine had the worst time of it when she had her baby and couldn't nurse her because of a breast infection that wouldn't go away. I told her I would do some research and see if I could come up with something. It's taken a whole year, and the kid is now a bit too old for it, but it's kind of exciting that it will be introduced to the public by the first day of spring, if all goes well."

"Wow! I am quite impressed. What's it called? Tassiebaby?"

"How did you guess?"

Irene chuckled. "Just a thought. I absolutely love the idea. So, Ms. Inventor, you will be mighty busy for a bit."

Helena sighed. "Guess so."

"This is not a dream, is it? What we have

experienced...something that will go away when we wake up and get ourselves out of the land of Oz?"

"It feels like a dream, doesn't it? I mean the whole story, with the emerald suitcase..." Helena's voice trailed off. "I was wondering, just so we can say to ourselves, 'no, this is not a dream,' what if..." she stopped.

Irene waited.

"What if we just immerse ourselves ourselves in our own busy lives for the next few weeks, and not contact each other, not blemish this space we have created with our demanding jobs. And what if, on the first day of spring, we call each other and reconnect all over again?"

"You mean no phone, Skype, text, or anything?"

"Yeah, what do you think? Crazy beyond crazy?"

"Yes, absolutely. Actually, though, it kind of makes sense. All we'll do is miss each other and I know that is all I would talk about, so I would be either whining and pining, or relating to you all my busy-day-ness."

"And all I'll want to do is to jump on the next plane and be with you, and I won't be able to, so I would be complaining and complaining..."

"And then our conversations will lead us nowhere, and then what?"

They both laughed.

"Okay, let's try."

"Really?"

"Yeah. Let's. I'm game. But the first day of spring is your product launching day."

"Precisely. The focus work will be done by then. And I know all I will want then is you."

The conversation ended there as lips and hands

took on their own life, and their hunger for each other flowed hot, cascading between them, erupting and climbing, falling, and climbing again until for that time, for that day, they fell asleep, curling sweetly between the sheets, one body, one being connected to the other.

Chapter Eight

Four o'clock met the world with darkness, a bleak sky that had not yet risen to the day. *The Four Seasons* greeted that day on Helena's phone, Vivaldi beckoning the world to wake up and forge ahead, do what one must with grace. Helena was tempted to hit the snooze button, and her brain kicked in and said *no, today is not the day for a prolonged snooze.* She placed her lips on Irene's, straddling her, pressing ever so gently into her as she scanned her face, watching her become awake, a gradual ascent from the deep world of sleep she was immersed in.

"Mmmmmm," she murmured. It appeared that her lips were not yet ready to engage.

Helena kissed her cheeks, her eyebrows, her nose, her forehead, her chin, and returned to her lips, where, this time, Irene kissed her back.

"Mmmmmmmmmmmm," she repeated, as her arms folded around Helena's waist, pulling her in.

Sadness laced their kisses, the urgency abating. "I haven't packed my bag yet," Irene said quietly; her voice seemed to be inside her throat.

"Let me do it for you. You take a shower and get dressed."

Irene leaned her lips into Helena's. "You are the angel of the seasons, winter, summer, and the other two..."

They both laughed, yet sadness laced the sounds.

"Come on, gorgeous. Time to get up. Planes are waiting."

While Irene let the hot water flow everywhere, Helena scrawled something on a piece of paper and slipped it inside the suitcase. Then she carefully folded all of Irene's clothes that had, somehow, been tossed all over the room. When Irene was dressing, the remaining items went in, the zipper got closed, and the emerald-green suitcase sat waiting by the door. Helena threw on her clothes, and together they shut the door to the cabin and got into the car, driving down in the still night sky to the front office. Sitting on the counter were two bags, one labeled "Helena" and one labeled "Irene." They looked inside to find that warm muffins and a cup of freshly brewed coffee sat resplendently in each bag.

"I just love this place. They are the kindest people you ever could meet." Irene found a postcard and wrote, "To all the people who work at this lodge: Thank you. Thank you for your amazing generosity, kindness, and for providing me with such a magical stay. We will return here, and return here, and return here for every passing monumental moment in our life…Thank you again. Irene…and Helena."

They got in the car. In silence, Helena drove, and Irene stared at the beginnings of the morning, gray skies in all shades welcoming the start of a day.

In a daze, they arrived, the plane preparing to leave just a few minutes later.

Irene and Helena embraced, holding tightly to the other, grasping on to the tender places, the softness that had held them for the last few days. Their kisses were incessant but brief, hints of a hunger that would have to wait. One last embrace, and with a nod, Irene grabbed her bag and took it to the flight attendant, who put it in the hold of the plane. Meeting four other passengers, sleepy-eyed souls preparing for their journey to Hobart, Irene walked up the stairs, turned around, and looked out at Helena whose eyes were focused on her. With no words, their gaze held them, as Irene stepped into the plane.

Helena watched the last footsteps of Irene as her hair blew everywhere, her saddened face, her dazed expression that invaded her being as she disappeared into the folds of the plane. Her face was wet with tears as she continued to stare at the plane that gained momentum, preparing to leave the earth for the sky. Then it happened, movement on a runway, gaining speed, and off into the air it went. Helena felt Irene's kisses on her cheek as if they were just placed. She felt Irene everywhere, her smell surrounding her, her voice, soft, a gentle song, as the plane disappeared and as she walked back to the car, her footsteps slow, dragging dirt. Her foot kicked at it as her tears continued.

❧❧❧❧

Irene couldn't think or feel as numbness invaded her, creeping around her, stilling all her senses. She stared out the window but couldn't see, her eyes a blank cavity inside her head. Below, Tasmania drifted by, a day beginning its slow progression. The plane landed in Hobart, and mechanically she got on the plane to Melbourne, got in her seat, and again, stared out at the blank world. In Melbourne, there was no time for anything except a quick pee, and again, she entered a plane that would take her through hours and hours of oceans until finally, Seattle would enter her world, bodies of water, mountains, and the Space Needle, welcoming her home. She didn't care about any of it, and shortly after the plane took off, Irene fell asleep. Sleep took her away, a dreamless, restless slumber that did not arouse her until somewhere over the Rocky Mountains. She opened her eyes. They were flying over Colorado. She smiled, her first smile in hours, as she felt Helena's kisses, her breath on hers. Tears came down, huge puddles of water erupting from her eyes. She sat and stared at the snowy peaks, letting the tears do what they needed to do as she smiled to herself. *My next plane trip will be to Boulder.* Then she wiped her eyes, sat up, and counted every minute of the last hour until the plane would land.

Now, all she wanted was home.

Seattle stood, just like it had when she left, but the snow on the ground had long since melted. In the customs line at Sea-Tac, Irene waited, wanting to get through quickly, as her only thoughts then were of home. There was a strange feeling in the air, and she noticed dozens of security officers, way more than usual. When it was her turn to normally breeze through the line and be welcomed back to her home country, on this day they scrutinized her passport and looked her up and down, staring at her last name.

"Where are you coming from?"

She answered.

"What kind of work do you do?"

She answered.

"Did you have any encounters with any Iranians while you were away?" the customs officer asked.

She gasped. *So, this is where our country is going?* Anger boiled up inside of her and focused on her mother's family. They had all voted for him, the one whose name she couldn't bring herself to utter aloud, whom she called "the dangerously frightening ignoramus in the White House."

"No," she answered, hiding her seething rage.

"Do you have any laptops or iPads in your possession?"

"No," she answered, urgently having to pee, her upset growing with each moment.

The officer scanned her passport, yet again, on a different database. Again, he looked her up and down. Then, with a gruffness, he stamped her passport and handed it back to her.

Tears welled up in her eyes as her only focus was on getting home. She got into an awaiting Lyft car, and within minutes she turned her key in the lock, welcomed by a frigid house, winter invading each crevice. She turned on the hot water in the bathtub, cranked up the heater, turned on her electric blanket, and, throwing her emerald-green suitcase containing her summer clothes into the corner, fell into the steaming bath. She thought about food but didn't feel at all hungry. Her body only wanted bed, and toweling off, she took her numbed body to the sheets.

≈≈≈≈≈

Monday morning hit like a gloved, spiked hand. Winter was thriving with a cloudy sky and a morning temperature of 37 degrees. It wouldn't get much warmer all day. Automatic pilot propelled Irene, dressing her in a multitude of layers, getting her to her neighborhood café for eggs and toast and a cup of coffee, and then to a classroom of awaiting students, notebooks, and iPads.

"Welcome back, dear students," she began.

As she spoke, her tanned skin, the glow on her face emanated throughout the room. She noticed her students fervently tweeting each other. "I enjoyed reading your essays. They were illuminating, as they always are, giving me insight that I hope to give back to you."

The class smiled, staring at her expectantly; some students gazed more closely at her, their eyes fixed on her face.

"Let's leave winter for a bit and maneuver our way toward spring, but as we do so, let's focus on the work of Hildegard von Bingen. One of you wrote about her, comparing her to J.S. Bach, an interesting juxtaposition of musical styles. I thought I'd play you a bit from each of their works and let you decide if indeed there is a similarity. They were both geniuses, masters in their time. But I want you to discern and listen carefully, and I am awaiting your masterfully created soliloquies on what you have picked up."

Irene played a passage from Hildegard von Bingen, letting the monochromatic line of the Gregorian Chant fill the room. She, herself, listened and imagined making love to Helena, their bodies connected as one. Her nipples hardened as Helena, in her mind, was all over her. Thank goodness she was wearing four layers of clothes so her students wouldn't notice. She looked at her students' faces, a sense of the sublime painted all over them. She smiled, knowing that she was introducing them to some of the finest music ever written.

Then she played Bach, from his solo partitas, the violin soaring to elegance, a raw example of an exercise that soared to spiritual heights. In each segment, there was silence in the room as mouths dropped from the perfection of each note.

She left them in silence, and then broke it after a minute.

"Okay, your turn. I expect brilliance from all of you."

"It's sexy," a voice from the back uttered.

The class erupted in guffaws.

"Care to describe, in words that are appropriate and eloquent enough for the university?"

"It's raw. Beautiful. It's making love, this music, both passages, in the nakedness of the soul. It's the baring of one's self with another, the union of two beings who are in love. It is flawless, the one line of Hildegard, uniform, beauty inescapable, and then with Bach, it soars to heights that one cannot even reach. Like a prayer, love."

Irene nodded her head, impressed by this student's interpretation.

"Can you do something for me, oh beloved students…Can you never lose your poetry and your excellent way of description?"

The class again laughed, knowing this praise was true. They were a class of poets, loving every minute of it.

Another student spoke up. "I see all the seasons in this music. I felt them all as they intertwined in my head. Bach puts in the adversity and the beauty, the tempestuous frenzy and the frolicking sweetness of winter, spring, summer, and fall, and von Bingen lays out the land, like on a farm, the earth being plowed after a hard rain, the trees blossoming, each one bearing a fruit."

Irene nodded again. The class did, too. There was

silence. They did that to each other, this class, moved each other with words, beyond words.

"Let music continue to always inspire you like this. See you next week."

The class lingered for a bit as they always did, laughing and telling stories. Irene loved to hear the bits that filtered through her ears. Then the room was quiet, everyone gone.

In the silence, she felt jet lag hit her, a stone thrown her way, making her want to run into a field, sinking into the earth, and sleep. She did not know how she did it, teach. *It must be something in my blood.* She had four more classes in a row. For each one she needed to be on, and somehow, she was. She found it rather miraculous.

When the last class had left, she sank into her chair, afraid she wouldn't be able to get up. A half hour passed, and somehow, she made it to her feet, to the bus stop, and to her front door. There was a brown bag perched against the door. In it was a container of God knows what, something that smelled delicious. A little note inside said, "Welcome Home. Bob." Irene smiled, went inside, and ate whatever it was, full of little chopped up vegetables and other vague things that slipped into her mouth like ambrosia. Putting the container in the sink, she threw off her clothes and climbed into bed, sleep hitting her immediately like a storm that had been waiting all day.

≈≈≈≈≈

The rest of the week blurred itself into one singular lump. The emerald-green suitcase lay in the corner of Irene's bedroom, forgotten and zipped up, impervious to the cold of winter that lay surrounding it, the chilly house where Irene rarely put the heat on, to save energy, she always said. Routine took over Irene's life: wake up, coffee and breakfast, teach, come home and run, make dinner, crash into bed. She texted Bob that she was home safely, thanking him for the dinner—delicious. He had texted back that when she was alive again, perhaps they could sit down for a real dinner, as he wanted to hear all about her trip. She had sent back a simple smile, hoping that the eventual dinner with Bob might bring her out of this mechanical existence.

The day she returned she texted Helena she had arrived safely. Helena sent back a text with a kiss, and a hug, and an emoji with tears flowing down. She sent back the same. Since then, as they vowed they would try to do, they had not communicated.

Saturday arrived. Irene woke up around three in the afternoon, wondering where she was. She looked around, and saw that her comfortable bed, home, surrounded her. She looked out the window at the pale, darkened, and damp sky. Her body felt like it was returning to normal, but her heart felt stuck in her throat, like it had been freed from an iron clasp, and now, it was again trapped, unable to walk or stand. She emerged from her home, and in the rain her body, nimble and strong, ran for miles, as if it needed to rediscover Seattle all over again, her heart a blurred mass of sadness, needing release.

Hours later, sweaty and exhausted, she returned home, her heart no better and her body ready for a shower and bed.

The first week of March arrived with a deluge of rainstorms. It was Saturday, and Irene had been home for nearly two weeks. She picked up the phone and called Bob.

"Hiya."

"Well, the Tasmanian princess has surfaced." He chuckled.

"Hey there. Nice to hear your voice."

"Dinner tonight?"

"Sure. Where?"

"The place around the corner from you. The Golden Crane?"

"Perfect. Our usual? seven?"

"Marvellllllllous."

⁂

"So, you begin. This might take a while." Bob laughed, his beard bouncing with his smiling mouth.

"No, you start."

"Nope, the princess must begin. I insist. So, I can tell, though, you're in love. Sorry, I am stealing your punch line. Okay, I'll shut up. Start at the beginning."

Irene just stared at her best friend and laughed. It was good to be back home, she realized.

She did start at the beginning, the very beginning. She wanted to draw out the story, as she had an avid listener, staring at her, but also, she wanted to just tell this story, relive it, as it was not only a beautiful one, but it was hers.

An hour later, dinner done, she finished, her face a pool of tears, and Bob's, too. He took her hand and cried like a baby.

"This is the most stunning story I have truly heard in all my years and, this story happened to my best friend, dearest Irene. No wonder you're glowing. Ah, I am such a puddle, look at me, I am so happy for you."

Irene smiled and kept beaming, her smile like a fixed object in time, an expression of something that would never change. She realized then that it was not just a story she was telling. This was her life, and there was someone, not very far away who was waiting for her.

"So, dearest Bob, tell me yours." Irene took her hand away as they ate their desserts, cake with ice cream.

He blushed.

"Oh, so, the bear has something to tell." Irene chuckled.

"Kind of." Irene smiled as she witnessed shyness take over her best friend.

"So..." he began. "I wrote the book. We lost power, and with candlelight and no sleep for five days and five nights, I wrote my next novel."

Irene laughed. She could totally picture it, her obsessive friend Bob. When he was on a roll, he was on a roll.

"My first almost completely erotic gay romance novel. I couldn't stop writing, as there was sex scene after sex scene, and I was just totally into it.

"When I was done, I slept for twenty-four hours, and then I called my publisher friend Harry. I sent it to him, and the next day he phoned and asked to meet me. He said he just loved it, wanted to devour it, and he wanted to take me to dinner to celebrate. We ate, we drank, we ate, we drank, and the evening turned into the night, and I went to his place and we had the best sex I've ever had. In the morning, we couldn't stop. So, now we are dating. He's single now, just barely, and who knows?"

He stopped, looked in Irene's eyes that were bubbly, matching her face, lit up and laughing.

"So, Harry. I always knew that something would happen between you two. He was with that guy Lester for far too long. It's good to know that there's hope for ending a bad relationship so you can start something that is hot and perfect. And I know you have been, on some level, waiting for him for years."

"Yeah, I guess I have. You know me too well."

She smiled. "You two probably would have gotten together anyway, but here's to your sexually mad new novel that sped up the process." She held up her water glass and clinked it with his.

"And here's to your lovely new relationship. I hear wedding bells. Please let me be the best man."

"You'll be the only man there, probably." She laughed. She told him about their agreement to not communicate until the first day of spring.

"You two are insane! Completely. You'll be laughing about this insane idea of yours when you are ninety-nine, sitting in your rocking chairs over Wineglass Bay."

They began guffawing that couldn't stop, one feeding off the other. Other patrons looked over and stared, but nothing could put a lid on their laughs and giggles, until the waitresses started to put the chairs on top of the tables, and the closed sign was hung on the door.

Chapter Nine

Helena got out of her truck, looking at the cows huddled in the snow. Spring would take a while this year to come, she thought, seeing that it was an exceptionally cold winter. Returning from Tasmania hit her hard, a building of bricks tumbling around her, bouncing off her feet. While she was standing there, somehow, she felt Irene still present with her, the smell of her in her car, on her clothes, her laughter still echoing in her mind. The journey home, the long flight, seemed to create an eruption of this sweetness in her mind, and when she returned to the Colorado she loved so well, she felt an emptiness, a missing piece. Her everyday tasks, the launching project in front of her, the animals welcoming her, all seemed laced with a vacancy in her brain and in her heart. Nothing of the old made sense to her anymore, it was just what she had to do. Irene had gone inside and had opened a window, the one that Helena had painted shut so many years ago when Ines died.

She had met her when they were both young, in high school. They were first loves for each other, and the newness of it all overtook them both. They would get married one day, they said, upon graduation. Ines was to go to Spain, to visit her family, her roots, and Helena was to forge a path at the University of Colorado. Six months later they would reunite and live together. Ines would find a job, and they cemented this vague notion of being together with a night full of passion that would leave them with I love yous painted everywhere on their hearts.

Two days later, Helena received a call from Ines's aunt. Ines was among the dead from the plane that had crashed over the Atlantic.

Helena was never able to say "I love you" to anyone after that phone call, and over so many years her heart closed off entirely from anything but flings, superficial bouts of sex-filled nights with other women.

As she stared at the cows, their complacency surrounding a certain form of contentment, she thought of Ines for the first time in decades, realizing how time had a way of covering up grief, paving a path that had its vortex submerged in sadness. She never realized how sad she had been; it just was an inherent part of her makeup, a pigment of her skin that she never bothered to examine. Her work had taken on a life of its own, demanding her, consuming her, and love had not even been part of anything she imagined for herself.

As she continued to gaze at the billowy winter clouds that enveloped the sky, and as she breathed in the freshness of the altitude, she noticed a fleeting sensation: Ines, disappearing, a spiritual release, as Irene entered, her face smiling, her eyes lit up with something intangible that felt like love. She, they, craved it. Sex, yes, they were hungry for this, over and over, their incessant appetite for the other, but beyond this, in the deeper realms of the open window, there was between them a starvation for love, a waiting for decades for just the right person to love, to open that window, to let in the light.

Helena smiled, feeling the tears well up, different

than the sad ones when Irene left. She put her hand to her heart and felt it beating, finding this so normal, this longing to be loved, this longing to love again.

She wondered if Irene had found her note in her suitcase, the emerald-green suitcase that was the beginning of the chipping away of the paint on the window.

⚘⚘⚘⚘

The spring after the disastrous election approached with a fervor of marches and protests all over the world, many spurred on by the #Resist Movement. Irene felt her own anger bubbling up again, especially after the airport incident, which mostly she had forgotten about as she had immersed herself in her everyday life.

At the same time, Irene discovered the first snowdrops in her garden, always the sign for her that spring was indeed beginning its gradual ascent from the earth. This year, even more she felt the contrast between the blemished world around her and nature's vital presence, new growth pushing itself forward, inspiring people to do the same.

And then there was Helena. In one week, the insane agreement between the two of them would end, and they would be able to talk. Irene had longed for her voice each day, just to hear her words, the way she wrapped phrases together, making her laugh or cry, or want to be held, or want to just plain devour her.

PART TWO: SPRING

Chapter Ten

M arch in the Pacific Northwest is a deceiving month, a taunting of the mind, a seduction into the vast world of what lay ahead. Spring emerges, gradually, in the tiniest increments, as the bitter cold of winter still permeates the ground. The days begin to elongate, and the promise prevails as woolen underwear still clings to the skin, the hats and gloves and boots of life still sit at night by the front door.

Snowdrops were followed by crocuses, as tiny, tightly held buds emerged in Irene's garden. This was the time of year when she ventured out every day to inspect, welcoming new growth, the return of life after the long deluge of winter.

The week before the first day of spring brought to Seattle frigid temperatures, plunging into the 20s at night, followed by crisp, sunny days of lows to the mid-40s. The sun beckoned Seattleites out into the streets, reveling in the blues of the sky, the brilliant diamonds on the water that surrounded all. Ah, the return to light, they said to each other, the blessed return to light. Some in T-shirts and shorts, flip-flops even, dancing in the streets, rejoicing spring and its royal entourage.

Irene saw it all in her classes, on her runs, loving this city and its idiosyncratic nature, its love of light in a darkened world. She knew she had made roots here, ones that danced with freedom to be herself. She longed to show it all to Helena. Their world was entranced by Tasmanian soil, a mere beginning to other realms. She wanted to share her world with her, and she wanted Helena to share her world with her. She felt worlds opening, spanning hemispheres, states, cities, for the heart sees no boundaries, she felt as she biked to work that day, bundled up with a multitude of layers, feeling buoyed by others smiling in the streets.

And then it was Monday the twentieth of March, and spring had made its royal entrance. Irene woke up to a crisp day, feeling energized, full, joyously delighted with the morning as she opened her eyes, and said simply, out loud, "It's spring!"

Sitting up in bed, staring at the sky, she waited for her phone to wake up. When at last it did, there was a ping and a zing, and a message waiting for her.

Good morning gorgeous. Happy Spring! Phone me when you are awake.

Irene's heart leapt, danced a somersault, and she pressed the Helena button.

"Hi, you."

"Hi, gorgeous. Happy spring."

"Mmmmmmmmmmmm," Irene murmured, loving this voice on the other end.

"Just wake up?"

"Yep."

Silence took over as she imagined waking up together, no words, kisses only.

"We made it. Are we crazy or what?"

"More than. Yes, we are decidedly crazy."

"Did you launch Tassiebaby?"

"Yeah. Today. As we speak."

"Wow. Congratulations. This is a big, I mean a huge, time for you."

"In more ways than one…" Helena's voice was like fire, sultry, wrapping itself around her. Irene felt weak sitting in her bed.

"I wish you were here," she said simply, her voice soft, pliable, wanting.

"Can I fly out this Friday, stay until Sunday?"

"Yes."

"There's nothing I want more."

"Me, too." Insistence took over, as she put her fingers to her nipples, feeling them harden, her breath deepening as the fire inside her consumed her.

"I want you, Irene." Helena's voice matched the pulsing that reigned all through Irene. "I have wanted you every day since that day the doors of the plane closed you in."

Irene moaned, finding words so inadequate. At once, she detested the phone, and wanted to throw it on the floor.

"Oh God, I am so not into phone sex. Just make that flight and get yourself here."

They both laughed.

"Okay, okay, I'm doing it now." Helena chuckled as she let her fingers flip through airline websites.

"Here's one. Looks like there is a sale for next weekend. That's always nice. How about this? Delta arriving at six thirty on Friday. When do you get off work?"

"Five thirty or so. Six thirty is perfect."

"Okay, just reserved that. And what about Sunday at five?"

"I think I'd rather censor my expletives on that one."

They laughed.

"You would not want me to leave Monday morning when you are supposed to be at work."

"Oh, shush. Stop telling me what I want to do and don't want to do." Irene laughed, and felt like dancing out in the streets with the thought of Helena being in her house less than a week away.

"Okay, done, paid for. No turning back, ticket is non-refundable."

They laughed together, the idiocy of that statement filtering through them.

"Do you have a day of celebrating ahead?"

"Oh, yeah, I guess so, I am more celebrating the fact that my reservation number is HJY789. Hey, how has teaching gone since you got back? Tell me how you've been."

"Fine, I guess. My students are brilliant, and I go on automatic pilot with them, so it's a good relationship. I come home each day wrecked and fall into dreamless sleeps. In between I think only of you. Had dinner with Bob. He cried when I told him our story. So, yeah, life tumbles on. How about you?"

"Well, the cows keep mooing. I swear, they are the most contented cows that must exist in the northern hemisphere. It's been full-on since I got back from Tasmania, and in the moments of quiet, I ponder what happened between us, beyond kissing you. Something deeply huge has happened, transforming what was to what is, and I know what will be."

"Yes, I feel it, too. Some monumental energy in the universe has shifted. We've called it doom here since January, and I imagine Colorado feels the same. But I believe that for every bit of doom and chaos and ugly bits of darkness that exist, there is, metaphorically, on the other side of the planet, on a different hemisphere, the most resplendent light imaginable, an energy force that only brings joy. We touched into that together, didn't we?"

"You say it beautifully."

"Hmmmmmmm."

"Ditto that."

"Do you have to leave?" Irene sensed Helena's schedule creeping into her day.

"Yeah, oh intuitive one."

"Well then, enjoy every moment. You have worked hard for this."

"We have worked hard, each of us, for this moment in our lives, meeting each other."

"It's bigger than a phone call."

"I love your voice."

Irene smiled, finding again that sensual being, wrapping herself around her.

"Mmmmmmmmm. Bye."

"Bye, gorgeous. See you in less than a week."

"Yes."

And with that yes, that sweet, lilting yes that spoke more than just the three letters it was given, they hung up, floating into their days.

🌿🌿🌿🌿

Irene danced into the shower, singing. She forgot how she loved to sing, and the more she sang, the louder she sang, to the point where if her volume got any higher, the neighbors next door might have come knocking, asking for publicity rights.

When she emerged from her operatic cleanse, there was a message waiting for her on her phone, the green light flashing, making her soprano voice even higher as still the Queen of the Night aria from *The Magic Flute* continued.

Did you get my note?

What note?

The one in your suitcase.

Irene gasped.

Oh, my. Ummmm...you'll never guess. I haven't even opened the suitcase since I came back. It is sitting in my room covered in a heap of laundry. It's my new and improved laundry shelf. LOL.

LOL.

Irene imagined Helena was truly laughing on her end. Irene was, too. She thought of how she always threw her clothes all over the room, like autumn leaves, letting them disperse everywhere.

Shall I look at it now?

Sure.

Irene went over to the infamous heap and threw everything off, watching a month's worth of dirty, rather fragrant, clothes tumble to the floor.

She opened the latch and took a whiff of Australia, making her smile. She laughed hard at herself why she hadn't done this earlier. She picked up each article of clothes, smelling sand, and water, and above all, Helena. Tucked into one of the unused pockets was indeed a piece of folded paper, the name of the lodge printed on the top. "*I love you,*" it read.

Irene held the paper to her chest, tears welling up in her eyes.

She pressed the send button on her phone.

I love you, too.

☙ ☙ ☙ ☙

Having an entire day to herself, being that her TA was taking over her classes for the day, part of her Master's thesis compulsory practicum, Irene decided she had no other option than to do the laundry. She began the task with a dance around her home, to her own songs that came out voluminously from her mouth, her diaphragm finding air in it that she never knew she had. While the clothes jumbled and tumbled around her machine, Irene looked at her home with a ceremonious sigh, realizing she really hadn't cleaned it properly for so many months she had stopped counting. She spent hours that day wiping and sweeping and folding and picking up things she didn't even know existed. By nightfall, she looked around at a home she didn't recognize. Aching from her efforts of the day, she collapsed in the bath, glad she didn't choose housecleaner as her profession.

On Tuesday morning, she greeted her students with a ceremonious "Happy spring."

They all seemed to have a glow about them as they poised their hands over their keyboards, ready for that week's inspiration.

Irene smiled as she began. "Okay, which one of you with a gorgeous voice can hum, or even whistle as much as you can of Vivaldi's spring concerto from *The Four Seasons*, the famous first movement, 'Allegro in E Major'?"

Hands flew in the air, begging for their own grandiose musical moment.

The first one was a whistle, each note perfect, the staccatos where they should have been, and a luscious vibrato on the hanging notes. The class applauded with gusto.

The next was a high soprano, the student singing the main melody after which she did a harmony version, after which she did her own cadenza, obviously improvising on each part. Again, ravenous applause.

The third and final rendition was an impromptu band, where some students played percussion with their knuckles on the desk, making djembe-like sounds, while other students used mouth music, and the soloist juxtaposed his sultry baritone voice of the melody with accompanying rhythms, creating a mélange of sounds, spanning the hemispheres and the generations with their own version of the Baroque classic. A standing ovation resulted from this interpretation.

Irene beamed as she began her lecture, bringing in differing classical styles from composers who wrote timeless pieces for spring, focusing on Aaron Copeland's *Appalachian Spring*, Igor Stravinsky's *The Rite of Spring* and Robert Schumann's *Symphony Number One*, the "Spring" Symphony.

The students hung on her words, as their brains were engaged in their next assignment: take the music and the style in which it was written and describe spring. They immediately turned to Vivaldi, using his music as the base, spring at its most known. She wanted them to ponder what spring was, why composers sought out this season to write a plethora of music about, and what the listeners needed to learn about spring in all this music. Irene loved it when she saw the wheels turn in the minds of her students, when they could take new things that they were learning and incorporate them on many levels. She mostly just loved it when her students just loved music, taking it all in, letting it change their lives, even on the tiniest level.

Chapter Eleven

Five o'clock on Friday arrived easily. Irene knew how to pass time. Focus on the moment, keep yourself insanely busy, don't look at the calendar except to know what you must do that day, eat well, exercise every day, and get yourself completely exhausted so that by the end of the day all that is left is the act of sleeping soundly. Her recipe for getting herself to the moment when she was to leave work and get to Sea-Tac worked amazingly well. She was well rested, relaxed, and her calm and grace were at their peak. On top of that, when she got into the Lyft car, she realized she had absolutely nothing to do that weekend but to spend it with Helena. It was her gift to herself.

The plane was right on time.

Irene knew, even before she saw her, that Helena was coming her way. Her heart began beating fast, and her legs slightly wavered. She had to hold on to a post to steady herself. When indeed Helena approached her, and her smile radiated throughout her, Irene ran to her, her muscled legs carrying her all the way to her arms which folded around her, holding her tightly. Their eyes locked for a moment, sending waves of desire back and forth, and then their lips got hold of one another, frantically meeting, their incessant pull toward each other pushing away anything and everything as they longed to be inside of one another, effortlessly merging there at the airport.

When they could barely bear to tear themselves apart, they laughed, quietly at first, then at a greater volume. Arms around each other, they went to the bathroom, entering a stall together, letting their hands and lips travel anywhere, longing for the other with a famine, a fiery surge that was uncontainable. Without making a sound, they came and then again, begging for more, and leaving the stall, giggling, holding each other, they made their way to the Lyft waiting area. They slipped into a car and soon arrived at Irene's front door.

"Dinner first, around the corner is a lovely little place, and then, my home?" Irene asked, knowing that once they settled into her home, they would have absolutely no desire to leave it.

"Beautiful idea."

Hand in hand, they walked to Scraps, one of Seattle's favorite local bistros, making the best comfort food that locals couldn't get enough of. Fortunately, they found a table without a wait. That was a rare treat. They shared house-made gnocchi with foraged mushrooms, and a pan-roasted halibut with fiddlehead fern and a carrot-ginger sauce, a meal that melted on their tongues. Without hesitation, they shared a dessert, a coffee pots de crème with maple cream and hazelnut sauce, sliding spoonfuls into each other's mouths and imagining it on their bodies, their tongues slipping freely. They rarely spoke, savoring every bite of their meal.

Their bellies satiated and deliciously happy, they took each other's hands again, and walked the eight blocks to Irene's home.

"Here it is. My home. Welcome."

Helena took Irene into her arms, and held her

close, wrapping herself around Irene. Their lips met fervently as Helena removed Irene's jacket and then her own. Irene took her hand and led her to the bedroom, where their hands and lips grabbed each other pulling at one another with a ferocity that made their legs weaken. Clothes got ripped off, all the many layers, one by one, as their bodies came together, Irene pulling Helena under the sheets. In the cold room, they were combustible, their heat almost suffocating as lips tore at lips and necks and nipples and any place they could. Their starvation for the other could not be met enough as they groaned and ached for each other, their nails digging in like animals wanting, devouring. Their mouths sucked and pulled and licked and swirled, and they teased, and they taunted each other, each one taking control of the other, pushing and pulling, their evenness in the match. They forbade orgasm at first, almost getting there, then pulling back, grunting like beasts, their nipples taut, the waves of the river between their legs flowing, gushing, spilling over into every crevice of their bodies. Then they gave way, letting release happen, and letting it happen over and over, their screams penetrating the spaces of the sheets as they refused to yield to an end.

Then there was silence, the last roar echoing through them as they held each other tightly, tears streaming down their faces, nearly endless tears, as they folded into each other even more, this sharing of tears, this silence letting down walls, thickened walls of much of a lifetime waiting for the other.

They fell asleep for hours, holding each other. They were in each other's dreams, a complete merging of one to another as love moved into the spaces of sleep.

❧❧❧❧❧

Blue skies met their eyes the next morning.

"Hi, you," Irene murmured, slowly entering the world of the awakened beings.

"Good morning, gorgeous." Helena pulled Irene closer.

"It's a beautiful day. I'd like to take you out, show you the city. After the hard rains from the last few days, it smells so beautiful."

"I'd love that. I would absolutely love to see your city."

"Would you now?" Irene rolled over and straddled Helena, pressing into her, giving her a short kiss on her cheeks.

Helena breathed hard. "Tell me what you like the best?"

Irene took her lips to Helena's ear, blowing a cool wisp of air into it. "The way the sky meets the water, and the mountains almost laugh, their peaks covered with snow."

Helena's nipples became toys for Irene, as she took her fingertips and grazed them, her hips pressing into the flow of nectar that Helena was creating for her.

"Kiss me. Now," Helena demanded, her breath rapid.

Irene lowered her body, giving Helena one slow, deep kiss, then pulled away. Helena grabbed her, caressing Irene's inner thighs, as Irene laughed, loving this morning play.

"So, tell me what you want to see," Irene teased, seeing if Helena could mouth out anything.

"I....I..." Helena breathed hard, unable to make a word emerge.

Irene laughed, pressing harder into her, the
folds of her, her own juices blending into Helena's.
Irene loved the feel of her breasts, full and round as
her hardened nipples circled around Helena's. Helena
moaned incessantly as Irene starved her, loving the
power she held over Helena's desirous body. Irene took
her lips and moved them down through the curves
of Helena, lapping up stray nectar as she landed on
Helena's labia, her tongue circling around it, teasing
and taunting. Irene felt Helena writhe under her
tongue, her moans deeper in her throat as Irene tasted
and licked and thrust her tongue deeply inside. Helena
screamed, loud, and Irene continued to thrust and pull
and then soften, as Helena quieted, and Irene moved
up to hold her in her arms.

Softness enveloped them as the morning
meandered. Irene took Helena's hand and turned
it over, her palm up, stroking it, and studying it
assiduously.

"You have loved someone. Deeply. A long time
ago. She died. Many years ago."

Helena looked carefully into Irene's eyes. "How
did you know this?"

"Your palm. My grandmother, my father's
mother, taught me this when I was little. She was a
palm reader in Iran."

"Her name was Ines. I was so young. I did love
her, we were crazy about each other."

"How did she die?"

"Plane accident. She perished along with her
parents."

"Oh my God, I am so sorry."

"I didn't think I could ever love again."

Irene watched her, studied her face.

"When I wrote you that little note, I felt a huge window open again."

Helena stroked Irene's soft skin, her fingertips making circles.

She stopped, looked deeply into Irene's eyes. Tears began to well up. "I love you, Irene."

Irene held her gaze, felt her own tears inside, welling up. "I love you, Helena."

Their hands held each other, as their lips met, their tears mixing, their faces wet with the emotion that they felt, the hugeness of love.

"Have you loved before?" Helena said, this time studying Irene's face.

"Yes," Irene said in a quiet voice. "I, too, have experienced death."

Silence covered these words, leaving them exposed, naked.

"He was one of my father's students," she began. "From Iran. He came to the house often when I was little. He was a prodigy of my father's, brilliant. When my father died, he disappeared for many years, returning to Iran. One day, as I was studying at the university, several years after my dad passed, he emailed me. He had returned to New York and he was teaching at NYU, where I was a student. We met, had coffee. We fell instantly in love, crazy beyond crazily in love. I became pregnant. Then, like your Ines, he died in a plane crash, coming back from a trip to Iran. I lost the baby. Like you, after that, I closed off my heart, not allowing love back in."

Helena and Irene lay together, each holding their own pain and the other's, stroking each other's hair and cheeks, finding the need to touch, to connect through that opening of the heart, hands on the body, nurturing the other.

They sighed, knowing the past never really left, yet also knowing that the heart could and wanted to love again.

"The baby?" Helena asked.

"For two months I was pregnant. The doctors didn't know the sex yet, but I knew it was a boy."

Helena sighed as Irene stared off, looking out the window, wanting to change the subject.

"And being a lesbian?"

Irene laughed. "Bob told me I was a lesbian."

"Really?" Helena giggled.

"Yeah, one day, shortly after we met, he blurted out, 'Irene, you're queer, you know.'

"'I am?' I said.

"'Yep. As queer as they come.'

"'But what about Ari?' I asked.

"'Yes, that was real. But that was your past life. Some people are born gay, and some people become gay later in life. There's no recipe for it, it just is.'

"I looked at him, and then I looked at my own life, and realized he was absolutely right. I had a few lovers, women, and realized Bob was spot-on. The missing piece was love, though. So, I just stopped seeing women altogether. I kept breaking their hearts, as I couldn't love them, and they needed this.

"Something happened with you and me, Helena. Like you said, a window opened. Maybe on some level our shared experience, even if we didn't know it when we met, but on some level, that shared understanding paved the way to unlatching the bolt. Plus, and I think this is the greatest thing, we are, on a planetary, spiritual level, connected. It was fate that brought us together."

They stared at one another, their gazes piercing, their eyes still wet from those admissions of the soul. Their lips found each other's then, and with no more words to say, with the truth out, that naked window opened, they fed each other, their bodies wanting and their lips feeling the thread of connection. They danced in that bed, alive with a rhythm that accompanied their moans and their screams, and then their quiet reigned as they solidified something so entirely real, so much the source and the depth of that miracle of finding love again.

෯෯෯෯

"You'll never guess what I found at my local co-op yesterday." Irene smiled, dreamily, sitting up in bed and looking out at the window at the blue skies, then bounding on top of Helena, puppylike.

"Hmm?" Helena bantered back, stroking her buttocks, her eyes bright and playful back.

"Tassieyogo. I made a request for it last month. They said they would contact the distributor and try to see if they could carry it regularly in their stores. I got a phone call a few days ago telling me that the product is in. I danced in the store when I saw it on the shelf. Took it home, and my god, it is divine. So, now, in my fridge, I have the entire collection of Tassieyogo, in all three flavors they were able to get for now."

Helena laughed, pulling her to her, kissing her cheek.

"Would you like me to bring you a bit of breakfast in bed, highlighting the piece de resistance?"

"Oh my, what luxury. Sounds wonderful."

"I'll be back soon."

Putting on her robe and turning up the heat, as

it was literally freezing in the house, Irene banged a few dishes around, made a strong pot of coffee, and in a few minutes, was back in the bedroom with a tray of containers of yogurt, bowls of different kinds of homemade granola by local artisans, and a plate of chopped bananas.

"What a feast! Thank you." Helena reached for Irene's lips and let hers graze them, as Irene laughed and spread out the tray on the bed.

"I think I like the mango flavor the best," Irene commented, sampling the vanilla, raspberry, and mixed berry.

"I don't agree. I like the mixed berry. Of course, I like them all. I guess I should, shouldn't I?" They were feeding each other, spoonful by spoonful, playfully using their tongues to clean up the mess they were making on each other's faces.

They managed to finish up every one of the yogurts, all the granola, and all the bananas.

"Well, I guess we were hungry." Helena laughed.

"So, I had an idea. A few," Irene said, changing the subject. "What if we take our time and discover a bit of Seattle today. Let's rent a car for the weekend. I can show you the places I love in the city. When we are done, we shop for a bit and then we come home and make dinner together. I would love to make Fesenjan with you. It takes a while to make, but I haven't done it for ages, and I so want to cook with you. It is one of my favorite dishes of all time, and I have my dad's recipe in my head from three generations."

"I love it. Every bit of it. Cooking with you sounds just divine. And I just love Fesenjan."

"You've tasted it?"

"Of course. I am not as dumb of a white girl as

you think." They both laughed. "We had some Iranian neighbors when I was little. We often invited each other for dinner, and they, too, loved to make Fesenjan. I loved the pomegranate part, the mixture of sweet and savory."

"Me, too, and the nuts. Ah, just thinking about it makes my mouth water. And of course, the saffron rice that goes with it."

"Okay." Irene changed the subject again. "Shower and go?"

"Perfect."

They stepped into the hot pouring water together, soaping each other, letting the bubbles slide down their bodies, slipping themselves around each other, kissing, embracing, wanting more.

In the car, Irene became the ultimate tour guide, driving here and there, with no real destination as her guide. She called it "Intuitive Seattle," seeing the city without a map. They drove through neighborhood after neighborhood, curving around terraces of manicured homes, and neighborhoods where manicuring was a laughable matter. They went up and down First and Second Hill, viewing the many tent cities that had sprung up everywhere, people's entire lives contained in a single tent and an adjoining grocery cart. There was a somberness to it, these homes, lives dispersed into tents clumped onto the cold pavement.

Later, they laughed at the abundance of marijuana shops and Starbucks that adorned almost every corner. It was clear what Seattleites adored. And everywhere on that crystal-clear day, there were the mountains that towered above and beyond, Mt. Ranier of course, but also the Olympic Range to the west, the snow glistening. The water, always the water that reflected the many aspects of life, surrounded all, like a decoration, filtering in and out of islands and the many other land forms of the Puget Sound. Earth and sky and water and air felt alive that day as spring was becoming in front of their eyes. They walked in gardens, watching the daffodils, still tightly folded, begin their progression toward the sun, and the rhododendrons, too, exposing little of themselves, yet showing their buds, not yet ready to flaunt any of their magnificence.

As the sun moved through the sky and folded itself around back into the landscape, Irene and Helena stepped inside the co-op, ready to get what they needed for the feast they were to prepare that evening. Hand in hand, they walked in to the plethora of organics. Irene felt pangs of guilt run through her as she imagined the fine meal she and Helena would make, her imaginings juxtaposed with images of the nameless, hungry faces inside the tents, staring back at her.

≈≈≈≈

The kitchen turned into a whirlwind of chopping, stirring, mixing. Food was everywhere, on the floor, and all over the counters, as the smells of onions and cardamom filled the kitchen, the nuts, the pomegranate juices, and saffron spilling out and flowing. In between knives chopping and the food processor blending, Irene and Helena had entered a tranced state of ecstasy. Completely sober, they felt stoned, starving for each other all over again, their lips on lips, their hands reaching for each other's hips, their bodies swaying to music on the stereo, "cooking music" Irene called it, digeridoo, with djembes in the background, a pulse and a connection to the earth. As they stirred what was in the pot, the two danced, tasting what was cooking and tasting each other, their arms wrapped around one another, feeling the heat they were making. Irene, leaning against the counter, pulled Helena toward her, writhing underneath Helena's kisses as they swayed, their hips together, pressing into each other as the music slipped inside of them, weaving a rhythm around their own moans as they teased each other.

Irene put a lid on the pan, lowered the flame, and took Helena's hand, leading her to the sofa. The wood stove had made a comfortable heat in the living room. She added a few more logs and, taking off her shirt, lowered herself down to Helena, swaying on her as Helena took her nipples and sucked to the rhythm of the drums. The beat was intense, throbbing, matching their hunger. Irene breathed hard as she unbuttoned Helena's shirt, exposing her breasts, letting the fullness of them grow, burying her head in between them, her legs folded around Helena's, sinking into each other. Laughing, breathing hard, wanting, they rolled off the couch onto the floor, tearing each other's clothes off as their heat intensified, the music resounding through their bodies as the aroma of cardamom and pomegranate filled the room.

෴෴

"I think it's time to finish up the rice, make a salad, and eat," Irene whispered some time later, feeling the need to get up and add another log.

"Let me get the fire roaring. My turn." Helena helped Irene up off the floor that had become chilly.

"This is amazing," Helena said, her fork in her mouth, tasting the saffron rice mixed with the Fesunjun. "It just melts in the mouth, better than what I remember as a child."

"Three generations of making this, plus a bit of our passion thrown in." Irene laughed, smiling at the results of their creation.

"This will be a dish we will be making for many, many more years together." Helena raised her wineglass, clinking it with Irene's.

"Here's to our beginning." Irene teared up, feeling in her the largesse of their toast, the entrance to their world where love seemed to reign like the inevitable blossoms in the spring.

They were each quiet for a moment, taking it all in. So much had happened in only a few months. They both had tears now. The music had stopped, and there was a tiny patter of rain that had taken its place, dancing against the windows. They looked at each other, deeply gazing into the eyes of the other, noting the glow that resided in their faces. They sighed together, smiling, knowing that this feeling would never end.

Washing the dishes, Helena leaned into Irene, breathing her in. When they entered the kitchen, their laughter took on a voice of its own as they walked in to a major disaster. Food and sauce, the blood-red pomegranate, was everywhere. When finally the dishes were all in the sink, Irene offered to wash as Helena dried. Each time there was a new dish, she rushed at the opportunity to join Irene again, each time kissing her in a new place as Irene moaned, her arms up to her elbows in soap suds.

When the kitchen was spotless, they lit candles, drew a bath, and sank into the hot water, letting their bodies curve around each other, their lips starving again for the other. Helena moved on top of Irene, letting the sway of her body glide itself with the waves she made, water flowing everywhere, all over the floor, as the fire between the two grew and grew, their kisses unable to cease as Helena pressed into Irene. Irene held on to her, grabbing her, splashing water everywhere as they laughed and screamed and moaned, their breasts hard and hungry.

They added more water, not wanting to leave their aqueous cave. Irene curled up against Helena, watching the flicker of the candles, loving the faint light they gave. Helena poured water from her hand onto Irene, letting the soft flow bathe her. Irene purred. Never in her life had she ever been this happy, this utterly content.

Her mind moved to something that she had been pondering for the past week.

"What do you know about Laure?"

"You mean Laure Lyons, my grandmother's lover?"

"Yes, I mean, do you really think she drowned herself in the river?"

Helena was quiet and looked as if she was pondering Irene's question.

"Because I have been thinking, what if your grandmother was not delirious, demented, or any such thing when she lay dying? What if Laure is still alive, and the story was not entirely true, or even true at all that she killed herself? Her family hated Hillary because of what they deemed was her seductions, when in fact Laure seduced your grandmother...What if they fabricated the story of her suicide? And what if your grandmother knew this, but didn't let on?" Irene was rather breathless with her postulations.

Helena was quiet again. She seemed to be taking it all in.

"I don't know, the suitcase, the letters, the money.

It sounds to me like she was getting ready for a trip. To France. Do you think that really she hid all this stuff in her suitcase out of dementia?"

"This idea never occurred to me. But how can we find out? Everyone is dead."

"The internet. We must do a search on Laure Lyons. She was a well-known poet?"

"Not exactly. She was a clandestine poet. I think her poetry was rather racy for the time."

They chuckled.

"With lesbian themes, perhaps?"

"Oh, I am imagining so much more. Perhaps there were even some mentions of kissing, maybe a breast or two." Helena laughed. "I wonder what this poetry could have even entailed."

The water was getting cold. Irene stepped out gingerly, giggling at the lake on the floor. She put out a towel to dry it, grabbed one for herself, and one for Helena.

They went to the bedroom, where Irene picked up her phone. She googled Laure Lyons.

There was nothing on the first page that matched.

She scrolled down, her eyes on a quest. She moved to the bed, and Helena wrapped herself around Irene as together they looked at the tiny screen, completely immersed in this new sleuthing.

She found a listing, in French.

She read it in its entirety.

"Wow!" She exclaimed.

"You understand French?"

"Yep. You'll never believe what this says."

"What? What? Tell me!" Helena nuzzled her nose into Irene's neck.

"It says that she was part of the underground

women's movement in Paris, that she was known in 'homosexual' circles as an advocate for women. It says she was a brilliant poet and essayist, and that she died quite old, at the age of eighty-five in Paris and was survived by her longtime companion, Elise Maillon."

Helena laughed, her belly shaking. Irene joined her.

"Wait. Wait," she said. She pulled out her phone and googled Elise Maillon.

She scrolled down and saw two Elise Maillons. One in Quebec, a hair stylist, and one in Paris, a neurosurgeon. Both were still alive, apparently.

"Ah, a younger girl she found. This is fascinating…Shall we contact Elise?"

"But why would Elise want to know about Hillary? The *other* woman…"

They both guffawed and couldn't stop laughing.

"You think Hillary knew all this, and about Elise?"

"Makes you wonder, huh?" Helena grabbed Irene, pulling her closer.

"My guess is that she didn't know about Elise. If your theory is correct and she was planning a trip to Paris, she probably thought Laure was single, or at least still married to the man her family threw her to.

"You know, I kind of feel like writing to Elise. I sense there is more there, and I am curious. Maybe she does want some information about Hillary. Maybe there's a story there."

"Ah, you are insatiable, aren't you? Your curiosity is infectious. Now how do you know French?"

"Oh, I lived there for a year. Picked it up quite fast, actually. I took some music classes at the Sorbonne, after Ari died and I miscarried. It was the best thing for me to do, and it helped my music career hugely. But anyway, what do you think? Is it worth digging up any possible skeletons in your family closet?"

Helena stroked Irene's hair. She kissed her neck, slow, gentle and deep.

"Wonderful. I'm in," she muttered.

Irene put down her phone, smiling.

"Come here, you," Irene said quietly, her voice insistent, pleading.

Helena rose to sit up, gently pushing Irene down onto the bed, straddling her. Irene's nipples hardened in an instant, her clitoris throbbing. She grabbed Helena's hands, and Helena pinned them down as she placed her lips on hers, thrusting her tongue inside her mouth as Irene deliciously writhed underneath her, her moans intensifying. With a grunt that could only have been of a primordial nature, Irene released her hands and rolled herself on top of Helena, now pinning her down with her muscled thighs. Back and forth the two women did this, establishing their dominance, their lips pressed together. They laughed, they moaned, they screamed over and over as their game continued throughout the night, until finally all was hushed, and sleep took them, their arms around each other tenderly, as the rain continued its softened patter outside.

❧❧❧❧

It was afternoon when their eyes opened to the world, the rain a constant hum that had not once subsided.

"Mmmm," Irene sleepily murmured, feeling Helena's lips on the palm of her hand.

"Good morning, gorgeous."

"Mmmm," Irene repeated, cozying inside

Helena's arms wrapped around her.

They took a few moments to lay quietly, the rain accompanying their wake-up sighs.

Their bladders called for attention, and each one got up to the darkened house and let nature call forth release.

"It's almost one o'clock." Helena sighed, the lack of light in the northwest not giving any indication as to the time of day. "I have to leave in a few hours for the airport."

"Don't remind me. Hungry?"

"Famished. More yogurt in bed?"

"Of course."

"I do like encores of lovely performances."

They both got up and went to the kitchen. Helena made the coffee and Irene got out the new yogurts they had bought yesterday along with some more granola, dried fruits, bananas, and a few strawberries. She arranged them all on a platter, like a flower, the petals of many colors, art on a plate.

"Beautiful," Helena commented, pushing Irene's wild, sleep- and love-filled hair away from her eyes, kissing her forehead.

They went back to the bedroom, cranked up the heat, and, naked, fed each other on the bed, laughing with abandon, forgetting completely about any imminent departures. When their bellies were satiated, Helena lathered yogurt all over Irene, listening to her giggles of ticklishness, as Helena's tongue lapped up every bit, every corner of Irene's skin.

"I smell like a milk factory." Irene laughed.

When Helena had, like a cat, fastidiously cleaned up all of Irene, their laughs subsided as their lips took over, ravenous all over again, their tongues thrusting inside the other's mouth, a desperation that filled them as their bodies tightened together, their juices flowing, gushing around their thighs. Back and forth they pushed each other against the softness of the bed, the pillows, their wants insatiable, their moans filling every space, and still they couldn't get enough of the other. Time meant nothing to them as they wailed and screamed, their bodies starting over each time with a newness, a desire to never let go.

There was one last scream, echoing in the room, a last gasp, and then only the rain sounded, the soft reminder of a world, a life outside.

Helena looked at the clock.

It was five minutes to three.

"We have to leave in ten minutes," Irene pronounced, her voice sad, small.

They got in the shower together, quickly removing residual yogurt, and in five minutes, bodies were dried, clothes were on, and they were out the door, Irene expertly maneuvering the car through Sunday afternoon lollygaggers.

She pulled into the departures curb at Sea-Tac at 3:45 p.m.

"You better rush. Your plane leaves in just over an hour. Text me, please, when you are home."

Irene looked at Helena, their tears welling up in their eyes. She could barely see through them.

They embraced, emotion filling their touch, and one quick kiss later, Helena rushed off through the afternoon crowd as Irene drove away, the airport police not giving her a moment to sit with it all.

Feeling full yet empty, Irene arrived home, threw on her running clothes, and let her body move through the streets, forcing her tears to hush as she let herself get completely exhausted. She stopped at her burrito place and sat on a bench at the azalea path in Washington Park, eating her food and letting the light rain bathe her. She looked out at the buds of awaiting blossoms as she still felt Helena's touch on her, her skin hot and desirous.

She smiled, watching the rain, the darkened sky, yielding little light, as she thought to herself that all this was because of a suitcase. She felt her body pulse, letting it all just surround her, this euphoric feeling that had now invaded every strand of her existence.

☙ ☙ ❧ ❧

Helena sat in her seat, watching Seattle's clouds disappear, the plane pushing itself through them, the thick mass of gray, to the awaiting blues of sky.

Irene's voice echoed in her ear. In her mind, Irene slithered around her body, awaiting her.

The weekend was like a film she didn't want to end. Her gaze focused out the window. The world below seemed like a passing thread, a figment of life that no longer belonged to her. Her hands shook as she took a gulp from her water bottle. She felt her heart beating, fast, uncontrollable, as Irene filled her thoughts.

What is happening to me? Is this me, or a fantasy version of me? Did this weekend really happen, did this woman come into my life and change everything I ever knew about myself? Her mind dipped to the passion between them. She didn't know this about herself. Lovers had called her boring in the past, unexciting in bed. They had mocked her, telling her that her head was too full of yogurt to know what was what, what really mattered. When she was with Irene, everything shifted, something inherently, vastly different, became triggered, a hungry animal, starved for what she and Irene created together.

Is this lust or love? she wondered. What was the difference? At what point did one bleed into the next? Can one love more than one person in one's life? Had she really loved Ines, or was she too young to really know love back then, when she was barely out of her own adolescence? Did she have to wait all these years to finally find love, be ready for it?

She took another gulp of water, found her heart quiet, her hands relax. As she continued to stare out the window, the mountains of home beckoned her eyes toward her life on the farm. She felt something different inside of her, shifting like the turn of the seasons. Coming back to the scent of her, her cows, all that she created, she experienced in her an inability to want to return to what was. Now, her life seemed to be irresistibly moving toward the sharing of this solitariness with another. Now, the scent of Irene was everywhere, on her, in her, forging a path toward the merging of herself with another.

Now, for the first time in decades, she wanted more than yogurt.

❧❧❧❧

I'm home. Your lips are around me. Everywhere there is you. I am stunned by this. I am hungry for it. When can I see you next?

Irene smiled, held her phone in her hands, clutching it to her heart.

We have given a new synonym to "missing you" haven't we? You are everywhere in my home. I can't go into any room now with wistfulness. When are you free again to come out here? I can't wait more than two minutes. I just remembered. I have papers to grade the next two weekends. And then the weekend after that, I am supposed to be in Vancouver presenting a paper I have to write.

One month then.

Oh God, is there eternity? For if there is, it is in front of me now."

Me too.

I don't want sexting either.

A howling with laughter emoji came up on her screen.
Irene pressed send after howling back.

Sleep well, gorgeous.

You too. Dreams upon you, may they be sweet.

Smile.
Smile back.
Irene made her way to the bedroom, sniffing as she entered. The smell of slightly fermented yogurt was everywhere. She took off the sheets and covers, throwing them in the washing machine. Grabbing her sleeping bag, she curled up in it and sighed, falling into a deep sleep, the rain stopping now as a brilliant moon lit up the sky.

Chapter Twelve

Spring happened in Seattle like it always does. There was a progression of things, this unfolding, this opening to the world, from tightly balled masses of growth, to the tenderness of a flower, leaves emerging out of nowhere, it seemed, and suddenly the towering red cedars had company, and green appeared everywhere.

Irene felt this, her step light, her body a cavern like a flower, one of Georgia O'Keefe's, full of passion and an insistency, movement toward the light, the ever-present elongation of the days and the nights. Her teaching was alive, more vibrant than ever, her cheeks flushed with an exuberance of music that spilled out into the corridors of her classes. Students were on waiting lists now to attend her classes, and sometimes just snuck in, sitting on the floor in the back of the lecture hall to listen to her words, her inspiration. Because of her teaching, music had become a quintessential part of the University of Washington student experience. Other faculty members did not fail to notice this. That day, in her work mailbox was a letter announcing to her that the Music Department had awarded her "Outstanding Teacher of the Year."

Later, Irene held this letter in her hand, deep in thought about the power of teaching, how teaching was itself an act of love, of inspiration, coming from a place that seemed nebulous to her, yet was, entirely real. She smiled as her phone rang. *Helena.*

"I am at the airport," she said, her voice a mixture of nervousness and delight.

"Which one?"

"Yours."

Irene laughed. "Are you serious?"

"Would I ever lie to you? I will grab a car. Be at your house in a bit."

Click.

Irene stared at the phone as if it had a life of its own, as if it were making up a fable, with clues, and all she had to do was to get herself home in one piece.

She called her favorite pizza place and ordered a pie to go. In forty minutes, pizza in hand, her key was in the front door. The car was just pulling up, and out stepped Helena, her shirt tossled, her hair a mess.

She looked positively sexy.

Irene just about dropped the pizza she was holding, just about saw little mushrooms and olives fall helplessly to the ground.

"Can I help you, ma'am?" Helena grabbed the pizza, took the key, and let them in, while Irene just stared incredulously.

Just in the entryway, Helena dropped her backpack to the floor and carefully put the pizza box on a chair. She grabbed Irene, their bodies a massive conglomerate of fire. Helena took Irene's hand and led her to the bedroom, where her hands couldn't move fast enough, removing her clothes. They tore at each other, animals, their nakedness not enough as the fire between them consumed every particle of their organisms. Screams followed screams until the silence of the evening wrapped around them, cuddled like primates, wanting only the softness of each other.

Irene purred as Helena went to the kitchen and brought back the pizza, two plates, and a bottle of wine and two glasses, everything set on a tray, with a letter poking out.

Irene purred louder, laughing.

"What's this?" she asked, her hands in Helena's hair, running her fingers through her curls.

Helena nodded for her to read it.

Dear Ms. Helena Hanover,

After hundreds of nominations, your company has been awarded the best Colorado business of the year. We have noticed that sales and stock of Tassieyogo have climbed extremely high this past year, especially over the past few months, that I, on behalf of the state of Colorado, would like to declare a statewide yogurt day, allowing the public to get turned on to the delectable tastes of this amazing product. We have been informed that the United Nations has been expressing interest in your Tassiebaby product. I would like to offer you any support I can with this venture and provide any matching funds that you might need so that your product can be available for worldwide distribution to underdeveloped nations. Please let me know how I can assist you.

With respect and appreciation,
Simon Brazelton, Governor of Colorado

Irene focused on the words on the page, smiling, tearing up, and kissing the piece of paper.

"This is completely amazing. Wow! congratulations, darling."

Helena beamed.

"Is this why you are here?"

"Booked a flight just a few hours ago. I had to see you. I leave at four tomorrow morning for a six o'clock flight. I have a meeting in Denver at ten."

She opened the bottle of wine, poured a glass for Irene and a glass for herself.

Irene held up her glass, toasting her, their glasses kissing as their lips found each other's, not wanting to let go.

They fed each other pizza, eating the entire pie, and then let their hands and mouths devour each other, their bodies celebrating until the wee hours of night when they finally quieted, and all was still as smiles entered their sleep, their dreams translucent as fireflies on a warm summer evening.

And then it was four o'clock, the alarm rang, and Helena was out the door, and again, Irene stood in an empty house, remnants of pizza and the memories of a deliciously sex-filled night swimming around her.

☙❧☙❧

Friday morning rolled into focus. Irene was packing up her things, getting ready to fly up to Vancouver to present at the Musical Educators conference the next day. As she was zipping up her bag, her phone rang. It was Bob. He had been in la-la heaven, and so had she, and except for occasional texts, they had rarely seen each other. Seeing his name on the screen lit up her worried face. She had missed him.

"Salut."

"Bonjour, mon amour..."

"How goes? Oh, that's right, you're flying up to Vancouver to be *la voix celebre*."

"Oh stop. I'm a bit worried, actually. My mind has not been totally wrapped around this presentation. I've been a bit...um...distracted." She giggled.

"Oh, don't worry, love, just ad-lib. You know you're good at being the charming, erudite one. Words just flow out of you like honey." He laughed at his little joke.

Irene laughed, tried to stifle it, and then ended up guffawing. Nothing like seeing oneself and not taking oneself too seriously.

"Hey, just thought of something. Harry and I were talking about going for a little drive this weekend. We hadn't decided where. What if we get ourselves up to Vancouver and meet you? Have a bit of dinner or something."

"What a great idea. I love it. I have been dying to see Sir Harry again."

"Fab, darling. What time are you done?"

"Two."

"Oh my, that's perfect. Call me when you are free. If you're up to it, we can stroll in the UBC Botanical Gardens. I've been wanting to put my feet on that soil for ages."

"Ah, me, too. April is such a good month to see what's happening with all the blossoms. Oh, let's do it. I'll meet you there. Say, three o'clock? Want to get there before they close."

"*Parfait, ma cherie.* Have a good flight and remember how charming you are."

Irene just laughed. Sometimes with Bob you couldn't do anything but.

❧❧❧❧

Saturday at ten arrived, and Irene stood in front

of the podium. It was quite wonderful to be standing in front of a group of Canadians—Vancouverites at that. There was something entirely refreshing about being away from the US, in a country that, for her, always spelled out warmth and compassion. Especially now. When she landed at the airport and saw First Nations art everywhere, she breathed a sigh of relief.

She began. Her talk was on the parallels between world and classical music. She talked about the blend of the digeridoo and Vivaldi that she had heard in Melbourne, and she spoke of her grant that had just been accepted, to incorporate First Nations music with the greats of the Baroque era. She had been awarded $10,000 by the NEA to go to Australia to teach, and also take courses from the National Aboriginal Music Foundation and bring this new knowledge back to the US to incorporate into her coursework at UW. The participants were enthralled by her work, her enthusiasm. Canada had, for decades now, been supporting the art and music of First Nations. But her proposal—to make a joint relationship between styles of music that appeared to be so vastly different—seemed brilliant. Canadians were always at the forefront of being peacemakers, of brainstorming ways to blend ideas, customs, and mindsets. Irene's proposal fit right in, and they warmly embraced her, wanting her to speak over the time allotted, and continued to ask questions in the open mike session after lunch.

As Irene basked there in Vancouver, she remembered that day she received the letter from the NEA. It was the day Helena surprised her with her letter from the governor. She was going to show it to her, but she did not want to overshadow the excitement of Helena's big day. She was going to tell her the next day, but then Helena had to leave so early in the morning. The letter, she decided, would wait until the following weekend when Helena would be with her again.

Irene would be returning to Australia. She hoped somehow Helena would join her.

The conference over, Irene hailed a cab, and met Bob and Harry in the parking lot of the Botanical Gardens. It was a gorgeous spring day and the rain was holding off until Sunday evening, the forecasters said. She hugged her best friend, and hugged also Harry, remembering him from years ago when they met at a party. Both men were glowing, their faces showing how delighted they were making each other.

"You two look positively, stunningly happy," she remarked.

Their white faces turned crimson, the color of the rhododendrons that would be opening next month.

"Ah, the wonders of oxytocin," Harry remarked as all three nodded and laughed.

They made their way into the garden, met by a splendorous display of spring foliage under the canopy of old-growth cedars.

"Mmmmm," they exclaimed in unison at the fresh aroma of the forest beckoning them on tiny pathways that meandered around the acres and acres of exotics and natives.

All of them horticulturists, they pointed out plants they wanted in their gardens, their dream gardens that looked just like this one.

"Why don't we move here, build one of those tiny houses, and hide it in these woods?" Bob giggled.

"Yeah, right up the hill from the gay nude beach?" Irene poked him in the arm.

"Oh, that's right," Harry said, smirking. "Forgot

about that one."

Two hours later, without even noticing how time had zipped itself through the myriad of paths of forgetfulness, the garden's announcer told them to kindly make their way to the exit as the garden was closing.

At the exit, they stopped and chatted, and decided that dinner was next.

"I am dying to get some melt-in-the-mouth pho."

"Me too," Harry agreed. "Vancouver is truly the best, heads above Seattle, my friends."

"I'm afraid you're right," Bob said. "This city knows how to cook."

"Where to?" Harry asked in the driver's seat, their WA state license plate sticking out like a proverbial sore thumb.

"I have an idea," Irene chimed in. "Why don't we drive, see people's gardens for a bit? The Shaughnessy neighborhood has some magnificent ones. When we're ready, we head over to Main Street. There're good Vietnamese places over there."

"I love you, Irene. You always know what you want. And you know how to get it."

Harry and Irene guffawed together.

"Oh, come on, we are three peas in a pod. We're all like that," Harry added.

All three nodded, their passionate insistent natures caught in broad daylight.

"Wow. Look at that garden, *s'il vous plait*," Bob said, his voice sounding like a bird chirping.

"Yeah and look at that house. Have you ever seen something as gorgeous as that? Come on, darling one, we need to buy in Vancouver."

"Sorry, honey, our American passports won't

give us the ticket."

"Why don't you apply to teach at UBC?" Irene said, wanting to contribute to the boys' fantastical banter.

"Oh, come on, why would they hire *moi*?"

"Because you are a specialist in your field. There's only one of you."

"Yeah, that's for sure," Harry added, squeezing Bob's hand in such a way that Irene felt the energy from the two, knowing that under each of their pants something very hard was evolving.

She laughed.

"Oh, were we caught?" Bob asked.

"I'm afraid so. You are not so subtle."

The three broke into laughter as home and garden after home and garden continued to wow them. Sighing, Harry turned the corner and headed east. His stomach was rumbling, and he had a mission.

"I see you're ending the show, darling."

"Yep. Stomach called."

"As you can see, Harry's bodily needs control things at times," Bob commented.

Irene laughed and laughed. She, of course, couldn't relate.

A half hour later, steaming bowls of pho greeted them. They dug in, savoring the broth and all the unnamed things that were floating here and there.

"Is this not divine?" Harry bellowed out.

"Orgasm in a bowl."

The men slurped, and Irene, taking their lead, slurped too. She loved these two, and now she really had two brothers.

"Stick around, Sir Harry. You are delightful. You are so good for our Bob."

Harry took Bob's hand and kissed it.

"Caught again," Irene said, quietly, knowing there was a theatre piece happening under the table.

After dinner, at Irene's suggestion they drove out to Jericho Beach. Sitting on the sand, they looked out at the glorious Grouse Mountain, West Vancouver to the west, and downtown to the east.

"What a positively gorgeous, fabulous city this is," Harry said, curled up in Bob's arms.

"We have got to do this more often, come here all together. Next time, Helena will join us, right?" Bob added.

"Oh God, yes. She needs to be here, too."

"We both can't wait to meet the love of your life," Harry said.

"Wedding bells are ringing don't you hear them?"

"Yep."

Irene smiled at their banter. The mention of Helena's name made her wet, wanting.

"What about you two? I hear the glockenspiel."

"Well, actually..." Harry looked at Bob.

"Really?" Irene looked back and forth between them.

"This fall." Bob blushed.

"Well, here's to that." Irene held up an imaginary glass.

"W-we kind of decided just last night," Harry said, partially stammering.

Irene moved over and gave them both hugs.

"You are our bestest sister."

"And you are my bestest brothers."

They all laughed, smiling as the Vancouver sun set, and brilliant colors emblazoned the sky, highlighting the mountain and giving it a glowing sheen.

Chapter Thirteen

Helena held the phone in her hand, shaking. Her tears enveloped her face, and her heart was beating rapidly.

But there's no history in my family, I eat healthy, live a healthy life, I am crazily in love with the woman of my dreams. What is this, what kind of curse is this?

She remembered the words of her doctor, just minutes ago.

"Don't get alarmed, Helena. It's just a lump. We don't know what it is, but very often these things are benign. You'll need to come in on Friday for the biopsy, and rest the whole weekend afterward because it might be a bit extensive. If they find something they are concerned about, they could admit you for immediate surgery, but this is rather unlikely."

Friday. She was to fly out to Seattle on Friday. She had been missing Irene so terribly. Just a routine mammogram. She was feeling fine, more alive than ever in her life.

"Damn," she said out loud, throwing her phone on the ground, listening to the thud it made from her hand to the cement, a distance of perhaps ten feet from the hill she was perched on. She heard the glass shatter before she saw the damage, pieces of the phone splayed out in front of her.

She put her head in her hands and wailed, her screams echoing off the hillside, over to the grazing cows who looked over. Two of them turned around and moved toward her, and slowly, they approached her and nuzzled their mouths on her knee. Her tears fell in droplets on their heads like rain as they stood quietly, not leaving her.

Helena wanted to call Irene, and then she realized with the phone now broken, useless, she didn't even know her phone number. *Where have we gone that we don't even memorize our own beloved's phone numbers anymore?* When she got back inside, she thought she would email her—at least she still had that address on her laptop. She knew she had to go get a replacement phone, but she didn't even have it in her to get up from that spot to get herself inside.

Day turned to evening and still Helena had not moved, and neither had the two cows. No one was around, and no one would be looking for her. She had given everyone that Saturday off—everything was under control, she had told them. The clouds turned bright pink as the sun set, and gradually the world around her turned dark. Her mind had numbed, the tears still wet on her face. She was getting cold, but she still couldn't move. Her memories turned to the day Ines died, the phone call, the screaming, the helplessness. Then the flashbacks turned to when she was fifteen years old, the day she fell off her horse and lay there on the hillside, unable to move. No one was around then, either. Her dog, Lucy had found her, licking her senseless. She was insanely lucky, the doctor had said, hours later, after the dog had run back to the farm, barking like a mad wolf, getting the attention of her father who came running. One millimeter in either direction from where she fractured her spine would have been instant paralysis, the doctor had said.

The night became colder and colder as still Helena's own darkness crept inside of her, fear of the unknown, fear of death invading her like a monster, creeping at her insides like a toxic vine, numbing all rational thought. Wolves howled in the distance, smelling the cows that Helena had not taken to shelter for the night. There were calves present, clinging onto their mothers who smelled fear as the wolves edged closer.

One of the wolves, sensing freedom, approached a calf and stole it, his fangs digging in, as a chorus of cows mooed mournfully, helpless.

It was then that Helena snapped out of her darkness and ran, lightening propelling her feet as the storm edged closer, the clouds moving in furiously. She ran to the grieving cows and quickly herded them, her own tears stifled as she felt the tears of her bovine companions. Locked into the safety of their enclosure, she stroked the mama of the stolen, dead calf, apologizing over and over, knowing that human apology meant nothing to an animal in distress. The rain came down in pellets as the thunder crashed and lightening flashed across the sky as all of them, cows and human, wailed into the night.

❧ ❧ ❧ ❧

Helena finally arrived in her bed, and sleep took her quickly, a night of dreams where the death card was chosen, where cancer filled her unconscious mind.

It came, dark and bulbous, a black slug, creeping everywhere. She yelled out, and no one was there. It was creeping on her body, covering her breasts, swelling

*them up, hanging on tight. She couldn't breathe, and
little by little her body shut down, organs collapsing in
front of her eyes.*

Helena tore out of bed, running to the shower,
and scrubbed her skin raw, trying to get away what
came in her dream, what was growing in her body. She
raised her arm and put her fingers to her left breast and
felt the hardened mass, tugging at her skin, a ball of
what she felt was poisoned material, invading her. She
cried and cried, scared, letting the water flow endlessly
as her body shook uncontrollably.

She got on the computer and emailed Irene. It
was still the middle of the night for her.

"I broke my phone," she wrote. "I might have
breast cancer. They are doing a biopsy this Friday and
maybe they will admit me for immediate surgery if they
find something. Remember when you felt something
on my left breast in the bath that day? I will try to get a
new phone later today, maybe tomorrow. I love you."

She drummed her fingers on the desk, wondering
how long it would take to get a reply, wondering if
Irene was even awake. She didn't have to wait long; the
return email came through in mere minutes.

"Oh, my darling. Oh, my darling. I will be there
on Friday and stay as long as you need me." She quickly
thought of Bob, who might fill in for her classes.

"No, don't," Helena wrote back. "I don't want
you to see me like this."

"I know. But I couldn't bear to be away from
you."

Somehow, with those words, Helena felt better.
She was hungry for Irene, wanted her lips immediately
on hers, and ached everywhere for her. She put her hand

on her right breast, feeling its suppleness, arching her back, feeling herself, her wetness, her famine for Irene, and suddenly she came, calling out Irene's name.

"God, I love you," she wrote back when she had quieted, her body relaxed and hopeful.

"I love you," Irene responded. "We'll get through this. Now, go get that phone today. I will call you this evening. Get a massage, anything, but don't worry yourself sick on this."

Helena nodded. *She's right. Irene is my queen of practicality, and look at me, I am a mess, a blubbering mess who lets a cow die, who breaks a phone, who imagines death when it hasn't even come to my door. I survived falling off the horse. I will survive this.* She loved the way Irene said that "we" will survive this. There was something to that, like a warm salve to a cold edge, that together they were a "we" now, no longer facing challenges alone. She felt buoyed, energized, hope taking its wings around her as she got dressed and got herself to the Verizon store just as it opened.

✿✿✿✿

"So, everything is worked out. I will have to teach until two on Friday, but I fly out right after. Bob, dear Bob, said he would cover my classes next week, as many days as I need to be away. He said his TAs could cover the majority of his, and he would do a bit of dancing back and forth, like a vaudeville striptease dancer, he said, between his classes and mine."

Helena broke into laughter, uncontrollable. Irene joined in.

"I'm glad you noticed that bump the other day. It prompted me to call my doctor, and she ordered an immediate mammogram."

"I'm surprised I did. Usually when I am at your breasts, my famine takes over and my thinking brain is completely shut down."

Again, Helena guffawed. Again, Irene joined her, a game they were playing, a game that worked.

When they got off the phone, Helena smiled through her evening and even through the next few days.

Friday morning showed its talons with diarrhea episodes in the bathroom, several trips that ripped away all her energy.

Dragging her feet, her body heavy and void of color, she entered the outpatient clinic, signed the paperwork, and waited for her name to be called. She looked down at her phone. A message from Irene displayed itself with a happy blinking light.

Breathe. Again. You will be OK. I will be at the hospital or at your home at 8pm. When I arrive in Boulder, I will find out where you'll be, so no worries about texting me. Just focus in on relaxing, if you can. I love you.

Helena held the phone in her hand, smiling, as her name was called. She drifted into a quiet, happy place as she changed into a gown, waited again, and then, as they called her in and put an IV into her, still she was smiling and in a zone where only peace reigned. Soon, the anesthesia took over, and soon after that, the biopsy was complete. The afternoon wore on, and the anesthesia wore off, and Helena was ready to go home. She began to feel pain where the needle had gone in, and she longed to be home to rest.

The doctor came to her gurney, still sitting in the recovery room. He wrapped the curtain around her bed. Her heart leapt. Why the privacy, she wondered? She looked at his name tag: Herve Zilber, MD.

"Ms. Hanover, the biopsy report has come back. You have what appears to be a phyllodes tumor in your left breast. These things are very rare, and they start in the connective tissue of the breast. One in ten of these kinds of tumors is cancerous, and the rest are benign. Naturally, we will have to go in and surgically remove the tumor as well as the tissue around it. We will biopsy that, and we will all cross our fingers that what you have is perfectly benign."

Helena gulped, reminding herself to breathe.

"And if it's not?"

"Then we will have to do an emergency mastectomy. But let's not go there. Let's think optimistically. Now, because you will be given general anesthesia, you will need a twelve-hour fast. We will admit you momentarily and perform the surgery tonight. I have made a special arrangement with the surgeons to do it today, as they don't generally do these procedures on the weekends. Do you have any questions?" He held her hand gently, looking at her with kind eyes.

"How long will I be in the hospital, and how long is the recovery time?"

"Assuming we don't need to perform a mastectomy, you should be out of here by Monday at the latest. And recovery time is usually between four and eight weeks. But we'll give you all those instructions and recovery information later."

"Will you be the doctor in charge?"

"Not the surgeon, but the doctor in charge. I will

be here throughout the weekend to check in on you."

"Thank you, Dr. Zilber. Are you French?"

"Yes." He smiled.

He squeezed her hand one last time, then breezed away.

Irene was on the plane, Helena thought. She left her a quick message, telling her what the doctor had said, ending with an emoji of fingers crossing fingers.

Helena's mind numbed. She put her earbuds in and listened to monks chanting, letting herself calm, forgetting everything, and losing herself in meditation. The attendants came and moved her to a private room on the eighth floor, helping her get settled into her hospital bed. The late afternoon moved to the evening, and as nurses skipped her room with their dinner trays, still Helena remained in her quiet meditation. Evening had turned to the early night when Irene walked into the room.

Helena took out her earbuds and wept, feeling Irene's kisses cover her eyes, her cheeks, landing on her lips.

One minute later, the attendants arrived in the room, announcing that the surgeon was ready. They told Irene she could only go with them as far as the bottom of the elevator.

Irene held Helena's hand as they wheeled the bed out of the room, down the hallway, into the elevator. She squeezed it as Helena smiled, feeling Irene's strength and calm pour into her. As the elevator door opened, Irene told her she would be in her room, waiting.

She placed her lips on Helena's, and then whispered in her ear, "I love you."

"I love you," Helena said back, her voice shaky, holding back her tears.

As the attendants took over from there, Irene sat down on a nearby chair, letting her own tears flow, her own body shaking with fear, her stomach turned around and nauseous.

A hospital staffer approached her and told her she couldn't stay where she was, that she had to move. Irene slowly got up and headed to the front door of the hospital and stepped outside, feeling the chilly mountain air wrap itself around her neck. The look on Helena's face was imprinted in her mind—one of fear, yet also of love, devotion. She wept just thinking about that expression, and what it meant to really love someone in sickness and in health. There was nothing more that she would rather do than to be there for Helena during this time. Nothing else seemed to matter. In fact, in a few weeks, her term would be over, and she imagined living with her in Colorado, watching her heal, watching her come back to her original self.

"Oh God, please don't let it be cancer," she said to herself, wanting God to hear her, now more than ever. As she walked, she repeated this over and over, as if repetition would somehow change things. She had no idea where she was, and no idea where she was going, but she continued to walk, and like a mantra that led her out of her trail of misery, she prayed.

She found a park, a darkened park on a cold dark night, and she sat on a bench, letting her tears come, not stopping them, not caring if she was alone in a dark park in a town where she knew not a soul aside from the woman on the operating table. Two students walked by, lovers, obviously, engrossed in each other and completely unaware that a crying woman was sitting alone on a park bench. She thought to herself that they were the age her child would have been had he survived. She rarely thought about this, her mind so usually focused on the present. She had learned this from her father. "Don't focus on the past," she used to hear him say to her mother. He was such a happy man, and perhaps this is how he overcame the sorrows that all lives go through. Still, she couldn't help but wonder where her life would have led her, had her baby lived.

Her mind flipped back to Helena. She thought perhaps they knew by now. She had to get back to the hospital, but she had no idea where she was. She reached in her pocket, and her life-saving phone gave her directions how to get back toward Helena. She began with a walk, and then ran, her legs full of energy, a buoyancy that surprised her in her state. She felt an intuitive voice resounding in her that said, *Helena is fine. There is no cancer.*

She arrived at the hospital, sweaty and out of breath. Shaking, she went over to the information desk. The hospital volunteer looked up Helena Hanover, informing Irene that just two minutes earlier she had been moved to the recovery room. Irene told the woman that she was Helena's wife, and asked if she could please speak with the doctor. The woman wrote a message, paging the unit and the doctor, and announced that he would be down in a few minutes if she could just remain in the waiting room.

Irene, sweating even more, waited, staring at the fish swimming in the tank, oblivious to anything but their own circuitous motions.

Ten minutes later, a middle-aged, Middle Eastern man in a white coat approached Irene. His nametag spelled out Dr. Hashemi. *Iranian*, Irene said to herself, and smiled as he put out his hand and introduced himself.

"Great news, Irene. There is not one sign of cancer. We removed the entire tumor and quite a bit of breast tissue, did a thorough biopsy, and found everything to be completely benign. It was an extensive procedure, and she will need about eight full weeks of recovery time."

Irene sobbed, smiled and cried, reached out her arms and hugged the surgeon.

"*Moteshakeram*, thank you," she said, pulling away, wiping her eyes.

"*Khahesh mikonam*," Dr. Hashemi replied, beaming and nodding as he headed back to the elevator.

Irene danced to the elevator and up to the eighth floor. She knew Helena would be in the recovery room for a while, but she couldn't wait, and wanted to be in her hospital room, waiting for her. "Thank you, Allah, God, Goddesses, anyone who cared to listen tonight," she said to herself as her steps felt light, her smile radiating through her like the winter sun dazzling over the Puget Sound.

⁂

Irene sat in the chair in Helena's room, engrossing herself in the hundreds of pictures they had taken in Tasmania just a few months earlier. One photo after the other made her smile, laugh, and reminisce, and hours seem to pass effortlessly by. Finally, from a distance in the hallway, there was the sound of a gurney being wheeled, hospital attendants chattering. Helena, wrapped tightly in blankets, emerged through the door, her eyes closed, the expression on her face one of having had a severe trauma to her body. Her eyes were glassy, the paleness of her skin resounded. Irene's stomach lurched at seeing how agonized she was underneath the anesthesia. She walked over to her, taking her cold, clammy hand in hers, kissing it gently.

Helena attempted a smile, but it was evident that this was even hard to do. The anesthesia must have been quite strong, and Irene winced as she watched her struggle.

The attendants got her settled and then left the room as nurses arrived, checking her IVs and taking her vitals. Then they, too, left the room.

Helena opened her eyes for a moment and let her gaze sink into Irene's. Irene took her hand and brushed it through Helena's hair, stroking her forehead, letting her lips kiss Helena around the eyes, the cheeks, listening to the faintest moans coming from Helena.

"You have no cancer," she whispered. Helena smiled.

Helena closed her eyes again, dipping into a sleep as Irene sat by her, her hand holding Helena's, stroking it, not letting it go.

Nurses came and left for the next few hours as still Helena slept, and still Irene didn't let go.

Sometime in the middle of the night, Helena's eyes opened.

"Ow!" she cried. Her eyes were filled with pain, her body was shaking.

Irene got up and fetched a nurse.

The nurse came in, checked her vitals, and gave her pain medicine. A few minutes later, Helena was again asleep. Irene closed her eyes and found herself drifting away, her body escaping to Tasmania. In her dream she and Helena were making love, their bodies on fire.

Another groan of pain emerged a few hours later, and again Irene fetched the nurse.

Saturday blurred into Sunday, the pain severe and Helena's body only wanted to sleep. Doctor Zilber came and went and told Irene that her progress was quite good, that she did very well in the surgery.

On Sunday, the nurses made her get up, took out the catheter, and Irene watched Helena come back to the world of the living.

By Sunday afternoon, Helena was already sitting up. Color had begun to return to her face. Irene spread kisses everywhere, delighted.

"I have a secret to tell you," she giggled.

"Mmm?"

"I told the hospital staff on Friday night that I am your wife."

"I have a secret to tell you."

Irene looked in Helena's eyes, amused.

"When I did my admitting papers, I checked the box 'married.'"

"Well then, it's official. Will you marry me, Helena Hanover?"

"Oh my God, yes! Will you marry me Irene Alborz?"

"Yes! With every bit of me, for the rest of our lives and beyond."

Irene's lips met Helena's and they kissed, gently of course, but with waves of passion that sent each of them smiling.

"When?"

"After I am done healing from all this mess. When did the doctor say again that I will be back to normal?"

"He said eight weeks of recovery."

"So, what does that mean, in July I am fine, or in July, I can get up and take a wee?"

Irene laughed.

"I want to know when we can make incredible, passionate love again. That's all I care about. When is that magical day? Because that's when I want to get married. I don't want to marry the woman of my dreams and on our wedding night not do whatever in the hell I want with you."

Irene laughed and guffawed, but realized that wasn't very kind, because laughing hurt Helena's chest and then she groaned with intense pain.

"What am I going to do for eight weeks? That sounds like being in a penitentiary."

"Take up knitting?"

"Thank you, darling."

"Read? Books on tape? Listen to music?"

"Hmmm."

"I've been thinking. After this week, I will come every weekend. And then after Memorial Day, I'm done until the end of August. How about if I spend the summer here with you?"

"Well, that's a given. If you weren't going to suggest it, I was going to personally steal you away."

"You can't get on a plane for a few months. How were you going to do that?" Irene smirked.

"Oh, I don't know," Helena spouted petulantly. "Kiss me, Irene."

"Are you sure?"

"Oh, stop, just kiss me. Now."

Irene laughed, felt her nipples harden as she put her hand to Helena's right breast, stroking it, her lips deeply engrossed with Helena's. Their tongues lashed together, the beginnings of a fire.

"Ow!"

"Guess not," Irene chuckled.

"Damn!"

"It's only two days after surgery, sweetheart."

Helena's pain increased, and the nurse gave her more drugs. Sleep came to her, and several hours passed by.

Irene realized that she was quite exhausted. While Helena slept, she curled up next to her on her right side, making her body small. She fell asleep instantly, feeling Helena's warmth next to hers.

Dinner came, and then the nurse, waking them both up.

"I like you here in this tiny bed with me," Helena announced, a bit rested, once the nurse escorted herself out. "You're healing me."

"Love is healing you. That and a bit of oxytocin." Irene giggled. "We've got to kiss every day now. It's your medicine."

"I like that idea."

Helena ate her dinner, finally getting an appetite. She wanted to share what she had with Irene, but Irene refused. Not wanting hospital food, Irene got on her phone and found an Asian noodle place that delivered. She called them, and they said they would deliver right to Helena's room. She found that to be just the perfect thing, and that way she could share something delicious with Helena. Plus, she didn't want to leave Helena for one minute. She couldn't bear it.

Monday morning arrived and Dr. Zilber pranced into the room.

"So, are you ready to go home today?" he asked,

sounding like he was presenting Helena with a medal of honor.

"Yes, absolutely. This bed isn't big enough for two."

Dr. Zilber and Irene laughed together. He checked her out, examined the incision, and reminded her no strenuous activity and no sex for eight weeks. Then he winked at Irene, put in the discharge orders, and with thank yous and mercis all around, he dashed back out of the room, into the corridors of the hospital.

ﻬ ﻬ ﻬ ﻬ

At home, finally in bed after a very painful trip from the hospital, Helena sighed.

"Come here, you. Sleep with me."

"Absolutely. I am buggered out."

"Me, too."

On Helena's right side, Irene snuggled in, her arm around Helena, and together they fell into the deepest sleeps, snoring and dreaming, and then quiet as each rested and restored.

It was almost dark when the doorbell rang. Irene woke up with a start and met at the door a woman with flowers and a big pot of soup, and a loaf of fresh bread.

"Hi there. Sorry to bother you, I am the next-door neighbor, Olivia. I saw Helena is back from the hospital, and I made a pot of soup for you two. Some bread, too, from the local bakery. I know Helena loves this bread."

"Wow. Thank you." Irene beamed. "I'm Irene."

"Total pleasure to meet you. I have heard so much about you."

Irene beamed again.

"Thank you, truly."

"How's she doing?"

"No cancer, happily. But she's pretty tired and sore."

"Fabulous news! How long are you here till?"

"I have to leave Sunday. But I will return every weekend until Memorial Day, then I'll be here for the summer."

"Well, rest assured, while you're not here my husband and I will look after her, cook her meals, do whatever she needs. We think the world of her. I am so relieved it's not cancer."

"Me, too."

"Well, I don't want to take any more of your time. So happy to meet you."

"Likewise. And thanks again."

Irene closed the door, took the soup, ladled it into two bowls, and got the bread, some butter from the fridge, and went with a tray to the bedroom. She glanced around the house. It was nice, functional. It had good energy. Not a mess, like hers was often. She smiled to herself.

She helped Helena sit up to eat.

"Our first feast in this home. Welcome home, darling."

Irene didn't know why, but tears came to her eyes, big ones, as she looked in Helena's eyes, resting there, residing in that place of safety, of holding and being held, of making it through something very difficult and loving her even more.

※ ※ ※ ※

The days bled into each other, a blur of hours,

as Helena and Irene mostly slept, read, and watched movies together in bed. Neighbors and friends came by every day with flowers and meals, so Irene didn't have to cook even once. Breakfast was always yogurt, and there was plenty in the fridge. Life was about healing now, and everything that they did together reflected this.

"It's strange, but I don't want you to leave my sight," Helena blurted out on one of those days that blurred into the next.

"And it's strange, but I have absolutely no desire to go any farther than the kitchen to warm up food," Irene responded, curling up next to Helena, feeling the ever-present warmth between them. By Thursday, Irene helped Helena put on some clothes. They were going for a walk to see the cows. This was quite an effort, and when Helena was out the door, she winced.

"Hurts?"

"Yep. But the fresh air feels so good. God, I have missed this." She took a deep breath. Irene held her hand and together they walked slowly to the field, where the cows ran to her, the looks on their faces seeming like they had missed her. She let them nuzzle her right hand, and then the color washed away from her face.

"Back to bed?"

Helena nodded.

Finally, back in the comfort of the sheets, she collapsed into a sleep that led her into Friday, missing dinner entirely.

On Saturday, Helena's mother arrived. She busied herself around Helena, looking quite officious, as if she wore the crown entitled "the mother." She was kind enough to Irene, in a cold sort of way, subtly brushing her aside as she did her version of the "motherly duties." She shook her head, witnessing the dirty laundry that had been stashed in the dusty corners of the spare bedroom.

Irene excused herself for a walk.

An hour and a half later, Helena's mother was gone.

Helena breathed a sigh of relief. Irene just laughed. She crawled back in bed with her, holding her, kissing her, as together they felt again their little nest come back to its original state.

Chapter Fourteen

"You have to leave today," Helena said, her voice small and weak.

"Yeah, I guess I do," Irene responded, her body curled up against Helena, the cozy positioning they had developed and sunk into this past week.

"This may sound strange, but I need you." Tears welled up in Helena's eyes. She really had never felt this way, needed someone like this, and it caught her off guard.

Irene snuggled closer, sinking as she purred. The windows were open, and the beauty of the morning fluttered through the curtains, a light breeze cooling the air.

"You are everything to me, Irene." She kissed the top of her head as Irene purred. Irene took her hand and kissed it gently, resting her mouth on Helena's fingers. Helena moaned quietly as Irene kissed harder, sucking on each finger, letting her tongue envelop and caress as Helena moaned louder. In that moment, no doctor was in the room issuing orders as Irene moved her body and placed her lips on Helena's, her nipples hard underneath her silk nightshirt. Pressing into Helena, their kisses contained a small fire, as their tongues fought and tossed, playing, wanting. Helena moaned louder.

Then, as if there were a warning bell clanging in their ears, Irene removed her lips from Helena's as each one breathed hard, groaning, and then laughing.

"We don't want you in the ER, darling."

"Guess not. Damn it. Ow!"

"Yep. That's why. Seven weeks to go."

"Oh, shush. God, I'm tired after that little bit. I'm pathetic."

"Yep. You are. But I love you, oh pathetic one."

Irene assumed her position, curled up next to Helena, as they both fell asleep, drifting off to their own dream worlds. The early afternoon woke them with the dog barking next door. Irene looked at the clock and bounded out of bed as Helena looked on, and her face saddened knowing Irene had to get to the airport. Irene threw on some clothes and tossed her dirties into her bag, and, looking at Helena's face, she cried, too, as she called a cab.

"I made sure all your neighbors and friends are taking care of you morning, noon, and night until Friday. All you have to do is rest. I'll call you this evening when I get in. I love you more than this whole universe." She gave Helena a short kiss, as Helena tried to grab her, and winced.

"Rest, okay?"

"Yep. I will."

And with that, Irene zipped away, leaving Helena with her own pool of tears. Closing her eyes, she let her healing, tired, and sore body fall into her first solo sleep since the surgery. Sometime in the early evening, she awoke to her good friend Marilyn's entrance into the house, with a freshly made lasagna and salad for dinner.

"How goes, wounded one?"

"Ah, I'm a mess. Irene left a few hours ago. Didn't want her to go."

"Yeah, that's hard. She'll be back Friday?"

"I know, thank God. Man, when she kisses me, I lose myself. Then the pain comes back viciously, and I couldn't tell her how bad it really was. This thing better heal because my desire keeps growing for her."

"It will. It's only been a little over a week."

"Yeah, yeah, yeah…Hey, can you stay for dinner?"

"Sure. Let me get plates."

"How's the farm, Tassiebaby, everything?" Helena asked, her mouth full of noodles and cheese, a perfectly seasoned lasagna. "It's so weird to be completely out of the loop, and until this moment, I haven't thought once about it."

"Everything is fine. Stocks have risen like crazy, and we're getting more and more demand for it all over the world. Everyone has been asking about you. What should I tell them?"

Helena laughed. "I'm alive. Just stop there."

"We have all been so worried about you."

"I was worried about me."

"And you never worry."

"I guess so. You know me so well."

"Well, it's only been, what, twenty years?"

Helena smiled. "How's Joanne?"

"She's fine. She wanted to be here, but she had to babysit her nephew. We will come here together later in the week."

"Oh, yes, please, we'll have an 'I'm pathetic, but I didn't die' party."

Marilyn laughed. Helena joined her, and then realized again that laughing hurt. She winced.

"Ah, everything hurts. I'm such a mess."

"Okay, enough laughing for you. I better go, because I sure as hell don't want to engage you in painful laughing or unnecessary crying."

With that, Marilyn cleaned everything up and drove away. Helena rose to brush her teeth, which she realized she hadn't done in a few days. *How could Irene have handled my disgusting breath?*

Realizing that this was the first time she had been alone for several days, she felt an uneasiness in her steps, even in her breathing, which felt labored, tight, anxious. She looked around her room, smelling Irene everywhere, the earthy scent that wafted through healed her. She wondered if she would get better without her there. Images of her mother floated through her head, her visit earlier that week. Helena tried to brush her mother away, like a speck of dust in her hair, but she couldn't let go of the admonishing expression on her face that lingered in her mind, critical of Irene, but mostly it seemed she was critical of herself, the not-good-enough mother, and still she was useless around her daughter. Helena shuddered as she stepped into bed, wanting it to be different, as still her voice resounded inside of her, the one that called out, "Mommy, don't leave!"

As she pulled the covers up to her neck and picked up her book, she took a deep breath, and with the exhale, felt like she found in herself a moment in life where one had to admit that it is what it is, it was what it was, and life keeps going.

Feeling herself settle into the soft sheets, smelling Irene around her, she read for a few minutes, and then stumbled into a deep and lasting sleep.

❧ ❧ ❧ ❧

Irene moved through her week, glad she had

routines that distracted her from her gripping feelings of missing Helena. She recalled so vividly the brief visit with the surgeon who announced to her the benignness of everything. Life had sauntered its way through her relationship with Helena, from the sublime to the fearful, to the sigh of relief, and mostly to the consistency of love between them that continued to grow with each week that passed.

With this last thought, this sense of gratitude that filled her, she taught, inspiring even further her students.

Soon it was Friday already, and she was back on the plane.

⁂

The month of May passed quickly by. The routines of each week firmly in place, Irene taught her classes and Helena continued to heal; each had a full-time job. From Friday night to Sunday afternoon, Helena and Irene found themselves beaming, feeling overall exceedingly happy, side by side, not wanting to leave the other.

Soon, it was the day before Memorial Day weekend. Irene had finished her term and the year with the students, had graded all their exams, and that evening she packed up the emerald-green suitcase with things she would need for the summer. On Saturday morning, she made sure all the lights were turned off, the curtains pulled, and she turned the key in the lock. She skipped down the stairs, ecstatic with the notion that she would be having an entire summer with Helena.

PART THREE: SUMMER

Chapter Fifteen

Helena woke up on the Saturday of Memorial Day weekend with boundless energy. In a few hours Irene would arrive, suitcase in hand, and they would begin what she decided was going to be their own summer of love, their own psychedelic experience of loving each other. She reminisced on her own drug experiences with Ines. At the time, she couldn't imagine not being high when making love. Now, completely sober and off drugs, she experienced more of a high with Irene than any of those times in her twenties. One month after the surgery, she felt a burst of energy returning, the beginnings of getting back to her normal self, and she was elated. She felt a new lease on life swim around her, and as she began her day, making her breakfast, she experienced a sense about her that nothing now would ever be taken for granted. Life was precious, now more than ever. The still-present ache in her left breast reminded her of this, of how easy it was to ignore the preciousness of life. Just like that, her breast could have been removed, and just like that, she could have been that one in ten. Just like that, women all over the world *are* that one in ten.

It hit her then, that realization. She was among the lucky, but so many women in the world didn't get to fall in that category, having to lose those delicious breasts of theirs. As she stirred the milk in her coffee, she saw the imperativeness of doing something about this, this horrific thing called breast cancer. Tassieyogo would, as soon as she was fully back at work, be in the forefront of this, of donating millions each year to breast cancer research. Tassiebaby, that was, in just two months, earning its first million, would be the engine. She decided that every single dollar earned from this product would go toward this vital project. It made complete sense to her that a lesbian-owned business had in its mission a commitment to savor and to save the breast from disease.

As she sipped her coffee, she got on the phone to Marilyn, her best friend and product manager.

"Yo."

"How goes? How's the old booby?"

"That's what I wanted to talk to you about." There was urgency in her voice. "One hundred percent."

"One hundred percent what?"

"One hundred percent of all proceeds from Tassiebaby go to the education and research for breast cancer. I want us to be at the forefront of this, Marilyn. It's imperative. I woke up this morning and I felt like I was in the lucky group, and I want every woman on this planet to be in that same group. I want that fucking disease gone." Tears were streaming down Helena's face.

Despite her tears, she practically heard Marilyn's smile. Helena's words were powerful.

"One hundred percent, Helena. I'm with you. Let's do it. As soon as you're up to it, let's call a meeting and start it up. Get it going as soon as we can."

"Thank you, Marilyn. We will make a difference in this world, won't we?"

"You're damn right we will. And in our lifetimes."

"Yes," Helena said, wiping her tears.

"Irene's coming in later, isn't she?"

Helena beamed, listening to her name. "Yes. Yes. Yes."

Marilyn laughed. "How about we have a barbeque for you two, tomorrow or Monday, whichever you want?"

"Might rain Monday. Supposed to be gorgeous tomorrow. How about we do it then?"

"Perfect."

"Can we bring anything?"

"Just you and your Irene."

Helena laughed and felt her face flush.

"Hey, I love this idea of yours. And I am so glad you are doing better."

"Thanks. It's all because of your lasagnas."

Marilyn laughed. "Oh, it's a little more than that, but thanks. I do have fun making those things."

"See you tomorrow."

"Fabulous."

∿∿∿∿

The skies burst just as Irene got out of the car at Helena's front door. She was not used to this mountain behavior. As she got into the Lyft car at the airport, it was warm and sunny, and she had put her jacket in the suitcase, loving the fact that she could wear only a T-shirt. In Seattle, T-shirt weather hadn't quite arrived yet; the cold refused to budge. Spring was spring, and summer was summer, as if nature herself played by an obsessive set of rules.

Walking from the street to Helena's front door, she felt the cold rain on her head, shoulders, everywhere, drenching her. When she stepped inside the house and into the hallway, she made a puddle by her feet.

Helena bounded from the kitchen, staring at Irene's nipples protruding from her wet shirt. She laughed as she grabbed Irene, pulling her to her. Their lips met, their kisses frantic and joyous as Helena reached her right hand around Irene's tight buttocks and squeezed, their bodies hot and yearning for each other.

Their embrace lingered in the hallway as Helena, too, became soaked from Irene's clothes.

"How about we get you in the bath, oh luscious one?"

Irene nodded, laughing, and stripped off her wet clothes. Naked, she walked to the bathroom and drew the bath. She slipped in and Helena followed, as they kissed and held each other and savored the beginning of a deliciously long summer ahead.

When the water got cold, they took their warmed skin to bed, cuddling under the sheets, listening to the end of the rain shower, lulling them to a sweet sleep.

When they awoke, hours later, the sky was a brilliant blue, unaware that a few hours earlier a storm had played games in the atmosphere. Helena's lips found Irene's, and, sweetly at first, they kissed, then an urgency took over. Irene climbed on top of Helena, pressing into her as their bodies hungered for the other.

She felt Helena wincing, and rolled off as both groaned, tired of this nonsense.

"Three more weeks?" Helena whined.

"I'm afraid so. Or…we could make our own rules. As long as you wince, no. But when that stops, we are free as a bird. When is your next doctor appointment?"

"Next week. Friday."

"Okay, we'll ask then. Maybe he will bump things up a bit."

"Dinner?" Helena asked, changing the annoying subject.

"Sure. Are there leftovers, or are we making something?" Irene had gotten quite used to having wonderful homemade food always available every weekend when she was there.

"Saved the last bit of Marilyn's lasagna, just enough for tonight. Oh, tomorrow, she and Joanne invited us to a barbeque."

"Oh, wonderful. Those two are lovely. How fun!"

Irene put her arms around Helena, kissing her cheeks.

Bubbling, she announced, "I am so, so happy I am here with you for the whole summer. I am ready to explode!"

Helena beamed as she folded Irene into her, her own joy pouring out in her flushed cheeks.

At dinner, she told Irene of the plan she had made earlier that day.

Irene was, of course, delighted.

"Can I be a part of it?" she asked, unsure how much Helena wanted her to be involved in her work business. In her mind, she wanted to be with Helena all the time this summer, whatever that entailed, but she wasn't sure yet what that would look like, and how much space Helena would want just for her business, not to overlap with their relationship.

"I want you a part of everything. I sense your timidity, darling. It's crazy, maybe, but I want you everywhere. That is, everywhere you want to be. This is brand new for us, being together for all this time. I just can't get enough of you. Just seeing you walk in with your suitcase made me never want to ever see you leave."

They gave each other a look that said, *Oh God, please, let me do all I can to refrain from not attacking this woman like I want to.* They just laughed instead, and brought out movies to watch, distracting themselves with stories of animals and their babies, and detective stories. They didn't watch any film that had one inkling of romantic love in it, and they didn't go near ones that had lesbian characters.

At the barbeque the next day, the talk was only on the new ideas for Tassieyogo. All four women animatedly discussed the prospects, how they would do it, what their marketing would be, and what they thought they would earn each year. Based on their first quarter's sales plus the increase in sales after the announcement of their goals for this product, they projected five-year target revenue of $100 million. The United Nations World Food Program was still in talks regarding their desire to have Tassiebaby distributed worldwide in developing nations.

Adrenaline was flowing like lifeblood. They planned a follow-up meeting in two weeks. They saw how Helena still tired easily, and the three other women were all very protective of not burning her out. Indeed, Helena was visibly tired by the end of the evening. It was her first night out, and by the time she came home, she was pale and could hardly get herself to bed.

For the next several days, Irene and Helena stayed close to the bed and watched movie after movie, taking a plethora of cuddle naps each day. By Friday morning, this abundance of rest did an abundance of good. She looked strong, healthy, and when she hugged Irene that morning, Irene noticed she didn't wince once.

At the doctor's office, Dr. Zilber looked at the scar, did some tests, and exclaimed over and over how pleased he was at the results. After patiently being a patient for him, she asked him her burning question.

"Ah, the tiger in you has been painfully dormant, is that right?"

Helena laughed, her face turning bright red.

"I'd give it one more week, just to make sure nothing goes awry. It was major surgery, remember. And that is one less week than my original projection. Can the tiger hold off that long?"

Helena laughed and nodded, the crimson in her face remaining as the doctor congratulated her on her tremendous progress and wished her all the best. She thanked him for being such an excellent doctor. He smiled as he exited the room.

For the next week, Helena and Irene took walks in the mountains—short ones, and only those that had no hills. The wildflowers were emerging, and the colors and shapes were glorious. They would come home and cook together, and then sleep for long deep and restful hours until around noon the next day.

The week passed quickly, easily, and by the beginning of the following week, Helena appeared strong, healthy, and vibrant, her scar just a mere reminder now of the trauma that had occurred in her breast.

To celebrate, Irene bought an expensive bottle of Champagne, and they toasted and sipped and made dinner together, relishing in this freedom that had been handed to them. They got into bed and tentatively at first, they kissed, tiny kisses that felt sweet on the lips, the cheeks, the forehead, and from this space of holding back, the tiger lurked nearby, gradually loosening her claws, flexing her muscles as their kisses grew bolder, unleashed, surfacing again after a long hiatus.

The summer solstice began, the shortest night of the year, as Helena and Irene wailed into the night, their wails like wolves, calling to each other, their passion unbridled, giving in to the other, over and over.

Chapter Sixteen

Summer unleashed its hold on the universe in magnanimous ways for Helena and Irene. The first full day of the season, they decided to venture a bit farther in their mountain treks and, pulling on their hiking boots, backpacks filled with food and water and a pair of binoculars, they started on a trail that Helena had wanted to hike for years. The agreement was that as soon as Helena tired, they would rest, then turn around and head back. Irene smiled to herself at Helena's impishness coming forth like a petulant child being told what to do. She also saw how entirely smitten she was, and secretly, Irene basked in the fact that Helena rarely disagreed with her.

The trail began on even ground, a gentle flat path that meandered in the woods, aspen towering above as gentle columbines terraced the sides of the path, clusters of larkspur, mariposa lilies, and harebell penstemons reaching for the sun. The day was perfect, a cloudless sky and a light breeze as they walked quietly, smelling, looking, feeling the mountain air sit deeply within their lungs. Irene was surprised at how easily it was for her to acclimate to the high altitude, so different from her coastal, sea-level roots.

The woodland trail emerged to a landscape that took their breath away, a sweeping view of the mountains surrounding them, their snow-covered jagged peaks strutting into the sky. There was an endlessness that encapsulated them as they took note of their smallness in comparison.

They stood in awe, silent, hand in hand, bearing witness to the magnificence around them.

Slowly, Helena turned to Irene, looking in her eyes that were softened by this moment, yet alive in the magnitude of this breathtaking place.

"Irene, will you marry me?"

She smiled, her face lit up by the secondhand-ness of this question. She looked at the seriousness in Helena's face, comparing it to the fear that she felt the first time, right after the surgery. Her glance, her memories, flashed quickly by as she stared into Helena's eyes, feeling her own love pour from her, feeling Helena's swim around them.

"Yes," she said simply, the one-word-ness filling the space in between their two bodies.

Irene leaned into Helena, their lips touching, grazing at first, and then, as a falcon swooped overhead, their bodies pressed into each other as their lips found another fuel that propelled them deeper, deeper inside the other, tongues dancing as their bodies swayed, creating their own dance. They threw off their shirts and let their breasts dance together, the rhythm of their moans filling them as their wildness for each other danced through them. Their hands searched and found what they wanted as together, in that vast space that they shared with nature, they came and screamed, and came again, laughing and cooing, and celebrating the wonderment of their love, sharing it freely with the vastness of the mountains that held them.

Their shirts off, they continued hiking on the trail, which began its ascent, climbing through a more rugged terrain.

"I feel strong, stronger than really I have felt in ages," Helena remarked, apparently not experiencing any windedness as they propelled their bodies up the incline. "I love this feeling of hiking on the mountain," she continued. "I feel alive here, these mountains are so much a part of me. Did you know that these aspens have a root system that is intrinsically connected and stretches on for miles and miles, under the earth? Every time I think of this, I feel like there is a connection we all have, humans and animals, and trees and plants, and at some level, way at the depth of our own spiritual roots, nothing separates us."

Irene was quiet, pondering this, feeling something move inside of her as she did.

"It's powerful, isn't it? I mean, to conceptualize connectedness. It's true, we are all connected beings." She paused. "You know something? Your color has completely returned. I do sense a shift in you. It's subtle, but there is more of a wildness in you. I can really tell this is your home, my mountain woman."

Helena smiled as she grabbed Irene's hand and gave it a squeeze. "How is it for you, these mountains?"

"You know, I was thinking, I really don't know mountains, and in my mind, I think I am a bit wary of them because of this. But I love the feeling that I have being in them. I can completely see why they are part of your essence. I feel drawn to their energy. It is very much a woman's energy, so unpolluted from the city, from the world below which can zap a person's vitality. I am completely happy, and I would love to be a mountain woman with you."

Helena stopped, turned around and let the warmth of her chest caress Irene's. As the sun peaked in the sky and their desire for each other grew, their warm lips felt a hunger in them, the midday breeze floating hot currents through them as their bodies danced again together and as they listened to their own echoes off the canyon.

They walked on a bit, feeling their breath, their hearts pumping hard. They came to a flattened overlook, and as they looked out, they marveled at the altitude they had come to. In the Rockies, each time they climbed higher, the mountains followed them, their peaks reminding them that there was always a greater ascent.

"Lunch?" Irene suggested.

"Read my mind."

They spread out their shirts, and a jacket for a tablecloth, and then pulled out a loaf of fresh bread and some goat cheese, and white peaches from the farmer's market, whose juices dripped down and bathed their chins. They ate quietly, listening to the sounds around them, the winds whispering through the richness of the landscape. When they were done, they brushed off crumbs and Irene cozied up to Helena's bare chest as they sat still, Helena's arms wrapped around Irene as she purred, a contented cat on a mountain.

As she felt the softness, the firmness of Helena's arms, she thought about her own life, and the incessant energy of the city that affected everything she did. Without even realizing it, she had let her life become surrounded by a certain breathlessness. She existed with a feeling of perpetual motion, which had worked for her, and continued to work for most people around her. But being around Helena on her turf gave her a sensation of taking a breath, feeling grounded, slower, not needing to experience the fervency of sound and motion everywhere. She realized she had a lot to learn from being around Helena, and the more she got to know her, the more she saw an integral balance between them. She sighed, loving the peace between them, the comforting silence that calmed her mind, her soul.

Together they dozed as the sun moved through the sky, the lazy afternoon first day of summer becoming one with them, their hearts still, their breaths even and relaxed.

❧ ❧ ❧ ❧ ❧

As Irene slept, Helena rested her eyes, their bodies both still. All of a sudden, from the distance, a rattlesnake peered its head. It slithered toward them, its tongue thrusting in and out of its mouth, its sensory organs detecting its surroundings. In her sleep, Irene twitched. The snake edged closer, its curved sensual body an arm's length from the women. Still, she slept as the snake made its entrance into their space, quiet and unannounced.

Helena opened one eye and saw it, the snake's eyes peering directly at her own. Breathing calmly, she stared at the snake, smiling. In a conversation without words, it appeared that they communicated something to each other.

Helena watched it gently slither away, the same moment that Irene opened her eyes.

"What's going on, darling?" she said in a half-awake, half-sleep voice.

"Ummm, well, we just had a visit from a rattler. But before I describe it to you, we need to pack up quickly and start going back. I'll tell you more as soon as we are a distance from here."

Helena couldn't speak for at least thirty minutes

after they gathered their things and began their descent. "I've never done that before." Helena paused. "I looked straight in its eyes and found our common essence. Exactly what I was referring to earlier. It was a female, thank goodness, and they are usually less predatory, unless they have babies to protect. This one did not, I am imagining. You know, it was about three feet away from you. It's you I wanted to protect. I sensed that if you woke up you would have jumped, and that could have been disastrous."

"Oh my God, I am so sorry."

"No, don't be. It's natural to jump when one sees a snake. Especially a rattlesnake right next to you."

"Yeah, but I am such a city girl."

"Oh, stop that. You are far more than that, darling. I am glad you were sleeping through it all. I think had you been awake, even if you were completely silent, four eyes on that snake might have overwhelmed her. Besides, I think I was supposed to meet her. Just me and her. It was so powerful, I can't even begin to describe it."

Helena was quiet for a moment and appeared to be pondering the depth of this experience.

"I wonder if the snake knew," she began. "Two women, bare chested, resting in a loving way. I felt like it did, that she got it, the essence of our femaleness, the need to love and protect, in that split second there seemed to be a recognition of something so primitively mutual."

Irene looked at Helena and smiled, watching her ponder still, knowing that this experience would probably shape her for the rest of her life. In her own mind, she connected this experience with Helena's marriage proposal just a few hours earlier. These were all signs, she mused, blessings from one of nature's most powerful beings, the serpent. As Helena stared into the trees, Irene found herself gazing into them as well, letting the spiritual presence of the natural world lace itself around her heart, much like music had done for her all her life.

Chapter Seventeen

Summer moseyed along like an extended slow river, bending and twisting, a feeling of freedom displayed like a panoramic portrait upheld in the mind, the body letting itself sink into that place of the sublime.

Irene took up gardening, working the soil with her hands, letting the deliciously rich compost ooze into her fingernails. *There is nothing that beats a whole lot of organic cow shit,* she thought to herself as she experienced a feeling of euphoria, mixing everything together in the raised beds she and Helena had made, preparing to plant her vegetable starts. Often, she would look up and stare at the mountains, their peaks becoming now her familiar loved ones, always awing her with their magnificence. She breathed in the freshness of the air, filling her lungs with the pure oxygen that surrounded her. She was truly happy here, and never once did she even ponder her home, her life in Seattle.

Helena and Irene had easily created a comfortable rhythm of life together. On the days when Helena needed to be present on the farm and in meetings, Irene found her place either in the garden, or at her computer, where she had begun composing music, a passion of hers that she had always wanted to do. In her head, she had so many styles of music swimming around, and at her computer she began the exciting process of putting them to a score, listening in her mind to the outcomes from the notes she wrote down. The quiet of her surroundings and the pure air around her lent itself well to her composition, freeing up her creative skills like a wild bird, uncaged.

On days when Helena was not needed at work, they slept in and made love, their ferocious energy for each other never quieting. Sometimes entire days were spent in bed, alternating between sleeping and sex, their lips and hands continually searching, hungry, as their hearts swelled for each other with each passing day.

Some days they woke up early and started a hike which would last most of the day, choosing trails that would let them disappear into the mountain together, their lungs and their feet craving this connection with the nature around them that gave itself so freely. On those hiking days, shirts usually off in the later morning, their passion for each other blended with the femaleness of the mountains themselves, the shimmering aspens bearing delightful witness to it all.

One day, after Irene had lovingly planted all her organic vegetable starts, giving her little tomatoes and squashes all her prayers and blessings for their growth and production, she stood back as she sprinkled water on them, watching their tiny leaves sway in the breeze, and she sighed, smiling, thinking to herself how she never thought she would be doing this, her life turning around, stunning her with its exquisiteness, all because of an emerald suitcase, found in Melbourne, and opened in a cabin in Tasmania.

Smiling, she returned to the house for a glass of water, and saw Helena staring at her from the kitchen window. She handed Irene a glass of cool water. Irene gulped it down, then Helena took the glass from her and grabbed her sweaty body, ripping off her clothes one by one, as her lips pressed into the wetness from the water she had just drunk. Irene moaned, her knees unable to hold her weight as Helena picked her up and took her to the bed, pinned her down with the full weight of her, letting her lips sink into the firmness of Irene's nipples that grew with each sucking motion. Irene's sweat mingled with the flow of desire between her legs as pools of fluid bathed her, her moans increasing as her body writhed with a furtive, relentless energy. She dug her nails into Helena's back as she felt Helena's tongue lapping and licking, making them both suspended in fire, laughing and screaming and panting, their breaths deep and full, taken away in their bliss.

Chapter Eighteen

One day, when a drenching summer storm swooped down and watered the parched July earth, Irene checked her email on her laptop. She luxuriously only opened her emails about once a week, never expecting much anyway during the summer months, since most of her email was work related.

Nothing much was in her inbox, but, as she scrolled down there was a letter from a week earlier, from Elise Maillon. *That's interesting,* Irene thought. She had completely forgotten all about that woman and the letter she had sent her that week after she and Helena had talked about it in the bath. *When was that letter?* she asked herself. *Goodness, in April sometime, and here it is, three months later.* Irene had been so preoccupied with her present life that she had let go of the idea that Elise would contact her. And now, here was a letter. She opened it, reading in French.

Dear Irene. What a sincere pleasure to have read your email sent a few months back! My sincerest apologies for not responding sooner. I have a home in Greece, on Lesbos Island, where I run workshops, and each spring, I am there and so preoccupied with the work and the women, making sure everything is running smoothly, that I tend to neglect my regular email from April to June. I must say that when I received the letter the day before I was to leave for Greece, I was thoroughly delighted and found serendipity once again, bearing witness to small miracles. I am in the middle of writing a biography of the life of my late and beloved partner, Laure Lyons, and I have been searching for letters she sent and received before we met. Many times, she mentioned your partner's grandmother's name, Hillary Hanover, and the tragedy that befell their relationship, which perhaps your partner was never privy to. Laure's parents were very Catholic and very strict with Laure. It was quite surprising that they allowed her to go to Tasmania, of all places, to study. I never quite understood this. When they got word of Laure's involvement with Hillary, they immediately shipped her back to France and forced her to marry a heinous man, who took away all her liberties. She was not allowed to have a life beyond enslavement to him. Meanwhile, Laure's parents found Hillary's address and wrote her a letter, claiming Laure had killed herself. Laure knew nothing of this letter, and I only found out about this erroneous story a few years ago from someone who knew the sister of Laure's ex-husband. We found each other, Laure and I, at the market one day, instantly falling in love, and began a clandestine relationship. When Laure's husband was dead, and her parents, too, then we began to finally find freedom in our love.

As you might know from the internet, Laure and I founded a very influential underground women's/ lesbian movement in Paris, called Les Tigresses, and Laure, the beautiful poet that she was, was quite fond of doing the writing in our regular newsletters, continually empowering women and our love for women.

In my biography of her, I am of course including all this writing, but in the section on her earlier days, I want to include the correspondence between her and

Hillary, which, I am imagining, was quite stunning and passionate: those early days when she was just barely twenty, her first love for her professor whom she put on such a pristine and exotic pedestal, the Virginia Woolf scholar from Oxford, living in the woods in a remote region of Australia. Fascinating story, truly.

I would be so entirely thrilled to be able to obtain permission to use the letters you and your partner have discovered, and furthermore, I absolutely insist that you come to Paris, the two of you, and be my guests for a week or longer, as you desire. I have a palatial apartment here on the banks of the Seine, with a view of the Eiffel Tower, and I would be so humbly honored to have you as my guests.

Take all the time you need to ponder this but know that I was and am so thrilled to have received your letter—written in impeccable French, by the way—and I so look forward to hearing back from you, in the hopes that the three of us can meet someday soon.

> *With greatest respect and kindness,*
> *Elise Maillon.*

Irene sat in front of her computer screen, stunned. She texted Helena straight away.

Are you coming home for lunch today? If so, I have an amazing surprise to share with you!

Two seconds later.

You read my mind. I was just shutting down the computer, getting ready to head over to you.

Irene sent an emoji smile.

A short time later, Helena walked in the door, landing in the arms of Irene. She took her hand and led her to the office, where she translated the letter from Elise.

Helena's face dropped in awe.

"You were so right, darling. You knew that Laure hadn't committed suicide. This is juicy."

They both laughed.

"So, we're off to Paris." Irene laughed, kissing Helena.

"I guess we have to go, no choice there," she giggled, pulling Irene onto her lap, and kissing her neck. "What about a honeymoon in Paris?"

"Mmmmm...Delicious. But we haven't set a date to get married." She moaned lightly, as Helena continued to kiss the softest part of her neck, making her hum.

"Okay, so what day do we go and say I do... and make it all official and legal so we can go on our honeymoon?" she asked, breathing into Irene's ear, sending kisses through her ear canal.

"I love eights. Let's make it on an eight day."

"Well, July eighteenth is today. Kind of too late. July twenty-eighth might be too soon to gather people. What about August eighth or August eighteenth? August eighth will be eight-eight. Rather auspicious, no?"

"Perfect. August eighth, it is. Should we book the flight for that night?" she asked, her lips softly grazing Helena's, sending a shiver through her.

"That is the old-fashioned way, isn't it? The couple departs, drunk on champagne, leaving the wedding guests to clean up after themselves."

They giggled, their kisses full now, no longer teasing, as they tumbled to the carpeted floor of the office, the summer storm relentlessly spewing out life and nourishment all around them.

❧ ❧ ❧ ❧

As July slipped into August, plans happened simply. Things fell into place easily and quickly, the garden thrived, and their lovemaking twisted and turned, became deeper in meaning, the hearts swelling, enlarging, as Irene and Helena prepared for their union of one to the other.

Tassieyogo took care of most of the arrangements, having access to the best lesbian caterers and photographers and musicians in town. The wedding itself would be on the farm, in and old wooded grove on the far end of the property, with stunning views of the mountains in the background. The reception would be in the adjoining meadow, adorned with summer wildflowers. Rings were chosen, handcrafted by their friend and magical metalsmith, Ivy.

Irene opted for a Boho Chic look, finding in a shop in Boulder a Bohemian lace ivory-colored dress with a plunging neckline, tightly fitting around the hips, and falling loosely at the bottom. She would wear flowers from the garden in her hair, with a "why not, anything is possible" theme. When they shopped for her dress, and Irene put on the one that she would eventually choose, Irene laughed, thinking she saw Helena's breath catch seeing her in that dress. They made love in the dressing room, muffling their roars of delight.

Helena took five minutes to figure out what she wanted. She chose, in the same shop, a lavender-and-ivory blended vest made from a fine, soft silk, and ivory silken pants, fitting perfectly. They would be barefoot, they decided, wanting to feel the softness of the woods under their feet.

Bob and Harry would be the best men; everyone else invited was lesbian—or lesbian wannabees—from Helena's tight circle of Colorado women. Helena's mother politely declined the invitation, not being able to get out of Hong Kong, where she was "immersed in the prime development stages of their new concert hall she was designing, a building that would be the envy of the world," she wrote, unabashedly.

The flight from Denver to Paris would leave at eleven at night. They purchased business class seats that connected and would give them the freedom to touch each other the entire flight.

⚜ ⚜ ⚜ ⚜

The eighth of August arrived, a perfectly warm and stunning day, the temperatures in the low 80s midday, stunningly clear skies. The flowers in the garden waved in the breezes. Irene and Helena woke at the same time, rolling into each other, their lips greeting the morning with a mixture of hunger and sweetness, a flow between them that coursed through their veins.

"We're getting married today," they said together, rolling like tumbleweeds in that bed, their movements light and airy. They made love wanting every corner of the other, joining over and over, two beings as one. They felt like singing, and sing they did, in the shower, bathing each other; as they made breakfast, in between kissing, their voices in perfect harmony, like a transcendent chorus in the Australian outback, open land and the red-orange earth meeting their unbridled passion.

Helena helped Irene dress, kissing every part of her as she put on the dress that most likely would make Helena incessantly wet throughout the day. Helena got dressed, and then, with their friends waiting outside, having done absolutely everything so Irene and Helena wouldn't need to lift a finger, they were driven to the end of the farm, to the sacred grove, where everyone was giddily waiting.

Holding hands, with the gentle and celebratory rhythms of djembes and the digeridoo, Irene and Helena skipped and danced into the center of the grove, where a ring of aspen stood like women, their pale, white trunks holding fast into the earth and their leaves brushing the air, as if they were all witness to a female grooming act. At the center of the labyrinth their friends had made with stones, the minister stood, representing all the denominations of the world, the universal spirit of God, of the sages, of the beings of nature, of women loving women. Helena had known Pearl since she was a child, and she had told Irene that she had always wanted Pearl to marry her to the woman of her dreams. When Helena saw her, she cried.

They stood, with their friends circled around them, listening to the silence of the sacred space they had created, the rustling of the leaves reminding them of the interconnectedness of all living things. The quiet, the feeling of awe that spoke to everyone, brought up tears in almost all the guests.

"For in this moment of awe," Pearl began, "at the center is love, and we, in this sacred space, know how deeply Irene and Helena are in love with each other. We all have heard their story of meeting, of the emerald suitcase, and how instantly that connection grew to where they are today. As we gaze upon these two, we can all feel the power and the magic of love, the permanence of it, the perfection of it, and the exquisite beauty that emboldens the love between these two women."

"We come together," Pearl continued, after chanting a prayer in Farsi, set to a poem by Rumi, a prayer that Irene had heard her father sing to her mother many times, a prayer that made Irene cry, missing him in this greatest moment of her life. "To honor these two beautiful women: Irene Alborz and Helena Hanover. We come together to celebrate love in the purest sense. We come together, in these woods, in the midst of God, surrounded by the divine, the female, and mostly that feeling of awe, as we embrace these two and the miracle of finding one another in the realms of love and devotion. We come together, and cry and pray and drop to our knees at the beauty of these two and how deeply they care for one another. It was all because of a suitcase, but it was more than that. It was fate that brought them together, the mystical energy that connects two people, and lets them bond for life. For in these tears, there is such a celebration of feeling so moved and overjoyed that we are all here together, watching them share the infinite gaze of love."

Irene and Helena stood, indeed gazing at each other as if time stood still in that moment, and with Pearl and all their friends around them, their gaze spanned lifetimes of love, devotion, commitment, passion, and the intensity of the fire in their bellies.

With a nod from Pearl, after everyone had stopped to wipe their moistened eyes, Bob and Harry approached the couple, bearing two stunning pieces of gold in a velvet box. They handed Helena the first, and she slipped it on Irene's soft, welcoming finger. Then they handed Irene the second, and she quietly put it on Helena's hand. Their ringed hands clasped, feeling the smoothness of the gold against the seductively soft folds of their fingers, intertwined. They turned to Pearl, who looked at Helena.

"Do you, Helena Leah Hanover, take Irene Rumi Alborz, as your beloved wife, to have and to hold, in sickness and in health, until death do you part and beyond?"

"I do."

"Do you, Irene Rumi Alborz, take Helena Leah Hanover, as your beloved wife, to have and to hold, in sickness and in health, until death do you part and beyond?"

"I do."

"Irene and Helena, I now pronounce you legally wed."

As more tears fell from as many eyes as there were in that circle of love, Helena and Irene embraced, their lips gracing each other's with the joy of that moment, their passion exploding as they wanted more, the celebration of their love becoming legal, but in that moment, nothing else mattered more to them but that kiss, sanctifying all. Their friends clapped, wanting an encore, and Helena and Irene laughed as they grabbed each other and again, placed their lips on each other's, feeling their hunger, their lust for the other as well as the deepened love that had emerged from the two words "I do." The band then erupted in rhythms, the violin and the accordion, the cello and the mandolin, the djembes and the digeridoo all playing music that made everyone move and dance around the grove, their feet stomping up the dirt, filtering into the roots of the trees that stood, beautifying that celebration of love.

And the food, every dish and every snackable item was a work of art, a delicacy that slipped into the mouth, inviting passion that would meander its way throughout every one of the guests at that wedding. Champagne and non-alcoholic Pinot Noir grape juice from the Napa Valley flowed like orgasmic fluids. Everywhere in that meadow, there was dancing and kissing and couples sneaking off into the woods.

Helena and Irene did the first couple's dance as everyone stopped, gawked, and stared at the couple, the grace in their steps, the exhilarating beauty of Irene and how Helena brought it out, their love, their devotion, their eroticism like a poem from another era, slipped into the present day.

The hours passed, the celebration and the music and the drink and food not wanting to cease.

As the light changed and the sun began its impressionistic descent, Marilyn came up to Helena and whispered in her ear, "It's eight o'clock, darling; you have to leave in fifteen minutes to get to the airport. The limo just arrived."

Helena turned to Irene, who was dancing around everyone, her hair loose and flowing, her dress an orgasmic display of seduction and joy. With one simple nod from one spouse to another, hugs were given, and goodbyes were dispersed as Helena and Irene grasped hands, skipping away back to the house. Once inside, they lunged at each other as they tore each other's clothes off and stood naked, their lips and their tongues on fire for each other as they laughed and smiled and felt the heat rising, waiting for this moment. They came together, screaming and hollering as their friends outside chuckled and drank some more, danced and ate, the party not wanting to end.

Jeans and shirts thrown on, they grabbed their bags and stepped into the limo. Their friends all stood, waving goodbye as the car made its way to the airport.

𝒜𝒜𝒜𝒜

The mountains and highways flitted by as Irene and Helena kissed in the back seat, the taste of Champagne lingering in their mouths as they found a perfectly comfortable place, their lips on each other's lips, sipping still the ambrosia of their wedding, the most beautiful wedding they could ever have imagined.

Helena stopped, her mouth disengaging from Irene's, as she pulled out an envelope from her carry-on bag.

"I just remembered, before we get to the craziness at the airport, this arrived in the mail for you today. Marilyn gave it to me."

She handed a plain white envelope to Irene. The embossed printing return address was from the Counsel for International Exchange of Scholars Fulbright Scholarship Program.

Irene excitedly ripped open the letter and read it aloud.

"Dear Ms. Irene Alborz:

"On behalf of the Counsel for International Exchange of Scholars, we, at the University of Tasmania are extremely pleased and delighted to have you join us between the first of September through the thirtieth of

September 2017 at our Hobart Campus.

"Duties will include:

"Classroom teaching, three days a week in our ungraduate courses, department of music.

"Attending workshops, trainings, and symposiums related to the formation of our International Programme of the Integration of Aboriginal and Western Music Graduate level studies. (2 days a week.)

"We will provide off-site housing for you and your spouse, and stipend money for any other expenses you might have.

"In addition, we will provide flight and accommodations for you to attend Australia's Annual Conference on Music Education in Sydney, NSW, on the weekend of 14-15 September 2017.

"We so look forward to meeting you and including you as part of our faculty. We will have a formal meet-and-greet on the evening of the first of September at the home of our chancellor, Ms. Lucille Beckett.

"With kindest regards,
"Mr. Edmund LaPierre,
"Vice-Chancellor, University of Tasmania."

Irene resumed her kisses, her lips pressing into Helena's, as they felt again the heat of the implications of that letter.

"We're going back to Tasmania, darling one."

Still drunk from the wedding, this new bit of exciting news filtered through them with a fire that burned inside as Helena pulled Irene to her and their bodies squirmed with the delight of the moment. The mere thought of Tasmania enveloped all their senses as their kisses consumed the incendiary heat that emerged from the back seat of the limo. As the car arrived at the departures gate, and after giving the driver a generous tip, the newlyweds danced to the baggage check, deposited their bags, zipped through security, and sat hugging each other in the waiting area to prepare for the departure of their plane to Paris.

They each pulled out their phones to check any messages that might have arrived that week.

There were dozens of texts from their friends, wishing them bon voyage, telling them that they had the most beautiful wedding they had ever been to.

Helena had no interesting emails to report.

Irene had one from her department, telling her that they were entirely delighted about the arrangement that the University of Tasmania had made to "steal her away" during the month of September. They had arranged for her TAs to take over classes from the middle of September, when the term began, to the end of the month, so no need to worry about that. They couldn't wait to see her again in the first week of October.

"So, there you go." Irene beamed.

"Let me send a quick text to Marilyn, telling her I will be doing my Tasmanian visit in September, not October, as originally planned."

Within seconds, Marilyn sent her an emoji with a thumbs-up.

With everything all taken care of, Irene and Helena boarded the plane, taking their seats in the lavish business section, playing like children with all the buttons that made their seats do all kinds of fascinating things. The best part was that they could put their beds together and feel each other all night long.

Chapter Nineteen

The flight was a joyous blur, and mostly Irene and Helena slept through the miles over land and ocean, their hands clasping, the connecting thread through their in-flight dreams.

Before they knew it, Charles de Gaulle airport greeted them with a melodious cacophony of dozens of languages, the living and breathing of humanity from all parts of the world. One breath was all they needed to know they were in Paris, vibrant, pulsing, colorful Paris. They got a cab to take them to the flat they had rented in the heart of the Marais, where they would spend the first three nights, alone and unencumbered, before going to the generous home of Elise Maillon.

Evening in Paris greeted them as the car drove past suburbs, into the city and then into the Third Arrondissement. At eight in the evening, the August air was still heavy with the day's heat as the cobblestone streets crunched under the tires of the car. People were out, everywhere—dining, talking, laughing—cafés spilled over into sidewalks as glasses tinkled, and the sweet aroma of coffee and wine and desserts mingled with the savory, the homemade falafels and the spices of worlds beyond. Heels clicked on the roughened pavement, women dressed in fashions that stunned the eyes as men stood in doorframes and stared. The music of Paris was beyond any instrument, the rhythms of people everywhere doing, living, celebrating, being. It was music that tantalized the newcomer and in its own ways, stabilized the regulars.

Helena and Irene stepped out of the car on the Rue Vieille du Temple, hand in hand, feeling the aliveness greet them with a warm embrace. They took their bags up sixty well-worn stairs, curving up and up, until they reached the turret, their home all to themselves where they had a view of the city below and its vibrant cooing and singing self, as pigeons sat lazily on telephone wires and laundry lines.

"I like this place," Helena commented as they both looked around, feeling the age of the walls, the leaded windows, the old sit-down bathtub instead of a shower. Matisse was everywhere. The suite was called "Matisse in Paris," with the blue nude highlighting the small and cozy apartment, right over the luxurious bed.

"I do, too. It has everything we need."

They sat on the bed and looked in each other's eyes, gazing at the other as if the wedding had just happened again, with everyone around to witness.

Kissing each other's rings and letting their lips drift to each other's, they whispered to each other, "We are married now." Over and over they whispered as their clothes came off, bit by bit, and their breathing became full and deep with love, with a feeling of permanence that filled them, every pore of them. As Paris droned with the energy of life, Irene and Helena found and held and released passion in them over and delightfully over, making love, the sweetest, hungriest, most fulfilling love that perhaps they had ever made.

❧ ❧ ❧ ❧

They slept through the night, holding in them

their sacred vows, their talismans for their lives ahead interwoven like a braided candle, their passion like a hot, oozing wax that permeated everything they did.

In the morning when they arose, Paris was there waiting for them, giddily inviting them to join in. They threw on their clothes and raced down the stairs, their steps light, following the curves of the wood, the circular descent onto the street. Before opening the door to the world outside, they kissed, their heat swirling around their bodies, pulling into each other, excited about their day ahead, their lives together, now permanent, a feeling of grace sinking into them as they stepped out into the street, their hands interlocking, their smiles big and wide.

A café across the street greeted them, their bellies starving for food, for Paris, for a day of eating and drinking anything and everything delicious.

They ordered coffees, croissants, and of course, yogurts, giggling at each other, the warm buttery smoothness all over their fingers as they dipped the glutinous layers into their coffees.

Their hands still clasped, they meandered through the Third and the Fourth Arrondissements, winding their way, purposefully getting lost through neighborhoods, taking in sounds and smells and everything that had color around them. They ended up at the Seine and walked over bridges, and then meandered some more. For Irene, getting lost was not really lost, as she knew Paris so intimately from those many years ago when she lived there. For Helena, getting lost with Irene was part of the love of the city, for they shared this passion of not needing to know where they were going, but just being in the moment of excitement and surprise. Everything in Paris had a certain magical glow to it, and that first day they kept finding shops and gardens and people and food and churches and bridges over the Seine that made them want to never leave.

At night, when they returned to their little Matisse suite, they made love with an effervescent passion that sizzled with the lights of Paris still imprinted in their beings. Their bodies were hot in the sultry August air, and it only made their hunger for each other even more intense as they continued to discover that secret Paris inside each of them, coming over and over, each time even more rich and delicious.

They slept soundly, deeply, the kind of sleep that only sex and joy and magic can create, wrapping their bodies together into a softened gauze, a nest of warmth and comfort, a sweet balm on a summer's night.

For the next two days they explored, they ate, they drank, they slept, they made love; they lived Paris, and Paris lived in them.

On the fourth day, as planned, they arrived, suitcases in hand, at 88 rue de la Belle Etoile, home of Elise Maillon.

A sumptuous garden greeted them, an array of exotic plants and flowers that spread about them like a mini-jungle, a taste of the wild meeting the urban colors of the apartment itself.

Elise answered the door, a small woman with an elegance that spoke to them of years ago, her grayed hair in a bun, her face absent of wrinkles, instead shining with a buoyancy and a sense of grace like a dancer, an egret in a tree, waiting to take wing.

"*Bienvenue.* Ah, *bienvenue!*" she exclaimed, first kissing Irene on the cheeks, right and then the left, and then the right, three times, the Parisian custom, and politely and respectfully holding out her graceful, wrinkled hand to Helena, looking in her eyes with warmth and kindness. "Congratulations!" she continued in perfect English. "On your recent marriage. You both look so radiant, so happy!"

Irene and Helena blushed. "Yes, we are," Helena offered. Irene and Helena loved this woman instantly, her warmth, her generous spirit. From this first moment, they could tell they were all family, and everything they wanted to share, they could.

"Let me show you your room, and please come down for lunch when you are ready. Oh, it's truly such a pleasure to meet you!"

Irene rattled off something in impeccable French as Helena looked on and smiled. The two women prattled on, the language lyrical with its ebbs and flows of nuances, music emerging from the tongue. Helena's expression was one of admiration, and Irene loved the way that the buried French self of hers became unveiled again after so many years. Her mouth curved over each word like poetry, speaking French. As they spoke, Elise ushered them around the house, finally leaving the two alone in the guest room. The bedroom was palatial, with a stunning view of the Seine from the huge picture window that lined the room.

"This bed is probably the most comfortable bed I have ever sat on," Helena announced, returning the conversation to the banality of the English language.

Irene sat down next to her and whispered in her ear, "And I can't wait until tonight when we can do other things in it besides sit."

"Cheeky." Helena laughed.

Moments later, they ventured out of their room. "Let's see," Elise announced, seeing the two descend into the salon. "I think I have everything here. Sit. Sit." She was beaming, staring at Irene and Helena. Lunch was displayed around them in an array like peacock feathers, colors and shapes of foods folded out onto the table, making them feel like they were in Monet's garden in Giverny in the middle of May when everything was in bloom. Pâtés and breads and cheeses and quiches and fruits and cakes and wines and everything possible that was gastronomically exquisite beckoned their tongues, their voracious appetites. The conversation was all in English and covered every topic that they shared a love for: lesbianism, politics, poetry, music, literature, nature, travel, food, love, and of course, Hillary Hanover, the latter in which Elise seemed to feign interest.

"I normally like to do what we French call '*faire la sieste*' after lunch. Later, I would like to have my driver take all of us around the city to places that are part of the hidden magical world of Paris." Elise looked at Helena and Irene. Her statement was more of a command than a question.

"Absolutely. We'd love this," Irene exclaimed.

Back in the room, while Irene stared at the mesmerizing river, the Seine never giving away her seductive qualities, Helena folded her arms around Irene.

"Did you notice the subtle grimace on Elise's face when we talked of my grandmother?"

"Of course. Well, she was the bane of her existence."

"Yes, makes you wonder, though, why she wants us here and why she wants to write about her, digging up old skeletons."

"She does seem authentically delighted to have

us here. I get the feeling that as important a person that she is, she is actually quite a lonely woman."

"She must still be grieving the loss of Laure."

"Yeah, probably. The love of her life."

Irene continued to stare out at the river, mesmerized, as Helena moved to their one suitcase and methodically took things out and put them in the drawers of the dresser.

"What's this?" Helena asked, touching something in the infamous emerald-green bag.

"What's what, darling?" Irene asked dreamily, feeling rather sleepy, ready to roll over on the bed with Helena for a nice Parisian nap.

"I feel something in your suitcase, but I have emptied everything out and I am not sure what it is." Irene looked over, her eyes glazed from the wine and the jet lag, giving Helena a look of, "I'm too sleepy—go ahead and figure it out if you want."

Helena, inspected the bag carefully, and unzipped the hidden zipper where the whole story began, in the double-bottomed suitcase. In that same compartment where the letters and the money were kept, there was another zipper, she noticed, folded away quite inconspicuously. She carefully unzipped it, and there was indeed another hidden pocket, and inside was a small stack of letters, folded pieces of paper meticulously put inside a light blue envelope.

She looked over at Irene, who had moved over to the bed. Her eyes were now closed, and she had her hand out, waiting for Helena to join her. Helena was in deep thought for a moment, her eyes switching from the letters to Irene. She then put the letters back in the pocket, zipped it back up, and silently crawled onto the bed with Irene, folding into her as the two slept deeply, both in their own worlds yet connected by their bodies, entwined.

Two hours later, the heat of the day had waned a bit, and their eyes opened to each other's, smiling. Remaining in a half-groggy post-nap state for a while, they lay as still as corpses, not exactly sure where they were, except with each other, and they grasped the other's hand for a bit of grounding.

"Hmmm…I could sleep all day, wrapped against you," Irene murmured.

"Me, too. I think everything must have just hit us full-on. We have been in delicious places, and jet lag added to that."

"Mmmmmm. I kind of like the ebb and flow we go through. Our energies are quite similar, you know."

"You know, they really are. It makes being with you a natural extension of myself."

"Yes, in a self-centered way, we are all extensions of ourselves." Irene giggled.

"Yes, busted am I."

"Do I play on that one?"

Helena just laughed, and rolled on top of Irene, kissing her.

"Didn't Elise say she was going to take us on a *tour de Paris*?"

"Oh my gosh, I forgot. Yes, like now, I believe."

They jumped off the bed and splashed some cool water on their faces, then headed downstairs.

Elise was sitting outside on the terrace, drinking lemonade and reading a book. All was quiet around her.

"Are we disturbing your peaceful moment?" Irene asked, in soft, gentle, Parisian French.

"Quite the contrary," Elise responded in English,

putting her book down. "Help yourself to some lemonade. Did you have a nice rest?"

"Absolutely," Helena answered. "Your home is so beautifully quiet, and the bed is like heaven. Plus, I think it hit us how tired we were after all the excitement of the wedding."

"Tell me about your lovely wedding," Elise asked, her face alive with interest.

Irene and Helena took turns, back and forth, sharing with Elise all the details from the minute to the grand, of the most important day of their lives. It felt in that moment, as Elise sat, her expression one of being mesmerized and delighted by the story, that to Irene and Helena, Elise was like the mother that neither of them ever had. In the telling of their day, in the back of their minds, each of them held a deep longing, wanting their own mothers to have been present at the wedding. They had not spoken of this and had not even realized it until that moment when the story was shared, and the lemonade had been sipped, and here was a perfect stranger looking in their eyes with admiration and a sense of motherly pride.

As Irene and Helena were telling Elise their story, Helena noticed that Elise's face betrayed a kind of longing. There was a maternal expression in it, in the lines and the softness of her eyes. But there was also something else that she couldn't put her finger on. She wondered then about her relationship with Laure, and the mystery of it, the mystery of Elise herself. When they finished the story, Irene and Helena paused, smiling.

"I always wished I could have gotten married," Elise said in a quiet voice. Irene and Helena leaned forward, listening, waiting for more.

"It was hard to be a single physician. I had to hide all the time, continuously evading questions, for I was in an occupation which did not understand why a single woman would not marry a man. Whilst I had a vivid social life with all my activist women, we were all underground, and many of them were lesbians still married to men, not saying a word to their husbands about their underground life. When I met Laure, I was instantly smitten by her, wanting to devour her, own her, control her life. I had a boiled passion in me those first few years, a plaguing need to be loved that was not healthy. I don't know how she handled me on top of her married life. She had a wicked husband who controlled her every move, and there I was, her hidden lover who was just as cruel in my love for her.

"Gradually, I calmed down, yet our passion for each other was still as ferocious as ever. I tried to understand my jealousy for her husband. I always felt that we were just living in the wrong time, where real love had to be shoved in a corner, pushed aside, and what was allowed instead was a conformist acceptance of society's rules, as ugly as they were. The strange thing was that this was Paris, the home to all the Gertrude Steins and Alice Toklases of the world, yet still Paris couldn't refrain from being part of that world that dictates love and who we can and cannot show our affections to...In those moments when I did step back, seeing my life, I considered myself lucky that I could have those stolen moments with Laure, that I could have all the women around me and we could all make a difference in each other's lives.

"But still I yearned for the statement, that piece of paper that said we were seen and love was love.

"When finally Laure's despicable husband died

and we were able to sell her house and buy this home together, still, France had not allowed us to be legal. I wanted to marry her anyway, have a civil union, I did not care. Laure told me that she did not want to have anything that was not recognized by the courts. She believed it was coming, that time, and she insisted we wait."

Elise sighed; tears came from her eyes.

"I always wondered if there was more, if she was hiding something from me."

There was silence then, and Irene and Helena teared up, seeing the irony of everything, the subtle nuances of love. They saw how easy it was for them, stripped of the complications that Elise had faced. They looked in her eyes and saw her grief. Helena saw it even deeper, her own grandmother a monumental part of it. No words could have been spoken then that could console.

Elise broke the silence, changing the subject.

"Well, my darlings, let's go for a drive, shall we? I would so love to show you Paris—my Paris—the one I hide away for only the most special people."

They all got up, arm in arm, smiling, somehow needing each other like a family, two daughters and a mother, moving through something monumental, each needing Paris to distract them for entirely different reasons. The car awaited them. Elise's driver took the three everywhere that late afternoon. Paris was indeed revealed, like a woman disrobing, letting out her darkened hair, the unraveling of the seductress, showing her naked, tantalizing self.

They ended up, around nine in the evening, at a tiny Lebanese restaurant that Elise used to go to with Laure, a charming eighteenth-century building with stone floors and original beamed ceilings. Their tongues savored each bite of their tajine filled with vegetable and spices and dried fruit, sweet and sour melting on the palate, as the couscous, made light and fluffy, provided a seductive contrast. For hours, the three talked and laughed and ate and drank, forgetting everything that stabbed the heart, until yawns began, and the driver took them all home through the streets of Paris, never quieting in its magic, the jeweled city that had the ability to obscure even the most wretched.

⚜ ⚜ ⚜ ⚜

The next morning turned into the afternoon as Irene and Helena opened their eyes. There was a note slipped under the door.

"Hi there. Gone to the market and a few other errands. Should be back around 4 p.m. Help yourself in the kitchen. There is food everywhere. Hope you slept well. Elise."

Helena slipped back into bed. It was a rainy August Parisian day. She slid next to Irene, whose eyes were still slits, half in this world and half in another. The rain was a comforting sound, stilling the air with a cleansing. Helena kissed Irene's palm, putting her hand to her face. Irene murmured something quietly.

"Mmmmm…Wasn't there something the other day you wanted to show me?"

"Oh yes, I completely forgot. But first, you have to wake up." Helena kissed more places on Irene as she hummed and purred. Helena continued to kiss all the places that Irene loved, and Irene continued to hum and purr in each place.

"I guess someone is not getting up soon. At least it appears that someone is ensconced in being kissed in every possible place." Irene pulled Helena to her, and their lips joined, effortlessly, their lovemaking sounding like the rain at first, a constant patter on skin, the gentle need for release, letting go, and then the rain turned to fire, and the sweetness turned into something dragonish, full of an energy that could only be satisfied with claws on bare skin, tumbling to the floor, racing around the room, a game of chase, take me if you can. The house was all theirs, and the only sound came from their primitive groans and squeals and howls that perhaps the lonely bystander outside might have heard, but they didn't care. Their joy was just theirs and they were married now, and they were in Paris, and with one final scream, finally they were quiet.

☙☙☙☙

They showered and went downstairs for food, utterly famished.

"So…" Irene began, her mouth full of buttery crumbs, her *tartine* dissolving on her tongue. *This is surely homemade jam*, she thought to herself. *And the bread, the bread, no one makes bread quite like the French. This country is a gluten-free person's purgatory.* "So," she continued. Helena was staring at her with an amused expression. Irene was known to start a sentence, get lost in an inward thought, and then restart the sentence, as if now she was truly ready to press "play." "You were going to show me something. And we keep getting interrupted."

"Yeah, let me get it. I'll be right back."

Helena raced up and down the stairs, returning with the blue envelope.

"What's that?"

Helena explained how and where she found it. "I will show you where the extra hidden pocket was when we get back to our room, but I didn't dare open the envelope without you."

Irene's eyes twinkled. She loved how Helena didn't have a me-me-me attitude about life and relationships. She was quite moved that she had waited for her to open this treasured object. She pulled her to her and kissed her gently, feeling her closeness as they opened it together.

They were letters, distinctly love letters, a thin stack of them, from Laure to Hillary. The dates were clearly marked—most were before she had met Elise, and some were after.

"Oh, my," Helena exclaimed, quietly.

"Ummmm...these may not be what Elise wants to see."

"She already knows."

"I can still see Elise's face yesterday, defeat written so clearly on it, deception interlaced with the *joie de vivre* that she insists on living her life with. I have this vague feeling of hating my grandmother."

"Yeah, I can see why."

They looked at the clock. It was thirty minutes before Elise was supposed to get home.

"Let's take these upstairs. We should do some investigating first before considering if we want to show them to her."

They sat together on the bed, spreading the letters out as they started to read them aloud.

"*My dearest darling Hillary, I am missing you so much I feel the world has been torn apart. I cannot even begin to tell you how dreadful this life is for me. I am married to a monster who controls everything I do. I must write quickly and send this off to you as I am being watched constantly, and even getting to the post office is risky. Please know that in my heart I am surrounding you, I long for the softness of your skin, the hardness of your nipples that fit so perfectly in my mouth. Our love was perfect, just so perfect. Please be well. I am coming back to you, the first chance I can. Your Laure.*"

That was the first letter. Most of the following few letters said mostly the same things, with a few variations. All were ended by the same line: *I am coming back to you.* None of the letters had return addresses.

Then there was a long gap in the dates, a year and a half. This was when Laure met Elise, according to Elise's story the day before.

Then the tone changed.

"*Dearest Hillary, my life has bustled around a maelstrom of feelings, ideas, thoughts, and I have been so remiss in writing to you. I have joined an underground women's—mostly lesbian—movement, and we gather in cloistered homes, in secret, our husbands do not know any of this. I am dizzy with ideas, freedom from enslavement. I hardly sleep, eat, I am being thrown into the passion of Paris and its free thinking. In my quiet moments I think of you, wondering, missing the way your hair falls on your face when I kiss you. Your loving Laure.*"

"No mention of Elise," Irene commented. "According to Elise, they were head over heels with each other when they met."

Another big break in the letters ensued, another two years.

"*I am exhausted. My husband hounds me constantly, and the women I am with want me as well. No matter where I am, I am being ruled. We are making great changes for women, but it is with such a price on my heart. I think of you and my nipples harden, my breath quickens. I long to run to you where I can be free in the Tasmanian wildness, the wind rushing through our breasts as the snow falls, dipping into you at night, our breaths becoming one. One day, you and I will join again. I promise you. Your loving Laure.*"

Riveted, Helena and Irene read on, shaking their heads, intrigued, yet immensely sad for Elise. The next letter was dated several years later.

"*My husband died yesterday. I haven't felt this happy since I was with you. I long to run back to you, but the women need me here in Paris. The movement has grown to huge proportions. I am moving in with a friend. I miss you. Your loving Laure.*"

Several years later, the next letter.

"*Oh, Laure, I am sick. I tell no one, hiding myself from everyone, even the ones closest to me. I fear I am dying, my dearest Hillary. I pray every night that I can return to you, to heal what is in me, this raging anger that I have held for so long. You were my only grace,*

*my balm, my Australia. Oh, Hillary, to be in your arms
again, my darling. Your loving Laure."*

Helena and Irene held the last letter in their
hands, shaking, crying, feeling the lifetime of Laure's
pain, sensing the huge loss and pain that Elise must
have felt all along.

"Your grandmother was in no way delusional.
She had packed up her bag and was going to fly out
to Paris to find Laure after this last letter. Somehow,
though, she never made it," Irene announced after the
two had sat silently with all the letters strewn around
them, their tears flowing.

"I remember the day my grandmother died,"
Helena began, wiping away her tears. "Everyone was
convinced she was demented on top of the cancer that
had quickly spread to her entire body. When everyone
had left the room, my grandmother spoke to me, her
only granddaughter. She had mumbled something that
I couldn't decipher, and for years I wondered what
she had said to me. Now, sitting with those letters all
around us, the ones that have tormented me for years,
her words became clear. 'Find her,' she had said."

Helena, jolted to the present, looked at the
letters. "We can't share these with Elise. They would
completely ruin her, and at her age, especially."

"We must hide them quickly. Elise should be
coming home soon. Oh God, I hate deceit. Anyone's.
And now we must do it ourselves." Irene gulped, and
felt a pit of queasiness in her gut as Helena put all the
letters carefully back in the envelope and slipped them
in the extra hidden pocket in the suitcase.

"I can't believe I never noticed that pocket,"
Irene said, shaking her head

"It was strange, but I felt something that crinkled after I had taken everything out of your bag."

"Might have been better if we had never found it. Ignorance is bliss sometimes." Irene sighed, thinking of Elise and how much she adored Laure, yet also remembering when she said how she tried to control her, wanted her all to herself. "Laure was definitely a woman who wanted to be free in all ways, to live, to love, to write. Do you think your grandmother was truly that outlet, or was that in Laure's fantasy mind?"

"That's a good question. I think in the real world my grandmother was just as much enslaved as Laure. I mean, look at her. She wanted to follow Virginia Woolf and she was whisked away to Tasmania, which was as far removed from the vibrant world of London as you could find. My grandfather could never meet her needs for her own passion, her intellect, and yet she never divorced him, and stood by his side as the dutiful wife. Perhaps the world of Hillary and Laure was mostly a fantasy, a dream of finding that freedom to love in a time where this was so essentially impossible."

"No wonder Elise envies us, the time and place we live in, to marry whom we are crazy about, and no one has and will ever get in the way."

"And neither of us has one iota of a need to control the other. God, to want to possess another is such a dangerous notion."

"Except in bed, maybe, but that is an entirely different thing," Irene added, her small laugh mixing with the severity, the somberness of their discussion. Helena clasped Irene's hand, kissing it, when there was a gentle tap on the door to their bedroom.

Irene got up and when she saw Elise standing there, her small frame so unassuming and sweet, she couldn't help but hug her, giving her the warmest embrace since they arrived. Elise was a bit taken aback, yet with a quiet, knowing look, she returned the embrace with an equal amount of warmth, for in that moment no words were spoken, yet there was a female intuitive understanding: two generations removed, yet one connecting thread.

They all descended to tea and Elise talked about her day, and Irene and Helena about their trip to Tasmania and their upcoming journey for Irene's sabbatical. Elise was engrossed, fascinated by Irene's topic of study. They spoke of music and the arts for the longest time, and then Elise asked them if they wanted to go to a dance concert that evening. She mentioned that there was a performance by a company she had always heard about, the Bangarra Dance Theatre, an Aboriginal Australian world-renowned group that was currently touring Europe. Irene and Helena were delighted at the idea and they agreed to meet downstairs shortly, then go have a bite to eat first before the show.

An hour later, excited and bubbly to be going out on a "family date," the three women got into the car, and the driver, waking up from his nap took them out and away, far from the menacing letters of a few hours ago.

Mesmerized, the women sat at the edge of their seats, transported to a world 40,000 years ago that blended with a contemporary feel of story and dance, music and heritage. Something called to them as their bodies felt the pulse of the music and the movement, connecting them away from their brains to the land, to nature that inspired this richness on stage. After the performance they stood up, wanting more, and the group did encore after encore, a tradition in Paris, Elise pointed out. When they exited the theatre, they were exhilarated and did not want to go home. They sat at a café with a carafe of wine and some cakes, talking, laughing, and feeling the thrill of the dance inside of them.

Irene and Helena noted that Elise could certainly drink. That night was no exception.

After several glasses of wine, she quietly uttered, "Laure loved dance."

At the mention of her name, Irene winced. Helena kicked her gently under the table. They could not change the subject. Elise was demanding an audience.

She took a gulp of wine, her gentle sipping over. She was clearly drunk.

"You know, I never really had her. Her heart was always with Hillary."

Irene and Helena stared into Elise's eyes, wishing she would stop this, her drinking, sabotaging the beautiful evening. But then they saw the need Elise had to reveal secrets perhaps she had never shared. So, they said nothing and let her continue.

"She was so much older than I. What did I know of love? I knew how to try to possess someone I could never ever have. I gave her a home, I gave her stability, I gave her my body and my eternal devotion, but I could never give her what she had with your grandmother. I know she wrote her letters. I saw her go once to the post office with one, and she was acting strangely that day. I knew she never wanted me to know, but occasionally in her sleep she would mutter 'Hillary.' I never confronted her. I couldn't dare to. And no one until now has ever known how tormented I was for all those years. When you emailed me, Irene, I cried for days, wanting and not wanting to uncover all the secrets that broke my heart. I have been writing her biography. The world has wanted to know for years about Laure Lyons, and I have forbidden any biographer to come close to her. I decided I had to do this, though, write this book to unveil to the world. Yet I can't. I am just too weak."

She stopped. Took a huge gulp of wine. And then, she stared at Irene and Helena.

"Did you bring her letters with you?"

Helena kicked Irene, letting her know she would take care of this. Irene knew that it was time to back off, and that Helena would have to take the next step. She knew also that Helena was supposed to have found Laure's letters.

"Yes," was all Helena could say.

Elise pulled out her phone and called her driver. Within minutes he was there, they got into the car, and in silence, were taken back to Elise's home.

As soon as they got into the foyer, Elise, tired and drunk, said, "I need those letters now."

Irene looked over at Helena, noticing the leaden expression in her face, and felt tears well up in her eyes. She stayed with Elise while Helena went upstairs. Irene made Elise a cup of tea and kept an eagle watch on her, making sure she didn't put any more alcohol in her system.

Helena returned and handed the envelope to Elise. Slowly, she read one after the other of the letters, bawling, sobbing, screaming, as Irene and Helena held her. They held her as she asked for vodka and they refused to give it to her. They held her as she sobbed in their arms, the night becoming darker as the moon moved over their heads.

Then, the tears were done. Her impeccable hair and her fine clothes were plastered with moisture, her sweat and her tears mingling with the sourness in her breath from too much wine.

"We are burning them. Now," she announced. "Please help me up. I am so weak."

Together all three went outside to the warm and heavy August night, and made a fire in the pit, watching it grow. Helena and Irene then handed each piece of paper to Elise, witnessing her feed the engulfing flames with each word written by her beloved. They watched the papers turn black, all the words becoming obliterated, until they got eaten by the galloping flames and dispersed themselves into the sky.

They felt Elise loosen her grip, and they watched her dance around the flames, listening to the hysterical laughs that came from her. She pounded her feet on the earth, hard, like the dancers that evening, feeling the soil ground her, her own release ground her, her escape from decades of her imprisonment ground her. Her laughter turned to a guttural song, one which came from the depths of her being. She grabbed Irene and Helena, urging them to chant and dance with her, their steps mirroring each other as they danced for the freedom of their adopted mother, the one they cherished now and always would.

Elise spun around and around the fire as the moon radiated its light on her, like a privileged spotlight, letting her be the whirling dervish that she clearly needed to be. She spiraled in, and then spiraled out, letting out a moan that wailed into the night. Her music was her own and her dance as well, letting go.

As she spun, she tottered, held by the arms of Irene and Helena, who gently picked her up, folding her tiny body in their arms as they took her to her bed. They stayed with her until sleep came, brushing away the hairs on her forehead that were soaked with sweat.

Helena took Irene's hand and together they went upstairs to their bedroom. Feeling the exhaustion of what had just happened, the surprise turn in the day, they wrapped themselves around the other, clinging to each other like monkeys as they fell deeper and deeper into sleep, not moving their bodies once until two p.m. the next day.

Everyone woke up at the same time. Irene went in to check on Elise. She was just rising, smiling, her step light and buoyant as she greeted Irene, kissing her three times on the cheeks.

"You look happy," Irene said in French.

"I am radiant. I haven't felt this happy in years, truly. What we did last night was exactly what I have needed to do for so long I can't even remember. You were so amazing with me, my darlings. How are both of you?'

"Lovely, thank you. We just woke up as well. We slept hard and didn't even move one muscle."

"Oh, I am so glad to hear that. Well, get yourselves ready. We'll eat something and do whatever you two sweethearts want. It's your last day in Paris, so think about what you might want to do. The sky is the limit!"

"Okay. Perfect. See you in a few."

Irene reported back to Helena, who was steeped in water. Irene stripped off her shirt and joined her in the shower, letting the water cascade down and around them as their lips caught hold of each other, their hands reaching in places that showered ecstasy through their bodies. They squealed quietly, letting the flow of water muffle their shouts of joy, their own release.

They dressed quickly, meeting Elise in the kitchen. She had made the coffee for everyone, and the bakery across the street had delivered their daily loaf of bread.

"What else do you need in life to start your day?" Helena laughed, lathering butter and jam on her bread, sipping her coffee with milk, letting it all erase the night before.

"Well, the French have been eating their *tartines* with coffee for generations. It is one of the unhealthiest breakfasts around, but tradition is tradition." Elise laughed a hearty laugh, not one made of airs or pretense.

She was clearly a different person today. She seemed like she was about to elevate into the sky. She looked twenty years younger.

"So, my darlings. What will it be today, what strikes your fancy?"

Irene and Helena looked at each other and then at Elise and smiled, words not spoken, but delight on all their faces that they had all made it through last night, and all of them, as a result, felt a tremendous release, energy dissipated that had vanished completely.

"Well," Irene began. "We were interested in perhaps going to the Rodin centennial exhibition at the Grand Palais. And I know this is rather touristy, but what about a trip up the Eiffel Tower? And choice three is your favorite."

"Well, as for the Grand Palais, I have VIP passes, so if we get there right when they close at five p.m. we can go for free with no one around in the museum for up to ninety minutes if we choose. After that, we can go up the Eiffel Tower. And then, ummmm…well, I have two choices: either we take my private catamaran for a night river cruise with dinner of course, or we go to the Pompidou, where they are having a rather large-scale opening for their new wing. Or..." She smiled coyly. "We do it all."

"Shall we start then with the Rodin, since it is around four right now, and then let our inspiration and spontaneity and energy levels be our guides?" Helena asked.

"As for me, I have energy to climb the moon and back, thanks to you, my dearest souls. So, let's go. Are you all ready?"

"Completely."

At five minutes to five, Elise's car pulled up to the Grand Palais and a silent museum greeted them; the thousands of people that had meandered through the halls that day were completely gone. Rodin's genius was everywhere, marble after marble as they walked the hallowed corridors, feeling every bit of the splendor of his creations, the smoothness of his lines, the depictions of humans in all states of existence, pain turning to the sublime all in a pose.

Stunned and energized by this creative inspiration, they headed into the car to the Eiffel Tower, where it, too, was closing for the day, and it, too, allowed Elise and her party to ascend alone to the towering heights of majestic Paris. At the top, the three laughed and laughed, delight filling them like children who had never experienced such heights of the imagination.

"I would like to live to be a hundred!" Elise exclaimed, looking out at Paris, laughing like a young girl.

"Is that all?" Helena questioned.

"Oh, my goodness, no. I'll go longer as long as the spirit in me is alive and well."

"Well then, onward, past one hundred!" Irene

added, putting her arms around Elise as they all three huddled together, smiling, their cheeks red and full of life.

"And, I am not writing that book," she continued, her face gazing at the carpet of Paris all around her, the dazzling lights of the city serenading her thoughts.

Irene and Helena looked out, waiting for more.

But there was no more. Elise sighed upon her declaration, her own statement that would now let her live without the bondage that had encapsulated her. Paris was her lover, and as she stood there, at the top of the seductive tower, Irene and Helena saw her heart disrobe, one layer after another.

Then they all descended, slipping into the car that would take them to the Pompidou, where Elise was greeted with a red carpet, and where Champagne and artisanal edibles were handed out freely with an open, private tour of the new wing—*Art of the Southern World: An Exhibition of Aboriginal Sound, Color, Texture, Theatre, Music, Dance, from* Australia, New Zealand, and the Torres Straight. The three women bounced through the exhibition, beaming, stopping to have private conversations with some of the artists whose work Elise had purchased over the years with her multitudinous collections that adorned her walls, both in Paris and in Greece.

The night was still young as they then got into the car and arrived at the dock where Elise's boat sat waiting. For several hours and into the wee moments of the morning, they dined and danced and watched the stars twinkling in the sky and in Paris all around as the river meandered slowly around them. They were a happy three, their faces glowing with light, with the magic that is Paris.

At ten in the morning, just a few hours later, Irene and Helena, their bags packed, hugged Elise goodbye, heading into the car that would take them back to Charles de Gaulle airport. As they hugged and kissed, they knew that a familial love had been unveiled.

They felt something sink inside of them, the notion of letting go of that which was no longer needed. Irene looked at Elise as they stepped into the car, one glance as the Parisian put a hand to her heart and winked, and then, with a subtle wince, she moved inside the apartment. As the smells of fresh bread wafted through the air along with the cacophony of Paris, the car took off and sped through the streets toward the airport.

Chapter Twenty

Several hours later, Helena and Irene opened the door to their Colorado home in the mountains. Welcome home signs greeted them everywhere, with fresh-picked flowers from the gardens, bouquets upon bouquets greeting them from every room.

Hand in hand, they visited every room in the house, taking it in, the flowers, the signs, and then each other, savoring the moment, this homecoming after having been married and then whisked away to France. Time changes and jet lag escaped them both for that moment as they grounded themselves in one other. Their final room to explore, all over again, was their bedroom, where they stripped off their traveling clothes and opened the window to the summer breezes as they made love, sweetly at first, and then, as if they were getting to know each other all over again, their passion took on an explosive state of wonder, the awe of fire, playing with it, suspending it, lingering in it, until the breath could not stand it any longer and each let themselves be consumed by their flames, entwining like the roots that bound them to each other, infinite threads of connection that only rested until the next surge of passion.

And then they slept like they had always meant to sleep, curved and wrapped around each other like twins, yet not.

Their days, were lazy as the end of summer lingered like a book that had no end.

Yet, as the days grew shorter and shorter, their lives sped up and soon they were to be back at work, Helena at meetings, and Irene at her computer preparing for teaching in Tasmania. In a week, she would return to Seattle for a few days to align her TAs in preparation for her month away. Then she and Helena would be Australia bound, and with only an airplane to guide them, they would be switching from one season to the next; from the end of summer to the beginnings of spring.

In the evenings, Irene and Helena stopped everything and held each other while the sun dipped down, earlier and earlier, as it prepared itself for the oncoming autumn.

They picked vegetables from the garden, rich and ripe, oozing with the summer's sun. And then Irene was off to Seattle. Helena, as she waved goodbye, looked as if her arms were made of lead.

Irene felt a pit in her belly as she entered her home, as she smelled her house and opened all the windows to let out the mustiness. In one season, life had completely turned itself around for her, and now all she wanted to do was to meet with the TAs over the next few days, attend a mandatory faculty meeting, pack her bag, and turn herself around, back to her life with Helena.

After those three work days, she went for a run through her old neighborhoods. For several hours in that late August balmy evening she ran, and as her feet hit the pavement over and over, she knew in her heart that this would be one of the last runs she would ever have in the city of Seattle. The next morning, as she locked up her house yet again, she felt, like Elise, a release of the past, a monumental part of her life that she was done with. Her steps were light; she almost danced to Sea-Tac, to the plane that waited for her to get back to her wife, her new life, her destiny.

When she walked up the drive and saw Helena standing at the edge of it, waiting for her, she dropped her bag and ran to her, arms reaching out and hugging her, held her, and without words, told her she was not going back to the life that she had once led.

The next morning, rested and energized, Irene and Helena were again on an airplane, again in business class, but this time there was a seriousness about them. Gone were the days of meeting and courtship, done was the wedding and the honeymoon. Now, they were to begin their lives together, whatever that meant, wherever it would take them. Now, they were off to springtime in Tasmania.

What they knew for sure was that for one month, Irene was going to teach and Helena was going to be in meetings. On the weekends, they would explore Tasmania, returning of course to their place where everything began.

PART FOUR: SPRING/FALL

Chapter Twenty-one

Snow met them at the airport in Hobart, a late winter dumping. They had heard that Tasmania got wild winters, storms that blew in from Antarctica with winds and snow that froze the earth and the bones, making the state all that more far away from its Australian sisters. While September first marked the first day of spring in other parts of the country, it often took weeks for it to arrive in Tasmania.

Irene and Helena felt like they had entered a refrigerator when they got off the plane. They had left the balmy, warm, late-summer air of their home, and their minds were quite befuddled from the jet lag.

"Brrr...It is much easier to go from winter to summer, than summer to winter," Irene said, her arms hosting an array of goose bumps, her thin shirt covering barely nothing.

"I think we will need to go and find us some winter coats." Helena chuckled. Irene could see that she, too, was hosting an array of bumps on the skin. They got their luggage and taxied to their new home, a lovely one-bedroom, rather quirky, cottage in Sandy Bay, with a voluptuous overgrown garden and a deck overlooking the water. There was even a car that the university had loaned them, sitting in the garage, an immaculate specimen of a vehicle.

The place had a nice feel to it with artwork from around the globe displayed on the walls, and it had an eclectic energy that seemed like the old-world intellectualism had met the wildness and the idiosyncrasy of Tasmania. The ceilings were supported by old-growth timber, giving it a fairy-tale-like quality, a sense of enchantment.

Helena looked around and announced, "You know, I can't help but feel that this place makes me feel like the home my grandparents lived in. When they first arrived from London, I know they lived in a bohemian-styled artist cottage in a neighborhood by the sea. I remember she described it to me, and it sounded exactly like this. What do you want to bet that she lived right here in the home we are standing in?"

Irene giggled, imagining the idea.

"Maybe the only reason you met me was to get back to your roots."

Helena looked at Irene and shook her head.

"Sometimes, darling, you say these abrupt things that are so true."

"No, I'm not the subtle one, am I?"

Shivering in the cold house, Irene took Helena by the hand and led her to the very comfortable-looking bed.

"You have a job to do," she announced with her eyes twinkling. "You need to warm me up."

"Oh, do I?" Helena responded, beginning to kiss her neck as they lay fully clothed under the sheets.

The smells of a new home mixed with their own familiar smells as clothes got taken off, one layer at a time, their nakedness oblivious to winter, spring, summer, and fall, their own heat exploding in that bed as noisy birds outside announced the happenings of the day.

Twelve hours later, their eyes opened to a brilliant

sunny afternoon, yesterday's snow only in their memories. A cacophony of birds sounded outside, like a Mahler symphony, robust musical phrases that could only be announcing one thing: the beginning of spring.

Irene and Helena bounded out of bed, energized, happy, and they looked out at the garden that looked like a mélange of growth had happened overnight. Yesterday's naked vines showed their tiny buds, and spring bulb flowers had popped up out of the ground, ready for their upcoming show. As they stepped outside they could feel growth happening, smelling it as they breathed in, collecting new life in their nostrils.

Starving for food and for spring, they jumped in the car and sped off. They found the Salamander Market and dove into the abundance of fresh food choices. Gathering yogurts, coffee and picnic items, they again, with mercury under their feet, bounded back to the car and headed away from the CBD and the suburbs onto the highway.

Within minutes, they fell in love all over again with Tasmania, the wildness of it all, the undisturbed climate of an untroubled land, housing nature in its unbridled display of beauty. For the entire day, they drove and parked and ate and made love and drove and sat and watched and listened and felt something around them that brought back the memories of when they met, but also something more that they hadn't discovered then that they couldn't put their finger on.

"This is the world that is us," Irene announced as she looked out at the cascading cliffs dropping magnificently, dramatically into the sea. Helena nodded and kissed her then, the two realizing what it was that they both felt, this world, this landscape, the friendliness of the people, the progressive attitudes toward life and living, the interdependence between human and nature, passion ruling and spreading its wings everywhere, invigorating all.

"This is truly the world that is us," Helena murmured, repeating Irene's words as she unbuttoned Irene's blouse, their lips together, fondness enveloping them while the clouds quickly gathered, darkening the sky, and in seconds, raindrops plopped delicately on them, the cold taking over again, making them laugh and run back to the car.

☙ ☙ ☙ ☙

Life took on a feeling of normalcy after that. Irene went to work at the university, and Helena took the plane to Swansea and worked from there. On weekends, they would meet back in Hobart, exploring each other and the many cafes, the roads and trails that surrounded them.

One of those weekends, lying in bed late in the morning, Helena stroked Irene's hair and looked out at the garden.

"You know, I really do dislike Monday mornings, leaving you. There is always a pit in my belly, a feeling that this is not supposed to happen, this leaving-you thing."

Irene laughed. "I know. Me, too. I feel it the same way."

"You know, though, after it's over—the departure—it's okay. I get into my routine, and then I get excited about what I am doing. I just love these farmers here. They are so unpretentious, so kind, and open to discussion about changes and new developments in the yogurt-making business. Sometimes I feel so ridiculous, making yogurt. It seems so banal in the world. But then I step back and see that I am making more than yogurt. And while I have this project and that project all over the world, when I am with the farmers here in Tasmania, I feel this connection to the earth in an entirely different way. Being here gets me out of my head. It's like being in the mountains in Colorado, but here, there are people to connect with. And—you know me—I feel so shy usually around people, but here, for some reason, I don't."

She paused as Irene rolled her fingers through the locks of her hair.

"Something vast and huge is shifting inside of me, darling. I can't quite put my finger on it, it feels rather intangible. But I feel it, a settled feeling, a world that fits somehow with who I am. I feel contented. Truly. It's simple, yet it flows deeply inside of me. It's you, Irene."

"What do you mean?"

"It's us."

Irene looked at Helena, waiting for more.

Helena sighed.

"Ah, I'm not great with words."

"Don't let that stop you. Go on. What do you mean, it's me?"

"It's love. It's you. It's that feeling of being so full of something you have been starved for, and now you're not. And you know it. You know you will never be starving again."

Helena was crying then, the tears huge and wet, splattering all over, down her cheeks.

"Ah," she continued. "We can always count our losses, the huge ones, the ones that have made us the hungry monsters we have become. My mother, running away—I'll never forget those times where she looked at me with disgust in her eyes. We bury this stuff, you know, and then we wonder later why there is this emptiness inside of us, why we need to run away to the mountains to be far away from people."

The tears were voluminous then, streaming down her face. Irene put her arms around her and held her as they both cried, both letting out, both letting go.

Then there was quiet, the birds outside singing imperviously.

"I could say the same about you," Irene said in a quiet voice.

Helena stroked Irene's hair, the two women tenderly caring for the other's vulnerable heart.

"Automatic pilot was how I survived, before you. I suppose humans can all survive like this, but what is the quality of life? Now I understand why my mom disappeared emotionally after my dad died. She was so in love with him, and when he left, that piece never got replaced in her heart. There is something that happens in the heart when you find the one that is supposed to be there. I never knew until now. It opens, and there is the breath of the heart that beats like it's supposed to, with love."

As she spoke, Irene's hands did a kind of dance on Helena's skin, then in the air, like a bird in flight. There was levity, a lightness of being, a connectedness to yes, something that flowed deeply inside of her as she spoke, as she held Helena, as Helena sighed in her arms, as they made love afterward, their bodies entwined, their hearts completely met.

꧁ ꧁ ꧁ ꧁

Irene loved her teaching at the University of Tasmania and found a niche there amongst the eclectic mixture of students and faculty members. Every day in those first few weeks she was observed, and every day she was learning thrilling new information about Aboriginal music and stories and rhythms that she wove into her teaching. There was a vibrant history in the Aboriginal culture that she resonated with, and it brought her back to her Middle Eastern roots, the stories her grandmother would tell her about their origins, spanning centuries. When music connected a people, she felt, there was something in that population that corresponded with a soulfulness in their very being. The rhythms that she was learning, the deep guttural sounds of the digeridoo began to weave into her consciousness, into her unconscious self in her sleep, and they emerged in a soulfulness in her teaching. She saw it in her students' faces, this depth, this freedom from a certain kind of enslavement.

At the end of the second week, she was called in by the president and chancellor of the university, a graying woman who was half Aboriginal and half French.

"We have been scrupulous in our observations of you, Irene, these past few weeks, and never in the history of this university, except for a professor of English, years and years ago, never have we found such exemplary teaching such as yours." Lucille was beaming. Irene met her smile with her own, shyness taking over her face.

"We would like to offer you," she continued, "the position of Operating Director of our new Institute for Global Music in Swansea, a state-of-the-art campus that has sweeping views of the ocean and has a mission to provide students from all over the world a place to learn about and to blend music from all the cultures of the globe. We at the university have seen your work, glimpses of it, and we feel you would be the perfect person to lead our new program to international esteem." She paused and looked at Irene, whose eyes were moistened, holding back the flood of tears.

"If you agree, the contract would begin on the first of the year. I can email you the detailed job description for you to look over, and of course a contract for you to sign. We would consider you a tenured faculty member."

Irene had no words to express her feelings. It was one of those moments when everything in one's entire life was put on the table, all the joys and all the tragedies and everything else in between; one of those moments when all the pieces to everything one had worked on fit together, and the tide was coming one's way, gently, water cascading over the feet, lapping at the ankles, and it was all one could do but to go to one's knees and sink into the sun-warmed sand, kissing it, the earth, God, the forces of nature, of life, of one's own life and mostly of love, that permeable life-giving substance that held everything together.

With tears now freely flowing down her face, she could have kissed the feet of the woman who was offering her this position. She instead got up and hugged her, her arms weaving around her small frame, gratitude expressed in this hug, in this poignant moment of acknowledgment.

Irene let go, pulled out her tissues, and wiped her eyes.

"I guess that means yes, you'll accept our offer," Lucille said, laughing.

"Yes. Yes. I need of course to talk about it with my wife, but I know she will be dancing with me tonight,

Champagne glass in hand."

And with one final hug, Irene stepped toward the door. "By the way," she asked, "Who, if you don't mind me asking, was the English professor you were referring to?"

"Hillary Hanover."

Irene beamed and chuckled as she left the office of the president, dancing down the hallway to the music that was floating in her head, a mixture of djembes and a Straus waltz.

❧ ❧ ❧ ❧

At 5:00 p.m., Helena walked in the door. There were candles everywhere. The cottage looked like it was having a party. She smiled. From the backyard, spring flowers filling her arms, Irene emerged, giddy and light, ready to float up into the air at any moment. She hummed to herself as she put the flowers in water, as Helena stared at her.

"You better tell me the news right this minute before I take you into the bed."

"Oh, that wouldn't be so bad."

"Tell me. You've got to tell me, Irene, before I lunge at you."

She giggled.

Helena got closer, took the flowers in their vase and moved them aside as she leaned into her, and whispered, kissing her neck, her earlobes, and back to her neck, "So, what is your news?"

Irene moaned, her knees weak, her moans getting louder as Helena continued to kiss her, carrying her to the bed, undressing her, as they moved quickly, furiously, in need of the other.

Locked into each other's arms, hours later, Irene

murmured, "So, how would you like to live in Swansea starting in January?"

"Hmm?" Helena murmured back, her arms stroking the softness of Irene.

"I was offered a job, to be the head of the new Institute for Global Music in Swansea, part of the university. The president of the university, Lucille— you remember her—asked me to her office, and she said they liked my teaching so much they offered me a tenured faculty position."

Then the tears truly flowed, Helena's arms tightly woven around Irene, holding her as Irene released all her feelings, that moment where everything fits and then, feeling held and loved, where it was safe to let go, acknowledging this huge happening in her life, one that was altogether quite real and utterly amazing.

"Oh, my darling. Oh, my darling," Helena repeated over and over as Irene continued crying, this moment so huge. When the tears subsided, Helena recreated Irene's words. "The world that is us...is right here in Tasmania. They see your brilliance, they know. They knew we both belong here, you and I, and right down the road is our Freycinet Peninsula."

"And you?"

"It's perfect. I have always wanted to live here. And now, it is my dream truly coming true with you, together."

They pulled out the Champagne, and they toasted: to Irene's fabulous new job, to their love, their new life; and they danced and kissed and made love everywhere in that tiny cottage as Champagne swirled around their tongues, their bodies, their openings into their own world of the divine.

Chapter Twenty-two

The following weekend they spent in Sydney, where Irene attended the National Music Conference. On Saturday night, they had tickets to see Vladimir Ashkenazy conduct Beethoven's Ninth at the Sydney Opera House. They entered the grand space and Helena stared at the magnificence of the acoustically perfect concert hall. "This is the building my mother helped to inseminate." She paused as she gripped Irene's hand, the concert starting. Irene sat, transfixed, absorbed completely in this work of genius. Ashkenazy's conducting brought out the magnificence of this symphony. She had always wanted to hear a concert of this magnitude in this concert hall, where the acoustics soared to limitless heights, each note and each phrase transcending the instruments and the voices so that one felt that one was transported into a different realm entirely of the human existence. Irene clutched Helena's hand as together they felt the music pour through them, the aches of humankind juxtaposed with his concluding movement, the illustrious "Ode to Joy."

"And all was composed when he was entirely deaf," Irene said as the audience rose to their feet and applauded for nearly thirty minutes afterward.

As the applause waned, a lesbian couple sitting next to them glanced over and smiled, introducing themselves. "Amazing concert, wasn't it? Jayna and

Leslie, pleased to meet you," they said, together, as the four shook hands. "Do you live here in Sydney?"

Helena and Irene briefly told them their story.

"Hey, we'd love to go out for a drink and get to know you. We could tell you are music lovers and so are we, but we must rush home to relieve the babysitter. How about we give you our phone number and when you are settled in Swansea, give us a ring. We have a home out there, and it would be great to meet up when we are there, or when you are back in Sydney."

As the Aussies left quickly, Irene and Helena smiled. "New friends already. Wow. That makes me so happy."

"They seemed so nice," Irene added. "One of those gold kinds of friends, where the minute you meet them, you know they will be friends for life."

"Absolutely."

⁂

"So, my darling one, wonderful wife of mine," Helena whispered, taking off Irene's clothes, piece by piece, and kissing each body part she could find. "What if, next weekend, we look for a home to buy, a forever home?"

"Yes," Irene murmured, pulling Helena into her, finding her lips. "Yes, yes, yes."

Their passion merged into sleep, and the next day blended into the following, and the next day preceded the next. Soon, it was Friday, and Irene was on the plane to Swansea.

After dinner, they sat down at the computer, and looked at the house listings.

It had been fifteen years since Irene had done

this. When she bought her home on Capitol Hill, she had a vague sense of what she wanted and the third home she looked at, she knew that was it.

"I've never looked for my own home," Helena announced wistfully. "My home was my parents', and it's been the assumption that I would never leave it."

"Kind of like assuming one will never grow up, never change."

Helena sighed.

"Again, darling, you hit the nail and *ow* follows."

"Sorry."

"Oh, no. Never be."

A minuscule laugh followed, a transition, mostly, as the two perused the available homes.

"A home we will choose together, an *our* home. Now, *that* is a dream come true," Helena said, grabbing Irene and kissing her.

In bed that night as they held each other, Helena asked, "Are you ready to sell what you have had for fifteen years?"

"I am as ready to sell that home as I was to marry you. That home was important for me, and now, it is not. When I sell it, which I probably will in one weekend, I know I won't even be sad. It's that moving-to-another-stage-of-life feeling, like maybe a child has when it learns to walk, and it never wants to not walk again." Irene sank into Helena after saying this, feeling her arms around her, knowing that there was no other place on this planet she wanted to be.

"I know it's a bit different for you," she continued, "as you are not selling your home, and it will be your place to go to when you need to be back on the farm, or when we go together. But how is it for you to be considering a forever home that is not in your

Colorado?"

Helena dipped into the question and pondered. "I have been thinking about this, and actually, that while 'my Colorado,' as you say, I will be mostly leaving, I have dreamed about living here in Tasmania since I was a little girl. And I have dreamed about living here, not alone, but with the person I will love forever. It's funny, but it just fits so perfectly. It's kind of like watching a movie and you just want the couple who love each other so fiercely to let that love soar, and to let their dreams of being together happen. I'm simple that way, and I know, a bit corny, but sometimes in life simplicity is just the best thing in the world."

Irene rolled over and leaned into Helena, their bodies caressing each other. "I love that about you, your simplicity." Helena grabbed the softness of Irene's buttocks, her hand stroking it, its roundness. "I love... I just love the depth of you, the mysteriousness that I keep discovering. It's like you found me in absolutely exactly the right place, and I know I will hunger for you always, your intricacies, your brilliance, your beauty that stuns me to a place where there are no words."

"There's a mountain in you, Helena," Irene said, pressing into her farther, their lips touching. "You are the earth to me." Helena grabbed her buttocks tighter, pulling Irene in as their emblazoned lips became the fire that moved the mountain. It appeared that Helena couldn't get enough of Irene as Irene let her devour her, rolling around in that bed like the waves in a Tasmanian winter storm, untamed, their wildness calling to them over and over.

❧ ❧ ❧ ❧

The first home they saw the next day was it. It was an older home, with an architect's creative brilliance displayed in all its subtlety. When they walked in, they felt immediately at peace, inspired, and enchanted by the intricate woodwork, the beamed ceilings, the private nooks, the beveled glass. The kitchen had been carefully remodeled with all new appliances. The upstairs master bedroom had a sweeping view of the ocean, the greens and blues outlining the reddened sheer cliffs that surrounded all. The front garden was a magical oasis of an earthly wildness that Irene longed to dig into, with trees and ponds and flower-lined paths that sent out an invitation to curiosity. In the back, there was ample room for raised beds, and a southern sun exposure that graced all. They looked at the realtor, who looked at them with a seasoned expression that said she knew when a house had touched a buyer.

They made an offer.

Two hours later, as they were sitting on the beach, the same one where they first found each other, where they each knew, one to the other, that their futures were forever changed, that their love would effortlessly intertwine; the phone rang. Helena almost did not take the call as her hands were busy, finding Irene all over again. It was Irene who insisted, between her moans, that Helena stop and take the call.

They got the house. The realtor told them that never, in her thirty years of doing this business, had she sold a house in just two hours. She said she had such a strong feeling that they were the ones who were supposed to be living in that beautiful home, and when she told the owners this, they listened to her. The owners were her closest friends and they trusted her implicitly. It was agreed upon that they could move in any time after the fifteenth of December.

Helena hung up the phone and shouted to the seals nearby. Irene danced around her, her long hair swept away by the spring breezes, flying like her body that worked its way around Helena. They swung each other around and around, like whirling dervishes, their laughter and their kisses mixing with the sounds of the seals, asking for an encore. The rain fell, huge drops as the two continued their dance, letting the freezing water bathe them in their frenzied joy. When they were completely soaked, still kissing, wanting only their lips entwined, they quickly picked up their picnic things and ran to the car. Laughing, they drove back to their rented cottage and stripped off their drenched clothes and soaked in a hot bath, letting the warmth surround their lovemaking that continued well into that Saturday night, in the soft bed that let anything happen.

Chapter Twenty-three

Irene turned the key to her front door, the familiar key she had turned over and over for the past fifteen years. It was still home, and she dumped her things on the floor and went immediately to her bed. She was exhausted.

After finding her home—her forever home with Helena—that last week had been hard for her. She felt herself in an in-between place: in between jobs and homes and hemispheres and seasons. When she left Hobart, spring had taken her by the wings and created for her endless blossoms, openings, new beginnings. Now, almost twenty-four hours later but still on the same day, she arrived in Seattle where the bitter cold hit her neck, and leaves, ripped off trees, swirled around her. Power outages were reported everywhere from the early autumn storm that dizzied itself around the Puget Sound, making her house as dark as night when it wasn't yet night. Her plane made a layover in Denver, and when she said goodbye to Helena, feeling their eyes lock, not wanting to let go, her heart did somersaults, and she felt nauseous and thrown apart. Her mind knew this was temporary. They had gone over the plan. Helena would come the following weekend for Bob and Harry's wedding. The next weekend she would fly to Boulder while there was an open house with the realtor. Then, two weekends later, Helena would come to Seattle to help Irene pack up and ship boxes to Australia. That got her through October. Still, though, she felt her life squirm around her as her plane took off, leaving Helena, and soared into the air, back to the life that, in her heart, she had already left.

Her house was freezing. Her electric baseboard heater was non-functional, and she had zero energy to make a fire in the living room. She pulled out comforters and blankets and still more comforters and huddled in her bed until sleep finally took her away into the unblemished world of her dreams.

The next morning when she woke up the storm was still lingering, the power was still out, jet lag hung on her like an out-of-shape bra, and she had to be teaching her first class of the day in less than an hour. She had no idea what clothes she had thrown on, but something was indeed on her body as she raced out of the house, grabbed a cup of coffee from the café across the street, and took a Lyft to work.

Her students sat ravenously, joyously awaiting her return. She smiled, her warmth filling the space between her and them. In her smile, she realized she had no idea what she would be talking about that day.

She laughed as she began, always with a sense of grace and style. "Yesterday was spring for me, and today it is autumn. How fluid the seasons are, with just an airplane to transport one from one to another." Everyone laughed. They just loved her.

"Glad you're back," someone yelled out from the back.

"Nice to be back. It's rather befuddling to change seasons just like that, but it's good to be back."

She meant that. It was, after all, good to be back. She had forgotten that even when one has begun to say goodbye, the place where one is from will always be sacred in the heart, will always hold that magical place that grounds a soul, making it thrive.

"But the fact is, my dear students, we are all here now, and autumn is lashing out its fury outside. Some of you may have lost power. I did. It's Puget Sound Energy's wrath on humans in a blemished world."

Again, laughter.

"Let's go to the musical literature. What has been written and composed in honor and in celebration of autumn?

"Of course, we begin with Vivaldi, probably the most well-known. Here we are, in the midst of themes of the harvest, wine and ale overflowing that is juxtaposed with an inward melancholy, a folding in of the earth and a loosening of the skin, the leaves, falling and disappearing under the ground. The poem that inspired his autumn concerto:

'*The cup of Bacchus flows freely, and many find their relief in deep slumber.*

The singing and the dancing die away as cooling breezes fan the pleasant air, inviting all to sleep without a care.'

"While Vivaldi composed his concerto with the theme of the hunt, other composers have surged in the realms of a haunting beauty of this time of melancholy. Let's listen to Hillary Hahn's version of the Barber violin concerto, that is for me the epitome of this inward beauty that is ascribed to the season of autumn.

"And then, the element of wind and rain that is so present in the autumn, especially here in the Northwest where the rain doesn't seem to stop, in John

Adams's 'Shaker Loops.' In the violins, we can feel the leaves rustling in the wind, the rain falling.

"Here is another version of fall, a not very well-known Finnish composer by the name of Rautavaaara, a piece named 'Autumn Gardens.' You can feel the darkened shadows here. Listen, and imagine Finland, even farther north than where we are, and how darkness plays an important part in the topography and the psychology of the land and of course, the music.

"In the last century, George Winston was indeed at the forefront of evoking music that created a feeling, a mood. He composed an entire album called *Autumn*, titling his sections 'woods, longing, love, colors, dance, moon, sea, stars.' Let's listen and see if you can get a true taste of autumn from his music.

"From there, and finally, let's go to the soundtrack of the film, *The Village*. Again, we hear such rich haunting sounds, the music, in the strings, just makes you feel like running in the cold... Listen and feel the music, let it sink into you, too."

Irene paused after the last piece, which sank into everyone's core and left them speechless. As she observed that some students were crying, she imagined that they might be thinking of people they knew who died, some were imagining making love, and still others were visualizing being in that moment, standing in the rain, in a barren field, letting themselves get entirely soaked.

"Go home, my dear students. Feel the autumn enter you, listen to all this music again, and write a minimum five-page piece about one of them, or maybe two, interlocking the themes."

The class, for the first time, walked out silently into the rain, feeling the intensity of music. As they wrapped their scarves tighter around their necks, if even they had scarves, as they walked into the wind that whipped around every corner of campus, Irene hoped each of those students felt immune somehow to the cold, to the autumn's melancholic curse. She dearly hoped they felt happy, each of them, in their own ways, as some of them skipped through puddles, as others kicked leaves that fell around them, watching them dance, remembering the violin and its melodious resonance, reminding them of the beauty of it all.

❧ ❧ ❧ ❧

Helena looked out at her cows who came trotting like horses toward her, nuzzling her shoulder, licking her face. They had missed her. As she stroked each of them, making cooing sounds, she listened to the quiet of the mountain on that crisp autumn morning. She felt the leaves shimmering around her, dazzling bursts of gold that tumbled this way and that around her, feeding the blue sky as they flew upwards like birds.

She felt transported between two worlds: the one she was in now, her mountain home, where her solitary nature was perfectly met by her cows, where the pristine and quiet of her land surrounded her with an impeccability; and then, the one she was heading toward, the one of a wild and untamed nature, of land untended, a marriage that exploded with an unending passion, a hunger in her that, even just thinking about it, made her wet with desire. Somehow, though, these two divergent worlds created an infinite balance for her, one which filled each gaping hole with gold. She felt full. She knew she needed both to survive. She knew she couldn't sell this home—ever—that it was her place to come back to whenever she wanted to, with or without Irene. She also knew that Irene knew this about her, that she needed her land, her mountains, as much as she needed her. And she loved Irene even more, knowing that there was no jealousy, not even one tiny bit. There was an implicit trust between them, something she had never experienced with anyone she had ever truly loved. There was no reason not to trust each other. Thinking about this, her heart glowed, and she felt a warmth fill her, a love that she had never known in herself. As the wind picked up and the blue sky quickly turned gray, raindrops falling swiftly around her, she wiped away her tears, ones of a sweet feeling of happiness, a newness in her life that made her want to dance to the moon and back. Instead, she stood there crying, feeling all of it swirl around her, as she watched her cows amble away, grazing in the last of the summer's grass.

Chapter Twenty-four

With this ring, I do thee wed," Bob pronounced, his teary eyes fixed on Harry's with an expression of devotion. His tuxedo fit him perfectly and accentuated his roundness, his bigness, and his sex, which swelled as he cried. Irene was happy to see that Bob's lust for Harry would not disappear with their vows.

The rabbi stood back and watched, letting the two marry themselves. That was what they wanted.

"You are everything I ever wanted," Harry responded, his eyes glowing like fire, his flowing cloak draped seductively around his ankles. He was dressed like a pagan monk and wore a Star of David around his neck. Irene chuckled to herself, grateful that Bob had chosen a man who not only loved him deeply, but who also would not let the romance and sex fizzle out.

"*Siman Tov and Mazel Tov. Siman Tov and Mazel Tov.*" The rabbi chanted and circled around them as the rest of the congregation sang, Bob and Harry standing in the middle, holding hands, staring into each other's eyes, as everyone around them clapped in rhythm. First Bob, and then Harry put a gold ring around the other's finger, and then Irene came up and gave them the crystal glass that was wrapped in a fine silk cloth, one that Harry's parents and grandparents—and their parents and grandparents—had used when they married. Together, husband and husband, they stepped down hard on the glass as shouts of joy erupted around them. They then embraced, their big bodies wrapped around each other like bears as they kissed, not at all tenderly, but with a ferociousness that made everyone laugh.

Then came the chairs, two of them, and huge men held the eight legs as Harry sat on one of them, and Bob on the other, tottering, as the chair holders wove their way around the tree, a ginkgo in fiery yellow, October's finest display of majesty. Everyone clapped, singing *Hava Nagila,* dancing around them, weaving around their elevated bodies until it was time to put them down.

With one last embrace and a fiery kiss, the wedding was over. Harry and Bob signed the ketubah as the guests filtered toward the reception, food and drink overflowing in magnanimous amounts.

Music resounded around them, a mixture of klezmer and jazz and, of course, early music before 1600. Bob had found a group that could play every style of music in the books, and with their own improv, they made up the rest. The day was perfect, the early October crispness that warmed the earth as the afternoon progressed. The blue sky on that October 8 was a brilliant backdrop to the trees at the arboretum, a mélange of yellows and oranges and reds. Bob had told Harry that he always wanted to get married under a yellow and crimson canopy of leaves, and his wishes were granted.

The couple joined Irene and Helena, embracing them.

"So now it's your turn to have the most beautiful wedding that ever existed." Irene laughed, kissing Bob and Harry on the cheek. "Congratulations, darlings.

At one point there, I thought we would be listening to orgasms while everyone else was chanting in Hebrew."

Bob and Harry laughed like two lions, caught.

"So, what's this Tasmania thing, honey?" Harry added, looking sad. "You're leaving us."

"We're never leaving you. In fact, you do have plans to come to Australia often, don't you?"

Harry looked at Bob, and Helena looked at the two with an expectant gaze.

"If looks could kill. I hadn't thought about it. I might die of fright knowing Tasmanian devils are lurking," Bob said, laughing.

"Maybe we'll meet you in Colorado, your second home," Harry said.

"Deal." Helena winked.

"Hey, what about a reunion in Vancouver? November? Just the four of us," Irene added.

"Perfect. Love it. Vancouver Cultural Crawl? When the entire city opens their studios, end of November."

"It's a date," Irene stated, beaming. "Now go to your guests. Look at them, they are staring at you, wanting your attention."

With huge hugs, warmth exuding from four hearts, the big married men walked away, holding hands like little boys off to play.

Eating music turned to dance music as plates emptied and drinks continued to flow. Irene and Helena joined the circle dances, quickly learning the grapevine step that held the dancers together, weaving in and out of the circle as the accordion, the clarinet, and the fiddle played tunes that brought everyone back hundreds of years, to a time where men could only marry women. For the first couple of dances of the late afternoon, Harry and Bob took each other by the arms, holding each other close as everyone around them beamed and felt the normalcy of this, this beautiful expression of love.

After the sweetheart dance, the dance floor opened to anyone. Irene and Helena folded into the other, remembering their own wedding just two months before. They kissed and felt their skin touching, their bodies moving to the music, letting the heat between them grow with each cadence. It had been hard this past week being away from each other, and as they danced their bodies spoke of this, their longings, and yet also their contentment as they felt each other's rings, stroking them, sighing, as they smiled and let their feet move gracefully around the other, the softened autumn breezes caressing their skin.

※ ※ ※ ※

Irene locked the door and waited at the curb for the Lyft to take her to the airport. Her stomach was in knots that morning, yet she felt a breeze running through her brain, as if a window had opened and the curtains fluttered around her, freeing her. She had loved this house, and as she'd prepared this past week for the open house that weekend, she went through each room and reminisced. She remembered the day she bought it, when she had first been offered the teaching position at UW. She had fallen in love with it, its charm, its ability to hold her at the end of her day. She loved the garden where she had spent many an hour planting, weeding, watching life grow before her eyes. She loved the neighborhood, its diversity, its color, people living and accepting others for who they are. She remembered her readings of Buddhist non-attachment, not sure if she agreed with them entirely, but what she did know was that she had been extremely attached to this home, and as she waited at the curb that day, she realized that this attachment was no longer there. She had let go of this house, in her mind, and she had moved on. Selling it felt like the natural next step, as in taking an exhale after one had inhaled.

Later the next day, napping in Helena's arms as the chilly October mountain air filled their lungs, her cell phone rang.

They had received dozens of offers on the house, just an hour after the open house had ended. It was currently a seller's market, and the demand for Capitol Hill homes was huge. One of the offers was for double the amount listed, reaching more than $2 million.

"That's insanity," Irene exclaimed to the realtor. "So, tell me a bit about these prospective buyers."

"Well, they are a young couple, and they fell in love instantly with your home. She is a landscape gardener, and he is a new hire in the Islamic Studies department at UW, Harvard grad. She is very pregnant, thought that maybe she would be giving birth in your home during the open house. Gorgeous couple, and he is total eye candy," the realtor said, laughing.

"Amazing. What are their names?"

"Reza and Layla Majidi."

Iranian, Irene thought to herself as she smiled.

"I say we accept the offer."

"Sounds perfect. I will phone them straight away. To confirm, it will be available after the twentieth of December?"

"Yes, I finish the term on the fifteenth. I'll move out on the seventeenth and the cleaners will be here on the eighteenth, so, let's say the nineteenth it will be available."

"Lovely. And congratulations. That was the quickest sale I have ever made."

Irene had déjà vu, recalling that the realtor in Tasmania had said the same thing.

"Let's check in this week," the realtor added.

"Indeed. And thank you. Really."

"I have to say, Irene, that it really was an easy one. Wish there were more homes like yours."

Irene put the phone on the bed and crawled on top of Helena, kissing her like a puppy.

"Did you hear?"

"Yeah, I did. Amazing, huh?"

"Good thing I remembered to put away my dirty laundry before I left the house."

They both laughed, familiar with Irene's habit of forgetting dirty clothes, littering dusty corners.

"Congratulations are in order," Helena whispered in Irene's ear, rolling her over, straddling her as she moved her kisses along her neck, returning to her lips.

After making love and cuddling under the covers, not wanting to think about that in-between place she was in, her house almost gone, and their new one not yet ready, Irene blurted out, "Okay. Tell me something I don't know about you."

Helena laughed. "I don't think there is one single thing." She paused, laughed again, "What on earth made you think of that just now?"

Irene laughed. "My mind, it's weird that way, things just pop in."

"Your way of changing the subject, from selling the house, and we're not ready to move in to the new one, and you must go back to teach tomorrow, it's getting colder and colder, and we have to leave each other again?"

"Bingo." They both laughed, kissing each other.

"Okay, out of fairness, though, I will attempt to answer your question, if you do the same for me. Tit for tat."

"Fair enough."

They both were quiet, thinking hard.

"Okay, I have something," Helena began. "I have been to Africa."

"You have?" Irene asked. "I didn't know that."

"Well, you wanted me to tell you something you didn't know."

"Tell me all about it."

"I was little. I don't remember much. In fact, I didn't remember until just now. It was my dad's idea to go on a safari, and to have me see animals that I was in love with from my bedtime stories. And I don't remember the animals except that in the night, a big snake came into my room in the lodge we were staying in, and slithered on the bed, waking me. I didn't scream, but I looked at it in the eyes, and I felt like it was my sister. I had always wanted a sister. I was kind of a lonely kid. It was strange, but it felt like my twin. Later, I described the snake to the guy who ran the place, and he said that snake could have easily killed me. I never once felt that snake could have done anything to harm me. Just like that snake on the mountain, when you were asleep, this one just slithered away, as if we both had gotten something very big from that encounter, and then it parted before anyone woke up and scared it away...." Helena paused, seemingly remembering that moment as if it just had happened.

Minutes later, after they both pondered that

story, Irene said, "A snake lay on my belly once."

Helena looked at her, waiting.

"It was in a yoga workshop I went to in the Poconos. I was pregnant then. Barely. The workshop leader had a boa in her private cottage. I was mesmerized by it, but she said she rarely took it out during workshops. I begged her to. So, one day, after a rich morning of intensive yoga and meditation, there in the sun, I lay on the deck on my back, eyes closed. I was feeling so at peace, happy to be alive, happy to have a baby growing in me. She placed the snake next to me, carefully watching. I sensed the snake was taking me in, its tongue tasting the air I was breathing. Then, it slithered next to me, laying on top of my belly as I sighed and purred. I have never once felt so in love with an animal. I loved the way it felt on my skin, and I loved the being-ness we shared for those few moments until it slipped away..." Irene's voice trailed off, disappearing into the folds of her memories.

They both were silent then, as their hands took the form of a snake, quietly, sensuously caressing the other as their moans slithered around them, in them, their tongues dancing inside the other like a snake's, in and out, tasting the sweetness of the other. When they came together, deliciously, they felt connected by this serpent energy, the power, the mysticism, and the slipperiness bonding them, always deeper, into the folds of their existence, two snake women finding each other all over again.

Chapter Twenty-five

The middle of October in Seattle, while technically falling under the category of autumn, begins its early descent into the throes of winter. Gray skies follow gray skies, and rain follows rain. Leaves, once pubescent in their vibrancy for life, fall mercilessly to the ground, and the bare nakedness of trees erupts, sometimes all in a night if there is ample wind. The cold and damp sink into the skin, into the walls, and gardens become obliterated by a sea of dead brown leaves.

On one of those days that blended into each other, Irene began a run after work. It was a Monday, and that weekend Helena had flown in. For two solid days they packed boxes, Irene's entire life put into brown cartons that they shipped off to 86, Road of the Phoenix, 7190 Swansea Tasmania. Irene would miss her furniture, but to avoid exorbitant shipping costs, they limited themselves to only what would fit in a cardboard box. The rest she would donate. The night before, after Helena left, Irene was surrounded by a shell of a home, a kitchen that held only the bare essentials: one coffee mug, one plate, one bowl, and a spoon, fork, and knife. In her bedroom, she had just a few clothes, her oldest, flimsiest blankets and sheets, and towels. They had laughed themselves through the packing as the storm outside brewed insipidly, the power flicking on and off throughout the weekend.

In the middle of kissing, they fell asleep, their bodies wrecked with exhaustion. Conversation was entirely deadened as they flitted through Irene's house like birds, wings in eternal motion, collecting items for their nest, so very far away.

As Irene ran, the unusually dry, warm wind whipped through her, her body in motion, her exhaustion propelling her through the streets, one street at a time, as she only felt her feet on the pavement, hammering turning to lightened steps, as if she could fly. The more she ran, the lighter she felt, and the wind became only a balm to her tired self. When finally her feet approached her neighborhood, she smelled it before she saw it. Smoke billowed out into the sky as sirens blazed, their red lights flashing. Neighbors stood outside their homes, gawking, incredulous, as firefighters insisted they go inside.

The house next door to Irene's was burning to the ground.

An elderly couple had lived there for fifty years. Mabel and Bernie were the sweetest pair of two old birds, frail as anything, but still crazily in love. Bernie had Alzheimer's, and Mabel was beginning to lose her faculties. Their children came from time to time, but not often enough, and in the last visit, it was decided that before Thanksgiving they would both be sent to a care facility. This pronouncement made them furious. They loved their home; they had raised three children in it, had grown a fabulous garden, had entertained hundreds of guests, and they clung to this house with a ferocity that could not be matched.

As Irene approached a neighbor, he stated, nervousness in his voice, that he believed it was a kitchen fire. Ambulances arrived, but no bodies were taken out; the crowd of spectators assumed that they both had died in their home. From a distance, Irene watched the flames billowing out of the house. It would have been easy for the wild winds to change direction and consume her own home, just feet away from the one that was being eaten alive.

Dozens of firefighters amassed on that block. It seemed like the entire city of Seattle's firefighting crew was gathered that day to put out those flames, fighting nature's wrath, as smoke billowed everywhere, toxic fumes from every possible flammable substance that the couple had accumulated in their cluttered home and garage.

Irene closed her eyes and thought of Bernie and Mabel, the sweetness in their voices when she first moved in. She thought of all the pies Mabel baked and gave to the neighbors and to the homeless downtown. She thought of the affection the two shared, the sounds of their lovemaking on a summer's night, when all the windows were open. Her tears fell voluminously, like rain on a stormy day, large pools of water that accompanied her silent wailing.

As the smoke thickened, the police officers insisted that all neighbors retreat to their homes. Irene was ushered to a neighbor's down the street, where she stood on the second story for what seemed like hours, staring at her home, still standing, still protected from she didn't know what, as the wind gradually calmed, as the skies darkened, and as rain fell, tiny rivulets from the sky, descending.

It was 5:00 a.m., and finally the fire was pronounced controlled.

Neighbors emerged from their homes, approaching the blackened shell of a house that the last firefighters were still working on. Nothing remained but memories in people's minds, grief pouring out in a multitude of directions for the sweet couple who had died inside their beloved home just days before they would be forced to vacate it.

At around six, Irene hugged the last firefighters, thanking them profusely, as they packed up their hoses and drove away.

She walked inside her house, smelling smoke everywhere, the reminder of what had just been, and would be no longer. In the middle of the living room, in a home that was, for just a few more weeks, still hers, she bawled like a baby. Grief poured through her as well as survivor's guilt. She knew that with just a fleck of a breeze, her house could have been easily devoured.

Standing in the shower, she let the water absolve and dissolve, like the rain outside, letting all things go, fire and grief, endings and beginnings. She smiled as she imagined that old couple going off to a better place together; for all she knew, they had planned this whole thing together, holding hands as one of them lit the torch, whispering in each other's ears all the I love yous any couple that is in love for sixty years can whisper.

As she got dressed and got herself to campus, she forgot that she had not slept nor had eaten anything since lunch the day before. Mindlessly, she grabbed a yogurt at the corner store, and minutes later stood at the podium, to all the awaiting eyes. Once again, she had no idea what would come out of her mouth that day.

"The house next door to mine burned down last night. In it were my two lovely neighbors, an elderly couple, very much in love. Due to dementia, they were days away from being forced out of their home. As I watched the inferno erupt in front of my eyes, and as I grieved the couple, dying in their own home, as I watched the power of fire, I thought of music, the fire in music, the way sounds can not only mimic fire, but describe it—the crackling energy, the destructive forces within that ironically transform life to death and back again to life. I thought of Stravinsky's *Firebird Suite* and the 'Infernal Dance,' where monsters are filled with energy that transforms evil to good. I thought of how fire is itself a kind of music, a force that consumes, devours, indiscriminate in its hunger for destruction. Fire is loud—no one can talk over fire. Unlike rain and even wind, fire takes up combustible space, its music demanding and omnivorous. I want you all to close your eyes and conjure up music that makes you think of fire, or make music in your head that does this. Think of the instruments that would evoke this concept of fire."

After a few minutes of letting her students quietly evoke in their minds all that pertained to fire, she continued.

"Now, get into small groups, no more than five in a group, and create this music amongst yourselves. This may be in the form of composition, where someone is writing it down, or in the form of improvisation, but whatever form it is in, everyone gets to participate. I don't want to see one single student being left out. You can have a fire that never gets extinguished, or you can see transformation and an end to the fire. Your choice. All right, off you go."

Energized by this topic, the students quickly converged into small groups and talked and scatted and rapped and sputtered and sang and hummed and wrote down and did not write down their compositions.

At the end of class, they performed, not allowing a dry eye to remain in that room. They had gotten it, had captured the essence of fire and loss, Irene's loss, and loss in general of forces in society that consume and gratify at the expense of others, in fiery masses of contempt, destruction, and hatred. They connected fire to racism, to greed, to any -ism that perpetuated hatred. They connected fire to an uncontained energy, out of control. Some groups found balms to heal, to stop the fire, and some students let the fire rage, spewing out anger in the form of oppression and rage at feeling continually oppressed. The sounds that emerged from their throats was electric, primal, and one could feel the endless crackle of civilizations that have been killed and mutilated.

The music was trancelike and let everyone in that room feel connected to each other because of it. Their fire bonded one to the other, transforming them, letting the energy be wild, uncontained, and then, somehow in that space of the fire, there was a release, the letting go, the image of transcendence through fire.

And then the groups were done and quiet, reigned.

Class was over. The students wiped their eyes, some hugging Irene as they walked out into the rainy morning, shaken, yet at peace, music once again expressing and converging into the place of the sublime.

❧❧❧❧

Helena took her seat on the plane and looked out the window at the snow falling, a November first snow that blanketed the landscape, lightly dancing tufts of white painting the faded greens and browns of summer. She closed her eyes for a moment, realizing just how tired she was. She was excited about this trip to New York, planned for many months. Meetings had been arranged with global representatives at the United Nations, including members from UNICEF and the World Food Program. She would be meeting with people from Africa, the Middle East, and Asia, with her grant proposal to provide at no-cost, ongoing supplies of Tassiebaby, whose status on the world market had skyrocketed in the past few months since its launch into the market. The Bill and Melinda Gates Foundation was sponsoring her efforts, with encouragement and the resource-building support she needed.

As she closed her eyes, feeling the plane lift off from the runway, she saw her life swimming in front of her. Never in a million years had she fathomed that her passion for making yogurt, for living simply on a dairy farm, would produce such global acclaim. She had not grown up poor, but her family never had abundance. Now, her company was amassing close to a billion dollars in profits. The amount was staggering. She had never wanted to be rich. She wanted to have just enough and not more, just enough for her and for Irene. She, with her amazing business partners, had managed to steer the business toward a 25% profit base, giving the rest to global organizations and breast cancer research.

In just one year, she had met and married the woman of her dreams, had launched a product that had had immediate success, had bought a home, had hired an exceptional team to run the business while she was in Australia, and she was in the process of thinking about growing the business in Tasmania, focusing on exchanging product information with local yogurt makers, forming a cooperative organization to sell at home-grown local grocery stores in the state.

Her mind drifted toward sleep, her last thought focused on Irene, the softness in her eyes, her smile and her laugh that created music for Helena, a piece that she would always savor and crave. She smiled as sleep took her, her life feeling full, complete.

❧❧❧❧

"Darling, I think we are ready to cut the turkey."

"Indeedy," Harry responded, laughing with Helena and sharing their stories of spider fright.

Irene, who had been looking at the wedding photo album, approached the three in the kitchen. "God, it smells divine in here!"

"I think we have enough food to feed all the tent city residents in Seattle," Bob commented.

"How about we fix up some plates after dinner and do that?" Helena added.

"Love it!" Harry said, driving the knife into the cooked bird.

"Looks like you love knives, Sir Harry, just watching you. And yes, ditto on tent city Thanksgiving."

"Oh, yes. Harry and I have a knife fetish. They are rather sexy you know, phallic as can be, when you think about it."

"You boys are sick." Irene laughed. "Knives were definitely invented by men."

"In some cultures, women aren't even allowed to touch knives," Harry commented.

"Smart cultures." Helena laughed.

They sat down to dishes and dishes of food that overflowed their plates, colors and textures and smells wafting through the dining room.

"Here's to our friendship, the gilded kind that last forever," Harry said, raising his glass.

"And here's to you two, and your new life together in Tasmania!" Bob added.

"And here's to you two, your newly wedded lives," Helena continued.

"And here's a special one to Bob, for our beautiful friendship, and for him convincing me to follow my dreams, to get on that plane to an island where my future began." Irene teared up with her toast.

Everyone was tearing up by then, realizing the bigness of what each of them had done to find happiness, seeing the power of love that allowed those beautiful things to happen.

"Look at us. We are all puddles here," Bob exclaimed.

"We're all just softies here. Queers with big hearts," Harry added.

"Sounds like a name of a band." Helena giggled as everyone laughed and started eating.

No one talked for at least five minutes except to grunt and moan over the delectable blend of tastes in the mouth.

"Sounds like we are all having orgasms." Bob broke the silence.

"We need to come here every Thanksgiving, just to have these orgasms of the tongue," Irene joked. "You two can really cook!"

"I say that's a plan," Harry added. "Oh, I do like the idea! Every year you two pop over from Tassymania and we do this!"

"Hear, hear!" Bob raised his glass and the rest followed.

"And then we zip up to Vancouver the following day," Irene said.

"I can't wait for tomorrow. So, what's the plan?" Helena asked.

"How about if we leave super early tomorrow, so we can cross the border before the hordes arrive. The festival starts at five on Friday. I got us a fabulous three-bedroom Airbnb house at Point Grey, right next to Kitsilano," Harry said.

"Three bedrooms, is someone joining us?" Irene laughed.

"Harry thought that in case we have body music in the night, then we would have a bedroom in between us to be a sound stopper."

Laughter turned into guffaws as plates were cleared and desserts were eaten, again to the tune of moans and grunts.

❧❧❧❧

They packed up the car with paper plates of food, wrapped in foil. They drove over to the multitude of tent cities downtown. People were outside that night, as it wasn't raining, some shivering, some strung out, some slumped in corners, seemingly oblivious to the fact that almost all Americans that evening were inside, warm and snug, eating away.

Helena spotted a family, a woman with three children, sitting in front of a tent, playing with a dog with matted hair. She approached the woman, offering her plates of food as her children's sunken, hungry eyes perked up. Helena smiled as the four walked on, then found another woman with a newborn at her breast. The woman was shivering. Helena offered her a plate, to which her mouth opened, smiling, revealing no teeth. Two boys were kissing, emaciated teenagers, impervious to the world around them. Harry approached them, wishing them a happy Thanksgiving, looking like every gay boy's favorite dad. With the plate of food in their hands, they hugged Harry, devoured what was on the plate, and returned to kissing, blocking out the harshness of their reality, their tent, their home, all of their possessions sitting beside them. A young child approached Irene with pleading eyes. The child appeared to have no parents and seemed to go from person to person asking for attention. Irene gave her a plate, devastated by the sight. All their plates dispensed, the two couples walked silently to the car, feeling the tininess of what they had done.

"There is so much more I want to give them beyond these leftovers from our bountiful Thanksgiving," Helena said, her voice heavy.

"Exactly," Harry commented.

They put their arms around each other as they walked away, needing even more to accentuate their love for each other as friends. Sadness laced their gratitude as they stepped into the car, turning on the heat, and with no words to describe all this, they drove away looking behind them at the faces of those they might never see again, remembering forever those expressions of gratitude on that freezing night.

❧❧❧❧

In bed that night, Irene and Helena held each other tightly, not wanting to let go. As they felt the warmth of each other, they each seemed to have something terribly huge on their minds.

"I'm thinking of that child," Helena started, an urgency in her voice.

"Hmm?"

"She seemed like she had nowhere to go." She paused. "The look on her face was of such insistence. It's like she wanted to ask us something, or maybe it wasn't just us she wanted to ask, maybe it was the universe she seemed to be asking."

"What was it do you think she was asking?"

Helena paused. "Love maybe." She paused again. "Yeah, it seemed she was asking the world to love her."

"Yeah, I felt it, too. It was a pleading expression, wasn't it?"

"It was. It was all I could do to not sweep her off her feet and take her home with us."

They both paused, holding each other tighter.

Tentatively, Helena continued, moving her body to face Irene's. "Have you ever thought about having another child?"

"You read my mind. That's what came up for me when I saw that child. I felt my own inside of me, the one I lost. I think the soul of him screamed something to me."

"Really?"

"Yeah, it was quite profound. It shook me there on the sidewalk tonight."

"I saw you shiver. I thought you were just cold."

"I was. But it was more than that. I felt something quiver, like an earthquake inside of me."

"What was he saying?"

"The message itself seemed nebulous, but the essence of it was about a child. Wanting one."

"Do you mean in the form of pregnancy, a child coming from you?"

"I don't know. I might be too old. But the feeling is there. It's quite strong, Helena."

Irene paused. She felt tears well up in her eyes.

Crying, she grabbed onto Helena's hand. The words were in her throat, yet nothing could come out of her mouth.

"What is it, darling?" Helena stroked Irene's cheek, picking up the tears in her fingertips.

"I want to love a child with you. I want to have a child with you, Helena."

Helena was silent then as she closed her eyes and grabbed onto Irene's hand. Irene grabbed her hand back, squeezing it tightly, as the late November moon, a tiny sliver of it, reflected its way through the window.

Chapter Twenty-six

December blurred with the rain and cold, breath flying out of the mouth like dragons as Irene continued to bike to work most days, when she wasn't running so late that she needed a taxi to get to class on time. She preferred to let the world pass her by as she zipped through the streets, everyone readying themselves for Christmas.

On her bicycle, her life moved around her like a kaleidoscope, memories and feelings wrapped up in colors and shapes, constantly revolving and shifting as time moved forward. Hers was a life now of saying goodbye, of leaving particles of her eloquent, yet also humanly flawed, existence into the roots of her Seattle, her Pacific Northwest. *What does it mean to say goodbye, to leave the essential elements that once held a person together, so that one could forge a life with another a hemisphere away? What does it mean to let go of the past, of the present, to allow the future to take its beautiful hold?*

Memories of just a few weeks ago flooded her mind: Helena, Bob, Harry, and her, all together in Vancouver at Jericho Beach, overlooking the water, the mountains, the lights of Vancouver. They had spent the day immersed in art, food, and laughing and laughing, culminating with their feelings of togetherness, friendship, love. They all knew two of the four were soon to leave, which made their insistency on being real with each other that much more intense. They cried, laughed, and realized that Harry and Helena had just joined their tight pack, and because of that, their link was tighter, a bond that would never break. When they took leave of each other in Seattle on that Saturday night, knowing that the present was the present, and that at some moment in your life you have to realize that's all you have, they kissed, they hugged, they cried, and then, smiling, the four separated, each couple's arms around the other, into the cold of the night.

Everything rolled in the moment during those late autumn days. The future felt intangible for Irene, something illusive. Even the feelings she and Helena shared that night in bed felt like a distant dream, something to come back to when the present did not consume every particle of her life.

Mornings turned to night and then to mornings during that freezing December. Irene bicycled to her last day of work at the University of Washington. On her trip to campus that day, when snow lingered in the sky, ready for its first fall of the year, reminiscent thoughts flooded her tired yet exalted mind, memories of her beloved students, all the classes she had taught, the hours and hours of grading papers, but mostly of lecturing, of seeing her students' brilliance and motivation in their eyes, and deep down, a fierce passion for music. *Can one leave this,* she wondered, *let go of those eyes, the love between a teacher and her students? Can one trust that one has planted just enough seeds, has given just the right soil, and that the tree, the magnificent tree that has grown, can flourish and sustain itself, long after the teacher has gone?*

Irene walked into the music building in the early hours of the morning, and hundreds of people—faculty, administrators, students, and alumni—crowded the hallways, cheering her. Hundreds of instruments were picked up by gifted hands as "Auld Lang Syne" was played, and then, Vivaldi's "Spring" concerto, and then a piece she didn't know, composed by her students with voices of instruments from around the world, a piece that was at once melancholic as it was jovial, full of passion, transcendent into a divine space. Irene was a puddle, tears flowing uncontrollably down her face as she witnessed all around her not just the accolades that were given, but the gift from one to the other of music—of love in the form of music.

Someone offered her a chair as she listened to music by all those people who adored her, who were trying to say goodbye, but did not want to. An hour later, the instruments were put down, away, stored carefully into cases, as lives continued, and she started her day of lectures.

In all her classes that day there was laughter, tears, improvisational singing. The work had really all been done, and there was no more learning to be had on that day except one which emphasized following one's dreams, letting music be that soulful guide into places that mattered.

Later that afternoon, she scooped up a stack of mail addressed to her, the last mail she would ever receive at UW. Sticking out of the pile was a large Express Post envelope with a postmark from Iran. Overwhelmed by the day, she could not open it, and stuffed it in her bag.

As the early evening approached, the applause and the hugs were finally over. Irene gathered the bouquets of flowers and the hundreds of cards into her backpack, and she walked her bike off into the mostly silent streets, snow now falling in Seattle, crushing away sounds and leaving only the beauty of a quiet world and the stifled shouts of joy that emanated from the depths of Irene.

Chapter Twenty-seven

That night would be the last in her home. Before she got back from work, her arms laden with flowers, she went to the women's bookstore in town, approaching the lesbian couple who had owned the shop for fifty years, and presented them with the flowers, thanking them for still being around. Then, she quietly rode home, an empty shell that was still hers.

After she had put her bag down, the contents spilling out in all directions, all the cards and wishes she had received for a good life, as if by instinct, she crouched down in her bedroom and peered under her bed, something she hadn't done in years. It had occurred to her, as she was riding home, that under the bed was the only place in her home that she hadn't cleared out. Her hand reached under the bed frame and felt something covered in dust, a piece of wood and some broken glass. She pulled out the object, and there, staring at her, smiling, was her father, a photo of him taken most probably shortly after Irene was born. He was beaming and positively happy. The glass around the photo had all shattered, but the smile from her father radiated as if he was still alive.

"Oh, Dad, I miss you." Irene was bawling, kissing his cheek.

Why am I going to Tasmania? I need to be in Iran...Why haven't I been there? What has stopped me from being where my roots are, closer to my father than this country ever was...Am I following a dream, being with Helena? Is this real?

She looked at the picture, staring at the features, tracing her fingers along his cheekbones.

I have the same facial structure.

A mental picture of Helena entered Irene's brain then. She was smiling, her face a mass of love, her eyes warm, soft.

My father would have wanted me to love another, someone who could love me back, love me completely.

I want to be with Helena. More than anything...

She sat on the bed, looking at her father.

And I need to visit Iran. With Helena.

With that knowledge firmly planted in her head, she fell asleep, the photo cradled in her arms, her life coming together, pieces of it floating around her head, like delicate wisps of lace, like snow falling in a forest of cedars.

⁂

Very early in the morning she woke up, her head swimming with sleep dreams she could not remember. Her mind quickly became wide awake as she slipped into the bathroom, remembering then the letter from the day before.

She curled up back in bed and pulled the covers to her chin as she slipped open the thin envelope that was inside the big one, her hands shaking as she pulled out one piece of paper, Farsi words spilling out on the page like a painting.

Dear Irene, I have been trying to find you,

and after a google search, I found your University of Washington address. I emailed you several times, and my letters kept bouncing back. My husband suggested I write you a paper letter and send it by Express Mail to the University, in the hopes that you will receive this letter in a timely fashion. I hope these words come into your hands and find you well. I will be blunt and get to the point. Your father, may he rest in peace, had a daughter out of wedlock. Your mother never knew this. It happened before he even met your mother. Her name was Marjani. She is your half-sister, and she never stepped foot out of Iran. She married a man named Farrokh, and they had a daughter named Ziba, who married a man named Reza and they had a daughter named Noushin who is now five years old. Two weeks ago, Marjani, Farrrokh, Ziba, Reza, Noushin and I were on holiday in Shiraz. We had reserved online a special day trip that was to explore the countryside on what they said was a fancy tourist bus. That morning, however, Noushin developed a bad case of diarrhea, so I offered to stay back in the hotel with her. The bus, it turns out, had not been adequately serviced, the brakes failed, and the bus went tumbling down a steep hillside. Every single passenger and the driver died. Noushin's entire family is gone. I am a neighbor of theirs, a close friend for many years. The memorial service for the family, may they all rest in peace, is this weekend, on Saturday the 16th at 2pm at The Temple of Rumi, 76 Avenue Alborz, Tehran. We would like you to be there. Our family has known about you for all these years.

In loving memory of all your family, Fatemeh Karimi.

Irene put the letter down on the bed, her body

shaking, her feelings at first numb, recesses of lives, hers, theirs, the past and the present swooping down like vultures, trying to consume all. A family she never knew was hers was now gone on a hillside, just like that. She felt then anger, rage, a combustion of energy that she did not know where to direct. She got up and stomped around the house, her footsteps loud and ominous, her tears mixed in, salt invading her senses. *Why? Why?* Her thoughts felt useless, she felt useless. Everything came up, bile and tears, her body was sweating, water dripping from her temples as she sat down back on the bed and wailed.

Noushin. The image of the little five-year-old entered her consciousness, her tears quieting. *I must get to this child. The memorial is tomorrow.*

Without the time to ponder the hugeness of it all, she picked up her phone, and booked a flight to Tehran, leaving six hours later.

Chapter Twenty-eight

Helena paced the kitchen, the living room, the bathroom, the bedroom. She had never been a pacer, had not really known anxiety. Her life had been this farm, her job, a regularity that held such simple contents. As she put things into her suitcase, she quickly pulled them out. She gave up, stepping outside to breathe in the fresh mountain air. It had just snowed again, and the blanket of white mesmerized her, the fresh powder intoxicating. She slipped on her snowshoes and took off into the woods, called into the thick forest by an instinct that screamed to her. Crunching the soft white, she instantly forgot about the suitcase, about her life turning upside down, about leaving her home, her beloved mountains. Her feet carried her far up the mountain on trails she knew like her own voice. As her breathing grew more rapid, the elevation mixing with the ease of her own breath, she felt tears come down her face, gentle at first, then harder, as sobs developed. This mountain was like her lover, its voluptuous curves and heights had, from an early age, enticed her, seduced her, calmed her, been her source of companionship in her solitary states. Now she was leaving them, and felt a pang inside of her, a stab that she couldn't shake. *I can't leave this, my home, my heart…*She looked up at the looming clouds, darkened ghosts inviting storms. Everything had gone so smoothly, and the idea of moving all the way across the world felt effortless, as in a dream, a romance novel—until this moment. *I am choosing something over another, and I am afraid.* It was the first time she had felt this kind of fear, felt that indescribable emotion that prevailed in the sheer nakedness of loving another. As she looked down from the edge of the cliff, feeling her smallness creep around her, the majesty of the grand dame overbearing in its sheer magnitude, she asked her for a sign, some kind of reassurance, some inkling of a reminder that all would be okay. It was change, she realized, the mere thought of doing and going and living somewhere different. It was about giving up her solitariness; it was about her own fear of losing herself, this mountain, her lover. It was about challenging her own strength, her own vulnerabilities, letting someone else really see her, and live with her, and love her in all ways. Being loved by a mountain was a lot easier than being loved by a human.

She heard it before she saw it, the crunching on the newly fallen snow by footsteps that were indeed heavier than hers. She stood still, looked up, and saw its golden fur glistening in the early afternoon, the sun grazing its sleek body as it slinked toward her, sniffing her in the light breeze. In all her years, Helena had never encountered a mountain lion on the trail. This, she felt, was the sign she asked for, for loving the mountain meant meeting all the species that lived on it. In her hugeness, a docility permeated this majestic being, now standing still, staring at Helena, ready to lunge if necessary. She was hungry, and her meekness could turn instantly into a savagery that would meet her needs. Helena felt this, and instinctively raised her arms, high into the air, as if to touch the sky. As she stared into the eyes of this magnificent being, she slowly backed away, one step followed by the next, carefully descending the mountain, being led by the eyes of this creature back to her home, one last parting shot of the cat and then she turned around and felt the necessary jolt she needed to let her know that all would indeed be okay. It was the lion's territory now, and it was now her job to quickly pack her one suitcase and get on that plane to Seattle, departing in just a few hours.

She sprinted back to her home and threw herself in the shower, all the previous hesitation completely gone. *I want this. Irene, our life, our love. More than anything I have ever wished for, I am ready for this.* Everything that was laid out on the bed was going with her, and without even doing the usual methodical folding that she was used to, she tossed it all in, Irene-style, and chuckled as she did so, zipping it up, and setting it by the door just as Marilyn and Joanne approached, ready to take her to the airport.

They gave her a once-over.

"You don't look a bit nervous."

"Oh, believe me, I was, but the mountain lion chased it all out of me," Helena said, laughing.

"Mountain lion?"

"Yep, hungry one at that. I couldn't even put my things in my bag, so I headed up the mountain this morning."

"Now what would we have told Irene? Sometimes, dear, your brain is not quite on this earth." They laughed.

"I had to say goodbye. The cat understood, and she ushered me away. I got it. I am stubbornly in love with this mountain, and the lioness told me to leave this relationship for the human one."

They put their arms around Helena, tearing up. "We are going to miss you, sweetie. Only you could say things like that. You know your mountain will always be here for you, and we will be as well."

"I am going to miss you guys, too. I know this for sure. You have held me together in moments where I thought I would never be able to." They all stayed in a group hug for a few minutes just as a Mercedes SUV drove up.

It was Helena's mother.

"Oh my God, Mom," Helena said as she approached. "I haven't seen you in months. Haven't heard from you." She tried to hold back her resentment, her anger. Never once had her mother been supportive of anything that connected her to Irene. She had given up on her, and deep inside of her there was a bit of seething she tried to ignore.

"I am sorry. I have been steeped in the project in Hong Kong."

Helena had heard the story, the same one all her life; it was always about her work. She was itching to get in the car with her friends. She had a plane to catch. The lioness had told her to leave, and now she was ready. She had no time or energy for her mother, or even the guilt she could have felt for not wanting her there.

"I have something for you, sweetie."

Helena tried not to cringe, feeling her palms get sweaty.

She handed Helena a fancy gift bag. Helena opened it. It was a blank journal. Helena stared at it. She never wrote. Her mother had always wanted her to be a writer. Helena looked up at the blue sky, wanting to bolt. Her friends looked at her, silent invitations to make her exit and leave.

"I wrote something inside. Read it."

Helena opened the first page, like a young child obeying her mother, wanting to please her. Floods of memories invaded Helena's mind, as she fought back the tears, of when she was five, her mother leaving and moving away, leaving her, as she yelled out, "Mommy please don't go! Please!" She had watched her mother then get in her car and drive away from her home, from being a mother.

Darling Helena, she read to herself, her hands shaking. *The day I left this house was the day I became free. Maybe a bit of you is experiencing at this moment what I felt. I am truly happy for you in finding Irene, in finding your true love, which for you is your freedom. I know I have been a miserable mother—not even a mother at all. And I know you must bear severe scars from this. There is no forgiveness in a world where a mother abandons her child. I will always love you, and I cherish the fact that you have found love from another human being. Go now, go find her, and let your lives together be one of bliss.*

Helena stood, frozen, shocked at these words, the first time in all her life where her mother showed she knew her own daughter. Helena folded into the arms of the woman who had given birth to her, and finally, more than four decades later, had become a mother. She clasped the book to her heart as she climbed into the car, and waved to the woman who, at a closer look, was beautiful—standing there, tears flowing down her cheeks, throwing her a kiss, pointing at her heart and waving goodbye.

֍ ֍ ֍ ֍

In the backseat of the car, Helena could not speak, could not enter the frolicking banter of her friends. She closed her eyes and let the daydream fill her mind, her own cinema, how she wanted it all to be, the perfect good bye to an old life, as the new one fluttered in front of her.

I quietly knocked on the door to Irene's house, the last time I would do this. It was late, almost midnight, and Irene's lights were blazing. In a shell of the house, our tears echoed as if they were in a canyon somewhere, clasping each other, falling into each other's arms. Irene led me to her bed, the only thing except her suitcase that remained in the house. We stripped off each other's clothes as if it were summer, heat consuming our bodies, impervious to the melting snow outside, the freezing rain that permeated the sidewalks. Our hands grabbed onto each other, clinging with desperation, as our tongues fed each other, a ravenous presence as our bodies pushed and pulled, our mouths craving, our breathing heavy and full, our moans and screams blazing into the night.

We couldn't sleep, did not want to sleep. We only wanted each other, to feed each other, to be fed, to begin our new lives with this feeding, this nourishment, this merging of one body with the other, an infinite line toward wholeness, as the fire within could not and would not subside.

Finally, though, it did, one body sinking into the other, finding each other in sleep, holding, caressing in the place of dreams, beginning also a life there, in the slumber of the human heart, the intricate organ that folded into and nourished our two souls, tending to them as would a mother, rocking us, bathing us in the arms of sleep.

Morning moved to noon, and gradually we awoke, on almost the first day of winter, kissing each other to begin our day. Our flight would leave at 5:00 p.m., and the housecleaner would be there at two. As we showered and dressed, we each felt a sense of absolute completeness, a readiness to leave this home to begin something altogether new.

Irene, alone, went through the house, room by room, and stood quietly in the empty spaces. Then she put on her coat, slipped her bag over her shoulder, grabbed her emerald-green suitcase, and locked the door, putting her key under the mat, as she danced down the stairs and onto the sidewalk, next to the Lyft car where I was waiting. As we kissed each other, deeply and fully, the car sped away, into the wet cold streets of Seattle, the last reminders we would ever have of winters in the Northwest.

⇚⇚⇛⇛

Her daydream abruptly ended with the sound of her phone, Irene's familiar ring.

"Where have you been? I have been trying to reach you for hours." Irene's voice was insistent, breathless.

"What's going on darling? Are you okay?"

"Well, yes and no. I have been trying to reach you for the last three hours. I am at the airport."

"I am so sorry. I was on the mountain, and then my mom came over unexpectedly. I have been getting myself ready to meet you. I am almost at the airport myself." She paused. "You're at the *airport*? What in the world is going on?"

"My plane for Tehran leaves in one hour."

"Tehran. As in Iran?"

"Yes, don't be so daft. It's a long story."

"What in the world is going on?"

"I got a letter."

"Yes?"

"I read it early this morning."

"Yes?"

"I have a family in Iran I never knew about. It started with a sister. My dad had a daughter, my half-sister. No one ever told me."

Irene paused. Helena waited.

"So, in the letter, besides telling me that information, this woman, a neighbor of my sister's, tells me that the whole family, this sister, her husband, and their daughter and her husband, were all in bus wreck a few weeks ago, and they all died."

Irene was silent for a moment again, then continued.

"I have a niece. Her name is Noushin. She is five years old. She was not on the bus that day."

Helena gasped.

"The memorial is tomorrow at two. I must see Noushin."

"Oh my God."

"I am so sorry."

Helena was silent.

"The plane is boarding now. I will call you from Tehran."

"Helena? Are you there?"

"Yes. I am in shock."

"So am I. It will all work out. I must go to Iran." She paused. "Strange things happen every day."

Helena chuckled.

"I will go home then. Wait for your call."

"We will get to Tasmania. I promise."

"I love you, Irene."

"*God*, do I love you, Helena."

Chapter Twenty-nine

Irene stepped into the cab after her feet touched Iranian soil for the very first time. All her senses came alive the moment she landed. Already on the plane she heard only Farsi, English wafting away from her surroundings, replaced by the language of song and poetry, as her father used to call it. On land, sound was everywhere, traffic and horns blaring with abandon. Smells invaded every particle of her being. Saffron and mint, cardamom, turmeric, and ginger seemed to pour through every crevice of the air she breathed. Colors vibrated, she could feel the energy of them; all around her was the absence of black and white. The age of the buildings, the new with the ancient, held her gaze as she looked out the window of the car, mesmerized, feeling, in some primitive way, that after all these years of being on this planet, she was finally home.

The irony hit her as the car turned onto Avenue Alborz. Her namesake. Home. Farsi, a language she hadn't used since her youth, came back to her like syrup, flowing effortlessly from her tongue, as if she had never stopped using it.

The Temple of Rumi. Also, her namesake. She entered slowly, taking in the sumptuous beauty of the place, the ornate woodwork, the colors, the age and mystery of each stone. There was poetry everywhere; she felt entranced, like she had entered a sacred monastery of her own soul. There were dozens of people milling around, talking, laughing, crying, feelings not held in. It was a gathering of all generations, from the tiny to the old, and love seemed to permeate every corner of that temple.

Irene scanned the crowd, eager to find only one person. There was a group of children in the back corner of the grand space, behind some wooden arches, ornate latticework seemingly flying out of nowhere. It was easy to spot her, the small girl with the sunken face whose dark, thick hair laced her eyes, covering them. She sat, surrounded by other children who laughed and jested. She seemed alone in her sadness.

Irene approached her, her steps slow and deliberate. It felt like she was walking in a dream, and there she was, this child, at the other end of it, waiting.

"Hi," she said, looking in the dark eyes of Noushin as she kneeled and met her face-to-face.

"Hi," the small voice said back. "You're pretty," she added.

Irene blushed.

"You kind of look like me." Noushin kept scanning Irene's face.

"You think?"

"Yep."

They both were silent, staring at the other.

"What's your name?"

"Irene. And your name is Noushin?"

"How did you know?"

"Your friend wrote me a letter. Your neighbor. She told me you would be here. I came here to meet you."

"Where did you come from?"

"America."

"Oh, that's far. Is that where you live?"

"I used to. Now, I am moving to Tasmania."

"I like that name." She paused. "Will you take me with you to this Tasmania? Fatemah said you are my auntie and that you might take me and take care of me, because that's what aunties do, she said." She paused, her head crinkled up, looking like she was thinking about something very big. "My mommy fell out of a bus, you know, and she died. Maybe I'll find her in Tasmania. Will you take me there and help me find her?"

Both were silent then, the weight of this statement filtering in the air.

Irene gulped. "I'm so sorry to hear that your mommy died."

"Can you help me find my mommy?" Noushin repeated.

Irene stumbled, not sure what to say. All at once, she remembered what her father had once recited to her. "I am going to quote something from a very wise man named Rumi, something you may not understand. He said, 'For those who love with heart and soul there is no such thing as separation.'"

They were both silent then. Noushin's face looked ponderous.

"I can love you and care for you, and always be there for you. The spirit of your mother will always be with you. You may not understand what I am telling you, but as you get older you will."

Noushin looked at Irene, not taking her eyes off this stranger's face who, she said, looked like her. Irene, her face warm and inviting, gazed at Noushin as she quietly slid into Irene's arms, as Irene folded her soft arms around the softness of this child whose face lit up and smiled. They stayed like that, in that gentle embrace that made Irene cry, tears flowing from her face to the head of the little one who needed a mother, who, in that moment, appeared to need exactly what Irene was there for.

"I need to talk to the adults now, since I haven't yet done that. I will come back and talk to you. I promise." Noushin looked pleadingly at Irene.

"Play with your friends. I will be back."

Irene walked over to the group of adults, still talking and laughing, still crying and still living.

"Hi," she said simply. "I'm Irene Alborz."

Silence filled the room.

"Oh, my God. It's you." A well-dressed woman with long, wavy hair approached Irene, hugging her. Then women and men of all ages came up to Irene and embraced her, crying, whispering in her ear, "Welcome home."

Irene felt their tears, felt her own homecoming, felt so much in those moments where mystery shrouded her, years of not knowing any of this. She was introduced to everyone, names that she would never remember, names of people who had apparently known about her since she was a child.

"You met Noushin?" Fatemah said, her arms around Irene.

Irene gulped. She knew she needed to move things along. She thought of Helena. She needed to phone her. She moved back to the present, where the love surrounded her, where she was welcomed into a world that felt so rich, yet so overwhelmingly new, and yet, as Fatemah had her arms around her, her strong perfume wafting in the air, Irene knew, in that moment, that she needed to leave. With the child.

"I would like to take Noushin with me," she said, emotion filling her voice.

"Ahhhh...we were so hoping you would say this." Fatemah hugged her again, this time her perfume and her sweat grew to such an intensity that swam through Irene, making her dizzy.

"Are you alone? Married? Are you in America?"

"I am married. And we are moving to Tasmania."

"Oh, what a relief you and your husband will be not in the US. I have heard that it would have been much harder now to get her in. Australia is perfect for you and..."

"Helena."

Fatemah gulped, turning red. She then took her hands and waved them in the air. "Oh, love is love." She hugged Irene again, her perfume getting stronger by the minute.

"We have everything prepared for you. In a file folder. My husband spent hours talking and doing research, and we have it all here, all the necessary documents filled out and ready for you to adopt this child and leave the country. Her passport. Everything. We found a copy of Marjani's will and in it, at the very bottom, she specified that if it ever happened that all the immediate family members were unable to care for Noushin, she wanted you to adopt her and take her as your daughter."

Irene gulped. "She did?"

"Yes."

"Why didn't she ever contact me?"

"She always said she didn't want to taint your father's reputation. It's such a long story. One that perhaps we can save for another day, a day where we aren't so surrounded by such grief."

"Of course."

Irene was quiet then, collecting her thoughts.

"I get the sense that Noushin doesn't quite understand what's happening in her life now. She is so young and so much tragedy has just fallen in her lap… and I'm not sure that I can explain it to her in ways she will understand." Her voice was almost breathless. "Are you sure this is what Marjani would have wanted? She didn't know me at all."

"We will talk to Noushin together before you leave. Marjani always wanted her to be with family, and she was adamant that if you two shared that, you would be the perfect guardian for her little girl. She knew you would take the best care of Noushin."

Irene was silent again, feeling overwhelmed by this last statement. "I need to use the restroom. Where can I find one, please?"

She was directed to the back corner, where she entered a stall and pulled out her phone.

"Hi."

"Ah, baby. How are you? I have been so worried about you."

"I'm fine. She's beautiful. They want me to be her mom."

"And…?"

"I want to be hers."

Silence filled the air.

"Ah, tell me what's next. I miss you. I need you." Irene was crying hard, tears falling onto her dress.

"I want that child, too."

"You do?"

"Yes, I have been doing a lot of thinking since yesterday."

"You have?"

"Yes."

"And?"

"I want that child with us. I want to be a mommy with you. A family, yes. That's what we'll be in Tasmania."

Irene couldn't stop crying, her face flooded with tears.

"Really?"

"Yes."

"They have all the papers together. I could leave tonight with her."

"Then do. Meet me in Sydney. Just tell me what flight you're on. We'll fly together to Hobart."

"Oh my God. My house. I just remembered."

"I've been there. I got everything out. Talked to the realtor. All taken care of."

Irene laughed. "You did?"

"Yep. Didn't know if you'd be able to get there. So, I just zipped over there yesterday."

"I can't believe you. Are you for real?"

"Think so."

"Thank you. I love you *so* much."

"I do think it's insanely mutual."

"We are rather insane."

"Yes, we are, and let that be our greatest asset... and our greatest vice."

They both laughed.

"I want your lips on mine."

"Oh, god, don't start. I have been wanting you."

"Mmmm..."

"Here's to our life. Our new family."

Irene's tears returned. "I'm on my way."

❧❧❧❧

Irene clasped the hand of a small child as they landed in Sydney, the grand expanse of dry summer hills welcoming them from the plane. At the airport, the immigration line was as simple as eating yogurt, almost. Irene breathed a sigh of relief as together, she and Noushin went from one line to the other, one smiling face to the next.

And then, when it was all over, there, at the meeting place, a smiling Helena stood, her feet running to Irene, picking up first a sleepy, long-haired child who instinctively nuzzled into her arms.

"I heard about you. Fatemah said that you are the other lady who will take care of me. You are Irene's friend." She paused. "I like you."

"Yes." Her eyes were warm and twinkled as she spoke. "My name is Helena. And you are Noushin, and I like you, too." she said in heavily accented Farsi.

Noushin smiled.

"How do you know Farsi?" Irene chuckled.

"That's what long plane rides are for." She smiled.

As Noushin kept her arms around Helena, Irene snuggled in too, purring, laughing.

PART FIVE: WINTER/SUMMER

Chapter Thirty

Once out of the Hobart terminal and into the heat of summer, they basked in the hot sun blazing their faces. Irene and Helena gulped, each feeling it, the hugeness of what they done together. It was different to visit, to teach for a month. Now, this was to be their home, and jet lag and the seasonal change—and the reality of what they had just done, not to mention starting a new family—hit them. They felt transported to an ethereal existence, an out-of-body state that existed in each of them.

"Do you feel like you are not really here?" Irene asked, standing at the curb, waiting for the cab to take them to their Airbnb.

"Yes, it's weird," Helena replied, holding on tightly to Noushin, asleep in her arms. "It's like my feet aren't standing here, and they are somewhere else, and I am not with them." She paused. "I'm standing here holding this beautiful, precious child who kind of fell out of the sky, no?"

"We have done something rather huge, you know," Irene said, her voice quiet. She grabbed Helena's hand, feeling its warmth, letting hers sink into it. She took a deep breath and exhaled, feeling something move through her, out of her—fear perhaps. They both looked at Noushin and sighed and smiled, watching sleep weave itself around her tired little body.

She looked over at Helena, who was staring at

something. From a distance, a group of people was approaching, a parade it seemed, marching down the road by the arrivals and departures doors of the small airport. They were all women, mainly topless, some on bikes, some walking, some on stilts, rainbow flags flying from their arms. Djembes made a beat that everyone was dancing to.

"Oh my God, it's a dyke march, here at the airport!" Irene exclaimed. Her hand tightened around Helena's as they turned to each other and kissed. "This is our new home, sweetheart. What an incredibly wonderful way to be welcomed to it!"

Mardi Gras beads were thrown to the bystanders who all seemed to pause and celebrate, as the usual hurry and mindless haste at the airport ceased. The practicalities of flights transformed to a myriad of colors and shouts, and a party of women who loved women stood out, letting everyone smile and cheer.

And then the parade walked and danced and marched away as spiritedly as they approached. Irene and Helena, holding a fast-asleep child, stepped into the cab and sped away, knowing now that this was their place, their happy home. And this was only the first day.

෴෴෴෴

The next day arrived with sun bursting in the windows. They had come full circle, from summer to summer, and now they were back, seasons intermingling throughout a year, each one with its own definition, each one sinking into the crevices of their being. As the three of them woke up in the same bed that morning, Irene and Helena giggled, realizing completely what they had just done, coming here, their suitcases sitting in the corner.

"Are we in your Tasmania?" Noushin mumbled, still a bit groggy from her jet-lagged sleep.

"We're in *our* Tasmania. And it's our first day all together," Irene said, pulling the child close. The three snuggled in the big bed, Noushin in the middle.

"Shall we go buy some beds and things today for our new home?" Helena said, half in English, half in Farsi.

"Yes!" Noushin screamed, jumping on the bed, her lithe little body almost levitating into the air.

"Your Farsi is pathetic, darling. We have to work on that." Irene laughed.

Helena reached over and kissed Irene gently on the cheek.

"My mommy and daddy used to kiss on the cheek like that."

Helena and Irene looked at Noushin, watching her expression, a mixture of sadness and contentment, as she fell back in the bed, letting her body curl between the softness and the gentle, embracing arms of her two new moms.

❧❧❦❦

That day they bought a car and furniture. They had found a store, a co-op that only sold furniture made by Tasmanians using local wood—handcrafted, gorgeous pieces that stunned Irene and Helena. They found two beds, a kitchen table and chairs, end tables, and a sofa. They bought a tent and three sleeping bags, as the furniture wouldn't be delivered for a week. They bought groceries at the outdoor farmers' (and really, everything) market on Saturdays that brought out hundreds and hundreds of people—Tasmanians with music, creative energy, and a love of life on that beautiful summer's day. In everything they did that day, Noushin's eyes were wide open, as if she, too, knew that she was starting over, and everything was to be noted.

A shop sign caught Irene's eyes as they were meandering through the streets of Hobart that afternoon. "*Les plaisirs des livres,*" it read. The pleasures of books.

"Give me a moment, darling, I have to go in that shop." Helena smiled, took Noushin's hand, and began to walk on as Irene felt instantly pulled toward the French book store, and as she entered, winking at Helena to let her know she might get irretrievably lost inside, she experienced in herself something that sank into her like cool, white curtains waving in the breeze on a spring day. She actually smelled Paris as she stepped in the shop, the blend of the old and the musty with an agelessness that inspired something deep within her from her past.

As if a magnet had forced itself into her consciousness, she gravitated toward the recent releases section, and there it was—a silver-white book with the Eiffel Tower in the background. *When Paris Was My Lover*, by Elise Maillon.

Irene gasped. She opened the book and flipped to the first page.

*To Helena and Irene, who inspired me to write **my** story, and not someone else's.*

Irene began to cry, a tear landing on the dedication page as the saleswoman came up to her.

"Are you okay?" she asked, warmth in her voice.

"Yes. I knew this woman."

"Elise Maillon? Her book is beautiful. It just came in last week, and I stayed up for two nights and couldn't put it down. It is such a shame that she passed away..."

"She did?"

"Yes, the day after she completed the book and sent it off to her editor, she died of a massive heart attack. Apparently, she'd had a heart condition for many months before then, and the doctors warned her to slow down, but she didn't heed this advice and wrote her autobiography in just three months."

Irene paid for the book and sat down in the store and began to read, speechless. Helena crept up quietly beside her.

Helena's face fell as Irene silently flipped the book back to the cover and then over to the dedication page.

"She winked at me as we were leaving. She knew that our visit was the start of something big for her," Irene said, her tears large and looming as Helena put her arm around her and as Noushin plopped herself in her lap.

"As soon as I saw that suitcase, that emerald-green icon sitting rather dilapidated in the corner of the room here in Tasmania, I just knew it would hold so much more than clothes." Helena's tears blended with her laughs as the shop patrons turned around, listening to the bizarreness of those words, the secrets held in the dusty corners of places unveiled.

Irene and Helena and Noushin left the shop, edging out into the warm sun as the Eiffel Tower prominently gazed at them from the treasure Irene held in her two hands.

ᢒᎥᢒᎥᢒᎥᢒᎥ

With their car full of odds and ends, food, and
the meager beginnings to their new life, they drove to
their new home. The rural country road felt to them
hauntingly beautiful, hugging coastlines that dipped
around steep cliffs, with sheer edges plunging into
the sea. They had heard that people died or got lost in
the wilderness in Tasmania because of one false turn
on a windy night, or not knowing the terrain before
wandering out on a day's hike. That day, though, was
like a sublime sheep's journey, winter a far-off memory
as they drove, breathing in the freshness of the air, the
green grass that sprouted all around them, the small
farms that dotted the road.

And then they arrived, driving slowly up the long
dirt driveway, in their new car that smelled of new
beginnings. They were all giddy. When they got out
of the car, Noushin leapt in the air and ran, laughing.
Irene clutched Helena's hand as the forested front
garden beckoned them, trees and flowers in bloom,
birds singing at full volume on that perfect day. They
picked up the key that was hidden under the brand-
new, homemade doormat. Together, they turned it in
the lock, laughing like children as they pushed open
the big door, hearing a squeak that reminded them
that this home held stories—many, in fact—and they
were only just beginning to discover them, yearning to
create their own. Flowers were set in vases throughout
the entire house, accompanied by a welcome home
card from the realtor. Noushin ran through the house,
her steps light and airy, as she laughed and raced from
room to room, coming back every few minutes to hug

her two moms.

As Irene and Helena walked in each room, holding hands, they stopped, felt the energy of each room, kissing in each one, loving each space and the promises each one held. From their bedroom on the second floor they looked out at the ocean below, a glistening endless sea of greens and blues, inviting serenity, hiding life forms that existed and had survived countless generations. A kangaroo hopped effortlessly on the steep hillside, gallantry displayed in her haunches as her two joeys hopped playfully behind her with their fearless antics, mocking the game of foraging, stopping for moments to paw at each other's faces.

It was then that Helena cried, thinking of the card her mother had written that she had shared with Irene that morning. Everything was a sign: starting a family; holding Noushin; the dyke march at the airport; the warmth of the people they had met that day in town; Elise's book; and now, the mama kangaroo and her children. She and Irene had come home to nest, to nurture, to play, to celebrate, to love.

There, in the empty bedroom, where soon a bed would sit, and hours of sleep and loving would occur, she took Irene into her arms, whispering to her, "Welcome home" as she uttered I love yous over and over, hearing in her ears the mirroring echo of I love yous, Irene's voice soft and gentle. The breeze of the afternoon gently wafted through the house, through all the open doors and windows, the sweetness of it accentuating their lips on each other's lips, that final resolution in the search for love, for home, for lives merging into that sacred space of finding another. They walked downstairs and stood at the front door, smiling, watching Noushin engrossed in her play outside in the garden, exploring all the forested areas in their front yard. Helena looked at Irene, motioning for her to sit next to her. They plopped themselves down on the soft grass and stared at the beauty around them, at a child who was as riveting as she was sweet. As the two women held each other's hands, they sighed, collectively feeling in awe of what they had accomplished. Their lips met quietly, tasting the sweetness of it all, their lives now folded around each other in a perfect braid, strands interwoven, an endless ambrosia that would embrace them for moments, for days and weeks and years.

The emerald-green suitcase glittered in the sunlight outside. Noushin had discovered it, and she took it from place to place in the lush garden. A multicolored bird then stood on it, calling to its mate, watching it fly toward her, bundles of grass sitting in its mouth. They then flew off together, ready to create their own masterpiece. Hidden in the thick bushes, a kangaroo stopped and watched the young child in her imaginative world, a little wisp of a being with a warm smile on her face. She looked up and stared at it, her gentle singsongy voice calling forth the furry animal to her own play.

Irene and Helena watched her and giggled, but Noushin took no notice of them, ensconced in a pretend tea party. The emerald suitcase had become a table, and not one now, but three kangaroos sat nonchalantly in the bushes nearby as the child hummed a tune, a song Irene knew that spanned generations and hemispheres. She found herself humming along with her daughter, as the birds in the nearby tree called to each other, making their nest.

Acknowledgments

Gratitude is a powerful feeling.
At first, one is just grateful for the muse, for that simple guiding force inside a person that allows for expression, and then, the gratitude circle becomes wider, and the rings of this labyrinthian experience grow in ways that are quite profound.

Sapphire Books is, like their name suggests, the jewel that has been part of the monumental experience of publishing this book. A huge thank you to Christine Svendsen, who chose to publish my manuscript, taking a risk and giving it a chance to live, to grow, to become what it is right now.

Thank you to my two editors, Nikki Busch and Heather Flournoy, who taught me so much about how to turn words into a beautiful art form, about what is needed in this process and what is not.

Thank you to Ann McMan, the cover designer. She is a magician and created the most stunning artwork I could imagine.

Thank you to the amazing L.J. Reynolds, the book designer, who transformed the completed and edited manuscript into the actual book that you are about to read.

The labyrinth expands when I ponder all the people who have loved me since the moment I was born and beyond.

It started with my parents. Their love transcends, and in the case of my late father, transcended everything pragmatic. Every evening at 7:45 pm I talk to my mom on the phone, her love each evening, her sweet voice, reminds me of what is vital on our earth. I have two amazing sisters, Vicki and Diane, who are my rocks, my mates, and together we three have a resilient sisterly bond. And then I have my nieces, Izzy and Leila, two beautiful, inspirational, brilliant and dynamic women whom I just adore. My family, I thank you always for your love, for that energy that ignites a soul, making us all feel a part of something vastly important.

I am so incredibly fortunate to have wonderful friends in this country and all over the world; they are also the jewels that buoy me, the emeralds that I hold in my heart. Some of these friends go back to when I was still a child. To every single one of you, to all my dearest friends, I thank you. I cherish you. Thank you to the late Marie-Laurence Houssay, a woman who exuded love in every connection, in every relationship she had with other human beings. She loved the art of the story, and I still have in my head her rendition of "*Il y etait une fois...*" Once upon a time... For in life, in writing, in love, it all begins with a story...

Thank you Suzy, who, every now and then, flies in and out of the screen of my phone, often in moments when I am stumbling, unsure of my footing. She always reminds me that in everything we do, when we push aside all the dusty layers, it is all about love. All of it. Especially the love we cultivate in our own selves.

There is so much that goes into creating a book. Lastly,

I bow to you, the readers, the ones who have known me all my life, the ones who have never known me, and the ones who will get to know me through my writing. For it is all a circle, one gives to the other and back again. That, for me, is beauty beyond the emerald suitcase.

Thank you.

About the Author

Heidi Harrison has always loved writing. At a very early age, she realized that words allowed for the exodus of her soul, a rhapsody, a sense of grace enveloping her. Writing has been her boulder, her stories the healing balm in a world that sometimes cries out for this.

Born in and raised in the San Francisco Bay Area, she now calls home the Northwest, where towering red cedars surround her, inspiring her imaginative mind. She holds a MS degree in Counseling Psychology, and a dual degree in Child Development and French, and she spent almost thirty years as a psychotherapist and a teacher of young children. She is also a classically trained violinist. She has traveled extensively between the hemispheres and has lived and studied in Paris and Vancouver, BC.

She has written several novels and children's books, countless stories, (fiction and creative nonfiction), and a full-length memoir. One of her more recent creative non-fiction pieces, "The Wild Horse" was recently published in the Spring 2018 issue of *Still Point Arts Quarterly*. In each of these works, she is inspired by imagination itself, by the beauty and power of words, relationships, the diversity of cultures, the human heart, and by the earth we all live in.

The Four Seasons is her first published novel.

www.heidimharrison.com
Twitter: @emerald_heidi
Facebook: Heidi Emerald Harrison

Other book's by Sapphire Authors

The Treehouse – ISBN – 978-1-948232-00-5

Camilla Thompson, a Humanities college professor who never did write that Great American Novel, hasn't seen her son Nico for two years.

One morning she drives to the house where her ex, Allison, is still raising Nico. Knowing that they are away for a week's vacation, Camilla begins to build a treehouse as a surprise for the son she's not allowed to see.

But Camilla's regrets, grief, and lack of construction skills aren't the only challenges she'll face. Old friends and unexpected visitors show up to help—and complicate matters. Free-spirited Taylor, Camilla's best friend, arrives with her lover, Audrey, whom Camilla finds herself falling for. Then Wallace, Camilla's Department Chair, disrupts everything with startling news that threatens to end Camilla's career.

At first an impulsive idea, the treehouse soon promises to be an oasis for Camilla's redemption that could free her for another chance at love and family. Then again, it might simply be just a bad decision.

CPSIA information can be obtained
at www.ICGtesting.com
Printed in the USA
FSHW02n1301090818
51294FS